DETECTIVE STORIES

Edited by
Deborah Shine

Illustrated by
Roger Fereday

octopus

CONTENTS

First published 1980 by
Octopus Books Limited
59 Grosvenor Street
London W1

ISBN 0 7064 1157 9

Printed in Czechoslovakia

50 393

THE IVY COTTAGE MYSTERY

Arthur Morrison

I had been working double tides for a month: at night on my morning paper, as usual; and in the morning on an evening paper as *locum tenens* for another man who was taking a holiday. This was an exhausting plan of work, although it only actually involved some six hours' attendance a day, or less, at the two offices. I turned up at the head-quarters of my own paper at ten in the evening, and by the time I had seen the editor, selected a subject, written my leader, corrected the slips, chatted, smoked, and so on, and cleared off, it was very usually one o'clock. This meant bed at two, or even three, after supper at the club.

This was all very well at ordinary periods, when any time in the morning would do for rising, but when I had to be up again soon after seven, and round at the evening paper office by eight, I naturally felt a little worn and disgusted with things by midday, after a sharp couple of hours' leaderette scribbling and paragraphing, with attendant sundries.

But the strain was over, and on the first day of comparative comfort I indulged in a midday breakfast and the first undisgusted glance at a morning paper for a month. I felt rather interested in an inquest, begun the day before, on the body of a man whom I had known very slightly before I took to living in chambers.

His name was Gavin Kingscote, and he was an artist of a casual and desultory sort, having, I believe, some small private means of his own. As a matter of fact, he had boarded in the same house in which I had lodged myself for a while, but as I was at the time a late homer and a fairly early riser, taking no regular board in the house, we never became much acquainted. He had since, I understood, made some judicious Stock Exchange speculations, and had set up house in Finchley.

Now the news was that he had been found one morning murdered in his smoking-room, while the room itself, with others, was in a state of confusion. His pockets had been rifled, and his watch and chain were gone, with one or two other small articles of value. On the night of the tragedy a friend had sat smoking with him in the room where the murder took place, and he had been the last person to see Mr Kingscote alive. A jobbing gardener, who kept the garden in order by casual work from time to time, had been arrested in consequence of footprints exactly corresponding with his boots, having been found on the garden beds near the French window of the smoking-room.

I finished my breakfast and my paper, and Mrs Clayton, the housekeeper, came to clear my table. She was sister of my late landlady of the house where Kingscote had lodged, and it was by this connection that I had found my chambers. I had not seen the housekeeper since the crime was first reported, so I now said:

'This is shocking news of Mr Kingscote, Mrs Clayton. Did you know him yourself?'

She had apparently only been waiting for some such remark to burst out with whatever information she possessed.

'Yes, sir,' she exclaimed: 'shocking indeed. Pore young feller! I see him often when I was at my sister's, and he was always a nice, quiet gentleman, so different from some. My sister, she's awful cut up, sir, I assure you. And what d'you think 'appened, sir, only last Tuesday? You remember Mr Kingscote's room where he painted the woodwork so beautiful with gold flowers, and blue, and pink? He used to tell my sister she'd always have something to remember him by. Well, two young fellers, gentlemen I can't call them, come and took that room (it being to let), and went and scratched off all the paint in mere wicked mischief, and then chopped up all the panels into sticks and bits! Nice sort o' gentlemen them! And then they bolted in the morning, being afraid, I s'pose, of being made to pay after treating a pore widder's property like that. That was only Tuesday, and the very next day the pore young gentleman himself's dead, murdered in his own 'ouse, and him goin' to be married an' all! Dear, dear! I remember once he said—'

Mrs Clayton was a good soul, but once she began to talk some one else had to stop her. I let her run on for a reasonable time, and then rose and prepared to go out. I remembered very well the panels that had been so mischievously destroyed. They made the room the showroom of the house, which was an old one. They were indeed less than half finished when I came away, and Mrs Lamb, the landlady, had shown them to me one day when Kingscote was out. All the walls of the room were panelled and painted white, and Kingscote had put upon them an eccentric but charming decoration, obviously suggested by some of the work of Mr Whistler. Tendrils, flowers, and butterflies in a quaint convention wandered thinly from panel to panel, giving the otherwise rather uninteresting room an unwonted atmosphere of richness and elegance. The lamentable jackasses who had destroyed this had certainly selected the best feature of the room whereon to inflict their senseless mischief.

I strolled idly downstairs, with no particular plan for the afternoon in my mind, and looked in at Hewitt's offices. Hewitt was reading a note, and after a little chat he informed me that it had been left an hour ago, in his absence, by the brother of the man I had just been speaking of.

'He isn't quite satisfied,' Hewitt said, 'with the way the police are investigating the case, and asks me to run down to Finchley and look round. Yesterday I should have refused, because I have five cases in progress already, but today I find that circumstances have given me a day or two. Didn't you say you knew the man?'

'Scarcely more than by sight. He was a boarder in the house at Chelsea where I stayed before I started chambers.'

'Ah, well; I think I shall look into the thing. Do you feel particularly interested in the case? I mean, if you've nothing better to do, would you come with me?'

'I shall be very glad,' I said. 'I was in some doubt what to do with myself. Shall you start at once?'

'I think so. Kerrett, just call a cab. By the way, Brett, which paper has the fullest report of the inquest yesterday? I'll run over it as we go down.'

As I had only seen one paper that morning, I could not answer Hewitt's question. So we bought various papers as we went along in the cab, and I found the reports while Martin Hewitt studied them. Summarized, this was the evidence given—

Sarah Dodson, general servant, deposed that she had been in service at Ivy Cottage, the residence of the deceased, for five months, the only other regular servant being the housekeeper and cook. On the evening of the previous Tuesday both servants retired a little before eleven, leaving Mr Kingscote with a friend in the smoking or sitting room. She never saw her master again alive. On coming downstairs the following morning and going to open the smoking-room windows, she was horrified to discover the body of Mr Kingscote lying on the floor of the room with blood about the head. She at once raised an alarm, and, on the instructions of the housekeeper, fetched a doctor, and gave information to the police. In answer to questions, witness stated she had heard no noise of any sort during the night, nor had anything suspicious occurred.

Hannah Carr, housekeeper and cook, deposed that she had been in the late Mr Kingscote's service since he had first taken Ivy Cottage—a period of rather more than a year. She had last seen the deceased alive on the evening of the previous Tuesday, at half-past ten, when she knocked at the door of the smoking-room, where Mr Kingscote was sitting with a friend, to ask if he would require anything more. Nothing was required, so witness shortly after went to bed. In the morning she was called by the previous witness, who had just gone downstairs, and found the body of deceased lying as described. Deceased's watch and chain were gone, as also was a ring he usually wore, and his pockets appeared to have been turned out. All the ground floor of the house was in confusion, and a bureau, a writing-table, and various drawers were open—a bunch of keys usually carried by deceased being left hanging at one keyhole. Deceased had drawn some money from the bank on the Tuesday, for current expenses; how much she did not know. She had not heard or seen anything suspicious during the night. Besides Dodson and herself, there were no regular servants; there was a charwoman, who came occasionally, and a jobbing gardener, living near, who was called in as required.

Mr James Vidler, surgeon, had been called by the first witness between seven and eight on Wednesday morning. He found the deceased lying on his face on the floor of the smoking-room, his feet being about eighteen inches from the window, and his head lying in the direction of the fireplace. He found three large contused wounds on the head, any one of which would probably have caused death. The wounds had all been inflicted, apparently, with the same blunt instrument—probably a club or life preserver, or other similar weapon. They could not have been done with the poker. Death was due to concussion of the brain, and deceased had probably been dead seven or eight hours when witness saw him. He had since examined the body more closely, but found no marks at all indicative of a struggle having taken place; indeed, from the position of the wounds and their severity, he should judge that the deceased had been attacked unawares from behind, and had died at once. The body appeared to be perfectly healthy.

Then there was police evidence, which showed that all the doors and windows were found shut and completely fastened, except the front door, which, although shut, was not bolted. There were shutters behind the French windows in the smoking-room, and these were found fastened. No money was found in the bureau, nor in any of the opened drawers, so that if any had been there, it had been stolen. The pockets were entirely empty, except for a small pair of nail scissors, and there was no watch upon the body, nor a ring. Certain footprints were found on the garden beds, which had led the police to take certain steps. No footprints were to be seen on the garden path, which was hard gravel.

Mr Alexander Campbell, stockbroker, stated that he had known deceased for some few years, and had done business for him. He and Mr Kingscote frequently called on one another, and on Tuesday evening they dined together at Ivy Cottage. They sat smoking and chatting till nearly twelve o'clock, when Mr Kingscote himself let him out, the servants having gone to bed. Here the witness proceeded rather excitedly: 'That is all I know of this horrible business, and I can say nothing else. What the police mean by following and watching me—'

The Coroner: 'Pray be calm, Mr Campbell. The police must do what seems best to them in a case of this sort. I am sure you would not have them neglect any means of getting at the truth.'

Witness: 'Certainly not. But if they suspect me, why don't they say so? It is intolerable that I should be—'

The Coroner: 'Order, order, Mr Campbell. You are here to give evidence.'

The witness then, in answer to questions, stated that the French windows of the smoking-room had been left open during the evening, the weather being very warm. He could not recollect whether or not deceased closed them before he left, but he certainly did not close the shutters. Witness saw nobody near the house when he left.

Mr Douglas Kingscote, architect, said deceased was his brother. He had not seen him for some months, living as he did in another part of the country. He believed his brother was fairly well off, and he knew that he had made a good amount by speculation in the last year or two. Knew of no person who would be likely to owe his brother a grudge, and could suggest no motive for the crime except ordinary robbery. His brother was to have been married in a few weeks. Questioned further on this point, witness said that the marriage was to have taken place a year ago, and it was with that view that Ivy Cottage, deceased's residence, was taken. The lady, however, sustained a domestic bereavement, and afterwards went abroad with her family: she was, witness believed, shortly expected back to England.

William Bates, jobbing gardener, who was brought up in custody, was cautioned, but elected to give evidence. Witness, who appeared to be much agitated, admitted having been in the garden of Ivy Cottage at four in the morning, but said that he had only gone to attend to certain plants, and knew absolutely nothing of the murder. He however admitted that he had no order for work beyond what he had done the day before. Being further pressed, witness made various contradictory statements, and finally said that he had gone to take certain plants away.

The inquest was then adjourned.

This was the case as it stood—apparently not a case presenting any very striking feature, although there seemed to me to be doubtful peculiarities in many parts of it. I asked Hewitt what he thought.

'Quite impossible to think anything, my boy, just yet; wait till we see the place. There are any number of possibilities. Kingscote's friend, Campbell, may have come in again, you know, by way of the window—or he may not. Campbell may have owed him money or something—or he may not. The anticipated wedding may have something to do with it—or, again, *that* may not. There is no limit to the possibilities, as far as we see from this report—a mere dry husk of the affair. When we get closer we shall examine the possibilities by the light of more detailed information. One *probability* is that the wretched gardener is innocent. It seems to me that his was only a comparatively blameless manoeuvre not unheard of at other times in his trade. He came at four in the morning to steal away the flowers he had planted the day before, and felt rather bashful when questioned on the point. Why should he trample on the beds, else? I wonder if the police thought to examine the beds for traces of rooting up, or questioned the housekeeper as to any plants being missing? But we shall see.'

We chatted at random as the train drew near Finchley, and I mentioned *inter alia* the wanton piece of destruction perpetrated at Kingscote's late lodgings. Hewitt was interested.

'That was curious,' he said, 'very curious. Was anything else damaged? Furniture and so forth?'

'I don't know. Mrs Clayton said nothing of it, and I didn't ask her. But it was quite bad enough as it was. The decoration was really good, and I can't conceive a meaner piece of tomfoolery than such an attack on a decent woman's property.'

Then Hewitt talked of other cases of similar stupid damage by creatures inspired by a defective sense of humour, or mere love of mischief. He had several curious and sometimes funny anecdotes of such affairs at museums and picture exhibitions, where the damage had been so great as to induce the authorities to call him in to discover the offender. The work was not always easy, chiefly from the mere absence of intelligible motive; not, indeed, always successful. One of the anecdotes related to a case of malicious damage to a picture—the outcome of blind artistic jealousy—a case which had been hushed up by a large expenditure in compensation. It would considerably startle most people, could it be printed here, with the actual names of the parties concerned.

Ivy Cottage, Finchley, was a compact little house, standing in a compact little square of garden, little more than a third of an acre, or perhaps no more at all. The front door was but a dozen yards or so back from the road, but the intervening space was well treed and shrubbed. Mr Douglas Kingscote had not yet returned from town, but the housekeeper, an intelligent, matronly woman, who knew of his intention to call in Martin Hewitt, was ready to show us the house.

'*First,*' Hewitt said, when we stood in the smoking-room, 'I observe that somebody has shut the drawers and the bureau. That is unfortunate. Also, the floor has been washed and the carpet taken up, which is much worse. That, I suppose, was because the police had finished their examination, but it doesn't help me to make one at all. Has *anything*—anything *at all*—been left as it was on Tuesday morning?'

'Well, sir, you see everything was in such a muddle,' the housekeeper began, 'and when the police had done—'

'Just so. I know. You "set it to rights", eh? Oh, that setting to rights! It has lost me a fortune at one time and another. As to the other rooms, now, have they been set to rights?'

'Such as was disturbed have been put right, sir, of course.'

'Which were disturbed? Let me see them. But wait a moment.'

He opened the French windows, and closely examined the catch and bolts. He knelt and inspected the holes whereinto the bolts fell, and then glanced casually at the folding shutters. He opened a drawer or two, and tried the working of the locks with the keys the housekeeper carried. They were, the housekeeper explained, Mr Kingscote's own keys. All through the lower floors Hewitt examined some things attentively and closely, and others with scarcely a glance, on a system unaccountable to me. Presently, he asked to be shown Mr Kingscote's bedroom, which had not been disturbed, 'set to rights', or slept in since the crime. Here, the housekeeper said, all drawers were kept unlocked but two—one in the wardrobe and one in the dressing-table, which Mr Kingscote had always been careful to keep locked. Hewitt immediately pulled both drawers open without difficulty. Within, in addition to a few odds and ends, were papers. All the contents of these drawers had been turned over confusedly, while those of the unlocked drawers were in perfect order.

'The police,' Hewitt remarked, 'may not have observed these matters. Any more than such an ordinary thing as *this*,' he added, picking up a bent nail lying at the edge of a rug.

The housekeeper doubtless took the remark as a reference to the entire unimportance of a bent nail, but I noticed that Hewitt dropped the article quietly into his pocket.

We came away. At the front gate we met Mr Douglas Kingscote, who had just returned from town. He introduced himself, and expressed surprise at our promptitude both of coming and going.

'You can't have got anything like a clue in this short time, Mr Hewitt?' he asked.

'Well, no,' Hewitt replied, with a certain dryness, 'perhaps not. But I doubt whether a month's visit would have helped me to get anything very striking out of a washed floor and a houseful of carefully cleaned-up and "set-to-rights" rooms. Candidly, I don't think you can reasonably expect much of me. The police have a much better chance—they had the scene of the crime to examine. I have seen just such a few rooms as anyone might see in the first well-furnished house he might enter. The trail of the housemaid has overlaid all the others.'

'I'm very sorry for that; the fact was, I expected rather more of the police; and, indeed, I wasn't here in time entirely to prevent the clearing up. But still, I thought your well-known powers—'

'My dear sir, my "well-known powers" are nothing but common sense assiduously applied and made quick by habit. That won't enable me to see the invisible.'

'But can't we have the rooms put back into something of the state they were in? The cook will remember—'

'No, no. That would be worse and worse: that would only be the housemaid's trail in turn overlaid by the cook's. You must leave things with me for a little, I think.'

'Then you don't give the case up?' Mr Kingscote asked anxiously.

'Oh, no! I don't give it up just yet. Do you know anything of your brother's private papers—as they were before his death?'

'I never knew anything till after that. I have gone over them, but they are all very ordinary letters. Do you suspect a theft of papers?'

Martin Hewitt, with his hands on his stick behind him, looked sharply at the other, and shook his head. 'No,' he said, 'I can't quite say that.'

We bade Mr Douglas Kingscote good-day, and walked towards the station. 'Great nuisance, that setting to rights,' Hewitt observed, on the way. 'If the place had been left alone, the job might have been settled one way or another by this time. As it is, we shall have to run over to your old lodgings.'

'My old lodgings?' I repeated, amazed. 'Why my old lodgings?'

Hewitt turned to me with a chuckle and a wide smile. 'Because we can't see the broken panel-work anywhere else,' he said. 'Let's see—Chelsea, isn't it?'

'Yes, Chelsea. But why—you don't suppose the people who defaced the panels also murdered the man who painted them?'

'Well,' Hewitt replied, with another smile, 'that would be carrying a practical joke rather far, wouldn't it? Even for the ordinary picture damager.'

'You mean you *don't* think they did it, then? But what *do* you mean?'

'My dear fellow, I don't mean anything but what I say. Come now, this is rather an interesting case despite appearances, and it *has* interested me: so much, in fact, that I really think I forgot to offer Mr Douglas Kingscote my condolence on his bereavement. You see a problem is a problem, whether of theft, assassination, intrigue, or anything else, and I only think of it as one. The work very often makes me forget merely human sympathies. Now, you have often been good enough to express a very flattering interest in my work, and you shall have an opportunity of exercising your own common sense in the way I am always having to exercise mine. You shall see all my evidence (if I'm lucky enough to get any) as I collect it, and you shall make your own inferences. That will be a little exercise for you; the sort of exercise I should give a pupil if I had one. But I will give you what information I have, and you shall start fairly from this moment. You know the inquest evidence such as it was, and you saw everything I did in Ivy Cottage?'

'Yes; I think so. But I'm not much the wiser.'

'Very well. Now I will tell you. What does the whole case look like? How would you class the crime?'

'I suppose as the police do. An ordinary case of murder with the object of robbery.'

'It is *not* an ordinary case. If it were, I shouldn't know as much as I do, little as that is; the ordinary cases are always difficult. The assailant did not come to commit a burglary, although he was a skilled burglar, or one of them was, if more than one were concerned. The affair has, I think, nothing to do with the expected wedding, nor had Mr Campbell anything to do in it—at any rate, personally—nor the gardener. The criminal (or one of them) was known personally to the dead man, and was well-dressed: he (or again one of them, and I think there were two) even had a chat with Mr Kingscote before the murder took place. He came to ask for something which Mr Kingscote was unwilling to part with,—perhaps hadn't got. It was not a bulky thing. Now you have all my materials before you.'

'But all this doesn't look like the result of the blind spite that would ruin a man's work first and attack him bodily afterwards.'

'Spite isn't always blind, and there are other blind things besides spite; people with good eyes in their heads are blind sometimes, even detectives.'

'But where did you get all this information? What makes you suppose that this was a burglar who didn't want to burgle, and a well-dressed man, and so on?'

Hewitt chuckled and smiled again.

'I saw it—saw it, my boy, that's all,' he said 'But here comes the train.'

On the way back to town, after I had rather minutely described Kingscote's work on the boarding-house panels, Hewitt asked me for the names and professions of such fellow lodgers in that house as I might remember. 'When did you leave yourself?' he ended.

'Three years ago, or rather more. I can remember Kingscote himself; Turner, a medical student—James Turner, I think; Harvey Challitt, diamond merchant's articled pupil—he was a bad egg entirely, he's doing five years for forgery now; by the bye he had the room we are going to see till he was marched off, and Kingscote took it—a year before I left; there was Norton—don't know what he was; "something in the City", I think; and Carter Paget, in the Admiralty Office. I don't remember any more at this moment; there were pretty frequent changes. But you can get it all from Mrs Lamb, of course.'

'Of course; and Mrs Lamb's exact address is—what?'

I gave him the address, and the conversation became disjointed. At Farringdon station, where we alighted, Hewitt called two hansoms. Preparing to enter one, he motioned me to the other, saying, 'You get straight away to Mrs Lamb's at once. She may be going to burn that splintered wood, or to set things to rights, after the manner of her kind, and you can stop her. I must make one or two small inquiries, but I shall be there half an hour after you.'

'Shall I tell her our object?'

'Only that I may be able to catch her mischievous lodgers—nothing else yet.' He jumped into the hansom and was gone.

I found Mrs Lamb still in a state of indignant perturbation over the trick served her four days before. Fortunately, she had left everything in the panelled room exactly as she had found it, with an idea of being better able to demand or enforce reparation should her lodgers return. 'The room's theirs, you see, sir,' she said, 'till the end of the week, since they paid in advance, and they may come back and offer to make amends, although I doubt it. As pleasant-spoken a young chap as you might wish, he seemed, him as come to take the rooms. "My cousin," says he, "is rather an invalid, havin' only just got over congestion of the lungs, and he won't be in London till this evening late. He's comin' up from Birmingham," he ses, "and I hope he won't catch a fresh cold on the way, although of course we've got him muffled up plenty." He took the rooms, sir, like a gentleman, and mentioned several gentlemen's names I knew well, as had lodged here before; and then he put down on that there very table, sir'—Mrs Lamb indicated the exact spot with her hand, as though that made the whole thing much more wonderful—'he put down on that very table a week's rent in advance, and ses, "That's always the best sort of reference, Mrs Lamb, I think," as kind-mannered as anything—and never 'aggled about the amount nor nothing. He only had a little black bag, but he said his cousin had all the luggage coming in the train, and as there was so much, p'r'aps they wouldn't get it here till next day. Then he went out and came in with his cousin at eleven that night—Sarah let 'em in her own self—and in the morning they was gone—and this!' Poor Mrs Lamb, plaintively indignant, stretched her arm towards the wrecked panels.

'If the gentleman as you say is comin' on, sir,' she pursued, 'can do anything to find 'em, I'll prosecute 'em, that I will, if it costs me ten pound. I spoke to the constable on the beat, but he only looked like a fool, and said if I knew where they were I might charge 'em with wilful damage, or county court 'em. Of course I know I can do that if I knew where they were, but how can I find 'em? Mr Jones he said his name was; but how many Joneses is there in London, sir?'

I couldn't imagine any answer to a question like this, but I condoled with Mrs Lamb as well as I could. She afterwards went on to express herself much as her sister had done with regard to Kingscote's death, only as the destruction of her panels loomed larger in her mind, she dwelt primarily on that. 'It might almost seem,' she said, 'that some-body had a deadly spite on the pore young gentleman, and went breakin' up his paintin' one night, and murderin' him the next!'

I examined the broken panels with some care, having half a notion to attempt to deduce something from them myself, if possible. But I could deduce nothing. The beading had been taken out, and the panels, which were thick in the centre but bevelled at the edges, had been removed and split up literally into thin firewood, which lay in a tumbled heap on the hearth and about the floor. Every panel in the room had been treated in the same way, and the result was a pretty large heap of sticks, with nothing whatever about them to distinguish them from other sticks, except the paint on one face, which I observed in many places had been scratched and scraped away. The rug was drawn half across the hearth, and had evidently been used to deaden the sound of chopping. But mischief—wanton and stupid mischief—was all I could deduce from it all.

Mr Jones's cousin, it seemed, only Sarah had seen, as she admitted him in the evening, and then he was so heavily muffled that she could not distinguish his features, and would never be able to identify him. But as for the other one, Mrs Lamb was ready to swear to him any-where.

Hewitt was long in coming, and internal symptoms of the approach of dinner-time (we had had no lunch) had made themselves felt before a sharp ring at the door-bell foretold his arrival. 'I have had to wait for answers to a telegram,' he said in explanation, 'but at any rate I have the information I wanted. And these are the mysterious panels, are they?'

Mrs Lamb's true opinion of Martin Hewitt's behaviour as it proceeded would have been amusing to know. She watched in amazement the antics of a man who purposed finding out who had been splitting sticks by dint of picking up each separate stick and staring at it. In the end he collected a small handful of sticks by themselves and handed them to me, saying, 'Just put these together on the table, Brett, and see what you make of them.'

I turned the pieces painted side up, and fitted them together into a complete panel, joining up the painted design accurately. 'It is an entire panel,' I said.

'Good. Now look at the sticks a little more closely, and tell me if you notice anything peculiar about them—any particular in which they differ from all the others.'

I looked. 'Two adjoining sticks,' I said, 'have each a small semi-circular cavity stuffed with what seems to be putty. Put together it would mean a small circular hole, perhaps a knot-hole, half an inch or so in diameter, in the panel, filled in with putty, or whatever it is.'

'A *knot-hole?*' Hewitt asked, with particular emphasis.

'Well, no, not a knot-hole, of course, because that would go right through, and this doesn't. It is probably less than half an inch deep from the front surface.'

'Anything else? Look at the whole appearance of the wood itself. Colour, for instance.'

'It is certainly darker than the rest.'

'So it is,' He took the two pieces carrying the puttied hole, threw the rest on the heap, and addressed the landlady. 'The Mr Harvey Challitt who occupied this room before Mr Kingscote, and who got into trouble for forgery, was the Mr Harvey Challitt who was himself robbed of diamonds a few months before on a staircase, wasn't he?'

'Yes, sir,' Mrs Lamb replied in some bewilderment. 'He certainly was that, on his own office stairs, chloroformed.'

'Just so, and when they marched him away because of the forgery, Mr Kingscote changed into his rooms?'

'Yes, and very glad I was. It was bad enough to have the disgrace

Mrs Lamb watched him in amazement.

brought into the house, without the trouble of trying to get people to take his very rooms, and I thought—'

'Yes, yes, very awkward, very awkward!' Hewitt interrupted rather impatiently. 'The man who took the rooms on Monday, now—you'd never seen him before, had you?'

'No, sir.'

'Then is *that* anything like him?' Hewitt held a cabinet photograph before her.

'Why—why—law, yes, that's *him*!'

Hewitt dropped the photograph back into his breast pocket with a contented 'Um,' and picked up his hat. 'I think we may soon be able to find that young gentleman for you, Mrs Lamb. He is not a very respectable young gentleman, and perhaps you are well rid of him, even as it is. Come, Brett,' he added, 'the day hasn't been wasted, after all.'

We made towards the nearest telegraph office. On the way I said, 'That puttied-up hole in the piece of wood seems to have influenced you. Is it an important link?'

'Well—yes,' Hewitt answered, 'it is. But all those other pieces are important, too.'

'But why?'

'Because there are no holes in them.' He looked quizzically at my wondering face, and laughed aloud. 'Come,' he said, 'I won't puzzle you much longer. Here is the post-office. I'll send my wire, and then we'll go and dine at Luzatti's.'

He sent his telegram, and we cabbed it to Luzatti's. Among actors, journalists, and others who know town and like a good dinner, Luzatti's is well known. We went upstairs for the sake of quietness, and took a table standing alone in a recess just inside the door. We ordered our dinner, and then Hewitt began:

'Now tell me what *your* conclusion is in this matter of the Ivy Cottage murder.'

'Mine? I haven't one. I'm sorry I'm so very dull, but I really haven't.'

'Come, I'll give you a point. Here is the newspaper account (torn sacrilegiously from my scrap-book for your benefit) of the robbery perpetrated on Harvey Challitt a few months before his forgery. Read it.'

'Oh, but I remember the circumstances very well. He was carrying two packets of diamonds belonging to his firm downstairs to the office of another firm of diamond merchants on the ground-floor. It was a quiet time in the day, and halfway down he was seized on a dark landing, made insensible by chloroform, and robbed of the diamonds—five or six thousand pounds' worth altogether, of stones of various smallish individual values up to thirty pounds or so. He lay unconscious on the landing till one of the partners, noticing that he had been rather long gone, followed and found him. That's all, I think.'

'Yes, that's all. Well, what do you make of it?'

'I'm afraid I don't quite see the connection with this case.'

'Well, then, I'll give you another point. The telegram I've just sent releases information to the police, in consequence of which they will probably apprehend Harvey Challitt and his confederate Henry Gillard, *alias* Jones, for the murder of Gavin Kingscote. Now, then.'

'Challitt! But he's in gaol already.'

'Tut, tut, consider. Five years' penal was his dose, although for the first offence, because the forgery was of an extremely dangerous sort. You left Chelsea over three years ago yourself, and you told me that his difficulty occurred a year before. That makes four years, at least. Good conduct in prison brings a man out of a five year's sentence in that time or a little less, and, as a matter of fact, Challitt was released rather more than a week ago.'

'Still, I'm afraid I don't see what you are driving at.'

'Whose story is this about the diamond robbery from Harvey Challitt?'

'His own.'

'Exactly. His own. Does his subsequent record make him look like a person whose stories are to be accepted without doubt or question?'

'Why, no. I think I see—no, I don't. You mean he stole them himself? I've a sort of dim perception of your drift now, but still I can't fix it. The whole thing's too complicated.'

'It is a little complicated for a first effort, I admit, so I will tell you. This is the story. Harvey Challitt is an artful young man, and decides on a theft of his firm's diamonds. He first prepares a hiding-place some-where near the stairs of his office, and when the opportunity arrives he puts the stones away, spills his chloroform, and makes a smell—possibly sniffs some, and actually goes off on the stairs, and the whole thing's done. He is carried into the office—the diamonds are gone. He tells of the attack on the stairs, as we have heard, and he is believed. At a suitable opportunity he takes his plunder from the hiding-place, and goes home to his lodgings. What is he to do with those diamonds? He can't sell them yet, because the robbery is publicly notorious, and all the regular jewel buyers know him.

'Being a criminal novice, he doesn't know any regular receiver of stolen goods, and if he did would prefer to wait and get full value by an ordinary sale. There will always be a danger of detection so long as the stones are not securely hidden, so he proceeds to hide them. He knows that if any suspicion were aroused his rooms would be searched in every likely place, so he looks for an unlikely place. Of course, he thinks of taking out a panel and hiding them behind that. But the idea is so obvious that it won't do; the police would certainly take those panels out to look behind them. Therefore he determines to hide them *in* the panels. See here'—he took the two pieces of wood with the filled hole from his tail pocket and opened his penknife—'the putty near the surface is softer than that near the bottom of the hole; two different lots of putty, differently mixed, perhaps, have been used, therefore, presumably, at different times.

'But to return to Challitt. He makes holes with a centre-bit in different places on the panels, and in each hole he places a diamond, embedding it carefully in putty. He smooths the surface carefully flush with the wood, and then very carefully paints the place over, shading off the paint at the edges so as to leave no signs of a patch. He doesn't do the whole job at once, creating a noise and a smell of paint, but keeps on steadily, a few holes at a time, till in a little while the whole wainscoting is set with hidden diamonds, and every panel is apparently sound and whole.'

'But, then—there was only one such hole in the whole lot.'

'Just so, and that very circumstance tells us the whole truth. Let me tell the story first—I'll explain the clue after. The diamonds lie hidden for a few months—he grows impatient. He wants the money, and he can't see a way of getting it. At last he determines to make a bolt and go abroad to sell his plunder. He knows he will want money for expenses, and that he may not be able to get rid of his diamonds at once. He also expects that his suddenly going abroad while the robbery is still in people's minds will bring suspicion on him in any case, so, in for a penny in for a pound, he commits a bold forgery, which, had it been successful, would have put him in funds and enabled him to leave the country with the stones. But the forgery is detected, and he is haled to prison, leaving the diamonds in their wainscot setting.

'Now we come to Gavin Kingscote. He must have been a shrewd fellow—the sort of man that good detectives are made of. Also he must have been pretty unscrupulous. He had his suspicions about the genuineness of the diamond robbery, and kept his eyes open. What indications he had to guide him we don't know, but living in the same house a sharp fellow on the look-out would probably see enough. At any rate, they led him to the belief that the diamonds were in the thief's rooms, but not among his movables, or they would have been found after the arrest. Here was his chance. Challitt was out of the way for years, and there was plenty of time to take the house to pieces if it were necessary. So he changed into Challitt's rooms.

'How long it took him to find the stones we shall never know. He probably tried many other places first, and, I expect, found the diamonds at last by pricking over the panels with a needle. Then came the problem of getting them out without attracting attention. He decided not to trust to the needle, which might possibly leave a stone or two undiscovered, but to split up each panel carefully into splinters so as to leave no part unexamined. Therefore he took measurements, and had a number of panels made by a joiner of the exact size and pattern of those in the room, and announced to his landlady his intention of painting her panels with a pretty design. This to account for the wet paint, and even for the fact of a panel being out of the wall, should she chance to bounce into the room at an awkward moment. All very clever, eh?'

'Very.'

'Ah, he was a smart man, no doubt. Well, he went to work, taking out a panel, substituting a new one, painting it over, and chopping up the old one on the quiet, getting rid of the splinters out of doors when the booty had been extracted. The decoration progressed and the little heap of diamonds grew. Finally, he came to the last panel, but

25

found that he had used all his new panels and hadn't one left for a substitute. It must have been at some time when it was difficult to get hold of the joiner—Bank Holiday, perhaps, or Sunday, and he was impatient. So he scraped the paint off, and went carefully over every part of the surface—experience had taught him by this that all the holes were of the same sort—and found one diamond. He took it out, refilled the hole with putty, painted the old panel and put it back. *These* are pieces of that old panel—the only old one of the lot.

'Nine men out of ten would have got out of the house as soon as possible after the thing was done, but he was a cool hand and stayed. That made the whole thing look a deal more genuine than if he had unaccountably cleared out as soon as he had got his room nicely decorated. I expect the original capital for those Stock Exchange operations we heard of came out of those diamonds. He stayed as long as suited him, and left when he set up housekeeping with a view to his wedding. The rest of the story is pretty plain. You guess it, of course?'

'Yes,' I said, 'I think I can guess the rest, in a general sort of way—except as to one or two points.'

'It's all plain—perfectly. See here! Challitt, in gaol, determines to get those diamonds when he comes out. To do that without being suspected it will be necessary to hire the room. But he knows that he won't be able to do that himself, because the landlady, of course, knows him, and won't have an ex-convict in the house. There is no help for it; he must have a confederate, and share the spoil. So he makes the acquaintance of another convict, who seems a likely man for the job, and whose sentence expires about the same time as his own. When they come out, he arranges the matter with this confederate, who is a well-mannered (and pretty well-known) housebreaker, and the latter calls at Mrs Lamb's house to look for rooms. The very room itself happens to be to let, and of course it is taken, and Challitt (who is the invalid cousin) comes in at night muffled and unrecognizable.

'The decoration on the panel does not alarm them, because, of course, they suppose it to have been done on the old panels and over the old paint. Challitt tries the spots where diamonds were left—there are none—there is no putty even. Perhaps, think they, the panels have been shifted and interchanged in the painting, so they set to work and split them all up as we have seen, getting more desperate as they go on.

Finally they realize that they are done, and clear out, leaving Mrs Lamb to mourn over their mischief.

'They know that Kingscote is the man who has forestalled them, because Gillard (or Jones), in his chat with the landlady, has heard all about him and his painting of the panels. So the next night they set off for Finchley. They get into Kingscote's garden and watch him let Campbell out. While he is gone, Challitt quietly steps through the French window into the smoking-room, and waits for him, Gillard remaining outside.

'Kingscote returns, and Challitt accuses him of taking the stones. Kingscote is contemptuous—doesn't care for Challitt, because he knows he is powerless, being the original thief himself; besides, knows there is no evidence, since the diamonds are sold and dispersed long ago. Challitt offers to divide the plunder with him—Kingscote laughs and tells him to go; probably threatens to throw him out, Challitt being the smaller man. Gillard, at the open window, hears this, steps in behind, and quietly knocks him on the head. The rest follows as a matter of course. They fasten the window and shutters, to exclude observation; turn over all the drawers, etc., in case the jewels are there; go to the best bedroom and try there, and so on. Failing (and possibly being disturbed after a few hours' search by the noise of the acquisitive gardener), Gillard, with the instinct of an old thief, determines they shan't go away with nothing, so empties Kingscote's pockets and takes his watch and chain and so on. They go out by the front door and shut it after them. *Voilà tout.*'

I was filled with wonder at the prompt ingenuity of the man who in these few hours of hurried inquiry could piece together so accurately all the materials of an intricate and mysterious affair such as this; but more, I wondered where and how he had collected those materials.

'There is no doubt, Hewitt,' I said, 'that the accurate and minute application of what you are pleased to call your common sense has become something very like an instinct with you. What did you deduce from? You told me your conclusions from the examination of Ivy Cottage, but not how you arrived at them.'

'They didn't leave me much material downstairs, did they? But in the bedroom, the two drawers which the thieves found locked were ransacked—opened probably with keys taken from the dead man. On

27

the floor I saw a bent French nail; here it is. You see, it is twice bent at right angles, near the head and near the point, and there is the faint mark of the pliers that were used to bend it. It is a very usual burglars' tool, and handy in experienced hands to open ordinary drawer locks. Therefore, I knew that a professional burglar had been at work. He had probably fiddled at the drawers with the nail first, and then had thrown it down to try the dead man's keys.

'But I knew this professional burglar didn't come for a burglary, from several indications. There was no attempt to take plate, the first thing a burglar looks for. Valuable clocks were left on mantelpieces, and other things that usually go in an ordinary burglary were not disturbed. Notably, it was to be observed that no doors or windows were broken, or had been forcibly opened; therefore, it was plain that the thieves had come in by the French window of the smoking-room, the only entrance left open at the last thing. *Therefore,* they came in, or one did, knowing that Mr Kingscote was up, and being quite willing—presumably anxious—to see him. Ordinary burglars would have waited till he had retired, and then could have got through the closed French window as easily almost as if it were open, notwithstanding the thin wooden shutters, which would never stop a burglar for more than five minutes. Being anxious to see him, they—or again, *one* of them—presumably knew him. That they had come to *get* something was plain, from the ransacking. As, in the end, they *did* steal his money and watch, but did *not* take larger valuables, it was plain that they had no bag with them—which proves not only that they had not come to burgle, for every burglar takes his bag, but that the thing they came to get was not bulky. Still, they could easily have removed plate or clocks by rolling them up in a table-cover or other wrapper, but such a bundle, carried by well-dressed men, would attract attention—therefore it was probable that they were well dressed. Do I make it clear?'

'Quite—nothing seems simpler now it is explained—that's the way with difficult puzzles.'

'There was nothing more to be got at the house. I had already in my mind the curious coincidence that the panels at Chelsea had been broken the very night before that of the murder, and determined to look at them in any case. I got from you the name of the man who

had lived in the panelled room before Kingscote, and at once remembered it (although I said nothing about it) as that of the young man
who had been chloroformed for his employer's diamonds. I keep things
of that sort in my mind, you see—and, indeed, in my scrap-book. You
told me yourself about his imprisonment, and there I was with what
seemed now a hopeful case getting into a promising shape.

'You went on to prevent any setting to rights at Chelsea, and I
made enquiries as to Challitt. I found he had been released only a few
days before all this trouble arose, and I also found the name of another
man who was released from the same establishment only a few days
earlier. I knew this man (Gillard) well, and knew that nobody was a
more likely rascal for such a crime as that at Finchley. On my way
to Chelsea I called at my office, gave my clerk certain instructions, and
looked up my scrap-book. I found the newspaper account of the
chloroform business, and also a photograph of Gillard—I keep as many
of these things as I can collect. What I did at Chelsea you know. I
saw that one panel was of old wood and the rest new. I saw the hole
in the old panel, and I asked one or two questions. The case was
complete.'

We proceeded with our dinner. Presently I said: 'It all rests with the
police now, of course?'

'Of course. I should think it very probable that Challitt and Gillard
will be caught. Gillard, at any rate, is pretty well known. It will be
rather hard on the surviving Kingscote, after engaging me, to have
his dead brother's diamond transactions publicly exposed as a result,
won't it? But it can't be helped. *Fiat justitia,* of course.'

'How will the police feel over this?' I asked. 'You've rather cut
them out, eh?'

'Oh, the police are all right. They had not the information I had, you
see; they knew nothing of the panel business. If Mrs Lamb had
gone to Scotland Yard instead of to the policeman on the beat, perhaps
I should never have been sent for.'

The same quality that caused Martin Hewitt to rank as mere
'common-sense' his extraordinary power of almost instinctive de-
duction, kept his respect for the abilities of the police at perhaps a
higher level than some might have considered justified.

We sat some little while over our dessert, talking as we sat, when there occurred one of those curious conjunctions of circumstances that we notice again and again in ordinary life, and forget as often, unless the importance of the occasion fixes the matter in the memory. A young man had entered the dining-room, and had taken his seat at a corner table near the back window. He had been sitting there for some little time before I particularly observed him. At last he happened to turn his thin, pale face in my direction, and our eyes met. It was Challitt—the man we had been talking of!

I sprang to my feet in some excitement.

'That's the man!' I cried. 'Challitt!'

Hewitt rose at my words, and at first attempted to pull me back. Challitt, in guilty terror, saw that we were between him and the door, and turning, leaped upon the sill of the open window, and dropped out. There was a fearful crash of broken glass below, and everybody rushed to the window.

Hewitt drew me through the door, and we ran downstairs. 'Pity you let out like that,' he said, as he went. 'If you'd kept quiet we could have sent out for the police with no trouble. Never mind—can't help it.'

Below, Challitt was lying in a broken heap in the midst of a crowd of waiters. He had crashed through a thick glass skylight and fallen, back downward, across the back of a lounge. He was taken away on a stretcher unconscious, and, in fact, died in a week in hospital from injuries to the spine.

During his periods of consciousness he made a detailed statement, bearing out the conclusions of Martin Hewitt with the most surprising exactness, down to the smallest particulars. He and Gillard had parted immediately after the crime, judging it safer not to be seen together. He had, he affirmed, endured agonies of fear and remorse in the few days since the fatal night at Finchley, and had even once or twice thought of giving himself up. When I so excitedly pointed him out, he knew at once that the game was up, and took the one desperate chance of escape that offered. But to the end he persistently denied that he had himself committed the murder, or had even thought of it till he saw it accomplished. That had been wholly the work of Gillard, who, listening at the window and perceiving the drift of the conversation, suddenly beat down Kingscote from behind with a life-preserver.

And so Harvey Challitt ended his life at the age of twenty-six.

Gillard was never taken. He doubtless left the country, and has probably since that time become 'known to the police' under another name abroad. Perhaps he has even been hanged, and if he has been, there was no miscarriage of justice, no matter what the charge against him may have been.

THE 'NICOBAR' BULLION CASE

Arthur Morrison

The Anglo-Malay Company's steamship Nicobar *was returning home after a trading voyage in the Far East, and was due to land at Plymouth with a small general cargo, and gold bullion to the value of £200,000. The presence of this bullion was a source of much conspicuous worry to Mr Brayser, the second officer, who was in charge of the bullion-room. He soon came to suspect the motives of every member of the crew, including the captain. He suspected Captain Mackrie of being in league with the steward, as they were often talking together, and he suspected the carpenter of having duplicate keys to the bullion-room padlock.*

It was January, and a fierce storm blew up in the Channel. Within sight of the Eddystone lighthouse, the Nicobar *was in collision with a steamer, and the crew and the few passengers had to leave the sinking ship and reach shore by lifeboat. Brayser was anxious about leaving the bullion, but Captain Mackrie told him to leave it. But the captain did speak to the steward, who then went below deck, as if to execute some order. The* Nicobar *sank within fifteen minutes, only a mile from the shore.*

Next day Lloyd's agent was steaming about in a launch from Plymouth, and soon a salvage company's tug came up and lay to by the emerging masts. There was every chance of raising the ship as far as could be seen, and a diver went down from the salvage tug to measure the breach made in the *Nicobar's* side, in order that the necessary oak planking or sheeting might be got ready for covering the hole, preparatory to pumping and raising. This was done in a very short time, and the necessary telegrams having been sent, the tug remained in its place through the night, and prepared for the sending down of several divers on the morrow to get out the bullion.

Just at this time Martin Hewitt happened to be engaged on a case of some importance and delicacy on behalf of Lloyd's Committee, and was staying for a few days at Plymouth. He heard the story of the wreck, of course, and speaking casually with Lloyd's agent as to the salvage work just beginning, he was told the name of the salvage company's representative on the tug, Mr Percy Merrick—a name he immediately recognized as that of an old acquaintance of his own. So that on the day when the divers were at work in the bullion-room of the sunken *Nicobar,* Hewitt gave himself a holiday, and went aboard the tug about noon.

Here he found Merrick, a big, pleasant man of thirty-eight or so. He was very glad to see Hewitt, but was a great deal puzzled as to the results of the morning's work on the wreck. Two cases of gold bars were missing.

'There was £200,000 worth of bullion on board,' he said, 'that's plain and certain. It was packed in forty cases, each of £5,000 value. But now there are only thirty-eight cases! Two are gone, clearly. I wonder what's happened?'

'I suppose your men don't know anything about it?' asked Hewitt.

'No, they're all right. You see, it's impossible for them to bring anything up without its being observed, especially as they have to be unscrewed from their diving-dresses here on deck. Besides, bless you, I was down with them.'

'Oh! Do you dive yourself, then?'

'Well, I put the dress on sometimes, you know, for any such special occasion as this. I went down this morning. There was no difficulty in getting about on the vessel below, and I found the keys of the bullion-room just where the captain said I would, in his cabin. But the locks were useless, of course, after being a couple of days in salt water. So we just burgled the door with crowbars, and then we saw that we might have done it a bit more easily from outside. For the coasting steamer cut clean into the bunker next the bullion-room, and ripped open the sheet of boiler-plate dividing them.'

'The two missing cases couldn't have dropped out that way?'

'Oh, no. We looked, of course, but it would have been impossible.

33

The vessel has a list the other way—to starboard—and the piled cases didn't reach as high as the torn part.'

'What have you done about the missing two—anything?'

'Wired off to headquarters, of course, at once. And I've sent for Captain Mackrie—he's still in the neighbourhood, I believe—and Brayser, the second officer, who had charge of the bullion-room. They may possibly know something. Anyway, *one* thing's plain. There were forty cases at the beginning of the voyage, and now there are only thirty-eight.'

There was a pause; and then Merrick added, 'By the bye, Hewitt, this is rather your line, isn't it? You ought to look up these cases.'

'All right,' he said; 'I'll begin this minute if you'll commission me.'

There was a tap at the door and Captain Mackrie entered. 'Mr Merrick?' he said interrogatively, looking from one to another.

'That's myself, sir,' answered Merrick.

'I'm Captain Mackrie, of the *Nicobar*. You sent for me, I believe. Something wrong with the bullion I'm told, isn't it?'

Merrick explained matters fully. 'I thought perhaps you might be able to help us, Captain Mackrie. Perhaps I have been wrongly informed as to the number of cases that should have been there?'

'No; there were forty right enough. I think though—perhaps I might be able to give you a sort of hint.'—and Captain Mackrie looked hard at Hewitt.

'This is Mr Hewitt, Captain Mackrie,' Merrick interposed. 'You may speak as freely as you please before him.'

'Well,' Mackrie said, 'if that's so, speaking between ourselves, I should advise you to turn your attention to Brayser.'

'Do you mean,' Hewitt asked, 'that Mr Brayser might give us some useful information?'

Mackrie gave an ugly grin. 'Very likely he might,' he said, 'if he were fool enough. But I don't think you'd get much out of him direct.'

'What, do you suppose he was concerned in any way with the disappearance of this gold?'

'I should think—speaking, as I said before, in confidence and between ourselves—that it's very likely indeed.'

'Why?'

'Well, he was so eternally cracking on about his responsibility, and pretending to suspect the stokers and the carpenter, and one person and another, of trying to get at the bullion cases—that that alone was almost enough to make one suspicious. He protested so much, you see. He was so conscientious and diligent himself, and all the rest of it, and everybody else was such a desperate thief, and he was so sure there would be some of that bullion missing some day that—that—well, I don't know if I express his manner clearly, but I tell you I didn't like it a bit. But there was something more than that. He was eternally smelling about the place, and peeping in at the steward's pantry—which adjoins the bullion-room on one side, you know—and nosing about in the bunker on the other side. And once I actually caught him fitting keys to the padlocks—keys he'd borrowed from the carpenter's stores. And every time his excuse was that he fancied he heard somebody or something. Whether or not I succeed in conveying my impressions to you, gentlemen, I can assure you that I regarded his whole manner and actions as very suspicious throughout the voyage, and I made up my mind I wouldn't forget it if by chance anything *did* turn out wrong. Well, it has, and now I've told you what I've observed. It's for you to see if it will lead you anywhere.'

'Just so,' Hewitt answered. 'But let me fully understand, Captain Mackrie. You say that Mr Brayser had charge of the bullion-room, but that he was trying keys on it from the capenter's stores. Where were the legitimate keys then?'

'In my cabin. They were only handed out when I knew what they were wanted for. There was a Chubb's lock between the two padlocks, but a duplicate wouldn't have been hard for Brayser to get.'

'Well, and suppose he had taken these boxes, where do you think he would keep them?'

'Impossible to say,' he replied. 'He might have hidden 'em somewhere on board, though I don't think that's very likely. He'd be much more likely to have "dumped" it—dropped it overboard at some well-known spot in a foreign port, where he could go later and get it. So that you've a deal of scope for search, you see. Anywhere under water from here to Yokohama;' and Captain Mackrie laughed.

Soon afterward he left, and as he was leaving a man knocked at the cabin door and looked in to say that Mr Brayser was on board. 'You'll be able to have a go at him now,' said the captain. 'Good-day.'

'There's the steward of the *Nicobar* there too, sir,' said the man after the captain had gone, 'and the carpenter.'

Brayser made his appearance, overflowing with information. He required little assurance to encourage him to speak openly before Hewitt, and he said again all he had so often said before on board the *Nicobar*.

The men whose movements should be carefully watched, he said, were the captain and the steward. 'Nobody ever heard of a captain and a steward being so thick together. One day I met the captain coming out of the steward's pantry, and then he bullyragged me for being there and sent me on deck. But before that he bullyragged me because I had found out that there were other keys knocking about the place that fitted the padlocks on the bullion-room door. Why should he slang and threaten me for looking after these things and keeping my eye on the bullion-room, as was my duty? But that was the very thing that he didn't like. It was enough for him to see me anxious about the gold to make him furious. Of course his character for meanness and greed is known all through the company's service—he'll do anything to make a bit.'

'But have you any positive idea as to what has become of the gold?'

'Well,' Brayser replied, with a rather knowing air, 'I don't think they've dumped it.'

'Do you mean you think it's still in the vessel—hidden somewhere?'

'No, I don't. I believe the captain and the steward took it ashore, one case each, when we came off in the boats.'

'It needn't be, on a black night like that. You see, the parcels are not so big—look at them, a foot by a foot and a half by six inches or so, roughly. Easily slipped under a big coat or covered up with anything. Of course they're a bit heavy—eighty or ninety pounds apiece altogether—but that's not much for a strong man to carry—especially in such a handy parcel, on a black night, with no end of confusion on. Now you just look here—I'll tell you something. The skipper went ashore last in a boat that was sent out by the coasting steamer that ran into us. I suspected he might be up to something, so I got hold of one of the boat's crew that fetched the skipper ashore, and questioned him quietly—pumped him, you know—and he assures me that the skipper *did* have a small, heavy sort of parcel with him. I've made inquiries at the railway station and I find that two heavy parcels were sent off yesterday to London—deal boxes wrapped in brown paper, of just about the right size. And the paper got torn before things were sent off, and the clerk could see that the boxes inside were fastened with hoop-iron—like those!' and the second officer pointed triumphantly to the boxes piled at one side of the cabin.

'Well done!' said Hewitt. 'You're quite a smart detective. Did you find out who brought the parcels, and who they were addressed to?'

'No, I couldn't get quite as far as that. Of course the clerk didn't know the names of the senders, and now knowing me, wouldn't tell me exactly where the parcels were going. But I got quite chummy with him after a bit, and I'm going to meet him presently—he has the afternoon off, and we're going for a stroll. I'll find something more, I'll bet you! I'll let you know some more soon.'

Brayser went, and Norton, the steward of the old ship, was brought into the cabin. He was a sharp-eyed, rather cadaverous-looking man, and he spoke with sepulchral hollowness. He had heard, he said, that there was something wrong with the chests of bullion, and came on board to give any information he could. If he might speak strictly confidentially he would suggest that observations be kept on Wickens, the carpenter. He (Norton) didn't want to be uncharitable, but his pantry happened to be next the bullion-room, and he had heard Wickens at work for a very long time just below—on the under side of the floor of the bullion-room, it seemed to him, although, of course, he *might* have been mistaken. Still, it was very odd that the carpenter always seemed to have a job just at that spot. He also believed that Wickens had keys that fitted the bullion-room door.

'Thank you, Mr Norton,' said Merrick, with a twinkle in his eye; 'we won't forget what you say. Of course, if the stuff is found in consequence of any of your information, you won't lose by it.'

The steward said he hoped not, and he wouldn't fail to keep his eye on the carpenter. He had noticed Wickens was in the tug, and he trusted that if they were going to question him they would do it cautiously, so as not to put him on his guard. Merrick promised they would.

'By the bye, Mr Norton,' asked Hewitt, 'supposing your suspicions to be justified, what do you suppose the carpenter would do with the bullion?'

'Well, sir,' replied Martin, 'I don't think he'd keep it on the ship. He'd probably dump it somewhere.'

The steward left, and Merrick lay back in his chair and guffawed aloud. 'This grows farcical,' he said, 'simply farcical. What a happy family they must have been aboard the *Nicobar*! And now here's the captain watching the second officer, and the second officer watching the captain and the steward, and the steward watching the carpenter! It's immense. And now we're going to see the carpenter. Wonder whom *he* suspects?'

Hewitt said nothing, but his eyes twinkled with intense merriment, and presently the carpenter was brought into the cabin.

'Good-day to you, gentlemen,' said the carpenter in a soft and deferential voice, looking from one to the other. 'Might I 'ave the honour of adressin' the salvage gentlemen?'

'That's right,' Merrick answered, motioning him to a seat. 'This is the salvage shop, Mr Wickens. What can we do for you?

The carpenter coughed gently behind his hand. 'I took the liberty of comin', gentlemen, consekins o' 'earing' as there was some bullion missin'. P'raps I'm wrong.'

'Not at all. We haven't found as much as we expected, and I suppose by this time nearly everybody knows it.'

The carpenter coughed again. 'Well, gentlemen, my story ain't a long one. All I've to say was what I 'eard on board, just before she went down. The passengers was off, and the crew was gettin' into the other boats when the skipper turns to the steward an' speaks to him quiet-like, not observin', gentlemen, as I was agin 'is elbow, so for to say. "'Ere, Norton," 'e sez, or words to that effeck, "why shouldn't we try getting them things ashore with us—you know, the cases—eh? I've a notion we're pretty close inshore," 'e sez, "and there's nothink of a sea now. You take one, anyway, and I'll try the other," 'e says, "but don't make a flourish." Then he sez, louder, 'cos o' the steward goin off, "they're the likeliest stuff, and at worst we can but drop 'em. But look sharp," 'e says. Then I gets into the boat, and that's all I 'eard.'

'That was all?' asked Hewitt, watching the man's face sharply.

'All?' the carpenter answered with some surprise. 'Yes, that was all; but I think it's pretty well enough, don't you? It's plain enough, what was meant—him and the steward was to take two cases, one apiece, on the quiet, and they was the likeliest stuff aboard, as he said himself. And now there's two cases o' bullion missin'.' With this, he left.

'Well,' said Merrick, grinning across the table at Hewitt, 'this is a queer go, isn't it? What that man says makes the skipper's case look pretty fishy, doesn't it? What he says, and what Brayser says, taken together, makes a pretty strong case—I should say makes the thing a certainty. But what a business! It's likely to be a bit serious for some one, but it's a rare joke in a way. Wonder if Brayser will find out anything more? Pity the skipper and steward didn't agree as to whom they should pretend to suspect. *That's* a mistake on their part.'

'Not at all,' Hewitt replied. '*If* they are conspiring, and know what they're about, they will avoid seeming to be both in a tale. The bullion is in bars, I understand?'

'Yes, five bars in each case; weight, sixteen pounds to a bar.'

'Let me see,' Hewitt went on, as he looked at his watch; 'it is now nearly two o'clock. I must think over these things if I am to do anything in the case. In the meantime, if it could be managed, I should like enormously to have a turn under water in a diving-dress. I have always had a curiosity to see under the sea. Could it be managed now?

'I *might* spot something,' he said; 'one never knows. And if I do anything in a case I always make it a rule to see and hear everything that can possibly be seen or heard, important or not. Clues lie where least expected. But beyond that, probably I may never have another chance of a little experience in a diving-dress. So if it can be managed I'd be glad.'

'Very well, you shall go, if you say so. And since it's your first venture, I'll come down with you myself. The men are all ashore, I think, or most of them. Come along.'

Hewitt was put in woollens and then in india-rubbers. A leaden-soled boot of twenty pounds' weight was strapped on each foot, and weights were hung on his back and chest.

'That's the dress that Gullen usually has,' Merrick remarked. 'He's a very smart fellow; we usually send him first, to make measurements and so on. An excellent man, but a bit too fond of the diver's lotion.'

'What's that?' asked Hewitt.

'Oh, you shall try some if you like, afterwards.'

Merrick went first over the ladder at the side, and Hewitt with much difficulty followed. As the water closed over his head, his sensations altered considerably. There was less weight to carry; his arms in particular felt light, though slow in motion. Down, down they went slowly, and all round about it was fairly light, but once on the sunken vessel and among the lower decks, the electric lamps were necessary enough. Once or twice Merrick spoke, laying his helmet against Hewitt's for the purpose of instructing him to keep his air-pipe, life-line, and lamp connection from fouling something at every step. Here and there shadowy swimming shapes came out of the gloom, attracted by their lamps, to dart into obscurity again with a twist of the tail. The fishes were exploring the *Nicobar*. The hatchway of the lower deck was open, and down this they passed to the orlop deck. A little way along this they came to a door standing open, with a broken lock hanging to it. It was the door of the bullion-room, which had been forced by the divers in the morning.

Merrick indicated by signs how the cases had been found piled on the floor. One of the sides of the room of thin steel was torn and thrust in the length of its whole upper half, and when they backed out of the room and passed the open door they stood in the great breach made by the bow of the strange coasting vessel. Steel, iron, wood, and everything stood in rents and splinters, and through the great gap they looked out into the immeasurable ocean.

They regained the upper deck, and Hewitt, placing his helmet against his companion's, told him that he meant to have a short walk on the ocean bed. He took to the ladder again, where it lay over the side, and Merrick followed him.

The bottom was of that tough, slimy sort of clay-rock that is found in many places about our coasts, and was dotted here and there with lumps of harder rock and clumps of curious weed. The two divers turned at the bottom of the ladder, walked a few steps, and looked up at the great hole in the *Nicobar's* side.

Hewitt turned away, and began walking about. Once or twice he stood and looked thoughtfully at the ground he stood on, which was fairly flat. He turned over with his foot a whitish, clean-looking stone about as large as a loaf. Then he wandered on slowly, once or twice stopping to examine the rock beneath him, and presently stooped

Merrick went first over the ladder at the side, and Hewitt followed.

to look at another stone nearly as large as the other, weedy on one side only, standing on the edge of a cavity in the claystone. He pushed the stone into the hole, which it filled, and then he stood up.

Merrick put his helmet against Hewitt's, and shouted,—

'Satisfied now? Seen enough of the bottom?'

'In a moment!' Hewitt shouted back; and he straightway began striding out in the direction of the ship. Arrived at the bows, he turned back to the point he started from, striding off again from there to the white stone he had kicked over, and from there to the vessel's side again. Merrick watched him in intense amazement, and hurried, as well as he might, after the light of Hewitt's lamp. Arrived for the second time at the bows of the ship, Hewitt turned and made his way along the side to the ladder, and forthwith ascended, followed by Merrick. There was no halt at the deck this time, and the two made their way up and up into the lighter water above, and the world of air.

On the tug, as the men were unscrewing them from their waterproof prisons, Merrick asked Hewitt,—

'Will you try the "lotion" now?'

'No,' Hewitt replied, 'I won't go quite so far as that. But I *will* have a little whisky, if you've any in the cabin. And give me a pencil and a piece of paper.'

These things were brought, and on the paper Martin Hewitt immediately wrote a few figures and kept it in his hand.

'I might easily forget those figures,' he observed.

Merrick wondered, but said nothing.

Once more comfortably in the cabin, and clad in his usual garments, Hewitt asked if Merrick could produce a chart of the parts thereabout.

'Here you are,' was the reply, 'coast and all. Big enough, isn't it? I've already marked the position of the wreck on it in pencil. She lies pointing north by east as nearly exact as anything.'

'As you've begun it,' said Hewitt, 'I shall take the liberty of making a few more pencil marks on this.' And with that he spread out the crumpled note of figures, and began much ciphering and measuring.

'There we are,' he said finally. 'And the nearest village to that is Lostella—indeed, the only coast village in that neighbourhood.' He rose. 'Bring me the sharpest-eyed person on board,' he said; 'that is, if he were here all day yesterday.'

'Well, really I believe the very sharpest chap is the boy. He's most annoyingly observant sometimes. I'll send for him.'

He came—a bright, snub-nosed, impudent-looking young ruffian.

'Yesterday,' said Hewitt, 'no doubt you saw various pieces of wreckage floating about. What were they?'

'Hatch-gratings mostly—nothin' much else.'

'I saw them. Now, remember. Did you see a hatch-grating floating yesterday that was different from the others? A painted one for instance—those out there now are not painted, you know.'

'Yessir, I see a little white 'un painted, bobbin' about away beyond the foremast of the *Nicobar*.'

'You're sure of that?'

'Certain sure, sir—it was the only painted thing floatin'. And today it's washed away somewheres.'

'So I noticed. You're a smart lad. Here's a shilling for you.'

The boy disappeared, and Hewitt turned to Merrick and said, 'I'm going to take a walk down to Lostella now—it's only two or three miles along the coast, but it will soon be getting dark.'

'But what sort of a clue have you got? I didn't—'

'Never mind,' replied Hewitt, with a chuckle. 'Officially, you know, I've no right to a clue just yet—I'm not commissioned. When I am I'll tell you everything.'

Hewitt was scarcely ashore when he was seized by the excited Brayser, who told him that the railway clerk had recognized Norton as being the sender of the packages, and he had found out that they being sent to Captain Mackrie's London address. He was going to London himself to pursue the matter further. With this, the zealous second officer dashed off without waiting for a reply. Hewitt looked after him with an amused smile, and turned off towards Lostella.

★   ★   ★   ★

It was about eleven the next morning when Merrick received the following note, brought by a boatman:

'DEAR MERRICK,—Am I commissioned? If not, don't trouble, but if I am, be just outside Lostella, at the turning before you come to the Smack Inn, at two o'clock. Bring with you a light cart, a policeman

—or two perhaps will be better—and a man with a spade. There will probably be a little cabbage-digging. Are you fond of the sport?— Yours, MARTIN HEWITT.

'P.S.—*Keep all your men aboard*; bring a spade artist from town.'

Merrick was off in a boat at once. His principals had replied to his telegram after Hewitt's departure the day before, giving him a free hand to do whatever seemed best. With some little difficulty he got the policemen, and with none at all he got a light cart and a jobbing man with a spade. Together they drove off to the meeting-place.

It was before the time, but Martin Hewitt was there, waiting. 'You're quick,' he said, 'but the sooner the better.'

'Have you got the stuff, then?' Merrick asked anxiously.

'No not yet,' Hewitt replied, 'but I think we're about at the end of the job—it's been a fairly lucky one. But I'll explain after.'

Just beyond the Smack Inn, Hewitt halted the cart, and all got down. They looped the horse's reins round a hedge-stake and proceeded the small remaining distance on foot, with the policeman behind, to avoid a premature scare. They turned up a lane behind a few small and rather dirty cottages facing the sea, each with its patch of kitchen garden behind. Hewitt led the way to the second garden pushed open the wicket gate and walked boldly in, followed by the others.

Cabbages covered most of the patch, and seemed pretty healthy in their situation, with the exception of half a dozen—singularly enough, all together in a group. These were drooping, yellow and wilted, and towards these Hewitt straightway walked. 'Dig up those wilted cabbages,' he said to the jobbing man. 'They're really useless now. You'll probably find something else six inches down or so.'

The man struck his spade into the soft earth, wherein it stopped suddenly with a thud. But at this moment a gaunt, slatternly woman, with a black eye, a handkerchief over her head, and her skirt pinned up in front, observing the invasion from the back door of the cottage, rushed out like a maniac and attacked the party valiantly with a broom. She upset the jobbing man over his spade, knocked off one policeman's helmet, lunged into the other's face with her broom, and was making her second attempt to hit Hewitt (who had dodged), when Merrick caught her firmly by the elbows from behind, pressed them together, and held her. She screamed, 'Peter! Peter! Come 'ee, come 'ee here!

Davey! They're come!'

A grimy child came to the cottage door, and seeing the woman thus held, and strangers in the garden, set up a piteous howl. Meantime the digger had uncovered two wooden boxes, each eighteen inches long or so, bound with hoop-iron and sealed. One had been torn partly open at the top, and the broken wood roughly replaced. When this was lifted, bars of yellow metal were visible within.

The woman still screamed vehemently, and struggled. The grimy child retreated, and then there appeared at the door, staggering hazily and rubbing his eyes, a shaggy, unkempt man, in shirt and trousers. He looked stupidly at the scene before him, and his jaw dropped.

'Take that man,' cried Hewitt. 'He's one!' And the policeman promptly took him, so that he had handcuffs on his wrists before he had collected his faculties sufficiently to begin swearing.

Hewitt and the other policeman entered the cottage, and found another man, younger, and fast alseep. 'He's the other,' said Hewitt. 'Take *him*.' And this one was handcuffed before he woke.

Then the recovered gold was put into the cart, and with the help of the village constable, who brought his own handcuffs for the benefit and adornment of the lady with the broom, such a procession marched out of Lostella as had never been dreamed of by the oldest inhabitant in his worst nightmare, nor recorded in the whole history of Cornwall.

'Now,' said Hewttt, turning to Merrick, 'we must have that fellow of yours—what's his name—Gullen, isn't it?' The one that went down to measure the hole in the ship. You've kept him aboard, of course?'

'What, Gullen?' exclaimed Merrick. 'Gullen? Well, as a matter of fact he went ashore last night and hasn't come back. But you don't mean to say—'

'I *do*,' replied Hewitt. 'And now you've lost him.'

★   ★   ★   ★

Back on the tug Hewitt explained to Merrick how he had uncovered the plot. Gullen and his confederates had visited the scene the day before Gullen was due to inspect the breach in the Nicobar's side. They had left a large white stone with a hook and a line attached on the sea bed, and joined the line to a float on the surface. As there was a lot of debris floating about on the surface they thought it would be safe to use a hatch-grating as a marker, but forgot that the Nicobar gratings were all plain wood, and theirs was painted white.

The next day Gullen dragged the boxes along the sea bed to the stone, and tied the line around them. That night the men returned. As the salvage tug was still there, they used a small rowing boat to come in and pick up the float, hoping not to be noticed. They took the float back to a larger fishing boat which had the weight to pull up the heavy boxes.

By making notes and marking them down on a chart he had been able to ascertain the direction the boat had gone in, and all indications pointed to Lostella.

'I made off toward Lostella. The tide was low and it was getting dusk when I arrived. A number of boats and smacks were lying anchored on the beach, but there were few people to be seen. I began looking out for smacks with white-painted fittings in them. There are not so many of these among fishing vessels—brown or red is more likely, or sheer colourless dirt over paint unrecognizable. There were only two that I saw last night. The first *might* have been the one I wanted, but there was nothing to show it. The second *was* the one. She was half-decked and had a small white-painted hatch. I shifted the hatch and found a long line, attached to the grating at one end and carrying a hook at the other! They had neglected to unfasten their apparatus—perhaps had an idea that there might be a chance of using it again in a few days, I went to the transom and read the inscriptions, "*Rebecca*. Peter and David Garthew, Lostella". Then my business was to find the Garthews.

'I wandered about the village for some little time, and presently got hold of a boy. I made a simple excuse for asking about the Garthews —wanted to go for a sail tomorrow. The boy, with many grins, confided to me that both of the Garthews were "on the booze". I should find them at the Smack Inn, where they had been all day, drunk as fiddlers. This seemed a likely sort of thing after the haul they had made. I went to the Smack Inn, determined to claim old friendships with the Garthews, although I didn't know Peter from David. There they were—one sleepy drunk, and the other loving and crying drunk. I got as friendly as possible with them under the circumstances, and at

46

closing time stood another gallon of beer and carried it home for them, while they carried each other. I took care to have a good look round in the cottage. I even helped Peter's "old woman"—the lady with the broom—to carry them up to bed. But nowhere could I see anything that looked like a bullion-case or a hiding-place for one.

'This morning I was at Lostella before ten, and took a look at the Garthew's cabbages. It seemed odd that half a dozen, all in a clump together, looked withered and limp, as though they had been dug up hastily, the roots broken, perhaps, and then replanted. And altogether these particular cabbages had a dissipated, leaning-different-ways look, as though *they* had been on the loose with the Garthews. As expected, there was a box below. The rest you saw for yourself. I think you and I may congratulate each other on having dodged that broom. It hit all the others.'

'What I'm wild about,' said Merrick, 'is having let that scoundrel Gullen get off. He's an artful chap, without a doubt. He saw us go over the side, you know, and after you had gone he came into the cabin for some instructions. Your pencil notes and the chart were on the table, and no doubt he put two and two together (which was more than I could do, not knowing what had happened), and concluded to make himself safe for a bit. He had no leave that night—he just pulled away on the quiet. Why didn't you give me the tip to keep him?'

'That wouldn't have done. In the first place, there was no legal evidence to warrant his arrest, and ordering him to keep aboard would have aroused his suspicions. I didn't know at the time how many days, or weeks, it would take me to find the bullion, if I ever found it, and in that time Gullen might have communicated in some way with his accomplices, and so spoilt the whole thing. Yes, certainly he seems to have been fairly smart in his way. He knew he would probably be sent down first, as usual, alone to make measurements, and conceived his plan and made his arrangements forthwith.'

'But now what I want to know is what about all those *Nicobar* people watching and suspecting one another? More especially what about the cases the captain and the steward are said to have fetched ashore?'

Hewitt laughed. 'Well,' he said, 'as to that, the presence of the bullion seems to have bred all sorts of mutual suspicion on board the ship. Brayser was over-fussy, and his continual chatter started it probably, so that it spread like an infection. As to the captain and the steward, of course I don't know anything but that their rescued cases were *not* bullion cases. Probably they were doing a little private trading—it's generally the case when captain and steward seem unduly friendly for their relative positions—and perhaps the case contained something specially valuable: vases or bronzes from Japan, for instance; possibly the most valuable things of the size they had aboard. Then, if they had insured their things, Captain Mackrie (who has the reputation of a sharp and not very scrupulous man) might possibly think it rather a stroke of business to get the goods and the insurance money too, which would lead him to keep his parcels as quite as possible. But that's as it may be.'

The case was much as Hewitt had surmized. The zealous Brayser, posting to London in hot haste after Mackrie, spent some days in watching him. At last the captain and the steward with their two boxes took a cab and went to Bond Street, with Brayser in another cab behind them. The two entered a shop, the window of which was set out with rare curiosities and much old silver and gold. Brayser could restrain himself no longer. He grabbed a passing policeman, and rushed with him into the shop. There they found the captain and the steward with two small packing cases opened before them, trying to sell—a couple of very ancient-looking Japanese bronze figures, of that curious old workmanship and varied colour of metal that in genuine examples mean nowadays high money value.

Brayser vanished: there was too much chaff for him to live through in the British mercantile after this adventure. The fact was, the steward had come across the bargain, but had not sufficient spare cash to buy, so he called in the aid of the captain, and they speculated in the bronzes as partners. There was much anxious inspection of the prizes on the way home, and much discussion as to the proper price to ask. Finally, it was said, they got three hundred pounds for the pair.

Now and again Hewitt meets Merrick still. Sometimes Merrick says, 'Now, I wonder after all whether or not some of those *Nicobar* men who were continually dodging suspiciously about that bullion-room *did* mean having a dash at the gold if there were a chance?' And Hewitt replies, 'I wonder.'

THE SECRET GARDEN

G.K. Chesterton

Aristide Valentin, Chief of the Paris Police, was late for his dinner, and some of his guests began to arrive before him. These were, however, reassured by his confidential servant, Ivan, the old man with a scar and a face almost as grey as his moustaches, who always sat at a table in the entrance hall—a hall hung with weapons. Valentin's house was perhaps as peculiar and celebrated as its master. It was an old house, with high walls and tall poplars almost overhanging the Seine; but the oddity—and perhaps the police value—of its architecture was this: that there was no ultimate exit at all except this front door, which was guarded by Ivan and the armoury. The garden was large and elaborate, and there were many exits from the house into the garden. But there was no exit from the garden into the world outside; all round it ran a tall, smooth unscalable wall with special spikes at the top; no bad garden, perhaps, for a man to reflect in whom some hundred criminals had sworn to kill.

As Ivan explained to the guests, their host had telephoned that he was detained for ten minutes. He was, in truth, making some last arrangements about executions and such ugly things; and though these duties were rootedly repulsive to him, he always performed them with precision. Ruthless in the pursuit of criminals, he was very mild about their punishment. Since he had been supreme over French—and largely over European—police methods, his great influence had been honourably used for the mitigation of sentences and the purification of prisons. He was one of the great humanitarian French freethinkers; and the only thing wrong with them is that they make mercy even colder than justice.

When Valentin arrived he was already dressed in black clothes and the red rosette—an elegant figure, his dark beard already streaked with grey. He went straight through his house to his study, which opened on the grounds behind. The garden door of it was open, and after he had carefully locked his box in its official place, he stood for a few seconds at the open door looking out upon the garden. A sharp moon was fighting with the flying rags and tatters of a storm, and Valentin regarded it with a wistfulness unusual in such scientific natures as his. Perhaps such scientific natures have some psychic prevision of the most tremendous problem of their lives. From any such occult mood, at least, he quickly recovered, for he knew he was late and that his guests had already begun to arrive. A glance at his drawing-room when he entered it was enough to make certain that his principal guest was not there, at any rate. He saw all the other pillars of the little party; he saw Lord Galloway, the English Ambassador—a choleric old man with a russet face like an apple, wearing the blue ribbon of the Garter. He saw Lady Galloway, slim and thread-like with silver hair and a face sensitive and superior. He saw her daughter, Lady Margaret Graham, a pale and pretty girl with an elfish face and copper-coloured hair. He saw the Duchess of Mont St Michel, black-eyed and opulent, and with her her two daughters, black-eyed and opulent also. He saw Dr Simon, a typical French scientist, with glasses, a pointed brown beard, and a forehead barred with those parallel wrinkles which are the penalty of superciliousness, since they come through constantly elevating the eyebrows. He saw Father Brown of Cobhole, in Essex, whom he had recently met in England. He saw—perhaps with more interest than any of those—a tall man in uniform, who had bowed to the Galloways without receiving any very hearty acknowledgement, and who now advanced alone to pay his respects to his host. This was Commandant O'Brien, of the French Foreign Legion. He was a slim yet somewhat swaggering figure, clean-shaven, dark-haired, and blue-eyed, and as seemed natural in an officer of that famous regiment of victorious failures and successful suicides, he had an air at once dashing and melancholy. He was by birth an Irish gentleman, and in boyhood had known the Galloways—especially Margaret Graham. He had left his country after some crash of debts, and now expressed his complete freedom from British etiquette by swinging about in uniform, sabre and spurs. When he bowed to the Ambassador's family, Lord and Lady Galloway bent stiffly, and Lady Margaret looked away.

But for whatever old causes such people might be interested in each other, their distinguished host was not specially interested in them. Not one of them at least was in his eyes the guest of the evening. Valentin was expecting, for special reasons, a man of world-wide fame, whose friendship he had secured during some of his great detective tours and triumphs in the United States. He was expecting Julius K. Brayne, that multi-millionaire whose colossal and even crushing endowments of small religions have occasioned so much easy sport and easier solemnity for the American and English papers. Nobody could quite make out whether Mr Brayne was an atheist or a Mormon, or a Christian Scientist; but he was ready to pour money into any intellectual vessel, so long as it was an untried vessel. One of his hobbies was to wait for the American Shakespeare—a hobby more patient than angling. He admired Walt Whitman, but thought that Luke P. Tanner, of Paris, Pa., was more 'progressive' than Whitman any day. He liked anything that he thought 'progressive'. He thought Valentin 'progressive', thereby doing him a grave injustice.

The solid appearance of Julius K. Brayne in the room was as decisive as a dinner bell. He had this great quality, which very few of us can claim that his presence was as big as his absence. He was a huge fellow, as fat as he was tall, clad in complete evening black, without so much relief as a watch-chain or a ring. His hair was white and well brushed back like a German's; his face was red, fierce and cherubic, with one dark tuft under the lower lip that threw up that otherwise infantile visage with an effect theatrical and even Mephistophelean. Not long, however, did that *salon* merely stare at the celebrated American; his lateness had already become a domestic problem, and he was sent with all speed into the dining-room with Lady Galloway upon his arm.

Except on one point the Galloways were genial and casual enough. So long as Lady Margaret did not take the arm of that adventurer O'Brien her father was quite satisfied; and she had not done so; she had decorously gone in with Dr Simon. Nevertheless, old Lord Galloway was restless and almost rude. He was diplomatic enough during dinner, but when, over the cigars, three of the younger men—Simon the doctor, Brown the priest, and the detrimental O'Brien, the exile in a foreign uniform—all melted away to mix with the ladies or smoke in the conservatory, then the English diplomatist grew very undiplomatic indeed. He was stung every sixty seconds with the thought that the scamp O'Brien might be signalling to Margaret somehow; he did not attempt to imagine how. He was left over the coffee with Brayne, the hoary Yankee who believed in all religions, and Valentin, the grizzled Frenchman who believed in none. They could argue with each other, but neither could appeal to him. After a time this 'progressive' logomachy had reached a crisis of tedium; Lord Galloway got up also and sought the drawing-room. He lost his way in long passages for some six or eight minutes: till he heard the high-pitched, didactic voice of the doctor, and then the dull voice of the priest, followed by general laughter. They also, he thought with a curse, were probably arguing about 'science and religion'. But the instant he opened the *salon* door he saw only one thing—he saw what was not there. He saw that Commandant O'Brien was absent, and that Lady Margaret was absent, too.

Rising impatiently from the drawing-room, as he had from the dining-room, he stamped along the passage once more. His notion of protecting his daughter from the Irish-Algerian ne'er-do-well had become something central and even mad in his mind. As he went towards the back of the house, where was Valentin's study, he was surprised to meet his daughter, who swept past with a white, scornful face, which was a second enigma. If she had been with O'Brien, where was O'Brien? If she had not been with O'Brien, where had she been? With a sort of senile and passionate suspicion he groped his way to the dark back parts of the mansion, and eventually found a servants' entrance that opened onto the garden. The moon with her scimitar had now ripped up and rolled away all the stormwrack. The argent light lit up all four corners of the garden. A tall figure in blue was striding across the lawn towards the study door; a glint of moonlit silver on his facings picked him out as Commandant O'Brien.

He vanished through the French windows into the house, leaving Lord Galloway in an indescribable temper, at once virulent and vague. The blue-and-silver garden, like a scene in a theatre, seemed to taunt him with all that tyrannic tenderness against which his worldly authority was at war. The length and grace of the Irishman's stride enraged him as if he were a rival instead of a father; the moonlight maddened him. He was trapped as if by magic into a garden of troubadours, a Watteau fairyland; and, willing to shake off such amorous imbecilities by speech, he stepped briskly after his enemy. As he did so he tripped over some tree or stone in the grass; looked down at it first with irritation and then a second time with curiosity. The next instant the moon and the tall poplars looked at an unusual sight—an elderly English diplomatist running hard and crying or bellowing as he ran.

His hoarse shouts brought a pale face to the study door, the beaming glasses and worried brow of Dr Simon, who heard the nobleman's first clear words. Lord Galloway was crying: 'A corpse in the grass—a blood stained corpse.' O'Brien at least had gone utterly from his mind.

'We must tell Valentin at once,' said the doctor, when the other had brokenly described all that he had dared to examine. 'It is fortunate that he is here'; and even as he spoke the great detective entered the study, attracted by the cry. It was almost amusing to note his typical transformation; he had come with the common concern of a host and a gentleman, fearing that some guest or servant was ill. When he was told the gory fact, he turned with all his gravity instantly bright and business-like; for this, however abrupt and awful, was his business.

'Strange, gentlemen,' he said, as they hurried out into the garden, 'that I should have hunted mysteries all over the earth, and now one comes and settles in my own backyard. But where is the place?' They crossed the lawn less easily, as a slight mist had begun to rise from the river; but under the guidance of the shaken Galloway they found the body sunken in deep grass—the body of a very tall and broad-shouldered man. He lay face downwards, so they could only see that his big shoulders were clad in black cloth, and that his big head was bald, except for a wisp or two of brown hair that clung to his skull like wet seaweed. A scarlet serpent of blood crawled from under his fallen face.

'At least,' said Simon, with a deep and singular intonation, 'he is none of our party.'

'Examine him, doctor,' cried Valentin rather sharply. 'He may not be dead.'

The doctor bent down. 'He is not quite cold, but I am afraid he is dead enough,' he answered. 'Just help me to lift him up.'

They lifted him carefully an inch from the ground, and all doubts as to his being really dead were settled at once and frightfully. The head fell away. It had been entirely sundered from the body; whoever had cut his throat had managed to sever the neck as well. Even Valentin was slightly shocked. 'He must have been as strong as a gorilla,' he muttered.

Not without a shiver, though he was used to anatomical abortions, Dr Simon lifted the head. It was slightly slashed about the neck and jaw, but the face was substantially unhurt. It was a ponderous, yellow face, at once sunken and swollen, with a hawk-like nose and heavy lids—the face of a wicked Roman emperor, with, perhaps, a distant touch of a Chinese emperor. All present seemed to look at it with the coldest eye of ignorance. Nothing else could be noted about the man except that, as they had lifted the body, they had seen underneath it the white gleam of a shirtfront defaced with a red gleam of blood. As Dr Simon said, the man had never been of their party. But he might very well have been trying to join it, for he had come dressed for such an occasion.

Valentin went down on his hands and knees and examined with his closest professional attention the grass and ground for some twenty yards round the body, in which he was assisted less skilfully by the doctor, and quite vaguely by the English lord. Nothing rewarded their grovellings except a few twigs, snapped or chopped into very small lengths, which Valentin lifted for an instant's examination, and then tossed away.

'Twigs,' he said gravely; 'twigs, and a total stranger with his head cut off; that is all there is on this lawn.'

There was an almost creepy stillness, and then the unnerved Galloway called out sharply:

'Who's that? Who's that over there by the garden wall?'

A small figure with a foolishly large head drew waveringly near them in the moonlit haze; looked for an instant like a goblin, but turned out to be the harmless little priest whom they had left in the drawing-room.

'I say,' he said meekly, 'there are no gates to this garden, do you know.'

Valentin's black brows had come together somewhat crossly, as they did on principle at the sight of the cassock. But he was far too just a man to deny the relevance of the remark. 'You are right,' he said. 'Before we find out how he came to be killed, we may have to find out how he came to be here. Now listen to me, gentlemen. If it can be done without prejudice to my position and duty, we shall all agree that certain distinguished names might well be kept out of this. There are ladies, gentlemen, and there is a foreign ambassador. If we must mark it down as a crime, then it must be followed up as a crime. But till then I can use my own discretion. I am the head of the police; I am so public that I can afford to be private. Please Heaven, I will clear every one of my own guests before I call in my men to look for anybody else. Gentlemen, upon your honour, you will none of you leave the house till tomorrow at noon; there are bedrooms for all. Simon, I think you know where to find my man, Ivan, in the front hall; he is a confidential man. Tell him to leave another servant on guard and come to me at once. Lord Galloway, you are certainly the best person to tell the ladies what has happened, and prevent a panic. They also must stay. Father Brown and I will remain with the body.'

When this spirit of the captain spoke in Valentin he was obeyed like a bugle. Dr Simon went through to the armoury and routed out Ivan, the public detective's private detective. Galloway went to the drawing-room and told the terrible news tactfully enough, so that by the time the company assembled there the ladies were already startled and already soothed. Meanwhile the good priest and the good atheist stood at the head and foot of the dead man motionless in the moonlight, like symbolic statues of their two philosophies of death.

Ivan, the confidential man with the scar and the moustaches, came out of the house like a cannon ball, and came racing across the lawn to Valentin like a dog to his master. His livid face was quite lively with the glow of this domestic detective story, and it was with almost unpleasant eagerness that he asked his master's permission to examine the remains.

'Yes; look, if you like, Ivan,' said Valentin, 'but don't be long. We must go in and thrash this out in the house.'

Ivan lifted his head, and then almost let it drop.

'Why,' he gasped, 'it's—no, it isn't; it can't be. Do you know this man, sir?'

'No,' said Valentin indifferently, 'we had better go inside.'

Between them they carried the corpse to a sofa in the study, and then all made their way to the drawing-room.

The detective sat down at a desk quietly, and even with hesitation; but his eye was the iron eye of a judge at assize. He made a few rapid notes upon paper in front of him, and then said shortly: 'Is everybody here?'

'Not Mr Brayne,' said the Duchess of Mont St Michel, looking round.

'No,' said Lord Galloway, in a hoarse, harsh voice. 'And not Mr Neil O'Brien, I fancy. I saw that gentleman walking in the garden when the corpse was still warm.'

'Ivan,' said the detective, 'go and fetch Commandant O'Brien and Mr Brayne. Mr Brayne, I know, is finishing a cigar in the dining-room; Commandant O'Brien, I think, is walking up and down the conservatory. I am not sure.'

The faithful attendant flashed from the room, and before anyone could stir or speak Valentin went on with the same soldierly swiftness of exposition.

'Everyone here knows that a dead man has been found in the garden, his head cut clean from his body. Dr Simon, you have examined it. Do you think that to cut a man's throat like that would need great force? Or, perhaps, only a very sharp knife?'

'I should say that it could not be done with a knife at all,' said the pale doctor.

'Have you any thought,' resumed Valentin, 'of a tool with which it could be done?'

'Speaking with modern probabilities, I really haven't,' said the doctor, arching his painful brows. 'It's not easy to hack a neck through even clumsily, and this was a very clean cut. It could be done with a battle-axe or an old headsman's axe, or an old two-handed sword.'

'But, good heavens!' cried the Duchess, almost in hysterics; 'there aren't any two-handed swords and battle-axes round here.'

Valentin was still busy with the paper in front of him. 'Tell me,' he said, still writing rapidly, 'could it have been done with a long French cavalry sabre?'

A low knocking came at the door, which for some unreasonable reason, curdled everyone's blood like the knocking in *Macbeth*. Amid that frozen silence Dr Simon managed to say: 'A sabre—yes, I suppose it could.'

'Thank you,' said Valentin. 'Come in, Ivan.'

The confidential Ivan opened the door and ushered in Commandant Neil O'Brien, whom he had found at last pacing the garden again.

The Irish officer stood disordered and defiant on the threshhold. 'What do you want with me?' he cried.

'Please sit down,' said Valentin in pleasant, level tones. 'Why, you aren't wearing your sword! Where is it?'

'I left it on the library table,' said O'Brien, his brogue deepening in his disturbed mood. 'It was a nuisance, it was getting—'

'Ivan,' said Valentin: 'please go and get the Commandant's sword from the library.' Then, as the servant vanished: 'Lord Galloway says he saw you leaving the garden just before he found the corpse. What were you doing in the garden?'

The Commandant flung himself recklessly into a chair. 'Oh,' he cried in pure Irish; 'admirin' the moon. Communing with Nature, me boy.'

A heavy silence sank and endured, and at the end of it came again that trivial and terrible knocking. Ivan reappeared, carrying an empty steel scabbard. 'This is all I can find,' he said.

'Put it on the table,' said Valentin, without looking up.

There was an inhuman silence in the room, like that sea of inhuman silence round the dock of the condemned murderer. The Duchess's weak exclamations had long ago died away. Lord Galloway's swollen hatred was satisfied and even sobered. The voice that came was quite unexpected.

'I think I can tell you,' cried Lady Margaret, in that clear, quivering voice with which a courageous woman speaks publicly. 'I can tell you what Mr O'Brien was doing in the garden, since he is bound to silence. He was asking me to marry him. I refused; I said in my family circumstances I could give him nothing but my respect. He was a little angry at that; he did not seem to think much of my respect. I wonder,' she added, with rather a wan smile, 'if he will care at all for it now. For I offer it him now. I will swear anywhere that he never did a thing like this.'

Lord Galloway had edged up to his daughter, and was intimidating her in what he imagined to be an undertone. 'Hold your tongue, Maggie,' he said in a thunderous whisper. 'Why should you shield the fellow? Where's his sword? Where's his confounded cavalry—'

He stopped because of the singular stare with which his daughter was regarding him, a look that was indeed a lurid magnet for the whole group.

'You old fool!' she said, in a low voice without pretence of piety; 'what do you suppose you are trying to prove? I tell you this man was innocent while with me. But if he wasn't innocent, he was still with me. If he murdered a man in the garden, who was it who must have seen— who must at least have known? Do you hate Neil so much as to put your own daughter—'

Lady Galloway screamed. Everyone else sat tingling at the touch of those satanic tragedies that have been between lovers before now. They saw the proud, white face of the Scotch aristocrat and her lover, the Irish adventurer, like old portraits in a dark house. The long silence was full of formless historical memories of murdered husbands and poisonous paramours.

In the centre of this morbid silence an innocent voice said: 'Was it a very long cigar?'

The change of thought was so sharp that they had to look round to see who had spoken.

'I mean,' said little Father Brown, from the corner of the room, 'I mean that cigar Mr Brayne is finishing. It seems nearly as long as a walking-stick.'

Despite the irrelevance there was assent as well as irritation in Valentin's face as he lifted his head.

'Quite right,' he remarked sharply. 'Ivan, go and see about Mr Brayne again, and bring him here at once.'

The instant the factotum had closed the door, Valentin addressed the girl with an entirely new earnestness.

'Lady Margaret,' he said, 'we all feel, I am sure, both gratitude and admiration for your act in rising above your lower dignity and explaining the Commandant's conduct. But there is a hiatus still. Lord Galloway, I understand, met you passing from the study to the drawing-room, and it was only some minutes afterwards that he found the garden and the Commandant still walking there.'

'You have to remember,' replied Margaret, with a faint irony in her voice, 'that I had just refused him, so we should scarcely have come back arm in arm. He is a gentleman, anyhow; and he loitered behind—and so got charged with murder.'

'In those few moments,' said Valentin gravely, 'he might really—'

The knock came again, and Ivan put in his scarred face.

'Beg pardon, sir,' he said 'but Mr Brayne has left the house.'

'Left!' cried Valentin, and rose for the first time to his feet.

'Gone. Scooted. Evaporated,' replied Ivan, in humorous French. 'His hat and coat are gone, too; and I'll tell you something to cap it all. I ran outside the house to find any traces of him, and I found one, and a big trace, too.'

'What do you mean?' asked Valentin.

'I'll show you,' said his servant, and reappeared with a flashing naked cavalry sabre, streaked with blood about the point and edge. Everyone in the room eyed it as if it were a thunderbolt; but the experienced Ivan went on quite quietly:

'I found this,' he said, 'flung among the bushes fifty yards up the road to Paris. In other words, I found it just where your respectable Mr Brayne threw it when he ran away.'

There was again a silence, but of a new sort. Valentin took the sabre, examined it, reflected with unaffected concentration of thought, and then turned a respectful face to O'Brien. 'Commandant,' he said, 'we trust you will always produce this weapon if it is wanted for police examination. Meanwhile,' he added, slapping the steel back in the ringing scabbard, 'let me return you your sword.'

At the military symbolism of the action the audience could hardly refrain from applause.

For Neil O'Brien, indeed, that gesture was the turning-point of existence. By the time he was wandering in the mysterious garden again in the colours of the morning the tragic futility of his ordinary

Valentin took the sabre and examined it.

mien had fallen from him; he was a man with many reasons for happiness. Lord Galloway was a gentleman, and had offered him an apology. Lady Margaret was something better than a lady, a woman at least, and had perhaps given him something better than an apology, as they drifted among the old flower-beds before breakfast. The whole company was more light-hearted and humane, for though the riddle of the death remained, the load of suspicion was lifted off them all, and sent flying off to Paris with the strange millionaire—a man they hardly knew. The devil was cast out of the house—he had cast himself out.

Still, the riddle remained; and when O'Brien threw himself on a garden seat beside Dr Simon, that keenly scientific person at once resumed it. He did not get much talk out of O'Brien, whose thoughts were on pleasanter things.

'I can't say it interests me much,' said the Irishman frankly, 'especially as it seems pretty plain now. Apparently Brayne hated this stranger for some reason; lured him into the garden, and killed him with my sword. Then he fled to the city, tossing the sword away as he went. By the way, Ivan tells me the dead man had a Yankee dollar in his pocket. So he was a countryman of Brayne's, and that seems to clinch it. I don't see any difficulties about the business.'

'There are five colossal difficulties,' said the doctor quietly; 'like high walls within walls. Don't mistake me. I don't doubt that Brayne did it; his flight, I fancy, proves that. But as to how he did it. First difficulty: Why should a man kill another man with a great hulking sabre, when he can almost kill him with a pocket knife and put it back in his pocket? Second difficulty: Why was there no noise or outcry? Does a man commonly see another come up waving a scimitar and offer no remarks? Third difficulty: A servant watched the front door all the evening; and a rat cannot get into Valentin's garden anywhere. How did the dead man get into the garden? Fourth difficulty: Given the same conditions, how did Brayne get out of the garden?'

'And the fifth,' said Neil, with eyes fixed on the English priest, who was coming slowly up the path.

'Is a trifle, I suppose,' said the doctor, 'but I think an odd one. When I first saw how the head had been slashed, I supposed the assassin had struck more than once. But on examination I found many cuts across

61

the truncated section; in other words, they were struck *after* the head was off. Did Brayne hate his foe so fiendishly that he stood sabring his body in the moonlight?'

'Horrible!' said O'Brien, and shuddered.

The little priest, Brown, had arrived while they were talking, and had waited, with characteristic shyness, till they had finished. Then he said awkwardly:

'I say, I'm sorry to interrupt. But I was sent to tell you the news!'

'News?' repeated Simon, and stared at him rather painfully through his glasses.

'Yes, I'm sorry,' said Father Brown mildly. 'There's been another murder, you know.'

Both men on the seat sprang up, leaving it rocking.

'And, what's stranger still,' continued the priest, with his dull eyes on the rhododendrons, 'it's the same disgusting sort; it's another beheading. They found the second head actually bleeding in the river, a few yards along Brayne's road to Paris; so they suppose that he—'

'Great Heaven!' cried O'Brien. 'Is Brayne a monomaniac?'

'There are American vendettas,' said the priest impassively. Then he added: 'They want you to come to the library and see it.'

Commandant O'Brien followed the other towards the inquest, feeling decidedly sick. As a soldier, he loathed all this secretive carnage; where were these extravagant amputations going to stop? First one head was hacked off, and then another; in this case (he told himself bitterly) it was not true that two heads were better than one. As he crossed the study he almost staggered at a shocking coincidence. Upon Valentin's table lay the coloured picture of yet a third bleeding head; and it was the head of Valentin himself. A second glance showed him it was only a Nationalist paper, called *The Guillotine*, which every week showed one of its political opponents with rolling eyes and writhing features after execution; for Valentin was an anticlerical of some note. But O'Brien was an Irishman, with a kind of chastity even in his sins; and his gorge rose against that great brutality of the intellect which belongs only to France. He felt Paris as a whole, from the grotesques on the Gothic churches to the gross caricatures in the newspapers. He remembered the gigantic jests of the Revolution. He saw the whole city as one ugly energy, from the sanguinary sketch lying on Valentin's table up to where, above a mountain and forest of gargoyles, the great devil grins on Notre Dame.

The library was long, low, and dark; what light entered it shot from under low blinds and had still some of the ruddy tinge of the morning. Valentin and his servant Ivan were waiting for them at the upper end of a long, slightly-sloping desk, on which lay the mortal remains, looking enormous in the twilight. The big black figure and yellow face of the man found in the garden confronted them essentially unchanged. The second head, which had been fished from among the river reeds that morning, lay streaming and dripping beside it; Valentin's men were still seeking to recover the rest of this second corpse, which was supposed to be afloat. Father Brown, who did not seem to share O'Brien's sensibilities in the least, went up to the second head and examined it with his blinking care. It was little more than a mop of wet, white hair, fringed with silver fire in the red and level morning light; the face, which seemed of an ugly, empurpled and perhaps criminal type, had been much battered against trees or stones as it tossed in the water.

'Good morning, Commandant O'Brien,' said Valentin, with quiet cordiality. 'You have heard of Brayne's last experiment in butchery, I suppose?'

Father Brown was still bending over the head with white hair, and he said, without looking up:

'I suppose it is quite certain that Brayne cut off this head, too.'

'Well, it seems common sense,' said Valentin, with his hands in his pockets. 'Killed in the same way as the other. Found within a few yards of the other. And sliced by the same weapon which we know he carried away.'

'Yes, yes; I know,' replied Father Brown, submissively. 'Yet, you know, I doubt whether Brayne could have cut off this head.'

'Why not?' inquired Dr Simon, with a rational stare.

'Well, Doctor,' said the priest, looking up blinking, 'can a man cut off his own head? I don't know.'

O'Brien felt an insane universe crashing about his ears; but the doctor sprang forward with impetuous practicality and pushed back the wet, white hair.

63

'Oh, there's no doubt it's Brayne,' said the priest quietly. 'He had exactly that chip in the left ear.'

The detective, who had been regarding the priest with steady and glittering eyes, opened his clenched mouth and said sharply: 'You seem to know a lot about him, Father Brown.'

'I do,' said the little man simply. 'I've been about with him for some weeks. He was thinking of joining our church.'

The stare of the fanatic sprang into Valentin's eyes; he strode towards the priest with clenched hands. 'And perhaps,' he cried, with a blasting sneer: 'perhaps he was also thinking of leaving all his money to your church.'

'Perhaps he was,' said Brown stolidly; 'it is possible.'

'In that case,' cried Valentin, with a dreadful smile: 'you may indeed know a great deal about him. About his life and about his—'

Commandant O'Brien laid a hand on Valentin's arm. 'Drop that slanderous rubbish, Valentin,' he said: 'or there may be more swords yet.'

But Valentin (under the steady, humble gaze of the priest) had already recovered himself. 'Well,' he said shortly: 'people's private opinions can wait. You gentlemen are still bound by your promise to stay; you must enforce it on yourselves—and on each other. Ivan here will tell you anything more you want to know; I must get to business and write to the authorities. We can't keep this quiet any longer. I shall be writing in my study if there is any more news.'

'Is there any more news, Ivan?' asked Dr Simon, as the chief of police strode out of the room.

'Only one more thing, I think, sir,' said Ivan, wrinkling up his old grey face; 'but that's important, too, in its way. There's that old buffer you found on the lawn,' and he pointed without pretence of reverence at the big black body with the yellow head. 'We've found out who he is, anyhow.'

'Indeed!' cried the astonished doctor; 'and who is he?'

'His name was Arnold Becker,' said the under-detective, 'though he went by many aliases. He was a wandering sort of scamp, and is known to have been in America; so that was where Brayne got his knife into him. We didn't have much to do with him ourselves, for he worked mostly in Germany. We've communicated, of course, with the German police. But, oddly enough, there was a twin brother of his, named Louis Becker, whom we had a great deal to do with. In fact, we found it necessary to guillotine him only yesterday. Well, it's a rum thing, gentlemen, but when I saw that fellow flat on the lawn I had the greatest jump of my life. If I hadn't seen Louis Becker guillotined with my own eyes, I'd have sworn it was Louis Becker lying there in the grass. Then, of course, I remembered his twin brother in Germany, and following up the clue—'

The explanatory Ivan stopped, for the excellent reason that nobody was listening to him. The commandant and the doctor were both staring at Father Brown, who had sprung stiffly to his feet, and was holding his temples tight like a man in sudden and violent pain.

'Stop, stop, stop!' he cried; 'stop talking a minute, for I see half. Will God give me strength? Will my brain make the one jump and see all? Heaven help me! I used to be fairly good at thinking. I could paraphrase any page in Aquinas once. Will my head split—or will it see? I see half—I see only half.'

He buried his head in his hands, and stood in a sort of rigid torture of thought or prayer, while the other three could only go on staring at this last prodigy of their wild twelve hours.

When Father Brown's hands fell they showed a face quite fresh and serious, like a child's. He heaved a huge sigh, and said: 'Let us get this said and done with as quickly as possible. Look here, this will be the quickest way to convince you all of the truth.' He turned to the doctor. 'Dr Simon,' he said, 'you have a strong head-piece, and I heard you this morning asking the five hardest questions about this business. Well, if you will now ask them again, I will answer them.'

Simon's pince-nez dropped from his nose in his doubt and wonder, but he answered at once. 'Well, the first question, you know, is why a man should kill another with a clumsy sabre at all when a man can kill with a bodkin?'

'A man cannot behead with a bodkin,' said Brown, calmly, 'and for *this* murder beheading was absolutely necessary.'

'Why?' asked O'Brien, with interest.

'And the next question?' asked Father Brown.

'Well, why didn't the man cry out or anything?' asked the doctor; 'sabres in gardens are certainly unusual.'

65

'Twigs,' said the priest gloomily, and turned to the window which looked on the scene of death. 'No one saw the point of the twigs. Why should they lie on that lawn (look at it) so far from any tree? They were not snapped off; they were chopped off. The murderer occupied his enemy with some tricks with the sabre, showing how he could cut a branch in mid-air, or what not. Then, while his enemy bent down to see the result, a silent slash, and the head fell.'

'Well,' said the doctor slowly, 'that seems plausible enough. But my next two questions will stump anyone.'

The priest still stood looking critically out of the window and waited.

'You know how all the garden was sealed up like an airtight chamber,' went on the doctor. 'Well, how did the strange man get into the garden?'

Without turning round, the little priest answered: 'There never was any strange man in the garden.'

There was a silence, and then a sudden cackle of almost childish laughter relieved the strain. The absurdity of Brown's remark moved Ivan to open taunts.

'Oh!' he cried; 'then we didn't lug a great fat corpse onto a sofa last night? He hadn't got into the garden, I suppose?'

'Got into the garden?' repeated Brown reflectively. 'No, not entirely.'

'Hang it all,' cried Simon, 'a man gets into the garden, or he doesn't.'

'Not necessarily,' said the priest, with a faint smile. 'What is the next question, Doctor?'

'I fancy you're ill, exclaimed Dr Simon sharply; 'but I'll ask the next question if you like. How did Brayne get out of the garden?'

'He didn't get out of the garden,' said the priest, till looking out of the window.

'Didn't get out of the garden?' exploded Simon.

'Not completely,' said Father Brown.

Simon shook his fists in a frenzy of French logic. 'A man gets out of a garden, or he doesn't,' he cried.

'Not always,' said Father Brown.

Dr Simon sprang to his feet impatiently. 'I have no time to spare on such senseless talk,' he cried angrily. 'If you can't understand a man being on one side of the wall or the other, I won't trouble you further.'

'Doctor,' said the cleric very gently, 'we have always got on very pleasantly together. If only for the sake of old friendship, stop and tell me your fifth question.'

The impatient Simon sank into a chair by the door and said briefly: 'The head and shoulders were cut about in a queer way. It seemed to be done after death.'

'Yes,' said the motionless priest, 'it was done so as to make you assume exactly the one simple falsehood that you did assume. It was done to make you take for granted that the head belonged to the body.'

The borderland of the brain, where all the monsters are made, moved horribly in the Gaelic O'Brien. He felt the chaotic presence of all the horse-men and fish-women that man's unnatural fancy has begotten. A voice older than his first fathers seemed saying in his ear: 'Keep out of the monstrous garden where grows the tree with double fruit. Avoid the evil garden where died the man with two heads.' Yet, while these shameful symbolic shapes passed across the ancient mirror of his Irish soul, his Frenchified intellect was quite alert, and was watching the odd priest as closely and increduously as all the rest.

Father Brown had turned round at last, and stood against the window with his face in dense shadow; but even in that shadow they could see it was pale as ashes. Nevertheless, he spoke quite sensibly, as if there were no Gaelic souls on earth.

'Gentlemen,' he said; 'you did not find the strange body of Becker in the garden. You did not find any strange body in the garden. In face of Dr Simon's rationalism, I still affirm that Becker was only partly present. Look here!' (pointing to the black bulk of the mysterious corpse); 'you never saw that man in your lives. Did you ever see this man?'

He rapidly rolled away the bald-yellow head of the unknown, and put in its place the white-maned head beside it. And there, complete, unified, unmistakable, lay Julius K. Brayne.

'The murderer,' went on Brown quietly, 'hacked off his enemy's head and flung the sword far over the wall. But he was too clever to fling the sword only. He flung the *head* over the wall also. Then he had only to clap on another head to the corpse, and (as he insisted on a private inquest) you all imagined a totally new man.'

'Clap on another head!' said O'Brien, staring. 'What other head? Heads don't grow on garden bushes, do they?'

'No,' said Father Brown huskily, and looking at his boots; 'there is only one place where they grow. They grow in the basket of the guillotine, beside which the Chief of Police, Aristide Valentin, was standing not an hour before the murder. Oh, my friends, hear me a minute more before you tear me in pieces. Valentin is an honest man, if being mad for an arguable cause is honesty. But did you ever see in that cold, grey eye of his that he is mad? He would do anything, *anything*, to break what he calls the superstition of the Cross. He has fought for it and starved for it, and now he has murdered for it. Brayne's crazy millions had hitherto been scattered among so many sects that they did little to alter the balance of things. But Valentin heard a whisper that Brayne, like so many scatter-brained sceptics, was drifting to us; and that was quite a different thing. Brayne would pour supplies into the impoverished and pugnacious Church of France; he would support six Nationalist newspapers like *The Guillotine*. The battle was already balanced on a point, and the fanatic took flame at the risk. He resolved to destroy the millionaire, and he did it as one would expect the greatest of detectives to commit his only crime. He abstracted the severed head of Becker on some criminological excuse, and took it home in his official box. He had that last argument with Brayne, that Lord Galloway did not hear the end of; that failing, he led him out into the sealed garden, talked about swordsmanship, used twigs and a sabre for illustration, and—'

Ivan of the Scar sprang up. 'You lunatic,' he yelled; 'you'll go to my master now, if I take you by—'

'Why, I was going there,' said Brown heavily; 'I must ask him to confess, and all that.'

Driving the unhappy Brown before them like a hostage or sacrifice, they rushed together into the sudden stillness of Valentin's study.

The great detective sat as his desk apparently too occupied to hear their turbulent entrance. They paused a moment, and then something in the look of that upright and elegant back made the doctor run forward suddenly. A touch and a glance showed him that there was a small box of pills at Valentin's elbow and that Valentin was dead in his chair; and on the blind face of the suicide was more than the pride of Cato.

THE TWO BOTTLES

Freeman Wills Crofts

Providential was the adjective Superintendent French always used when he told of his call on his old friend Mark Rudd precisely at the most critical moment of the latter's life. French was enjoying a week's leave in early spring and had set out for a tramp round Leith Hill. Rudd had built himself a bungalow among the pines, and there he lived with his wife, practising his hobby of sculpture. He was well-to-do and sixtyish. French found him bending over bottles, a basin and a heap of sand.

'Hullo, Rudd! Turned chemist in your old age?'

The old man was glad to see French and fussed about drinks and smokes. 'Sorry, Joan's not very well,' he said, speaking of his comparatively young wife. 'She's just back from a few days in London with her father, the doctor, and is lying down. But you'll see her later.'

French replied suitably, though secretly he was pleased. It was with Rudd that he had come to chat, and the presence of Mrs Rudd cramped both their styles. Presently he pointed to the table. 'What's the great work?'

Rudd turned back to his bottles. 'I've had some new cement stuff sent me,' he explained, 'and I was just going to try it. But you wouldn't be interested.'

'Yes, I should,' returned French, sensing regret in his tone. 'Let's see the doings.'

Rudd brightened up. 'It's a stuff called Siliconine. Chap invented it and sent me a sample to try out. It's in these two bottles, and as long as they're separate it keeps indefinitely. But when you mix them it begins to harden into silicon, taking about twenty-four hours to do it.'

The bottles were of the ordinary medicine type. French picked one up. It bore a typewritten label: 'Siliconine—A. This preparation contains acid and must not be allowed to touch the skin.' The liquid was clear and brownish. In the other bottle, which was marked 'B' and had a wide mouth, was a white powder.

'How do you use them?' French asked.

'You empty the powder into a basin and pour the acid on it. The powder dissolves and makes a viscous liquid. Then you add sand, stirring till all the grains are coated. You press the moist sand into the shape you want, and it hardens into sandstone or marble or granite, according to the sand you've used.'

'Sounds good.'

'Well, that's the claim. I've not tried it yet.'

'The acid may attack your basin.' French pointed to a chip in the enamel showing dark metal.

'I'll try that first.'

Rudd poured three or four drops from his 'A' bottle on the defective spot. It boiled and smoked.

'Bless us,' French grunted, 'you've got strong stuff there.' He took the bottle and put it gingerly to his nose. 'Vitriol, I imagine, but I'm not sure.' He recorked it, picked up the second bottle, and pushed the blade of his knife slowly through the contents. For some moments he sat motionless, evidently thinking deeply, then quietly he recorked the second bottle and slipped it into his breast pocket. His manner changed and he spoke more decisively. 'I'd like to try an experiment.'

Rudd was mystified, but French would not explain. He emptied a few grains of the powder into a saucer and placed it on the ground in the centre of a small grass plot. Then he tied a spoon to a fishing rod, put six drops from the acid bottle into the spoon, and, lying down, pushed the spoon towards the saucer and carefully emptied in the drops. There was an instant reaction. A sharp explosion eliminated the saucer.

'I thought that not unlikely,' he declared grimly. 'That powder's chlorate of potash, and mixed with vitriol, which, as you know is commercial concentrated sulphuric acid, it explodes. I suppose you realize you were about to make enough to blow yourself to kingdom come?'

Rudd was overwhelmed. He discussed the affair wonderingly, though it was some time before he reached the inevitable conclusion. At last he muttered shakily: 'Someone surely must have intended to murder me!'

'You don't mean it?' French returned. 'Well, someone did, and someone who knew your circumstances. That ingenious tale of the silicon spells "sculptor" all through. It was quite a scheme, for all incriminating evidence would have been destroyed.'

'I just can't believe it.'

'I find that sooner or later I'm forced to believe the evidence of my eyes.' French's voice was dry, 'Now, Rudd, pull yourself together. We've got to get the chap who did this. Let's see what we know. First, show me the letter that came with the bottles and the packings of the parcel.'

These were available and French noted that the letter was on the usual sheet torn from the usual cheap block, and was typed with the usual machine with identifiable defects. It purported to come from Ralph Spence, of Hillside Crescent, Battersea, and contained simply what Rudd had already stated about the action of the alleged invention, together with Spence's earnest hope that a man of Rudd's eminence would be so kind as to test it.

'I don't wonder he took you in,' said French. 'Where's your telephone?'

Rudd indicated the hall. In a few minutes French returned.

'I thought that not unlikely also,' he declared. 'There's no Hillside Crescent in Battersea.' He picked up the wrappings. 'Posted yesterday at Charing Cross. H'm. That's not hopeful. However, if we get a suspect from your statement, we'll nail him through the typewriter and probably the purchase of the chemicals. Very well, let that go for the moment and tell me about your enemies.'

'Enemies?' Rudd blinked. 'I have no enemies.'

'Haven't you? You've at least one, you know. Think again, old man.'

Rudd shook his head helplessly.

'Well, let's see.' French looked at him speculatively. 'You're a rich man, I always fancied, Rudd. Worth how much, if you don't mind? It's not curiosity.'

'Of course not. About fifty thousand, though I don't get much out of it these days.'

'And who would have got it if you'd mixed your bottles?'

'Some to my wife, my own money: the greater portion to my nephew, James Rudd, a family inheritance.'

'H'm. Tell me about him. Is he well-to-do also?'

'As a matter of fact he's hard up. I know because he wanted me to help him out quite recently. But I refused. It's no use. I've done it again and again and it's always the same. He just throws everything away at the races.'

'That so? What's his job?'

'He's a chemist in one of the big patent food firms: I forget which.'

'A chemist? Good Lord, Rudd, what more do we want?'

Rudd looked profoundly shocked. 'Oh, come now, French, you're not going to accuse him of such a thing. He's a bit of a waster, I admit, but a murderer! No, I couldn't believe that.'

'I don't accuse him. I don't know who's guilty. Can you think of anyone else?'

'Well, no,' hesitatingly. 'But then I shouldn't have thought of Jim.'

'Quite.' French began to pace the room, obviously lost in thought. Then he swung round. 'I believe we could find out at the Yard who sent that parcel, but I've an idea we might get the information more easily. Perhaps your nephew would tell us if he's guilty?'

'I suppose that remark has a meaning, but I admit I don't get it.'

'Never mind,' French smiled. 'I think we'll try it. But you'll have to do what I ask you.'

'I'm not the expert in murder. What do you want?'

'Having no locus standi here, I must first have a chat with the local police. Then I'll come back and tell you.'

French disappeared and the afternoon was well advanced when he returned. He was close about how he had spent his time, except to say that he had seen the Superintendent and asked for a constable to guard the bungalow during the night. 'Can you ring up your nephew?' he went on before Rudd could protest.

'Yes, of course; at his works.'

'Then do so. Be chatty and friendly. Say a Mr Spence has sent you— what he said he sent you, and ask your nephew whether as a chemist he ever heard of the stuff. Say you think the invention might be of great value in repairing weathered stone on buildings, and that you're much interested. Then go on that by a lucky chance your friend So-and-so—mention some big pot in your own line—is coming down to see you tomorrow, and you're going to let him do the actual experiment. That'll give the stuff a great test, and a great boost if it works. Finish by apologizing for troubling your nephew, and explain again that you had wondered if the inventor was a well-known man.'

'I suppose there's a meaning in that too, French, but again—' Rudd shrugged resignedly.

'Well, don't you see, old man, if your nephew's guilty that message will put him in a cleft stick. Some innocent stranger will be blown to bits and you, you who are able to put two and two together, will probably survive. That is to say, unless he acts promptly he'll be facing a conviction for a murder he didn't wish to commit and which wouldn't benefit him. What will he do? Just answer that for yourself.'

While Rudd was waiting for his call, which was a trunk, there was a step in the passage and Mrs Rudd appeared. French sprang up to greet her. She certainly seemed ill, with her pale face, absent manner and slightly twitching hands. But she spoke to him normally enough, apologized for being unable to entertain him, and asked him to put a letter which she gave him with those for the post. A brief word of conversation, a briefer smile, and she disappeared and he heard the door of her room close. He turned to speak to Rudd, but just then the call came through. Nephew Jim seemed somewhat taken aback by his uncle's inquiry, though he expressed interest in the idea. Both invention and inventor were, he said, entirely unknown to him.

The day dragged on without further incident, and then about dusk a constable arrived with a reporter's flash-lamp and camera, which he handed to French.

'Good,' was the response. 'Even if he gets away we'll have a photo of him in the act. Now come along to the studio and I'll explain what I want. See those two bottles? Put a private mark on them, so that you can swear to them again. I'll do the same. Right.' He replaced the bottles and turned to the window. 'Just to see that the sashes are hasped. They are. Then let's go outside.'

The studio was at the opposite end of the house to the porch and its window gave on the small plot of grass. Through the open door of the porch the wall containing the window was clearly visible. French walked up and down inspecting everything, after which he gave the constable detailed orders for the night. He was to watch the back door, ready on a signal to run out round the house and take a visitor to the studio in the rear. 'We're all right for an hour or two,' French went on to Rudd, 'then we must take up our positions.'

'Time for a drink,' said the old man hospitably, leading the way to the lounge.

They chatted for some time, then French made a move. Having placed the constable, he sat down himself in the porch before the slightly open door. Rudd, though protesting about the door, insisted on sharing the vigil. French would allow neither light nor smoking nor speech above a whisper. The night dragged. Time indeed seemed to stand still. It was cold and the breeze moaned eerily among the pines. Except for this and the occasional hoot of an owl, it was very still.

Twelve came and one, then two. French was chilled and cramped and growing increasingly uneasy. Had he made a mistake? Was this nephew either innocent or sharper than he had allowed for?

Slowly the night crept on. Three came and, after another aeon, four. When five struck and faint signs of light began to show in the east, French's chagrin was painful. He apologized grumpily to his friend and sent the constable home. But till the normal life of the bungalow had been resumed he kept watch himself.

Before going for a bath and shave he had a look round the studio. Everything there was as it had been the night before, the windows latched, the marked bottles, basin, sand and letter on the table. But the acid bottle seemed somehow lighter in colour. He picked it up. It *was* lighter.

Puzzled, he shook it. No, the colouring matter had not settled. Slowly he uncorked it and cautiously sniffed the contents. Then his jaw dropped and he stood staring helplessly. This was not vitriol, it was vinegar.

In a way he had expected something of the kind: it was the basis of his trap. Rudd's message would have convinced Nephew Jim that the explosive possibilities of the 'cement' were unknown; and if he were guilty, substitution of some harmless chemical for the contents of one or both bottles was the only way in which he could save himself. True, his plan would have failed, but he could not be convicted of crime.

But Nephew Jim had not made the substitution. No one had entered the studio. No one could have unlatched the window without breaking the glass.

As French found himself driven relentlessly to the only conclusion possible, he felt sick with aversion and loathing for what must follow. Rudd himself had been sitting with them all night: he could not have approached the studio. The woman who helped during the day had gone home in the evening. Only from one room could a secret visit have been paid.

Screwing up his courage, French went to the room and knocked. There was no reply and he opened the door. Entering, he stood in the middle of the floor and let his eye pass slowly over the contents. How within the bungalow could a powerful acid like vitriol be got rid of silently and without leaving traces? French did not believe it could be done. Therefore another bottle. . . .

For perhaps five minutes he stood, looking and pondering. Then faint marks in the grate attracted his attention. He went over. Yes, some soot had recently been swept back. Kneeling down, he put his hand up the chimney.

As he gripped and drew down a bottle of clear brown liquid, there was a scream from behind him. Joan Rudd was running across the room. She was brandishing a poker and descended on him like a fury. He sprang to his feet and in the nick of time seized her arms. To control her he had to use his full strength. She screamed and struggled and called down horrible curses on him, but at last he got her arms in a lock and she was helpless. Then all the fight seemed to go out of her

She was brandishing the poker and descended on him like a fury.

and she collapsed limply. As French laid her on her bed Rudd's appalled face appeared at the door.

'I'm afraid it's her mind,' French said with profound sympathy in his tones. 'Better ring up the doctor.'

French followed him to the telephone, and Rudd, thinking over the action later, could never make up his mind as to his friend's motive. But when French returned to the bedroom he gave an urgent call. Rudd hurried after him.

'Bad news,' French warned. 'Prepare yourself for a shock. She's taken prussic acid.'

Rudd gasped. 'Can't we do anything?'

French shook his head. 'I'm afraid it's a matter of a very few minutes. She's unconscious already.'

The doctor turned up quickly, but before he arrived the unhappy lady had ceased to breathe.

Later French propounded his theory, for the benefit principally of Rudd. 'It was no doubt the common case of a mentally unstable person turning against the one most loved. When she sent those chemicals one cannot suppose she was responsible. Then from her point of view things went wrong: I turned up and there was no explosion. She must have suspected me of interference and doubtless watched us both. She heard something about telephoning, came to learn what she could, and certainly hid and listened to the message. Not knowing that we had learnt what was in the bottles, she obviously understood what your nephew was intended to understand. To destroy the evidence was her only hope, and she hid the acid up her chimney, substituting vinegar. But when she saw me with the acid in my hand she realized I knew all, and took the poison.'

Though this view was officially accepted by the police and coroner, it did not wholly convince French himself. He had heard rumours about Joan and a neighbour, and he had a certain suspicion that freedom and money were what the lady sought. Having had his position regularized, he therefore made some inquiries. He traced her purchase of the vitriol from a London shop, 'to clean a sink with damaged glaze', and of chlorate of potash, 'as a weedkiller'. A sufficient quantity of potassium cyanide was missing from her father's surgery. Having once acted as his dispenser, she knew her way about, and no doubt believed that, even if he suspected, he would not give his own daughter away. The typewriter she had borrowed from a friend. The plan, French imagined, had been suggested by the nature of the nephew's profession. She probably calculated that he would be suspected, but that nothing could be proved against him. Finally French learned that the neighbour had been at his home when the parcel was posted. From these facts he concluded that only Joan was implicated. No use, therefore, in stirring up mud which would hurt his friend without serving the ends of justice. French's conscience was clear. Through his efforts his friend was safe and the guilty party was dead: what more could be desired of him?

THE STOLEN WHITE ELEPHANT

Mark Twain

The following curious history was related to me by a chance railway acquaintance. He was a gentleman more than seventy years of age, and his thoroughly good and gentle face and earnest and sincere manner imprinted the unmistakable stamp of truth upon every statement which fell from his lips. He said:

You know in what reverence the royal white elephant of Siam is held by the people of that country. You know it is sacred to kings, only kings may possess it, and that it is indeed in a measure even superior to kings, since it receives not merely honour but worship. Very well; five years ago, when the troubles concerning the frontier line arose between Great Britain and Siam, it was presently manifest that Siam had been in the wrong. Therefore every reparation was quickly made, and the British representative stated that he was satisfied and the past should be forgotten. This greatly relieved the King of Siam, and partly as a token of gratitude, but partly also, perhaps, to wipe out any little remaining vestige of unpleasantness which England might feel towards him, he wished to send the Queen a present—the sole sure way of propitiating an enemy, according to Oriental ideas. This present ought not only to be a royal one, but transcendentally royal. Wherefore, what offering could be so meet as that of a white elephant?

My position in the Indian Civil Service was such that I was deemed peculiarly worthy the honour of conveying the present to Her Majesty. A ship was fitted out for me and my servants and the officers and attendants of the elephant, and in due time I arrived in New York harbour and placed my royal charge in admirable quarters in Jersey City. It was necessary to remain awhile in order to recruit the animal's health before resuming the voyage.

All went well during a fortnight—then my calamities began. The white elephant was stolen! I was called up at dead of night and informed of this fearful misfortune. For some moments I was beside myself with terror and anxiety; I was helpless. Then I grew calmer and collected my faculties. I soon saw my course—for indeed there was but the one course for an intelligent man to pursue. Late as it was, I flew to New York and got a policeman to conduct me to the head-quarters of the detective force. Fortunately I arrived in time, though the chief of the force, the celebrated Inspector Blunt, was just on the point of leaving for his home. He was a man of middle size and compact frame, and when he was thinking deeply he had a way of knitting his brows and tapping his forehead reflectively with his finger, which impressed you at once with the conviction that you stood in the presence of a person of no common order. The very sight of him gave me confidence and made me hopeful. I stated my errand. It did not flurry him in the least; it had no more visible effect upon his iron self-possession than if I had told him somebody had stolen my dog. He motioned me to a seat, and said calmly:

'Allow me to think a moment, please.'

So saying, he sat down at his office table and leaned his head upon his hand. Several clerks were at work at the other end of the room; the scratching of their pens was all the sound I heard during the next six or seven minutes. Meantime the Inspector sat there buried in thought. Finally he raised his head, and there was that in the firm lines of his face which showed me that his brain had done its work and his plan was made. Said he—and his voice was low and impressive:

'This is no ordinary case. Every step must be warily taken; each step must be made sure before the next is ventured. And secrecy must be observed—secrecy profound and absolute. Speak to no one about the matter, not even the reporters. I will take care of *them*; I will see

Inspector Blunt would knit his brows and tap his forehead reflectively.

that they get only what it may suit my ends to let them know.' He touched a bell; a youth appeared. 'Alaric, tell the reporters to remain for the present.' The boy retired. 'Now let us proceed to business—and systematically. Nothing can be accomplished in this trade of mine without strict and minute method.'

He took a pen and some paper. 'Now—name of the elephant?'

'Hassan Ben Ali Ben Selim Abdallah Mohammed Moisé Alhammal Jamsetjejeebhoy Dhuleep Sultan Ebu Bhudpoor.'

'Very well. Given name?'

'Jumbo.'

'Very well. Place of birth?'

'The capital city of Siam.'

'Parents living?'

'No—dead.'

'Had they any other issue besides this one?'

'None—he was an only child.'

'Very well. These matters are sufficient under that head. Now please describe the elephant, and leave out no particular, however insignificant—that is, insignificant from *your* point of view. To men in my profession there *are* no insignificant particulars; they do not exist.'

I described; he wrote. When I was done, he said:

'Now listen. If I have made any mistakes, correct me.'

He read as follows:

'Height, 19 feet; length, from apex of forehead to insertion of tail, 26 feet; length of trunk, 16 feet; length of tail, 6 feet; total length, including trunk and tail, 48 feet; length of tusks, 9½ feet; ears in keeping with these dimensions; footprint resembles the mark when one up-ends a barrel in the snow; colour of the elephant, a dull white; has a hole the size of a plate in each ear for the insertion of jewellery, and possesses the habit in a remarkable degree of squirting water upon spectators and of maltreating with his trunk not only such persons as he is acquainted with, but even entire strangers; limps slightly with his right hind leg, and has a small scar in his left armpit caused by a former boil; had on, when stolen, a castle containing seats for fifteen persons, and a gold-cloth saddle-blanket the size of an ordinary carpet.'

There were no mistakes. The Inspector touched the bell, handed the description to Alaric, and said:

'Have fifty thousand copies of this printed at once and mailed to every detective office and pawnbroker's shop on the continent.' Alaric retired. 'There—so far, so good. Next, I must have a photograph of the property.'

I gave him one. He examined it critically, and said:

'It must do, since we can do no better; but he has his trunk curled up and tucked into his mouth. That is unfortunate, and is calculated to mislead, for of course he does not usually have it in that position.' He touched his bell.

'Alaric, have fifty thousand copies of this photograph made, the first thing in the morning, and mail them with the descriptive circulars.'

Alaric retired to execute his orders. The Inspector said:

'It will be necessary to offer a reward, of course. Now as to the amount?'

'What sum would you suggest?'

'To *begin* with, I should say—well, twenty-five thousand dollars. It is an intricate and difficult business; there are a thousand avenues of escape and opportunities of concealment. These thieves have friends and pals everywhere—'

'Bless me, do you know who they are?'

The wary face, practised in concealing the thoughts and feelings within, gave me no token, nor yet the replying words, so quietly uttered:

'Never mind about that. I may, and I may not. We generally gather a pretty shrewd inkling of who our man is by the manner of his work and the size of the game he goes after. We are not dealing with a pickpocket or a hall thief, now, make up your mind to that. This property was not "lifted" by a novice. But, as I was saying, considering the amount of travel which will have to be done, and the diligence with which the thieves will cover up their traces as they move along, twenty-five thousand may be too small a sum to offer, yet I think it worth while to start with that.'

So we determined upon that figure, as a beginning. Then this man, whom nothing escaped which could by any possibility be made to serve as a clue, said:

'There are cases in detective history to show that criminals have been detected through peculiarities in their appetites. Now, what does this elephant eat, and how much?'

'Well, as to *what* he eats—he will eat *anything*. He will eat a man, he will eat a Bible—he will eat anything *between* a man and a Bible.'

'Good—very good indeed, but too general. Details are necessary—details are the only valuable things in our trade. Very well—as to men. At one meal—or, if you prefer, during one day—how many men will he eat, if fresh?'

'He would not care whether they were fresh or not; at a single meal he would eat five ordinary men.'

'Very good; five men; we will put that down. What nationalities would he prefer?'

'He is indifferent about nationalities. He prefers acquaintances, but is not prejudiced against strangers.'

'Very good. Now as to Bibles. How many Bibles would he eat at a meal?'

'He would eat an entire edition.'

'It is hardly succinct enough. Do you mean the ordinary octavo, or the family illustrated?'

'I think he would be indifferent to illustrations; that is, I think he would not value illustrations above simple letterpress.'

'No, you do not get my idea. I refer to bulk. The ordinary octavo Bible weighs about two pounds and a half while the great quarto with the illustrations weighs ten or twelve. How many Doré Bibles would he eat at a meal?'

'If you knew this elephant, you would not ask. He would take what they had.'

'Well, put it in dollars and cents, then. We must get at it somehow. The Doré costs a hundred dollars a copy, Russia leather, bevelled.'

'He would require about fifty thousand dollars' worth—say an edition of five hundred copies.'

'Now, that is more exact. I will put that down. Very well; he likes men and Bibles; so far, so good. What else will he eat? I want particulars.'

'He will leave Bibles to eat bricks, he will leave bricks to eat bottles, he will leave bottles to eat clothing, he will leave clothing to eat cats, he will leave cats to eat oysters, he will leave oysters to eat ham, he will leave ham to eat sugar, he will leave sugar to eat pie, he will leave pie to eat potatoes, he will leave potatoes to eat bran, he will leave bran to eat hay, he will leave hay to eat oats, he will leave oats to eat rice, for he was mainly raised on it. There is nothing whatever that he will not eat but European butter, and he would eat that if he could taste it.'

'Very good. General quantity at a meal—say about—'

'Well, anywhere from a quarter to half a ton.'

'And he drinks—'

'Everything that is fluid. Milk, water, whisky, molasses, castor oil, camphene, carbolic acid—it is no use to go into particulars; whatever fluid occurs to you set it down. He will drink anything that is fluid, except European coffee.'

'Very good. As to quantity?'

'Put it down five to fifteen barrels—his thirst varies; his other appetites do not.'

'These things are unusual. They ought to furnish quite good clues towards tracing him.'

He touched the bell.

'Alaric, summon Captain Burns.'

Burns appeared. Inspector Blunt unfolded the whole matter to him, detail by detail. Then he said in the clear, decisive tones of a man whose plans are clearly defined in his head, and who is accustomed to command:

'Captain Burns, detail Detectives Jones, Davis, Halsey, Bates and Hackett to shadow the elephant.'

'Yes, sir.'

'Detail Detectives Moses, Dakin, Murphy, Rogers, Tupper, Higgins and Bartholomew to shadow the thieves.'

'Yes, sir.'

'Place a strong guard—a guard of thirty picked men, with a relief of thirty—over the place from whence the elephant was stolen, to keep strict watch there night and day, and allow none to approach—except reporters—without written authority from me.'

'Yes, sir.'

'Place detectives in plain clothes in the railway, steamship, and ferry depots, and upon all roadways leading out of Jersey City, with orders to search all suspicious persons.'

'Yes, sir.'

'Furnish all these men with photograph and accompanying description of the elephant, and instruct them to search all trains and outgoing ferry-boats and other vessels.'

'Yes, sir.'

'If the elephant should be found, let him be seized, and the information forwarded to me by telegraph.'

'Yes, sir.'

'Let me be informed at once if any clues should be found—footprints of the animal, or anything of that kind.'

'Yes, sir.'

'Get an order commanding the harbour police to patrol the frontages vigilantly.'

'Yes, sir.'

'Despatch detectives in plain clothes over all the railways, north as far as Canada, west as far as Ohio, south as far as Washington.'

'Yes, sir.'

'Place experts in all the telegraph offices to listen to all messages; and let them require that all cipher despatches be interpreted to them.'

'Yes, sir.'

'Let all these things be done with the utmost secrecy—mind, the most impenetrable secrecy.'

'Yes, sir.'

'Report to me promptly at the usual hour.'

'Yes, sir.'

'Go!'

'Yes, sir.'

He was gone.

Inspector Blunt was silent and thoughtful a moment while the fire in his eye cooled down and faded out. Then he turned to me and said in a placid voice:

'I am not given to boasting, it is not my habit; but—we shall find the elephant.'

I shook him warmly by the hand and thanked him; and I *felt* my thanks, too. The more I had seen of the man the more I liked him, and the more I admired and marvelled over the mysterious wonders of his profession. Then we parted for the night, and I went home with a far happier heart than I had carried with me to his office.

★   ★   ★   ★

Next morning it was all in the newspapers, in the minutest detail. It even had additions—consisting of Detective This, Detective That, and Detective The Other's 'Theory' as to how the robbery was done, who the robbers were, and whither they had flown with their booty. There were eleven of these theories, and they covered all the possibilities; and this single fact shows what independent thinkers detectives are. No two theories were alike, or even much resembled each other, save in one striking particular, and in that one all the eleven theories were absolutely agreed. That was, that although the rear of my building was torn out and the only door remained locked, the elephant had not been removed through the rent, but by some other (undiscovered) outlet. All agreed that the robbers had made that rent only to mislead the detectives. That never would have occurred to me or to any other layman, perhaps, but it had not deceived the detectives for a moment. Thus, what I had supposed was the only thing that had no mystery about it was in fact the very thing I had gone furthest astray in. The eleven theories all named the supposed robbers, but no two named the same robbers; the total number of suspected persons was thirty-seven. The various newspaper accounts all closed with the most important opinion of all—that of Chief-Inspector Blunt. A portion of this statement read as follows:

'The chief knows who the two principals are, namely, "Brick" Duffy and "Red" McFadden. Ten days before the robbery was achieved he was already aware that it was to be attempted, and had quietly proceeded to shadow these two noted villains; but unfortunately on the night in question their track was lost, and before it could be found again the bird was flown—that is, the elephant.

'Duffy and McFadden are the boldest scoundrels in the profession; the chief has reason for believing that they are the men who stole the stove out of the detective headquarters on a bitter night last winter—in consequence of which the chief and every detective were in the hands of the physicians before morning, some with frozen feet, others with frozen fingers, ears, and other members.'

When I read the first half of that I was more astonished than ever at the wonderful sagacity of this strange man. He not only saw everything in the present with a clear eye, but even the future could not be hidden from him. I was soon at his office, and said I could not help wishing he had had those men arrested, and so prevented the trouble, and loss; but his reply was simple and unanswerable:

'It is not our province to prevent crime, but to punish it. We cannot punish it until it is committed.'

I remarked that the secrecy with which we had begun had been marred by the newspapers; not only all our facts but all our plans and purposes had been revealed; even all the suspected persons had been named; these would doubtless disguise themselves now, or go into hiding.

'Let them. They will find that when I am ready for them, my hand will descend upon them, in their secret places, as unerringly as the hand of fate. As to the newspapers, we *must* keep in with them. Fame, reputation, constant public mention—these are the detective's bread and butter. He must publish his facts, else he will be supposed to have none; he must publish his theory, for nothing is so strange or striking as a detective's theory, or brings him so much wondering respect; we must publish our plans, for these the journals insist upon having, and we could not deny them without offending. We must constantly show the public what we are doing, or they will believe we are doing nothing. It is much pleasanter to have a newspaper say: "Inspector Blunt's ingenious and extraordinary theory is as follows," than to have it say some harsh thing, or, worse still, some sarcastic one.'

'I see the force of what you say. But I noticed that in one part of your remarks in the papers this morning, you refused to reveal your opinion upon a certain minor point.'

'Yes, we always do that; it has a good effect. Besides, I had not formed any opinion on that point, anyway.'

I deposited a considerable sum of money with the Inspector, to meet current expenses, and sat down to wait for news. We were expecting the telegrams to begin to arrive at any moment now. Meantime I re-read the newspapers and also our descriptive circular, and observed that our $25,000 reward seemed to be offered only to detectives. I said I thought it ought to be offered to anybody who would catch the elephant. The inspector said:

'It is the detectives who will find the elephant, hence the reward will go to the right place. If other people found the animal, it would only be by watching the detectives and taking advantage of clues and indications stolen from them, and that would entitle the detectives to the reward, after all. The proper office of a reward is to stimulate the men who deliver up their time and their trained sagacities to this sort of work, and not to confer benefits upon chance citizens who stumble upon a capture without having earned the benefits by their own merits and labours.'

This was reasonable enough, certainly. Now the telegraphic machine in the corner began to click, and the following despatch was the result:

Flower Station, N.Y.: 7.30 a.m.
Have got a clue. Found a succession of deep tracks across a farm near here. Followed them two miles east without result; think elephant went west. Shall now shadow him in that direction.
Darley, Detective.

'Darley's one of the best men on the force,' said the Inspector. 'We shall hear from him again before long.'

Telegram No. 2 came.

Barker's, N.J.: 7.40 a.m.
Just arrived. Glass factory broken open here during night and eight hundred bottles taken. Only water in large quantity near here is five miles distant. Shall strike for there. Elephant will be thirsty. Bottles were empty.
Baker, Detective.

'That promises well, too,' said the Inspector. 'I told you the creature's appetites would not be bad clues.'

Telegram No. 3.

Taylorville, L.I.: 8.15 a.m.
*A haystack near here disappeared during night. Probably eaten. Have got
a clue, and am off.*

Hubbard, Detective.

'How he does move around!' said the Inspector. 'I knew we had a
difficult job on hand, but we shall catch him yet.'

Flower Station, N.Y.: 9 a.m.
*Shadowed the tracks three miles westward. Large, deep, and ragged. Have
just met a farmer who says they are not elephant tracks. Says they are
holes where he dug up saplings for shade-trees when ground was frozen last
winter. Give me orders how to proceed.*

Darley, Detective.

'Aha! a confederate of the thieves! The thing grows warm,' said
the Inspector.
He dictated the following telegram to Darley:

*Arrest the man and force him to name his pals. Continue to follow the tracks—
to the Pacific, if necessary.*

Chief Blunt.

Next telegram:

Coney Point, Pa.: 8.45 a.m.
*Gas office broken open here during night and three months' unpaid gas bills
taken. Have got a clue and am away.*

Murphy, Detective.

'Heavens!' said the inspector, 'would he eat gas bills?'
'Through ignorance—yes; but they cannot support life. At least,
unassisted.'
Now came this exciting telegram:

Ironville, N.Y.: 9.30 a.m.
*Just arrived. This village in consternation. Elephant passed through here at
five this morning. Some say he went east, some say west, some north, some*

south—but all say they did not wait to notice particularly. He killed a horse; have secured a piece of it for a clue. Killed it with his trunk; from style of blow, think he struck it left-handed. From position in which horse lies, think elephant travelled northward along line of Berkley railway. Has four and a half hours' start; but I move on his track at once.

Hawes, Detective.

I uttered exclamations of joy. The Inspector was as self-contained as a graven image. He calmly touched his bell.

'Alaric, send Captain Burns here.'

Burns appeared.

'How many men are ready for instant orders?'

'Ninety-six, sir.'

'Send them north at once. Let them concentrate along the line of the Berkley road north of Ironville.'

'Yes, sir.'

'Let them conduct their movements with the utmost secrecy. As fast as others are at liberty, hold them for orders.'

'Yes, sir.'

'Go!'

'Yes, sir.'

Presently came another telegram.

Sage Corners, N.Y.: 10.30

Just arrived. Elephant passed through here at 8.15. All escaped from the town but a policeman. Apparently elephant did not strike at policeman, but at the lamp-post. Got both. I have secured a portion of the policeman as clue.

Stumm, Detective.

'So the elephant has turned westward,' said the Inspector. 'However, he will not escape, for my men are scattered all over that region.'

The next telegram said:

Glover's, 11.15.

Just arrived. Village deserted, except sick and aged. Elephant passed through three-quarters of an hour ago. The anti-temperance mass meeting was in session; he put his trunk in at a window and washed it out with water from cistern. Some swallowed it—since dead; several drowned. Detectives Cross and O'Shaughnessy were passing through town, but going south—so missed elephant. Whole region for many miles around in terror—people flying from their homes. Wherever they turn they meet elephant, and many are killed.

Brant, Detective.

I could have shed tears, this havoc so distressed me. But the Inspector only said:

'You see—we are closing in on him. He feels our presence; he has turned eastward again.'

Yet further troublous news was in store for us. The telegraph brought this:

Hoganport, 12.19.

Just arrived. Elephant passed through half an hour ago, creating wildest fright and excitement. Elephant raged around streets; two plumbers going by, killed one—other escaped. Regret general.

O'Flaherty, Detective.

'Now he is right in the midst of my men,' said the Inspector. 'Nothing can save him.'

A succession of telegrams came from detectives who were scattered through New Jersey and Pennsylvania, and who were following clues consisting of ravaged barns, factories, and Sunday-school libraries, with high hopes—hopes amounting to certainties, indeed. The Inspector said:

'I wish I could communicate with them and order them north, but that is impossible. A detective only visits a telegraph office to send his report; then he is off again, and you don't know where to put your hand on him.'

Now came this despatch:

Bridgeport, Ct.: 12.15.

Barnum offers rate of $4,000 a year for exclusive privilege of using elephant as travelling advertising medium from now till detectives find him. Wants to paste circus-posters on him. Desires immediate answer.

Boggs, Detective.

'That is perfectly absurd!' I exclaimed.

'Of course it is,' said the Inspector. 'Evidently Mr Barnum, who thinks he is so sharp, does not know me—but I know him.'

Then he dictated this answer to the despatch:

Mr Barnum's offer declined. Make it $7,000 or nothing.

Chief Blunt.

'There. We shall not have to wait long for an answer, Mr Barnum is not at home; he is in the telegraph office—it is his way when he has business on hand. Inside of three—.'

Done.—P. T. Barnum.

So interrupted the clicking telegraphic instrument. Before I could make a comment upon this extraordinary episode, the following despatch carried my thoughts into another and very distressing channel:

Bolivia, N.Y.: 12.50.

Elephant arrived here from the south and passed through towards the forest at 11.50, dispersing a funeral on the way, and diminishing the mourners by two. Citizens fired some small cannon-balls into him, and then fled. Detective Burke and I arrived ten minutes later, from the north, but mistook some excavations for footprints, and so lost a good deal of time; but at last we struck the right trail and followed it to the woods. We then got down on our hands and knees and continued to keep a sharp eye on the track, and so shadowed it into the brush. Burke was in advance. Unfortunately the animal had stopped to rest; therefore, Burke having his head down, intent upon the track, butted up against the elephant's hind legs before he was aware of his vicinity. Burke instantly rose to his feet, seized the tail, and exclaimed joyfully: 'I claim the re—' but got no further, for a single blow of the huge trunk laid the brave fellow's fragments low in death. I fled rearward, and the elephant turned and shadowed me to the edge of the wood, making tremendous speed, and I should inevitably have been lost, but that the remains of the funeral providentially intervened again, and diverted his attention. I have just learned that nothing of that funeral is now left; but this is no loss, for there is an abundance of material for another. Meantime the elephant has disappeared again.

Mulrooney, Detective.

We heard no news except from the diligent and confident detectives scattered about New Jersey, Pennsylvania, Delaware and Virginia— who were all following fresh and encouraging clues—until shortly after 2 p.m., when this telegram came:

> *Baxter Centre, 2.15.*
> *Elephant been here, plastered over with circus-bills, and broke up a revival, striking down and damaging many who were on the point of entering upon a better life. Citizens penned him up, and established a guard. When Detective Brown and I arrived, some time after, we entered enclosure and proceeded to identify elephant by photograph and description. All marks tallied exactly except one, which we could not see—the boil-scar under armpit. To make sure, Brown crept under to look, and was immediately brained—that is, head crushed and destroyed; though nothing issued from debris. All fled; so did elephant, striking right and left with much effect. Has escaped, but left bold blood-track from cannon-wounds. Rediscovery certain. He broke southward through a dense forest.*
>
> *Brent, Detective.*

That was the last telegram. At nightfall a fog shut down which was so dense that objects but three feet away could not be discerned. This lasted all night. The ferry boats and even the omnibuses had to stop running.

★ ★ ★ ★

Next morning the papers were as full of detective theories as before; they had all our tragic facts in detail also, and a great many more which they had received from their telegraphic correspondents. Column after column was occupied, a third of its way down, with glaring headlines, which it made my heart sick to read. Their general tone was like this:

'THE WHITE ELEPHANT AT LARGE! HE MOVES UPON HIS FATAL MARCH! WHOLE VILLAGES DESERTED BY THEIR FRIGHT-STRICKEN OCCUPANTS! PALE TERROR GOES BEFORE HIM, DEATH AND DEVASTATION FOLLOW AFTER! AFTER THESE, THE DETECTIVES. BARNS DESTROYED, FACTORIES GUTTED, HARVESTS DEVOURED, PUBLIC ASSEM-

BLAGES DISPERSED, ACCOMPANIED BY SCENES OF CARNAGE IMPOSSIBLE
TO DESCRIBE! THEORIES OF THIRTY-FOUR OF THE MOST DISTINGUISHED
DETECTIVES ON THE FORCE! THEORY OF CHIEF BLUNT!

'There!' said Inspector Blunt, almost betrayed into excitement, 'this
is magnificent! This is the greatest windfall that any detective organization ever had. The fame of it will travel to the ends of the earth, and
endure to the end of time, and my name with it.'

But there was no joy for me. I felt as if I had committed all those
red crimes, and that the elephant was only my irresponsible agent.
And how the list had grown! In one place he had 'interfered with
an election and killed five repeaters.' He had followed this act with
the destruction of two poor fellows, named O'Donohue and
McFlannigan, who had 'found a refuge in the home of the oppressed
of all lands only the day before, and were in the act of exercising
for the first time the noble right of American citizens at the polls,
when stricken down by the relentless hand of the Scourge of Siam.'
In another, he had 'found a crazy sensation-preacher preparing his
next season's heroic attacks on the dance, the theatre, and other things
which can't strike back, and had stepped on him.' And in still another
place he had 'killed a lightning-rod agent.' And so the list went on,
growing redder and redder, and more more and heart-breaking.
Sixty persons had been killed, and two hundred and forty wounded.
All the accounts bore just testimony to the activity and devotion
of the detectives, and all closed with the remark that 'three hundred
thousand citizens and four detectives saw the dread creature, and two
of the latter he destroyed.'

I dreaded to hear the telegraphic instrument begin to click again.
By-and-by the messages began to pour in, but I was happily
disappointed in their nature. It was soon apparent that all trace of the
elephant was lost. The fog had enabled him to search out a good
hiding-place unobserved. Telegrams from the most absurdly distant
points reported that a dim vast mass had been glimpsed there through
the fog at such and such an hour, and was 'undoubtedly the elephant.'
This dim vast mass had been glimpsed in New Haven, in New Jersey,
in Pennsylvania, in interior New York, in Brooklyn, and even in the
city of New York itself! But in all cases the dim vast mass had vanished

95

quickly and left no trace. Every detective of the large force scattered over this huge extent of country sent his hourly report and each and every one of them had a clue, and, was shadowing something, and was hot upon the heels of it.

But the day passed without other result.

The next day the same.

The next day just the same.

The newspaper reports began to grow monotonous with facts that amounted to nothing, clues which led to nothing, and theories which had nearly exhausted the elements which surprise and delight and dazzle.

By advice of the inspector, I doubled the reward.

Four more dull days followed. Then came a bitter blow to the poor, hard-working detectives—the journalists declined to print their theories, and coldly said, 'Give us a rest.'

Two weeks after the elephant's disappearance I raised the reward to $75,000 by the Inspector's advice. It was a great sum, but I felt that I would rather sacrifice my whole private fortune than lose my credit with my Government. Now that the detectives were in adversity, the newspapers turned upon them, and began to fling the most stinging sarcasms at them. This gave the minstrels an idea, and they dressed themselves as detectives and hunted the elephant on the stage in the most extravagant way. The caricaturists made pictures of detectives scanning the country with spy-glasses, while the elephant, at their backs, stole apples out of their pockets. And they made all sorts of ridiculous pictures of the detective badge—you have seen that badge printed in gold on the back of detective novels, no doubt—it is a wide-staring eye, with the legend, 'WE NEVER SLEEP'. When detectives called for a drink, the would-be facetious barkeeper resurrected an obsolete form of expression, and said, 'Will you have an eye-opener?' All the air was thick with sarcasms.

But there was one man who moved calm, untouched, unaffected through it all. It was that heart of oak, the Chief Inspector. His brave eye never drooped, his serene confidence never wavered. He always said—

'Let them rail on; he laughs best who laughs last.

My admiration for the man grew into a species of worship. I was at his side always. His office had become an unpleasant place to me, and now became daily more and more so. Yet if he could endure it I meant to do so also; at least, as long as I could. So I came regularly, and stayed—the only outsider who seemed to be capable of it. Everybody wondered how I could; and often it seemed to me that I must desert, but at such times I looked into that calm and apparently unconscious face, and held my ground.

About three weeks after the elephant's disappearance I was about to say, one morning, that I should *have* to strike my colours and retire, when the great detective arrested the thought by proposing one more superb and masterly move.

This was to compromise with the robbers. The fertility of this man's invention exceeded anything I have ever seen, and I have had a wide intercourse with the world's finest minds. He said he was confident he could compromise for $100,000 and recover the elephant. I said I believed I could scrape the amount together; but what would become of the poor detectives who had worked so faithfully? He said:

'In compromises they always get half.'

This removed my only objection. So the Inspector wrote two notes, in this form:

Dear Madam,
Your husband can make a large sum of money (and be entirely protected from the law) by making an immediate appointment with me.
Chief Blunt.

He sent one of these by his confidential messenger to the 'reputed wife' of Brick Duffy, and the other to the reputed wife of Red McFadden.

Within the hour these offensive answers came:

Ye Owld fool: brick McDuffys bin ded 2 yere.
Bridget Mahoney.

Chief Bat,
Red McFadden is hung and in heving 18 month. Any Ass but a detective knose that.
Mary O'Hooligan.

97

'I had long suspected these facts,' said the Inspector; 'this testimony proves the unerring accuracy of my instinct.'

The moment one resource failed him he was ready with another. He immediately wrote an advertisement for the morning papers, and I kept a copy of it—

"A.—xwblv. 242 N. Tjnd—fz328wmlg. Ozpo,—; 2 m. ! ogw. Mum."

He said that if the thief was alive this would bring him to the usual rendezvous. He further explained that the usual rendezvous was a place where all business affairs between detectives and criminals were conducted. This meeting would take place at twelve the next night.

We could do nothing till then, and I lost no time in getting out of the office, and was grateful indeed for the privilege.

At eleven the next night I brought $100,000 in banknotes and put them into the chief's hands, and shortly afterward he took his leave, with the brave old undimmed confidence in his eye. An almost intolerable hour dragged to a close: then I heard his welcome tread, and rose gasping and tottered to meet him. How his fine eyes flamed with triumph! He said—

'We've compromised! The jokers will sing a different tune tomorrow! Follow me!'

He took a lighted candle and strode down into the vast vaulted basement where sixty detectives always slept, and where a score were now playing cards to while the time. I followed close after him. He walked swiftly down to the dim remote end of the place, and just as I succumbed to the pangs of suffocation and was swooning away he stumbled and fell over the outlying members of a mighty object, and I heard him exclaim as he went down:

'Our noble profession is vindicated. Here is your elephant!'

I was carried to the office above and restored with carbolic acid. The whole detective force swarmed in, and such another season of triumphant rejoicing ensued as I had never witnessed before. The reporters were called, baskets of champagne were opened, toasts were drunk, the handshakings and congratulations were continuous and enthusiastic. Naturally the chief was the hero of the hour, and his happiness was so complete and had been so patiently and worthily and bravely won that it made me happy to see it, though I stood there a homeless beggar, my priceless charge dead, and my position in my country's service lost to me through what would always seem my fatally careless execution of a great trust. Many an eloquent eye testified its deep admiration for the chief, and many a detective's voice murmured, 'Look at him—just the king of the profession—only give him a clue, it's all he wants, and there ain't anything hid that he can't find.' The dividing of the $50,000 made great pleasure; when it was finished the chief made a little speech while he put his share in his pocket, in which he said, 'Enjoy it, boys, for you've earned it; and more than that—you've earned for the detective profession undying fame.'

A telegram arrived, which read:

> *Monroe, Mich.: 10 p.m.*
> *First time I've struck a telegraph office in over three weeks. Have followed those footprints, horseback, through the woods, a thousand miles to here, and they get stronger and bigger and fresher every day. Don't worry—inside of another week I'll have the elephant. This is dead sure.*
> *Darley, Detective.*

The chief ordered three cheers for 'Darley, one of the finest minds on the force,' and then commanded that he be telegraphed to come home and receive his share of the reward.

So ended that marvellous episode of the stolen elephant. The newspapers were pleasant with praises once more, the next day, with one contemptible exception. This sheet said:

> 'Great is the detective! He may be a little slow in finding a little thing like a mislaid elephant—he may hunt him all day and sleep with his rotting carcase all night for three weeks, but he will find him at last—if he can get the man who mislaid him to show him the place!'

Poor Hassan was lost to me for ever. The cannon-shots had wounded him fatally. He had crept to that unfriendly place in the fog; and there, surrounded by his enemies and in constant danger of detection, he had wasted away with hunger and suffering till death gave him peace.

The compromise cost me $100,000; my detective expenses were $42,000 more; I never applied for a place again under my Government; I am a ruined man and a wanderer in the earth—but my admiration for that man, whom I believe to be the greatest detective the world has ever produced, remains undimmed to this day, and will so remain unto the end.

A BABY IS MISSING

Alistair Cooke

I suppose everybody who ever stops at a news-stand on his way to work has at the back of his mind a very simple distinction between a good newspaper and a bad one, or better, between a 'heavy' newspaper and a 'light' one. It is a curious thing that the heavy newspapers in most countries tend to steer clear of the great human stories in the news, while the light newspapers eat them up. Surely it's odd that light newspapers should be the ones to take an instinctive interest in such profound things as murder, kidnapping, rape and infidelity: for surely the deepest human feelings are involved in such goings-on. The other curiosity is this: the people who write for heavy newspapers are just the people who, on their own confession, pretend to a superior taste of literature. They will brood long and talk strenuously over a murder in Dostoevsky, a pickpocket in Dickens, a spy in Joseph Conrad. But lift the murder or pickpocket out of literature and into Sheffield or Camden Town, and they assume no journalist worth the name would give his talent to such squalid stuff. The result is, it seems to me, that the best stories get badly written up, while the dull abstractions that are the same in all countries and all generations—politics, economics—are treated with solemn care.

Luckily, the United States is not yet blasé enough to keep up this artificial distinction between life and literature. With the result that the most serious newspapers in the country—and there are no better newspapers anywhere than the best three or four American dailies—always have in their active employ a small stable of feature-writers who are very much aware of the teeming life that is going on all around them. By teeming life, I'm not thinking of the special tempo or intensity of life in New York: I mean the daily life of the streets, the markets, the slums, the private joys and grief of anybody from the Mayor of New York to a couple of Puerto Rican immigrants who sleep out nights in an uptown garage.

In the spring of 1950 a story broke in New York which here, and only here, swept Germany and Congress, and the risk of war, right off the front pages of all the light and heavy newspapers. It seems to me to be one of the news stories of the century, and I think it's worth telling over to anyone who has ever felt a pang for somebody else's disappointed hopes.

It is a story about a coloured girl, eighteen years of age, and a coloured baby, ten days old.

The first day of spring that year came into New York with a spatter of snowflakes. The night of the 21st of March was no time to be out. It was raw and misty, and even the midnight movies on Broadway were doing poor business. That night a young coloured woman, a Mrs Holden, was taken by her anxious husband to an uptown Hospital, the Lincoln Hospital, and delivered of a premature baby. It was put in an incubator right away. It weighed two pounds and a few ounces at birth, and the doctors told the trembling couple they could do no more than their best. Nine nights later, the 30th of March, was a wheezing, freezing night. The night nurse of the incubator ward came in to see how the premature babies were doing, peeked at the thermostat, looked around and into the Holden incubator and—the Holden baby was gone. She brought an orderly and a doctor running. But sure enough the baby had vanished. When the parents arrived they were almost crazed, but the doctor had to tell them the pitiful truth: the baby then weighed two pounds, eleven ounces. If it had been taken outside on such a night, it might live for an hour, two hours at most. The parents shuffled off home. The doctor put a tentative stroke across the baby's progress chart. A police siren

The night nurse discovered that the Holden baby was missing.

whined outside and the next morning the tabloids reported a routine kidnapping. The FBI was called in, and that was apparently the end of the story.

Three weeks later, a pleasant housewife who lives way uptown was doing her housework one morning and listening to the radio. And up came that tune again, a pleasant jingle going the rounds of the dance-halls and the disc jockeys. A song called, 'Don't Call Me a Nosey Man'. This woman couldn't get the thing out of her head. She decided she would clean up a bit and go out and buy the gramophone record of it. She went to a little store on 125th Street in the heart of Harlem and asked the assistant to play it first. While it was jingling away, a chunky, strutting coloured girl in her teens strolled up and said, 'Oh, I *like* that record.' The housewife turned to look at her and suddenly knew the face. She had seen it once before, weeks ago. She looked again, and she knew it was the face of a girl holding a baby on a cold night. The housewife was sure it was the same girl, but whereas three weeks ago this girl had been a forlorn ignorant mother, she was now in the housewife's eyes a 'person wanted.' The housewife too read the newspapers. Before the girl could say another sentence the housewife dashed from the store and grabbed the nearest cop. He was an old-timer, he'd seen hysterical women before. 'Take it easy, lady,' he said; 'now what's all this about a blanket?' By the time he was up and on the job the teenage coloured girl was gone. Then a week after that, by a mad coincidence, a little strutting, chunky coloured girl went into a bus depot on 42nd Street. Of all things, she went up to a cop. She wasn't too consecutive in her story. It seemed she'd had some trouble lately in a store in Harlem. The cop motioned to another cop, who came up and said 'I know that girl; she lives in my hotel.' So she did, a seedy little place way over on the West Side. Well, the cops 'phoned the station-house and the FBI connected in no time, and the word went out over the police-car radios that a young coloured woman 'wanted' had hopped a bus on 42nd Street, the terminal for buses that serve the South. In fact, the girl had not taken a bus. She had wandered out of the bus station and gone across the street and over to her hotel. But by that time the FBI men were stopping traffic and dredging through bus stations from New York City all the way down to New Orleans.

Next day they found her, in a tiny hotel bedroom. She was married to a porter in the hotel. She wept out her story. She had done nothing wrong. She was unhappy because only lately she'd given birth to still-born twins. Please would they get out and leave her alone. At last she broke down and said it: she had kidnapped the baby. But the detectives knew as well as she did that the baby was dead. They had cast a roving eye around everything and tapped the tattered wallpaper for hidden panels and looked under this and that. All right, then, sorry, ma'am, they'd have to book her. Too bad about the baby.

They were at her door and on the way out when one of them held up his index-finger. From across the hall came a thin broken wail, like the complaint of a powerful kitten. The cops and detectives jumped across the hall and broke the lock on a small door and pulled the door open. The heat from inside came at them like a ten-pound roast. It was a room no bigger than a linen-closet. And there was the baby.

Now we can go back to the nipping, frosty night of the 30th March and straighten everything out. The girl, eighteen years old, had, as she said, just had stillborn twins. She was fairly frantic for a baby. And in the active misery of her loss she decided quite straightforwardly to go get one. On the afternoon of the 30th of March she somehow got into the Lincoln Hospital. I said, I think, she had a plump, confident strut. Well, the nurses and doctors thought, if they thought at all, that she was a charwoman, or kitchen worker, or something. She marched around the corridors, took elevators up and down, sallied into this room, this lab, that dispensary, and kept her eyes open. By nightfall, she had the premature-baby section very well located. She went there, walked straight in, unhooked a door, lifted the top of the first incubator she saw and took the baby out—two pounds and eleven ounces. She put it under her coat, took an elevator down and out onto the street. This is where the good Lord and neighbourly sense did more to help her than the split-second timing of a bank robbery.

She walked three blocks to the underground station, went into a rest-room, took off the bright red skirt she had on and wrapped it round the baby. The train came in. The conductor said, 'Lady, that's no way to warm a baby on a night like this. You better go and stop a cab and get a blanket some place.' She went upstairs and out and walked straight into a nearby apartment, and in no time was back with another woman holding a blanket. She thanked the woman, hailed a cab, put the squawling baby on the seat and started to put her red skirt on. The driver was mildly outraged. 'I'm sorry, miss,' he said; 'you can't dress in my cab.' They tossed it back and forth a while, and the cab-driver said, 'Just can't *do* it, ma'am.' But he knew a nice lady who'd let her dress at her place. So he drove her to the home of a friend, the housewife we met with the tune on her mind. There the girl dressed, thanked the housewife, and the taxi-driver drove her downtown to a bus terminal. Somebody who worked around there remembered this bulging sight when, three weeks later, the cops started to ask questions in the same terminal.

None of this answers the aching question: 'How did she possibly keep the baby alive?' When at last it was returned to the hospital, it weighed three pounds, one ounce, a gain of six ounces, and was squealing a little more lustily now. The doctors said—'a miracle.' An act of God, said another. Well, we all know that God helps them that help themselves. And what had this forlorn, half-crazed, illiterate coloured girl done to nurture this miracle? She had bought a twenty-five-cent book, a reprint about baby care, at a drug store. She had nosed around a clinic and talked with nurses. And when the detectives broke into the little room, they found some paper-backed books: 'The American Woman's Cook Book'; a Bible; 'The New Modern Home Physician'; two pulp magazines—'Ideal Love' and 'Love Should be Laughter'. They found a folding carriage lined with an electric blanket. There was an electric grill. By its side a row of baby formulas, and twelve bottles with those sterilized nipples that pop up without touching. A pan of water and sterilizing tweezers. The proper vitamin extracts. Baby powder, absorbent cotton, baby oil. And the essential feeding weapon, for a child that size: and eye-dropper.

At the hospital later an obstetrician, still full of doubt, said, 'But there were two things she *couldn't* know: the atmosphere around a premature that size has to be humid, and must be maintained strictly at 96 degrees.' 'Well,' said a cop who was on the expedition to get her, 'she had a pan of boiling water on the electric grill, steaming the place up like mad. And, oh yes—up against the inside lintel of the door was a thermometer.'

He remembered he had seen it and noted down the temperature.

He opened his pad now and turned the pages. It was right there. It had read precisely 96 degrees.

They brought the girl into court about a month or so later. Very reliable psychiatrists had looked her over and simply testified nothing but the truth: she was quite mad, a psychotic. And so, quite rightly, since psychotics are beyond the intelligent handling of life, not to say a threat to you and me, they put her away. The baby is at this writing a year old and very fit and laughing its head off.

THE GOLD-BUG

Edgar Allan Poe

What ho! what ho! this fellow is dancing mad!
He hath been bitten by the Tarantula.

—ALL IN THE WRONG.

Many years ago, I contracted an intimacy with a Mr William Legrand.
He was of an ancient Huguenot family, and had once been wealthy;
but a series of misfortunes had reduced him to want. To avoid the
mortification consequent upon his disasters, he left New Orleans, the
city of his forefathers, and took up his residence at Sullivan's Island,
near Charleston, South Carolina.

This island is a very singular one. It consists of little else than the
sea sand, and is about three miles long. Its breadth at no point exceeds
a quarter of a mile. It is separated from the mainland by a scarcely
perceptible creek, oozing its way through a wilderness of reeds and slime,
a favourite resort of the marsh-hen. The vegetation, as might be
supposed, is scant, or at least dwarfish. No trees of any magnitude are
to be seen. Near the western extremity, where Fort Moultrie stands, and
where are some miserable frame buildings, tenanted, during summer,
by the fugitives from Charleston dust and fever, may be found,
indeed, the bristly palmetto; but the whole island, with the exception
of this western point, and a line of hard, white beach on the seacoast, is covered with a dense undergrowth of the sweet myrtle so
much prized by the horticulturists of England. The shrub here often
attains the height of fifteen or twenty feet, and forms an almost

impenetrable coppice, burthening the air with its sweet fragrance.

In the inmost recesses of this coppice, not far from the eastern or more remote end of the island, Legrand had built himself a small hut, which he occupied when I first, by mere accident, made for his acquaintance. This soon ripened into friendship—for there was much in the recluse to excite interest and esteem. I found him well educated, with unusual powers of mind, but infected with misanthropy, and subject to perverse moods of alternate enthusiasm and melancholy. He had with him many books, but rarely enjoyed them. His chief amusements were gunning and fishing, or sauntering along the beach and through the myrtles, in quest of shells or entomological specimens—his collection of the latter might have been envied by a Swammerdamm. In these excursions he was usually accompanied by an old negro, called Jupiter, who had been manumitted before the reverses of the family, but who could be induced, neither by threats nor by promises, to abandon what he considered his right of attendance upon the footsteps of his young 'Massa Will'. It is not improbable that the relatives of Legrand, conceiving him to be somewhat unsettled in intellect, had contrived to instill this obstinacy into Jupiter, with a view to the supervision and guardianship of the wanderer.

The winters in the latitude of Sullivan's Island are seldom very severe, and in the fall of the year it is a rare event indeed when a fire is considered necessary. About the middle of October, 18—, there occurred, however, a day of remarkable chilliness. Just before sunset I scrambled my way through the evergreens to the hut of my friend, whom I had not visited for several weeks—my residence being, at that time, in Charleston, a distance of nine miles from the island, while the facilities of passage and re-passage were very far behind those of the present day. Upon reaching the hut I rapped, as was my custom, and getting no reply, sought for the key where I knew it was secreted, unlocked the door, and went in. A fine fire was blazing upon the hearth. It was a novelty, and by no means an ungrateful one. I threw off an overcoat, took an armchair by the crackling logs, and awaited patiently the arrival of my hosts.

Soon after dark they arrived, and gave me a most cordial welcome. Jupiter, grinning from ear to ear, bustled about to prepare some marsh-hen for supper. Legrand was in one of his fits—how else shall I term them?—of enthusiasm. He had found an unknown bivalve, forming a new genus, and, more than this, he had hunted down and secured, with Jupiter's assistance, a *scarabaeus* which he believed to be totally new, but in respect to which he wished to have my opinion on the morrow.

'And why not tonight?' I asked, rubbing my hands over the blaze, and wishing the whole tribe of *scarabaei* at the devil.

'Ah, if I had only known you were here!' said Legrand, 'but it's so long since I saw you; and how could I foresee that you would pay me a visit this very night of all others? As I was coming home I met Lieutenant G——, from the fort, and, very foolishly, I lent him the bug; so it will be impossible for you to see it until the morning. Stay here tonight, and I will send Jup down for it at sunrise. It is the loveliest thing in creation!'

'What?—sunrise?'

'Nonsense! no!—the bug. It is of a brilliant gold colour—about the size of a large hickory-nut—with two jet black spots near one extremity of the back, and another, somewhat longer, at the other. The *antennae* are—'

'Dey aint *no* tin in him, Massa Will, I keep a tellin' on you,' here interrupted Jupiter; 'de bug is a goole-bug, solid, ebery bit of him, inside and all, sep him wing—neber feel half so hebby a bug in my life.'

'Well, suppose it is, Jup,' replied Legrand, somewhat more earnestly, it seemed to me, than the case demanded; 'is that any reason for your letting the birds burn? The colour'— here he turned to me—'is really almost enough to warrant Jupiter's idea. You never saw a more brilliant metallic lustre than the scales emit—but of this you cannot judge till tomorrow. In the meantime I can give you some idea of the shape.' Saying this, he seated himself at a small table, on which were a pen and ink, but no paper. He looked for some in a drawer, but found none.

'Never mind,' he said at length, 'this will answer;' and he drew from his waistcoat pocket a scrap of what I took to be very dirty foolscap, and made upon it a rough drawing with the pen. While he did this, I retained my seat by the fire, for I was still chilly. When the design was complete, he handed it to me without rising. As I received it, a loud growl was heard, succeeded by scratching at the door. Jupiter opened it, and a large Newfoundland, belonging to Legrand, rushed in, leaped upon my shoulders, and loaded me with caresses; for I had shown him much attention during previous visits. When his gambols were over, I looked at the paper, and, to speak the truth, found myself not a little puzzled at what my friend had depicted.

'Well!' I said, after contemplating it for some minutes, 'this *is* a strange *scarabaeus*, I must confess; new to me; never saw anything like it before—unless it was a skull, or a death's-head, which it more nearly resembles than anything else that has come under *my* observation.'

'A death's-head!' echoed Legrand. 'Oh—yes—well, it has something of that appearance upon paper, no doubt. The two upper black spots look like eyes, eh? and the longer one at the bottom like a mouth—and then the shape of the whole is oval.'

'Perhaps so,' said I; 'but Legrand, I fear you are no artist. I must wait until I see the beetle itself, if I am to form any idea of its personal appearance.'

'Well, I don't know,' said he a little nettled, 'I draw tolerably—*should* do at least—have had some good masters, and flatter myself that I am not quite a blockhead.'

'But, my dear fellow, you are joking then,' said I, 'this is a very passable *skull*—indeed, I may say that it is a very *excellent* skull, according to the vulgar notions about such specimens of physiology—and your *scarabaeus* must be the queerest *scarabaeus* in the world if it resembles it. Why, we may get up a very thrilling bit of superstition upon this hint. I presume you will call the bug *scarabaeus caput hominis,* or something of that kind—there are many similar titles in the Natural Histories. But where are the *antennae* you spoke of?'

'The *antennae!*' said Legrand, who seemed to be getting unaccountably warm upon the subject; 'I am sure you must see the *antennae*. I made them as distinct as they are in the original insect, and I presume that is sufficient.'

'Well, well,' I said, 'perhaps you have—still I don't see them;' and I handed him the paper without additional remark, not wishing to ruffle his temper; but I was much surprised at the turn affairs had taken; his ill humour puzzled me—and, as for the drawing of the beetle, there were positively *no antennae* visible, and the whole *did* bear a very close resemblance to the ordinary cuts of a death's-head.

He received the paper very peevishly, and was about to crumple it, apparently to throw it in the fire, when a casual glance at the design seemed suddenly to rivet his attention. In an instant his face grew violently red—in another as excessively pale. For some minutes he continued to scrutinize the drawing minutely where he sat. At length he arose, took a candle from the table, and proceeded to seat himself upon a sea-chest in the furthest corner of the room. Here again he made an anxious examination of the paper; turning it in all directions. He said nothing, however, and his conduct greatly astonished me; yet I thought it prudent not to exacerbate the growing moodiness of his temper by any comment. Presently he took from his coat-pocket a wallet, placed the paper carefully in it, and deposited both in a writing desk, which he locked. He now grew more composed in his demeanour; but his original air of enthusiasm had quite disappeared. Yet he seemed not so much sulky as abstracted. As the evening wore away he became more and more absorbed in reverie, from which no sallies of mine could arouse him. It had been my intention to pass the night at the hut, as I had frequently done before, but, seeing my host in this mood, I deemed it proper to take leave. He did not press me to remain, but, as I departed he shook my hand with even more than his usual cordiality.

It was about a month after this (and during the interval I had seen nothing of Legrand) when I received a visit at Charleston, from his man, Jupiter. I had never seen the good old negro look so dispirited, and I feared that some serious disaster had befallen my friend.

'Well, Jup,' said I, 'what is the matter now?—how is your master?'

'Why, to speak de troof, massa, him not so berry well as mought be.'

'Not well! I am truly sorry to hear it. What does he complain of?'

'Dar! dat's it!—he neber 'plain of notin'—but him berry sick for all dat.'

'*Very* sick, Jupiter!—why didn't you say so at once? Is he confined to bed?'

'No, dat he aint!—he aint 'fin'd nowhar—dat's just whar de shoe pinch—my mind is got to be berry hebby 'bout poor Massa Will.'

'Jupiter, I should like to understand what it is you are talking about. You say your master is sick. Hasn't he told you what ails him?'

'Why, massa, 'taint worf while for to git mad about de matter—Massa Will say noffin at all aint de matter wid him—but what make him go about looking dis here way, wid he head down and he soldiers up, and as white as a gose? And den he keep a siphon all de time—'

'Keeps a what, Jupiter?'

'Keeps a siphon wid de figgurs on de slate—de queerest figgurs I ebber did see. Ise gettin' to be skeered, I tell you. Hab for to keep mighty tight eye 'pon him 'noovers. Todder day he gib me slip 'fore de sun up and was gone the whole ob de blessed day. I had a big stick ready cut for to gib him deuced good beating when he did come— but Ise sich a fool dat I hadn't de heart arter all—he looked so berry poorly.'

'Eh?—what?—ah yes!—upon the whole I think you had better not be too severe with the poor fellow—don't flog him, Jupiter—he can't very well stand it—but can you form no idea of what has occasioned this illness, or rather this change of conduct? Has anything unpleasant happened since I saw you?'

'No, massa, dey aint bin noffin onpleasant *since* den—'t was '*fore* I'm feared—'t was de berry day you was dare.'

'How? what do you mean?'

'Why, massa, I mean de bug—dare now.'

'The what?'

'De bug—I'm berry sartain dat Massa Will bin bit somewhere 'bout de head by dat goole-bug.'

'And what causes have you, Jupiter, for such a supposition?'

'Claws enuff, massa, and mouff too. I nebber did see sich a deuced bug—he kick and he bite ebery ting what cum near him. Massa Will cotch him fuss, but had for to let him go 'gin mighty quick, I tell you—den was de time he must ha' got de bite. I didn't like de look ob de bug mouff, myself, nohow, so I wouldn't take hold ob him wid my finger, but I cotch him wid a piece ob paper dat I found. I rap him up in de paper and stuff a piece of it in he mouff—dat was de way.'

'And you think, then, that your master was really bitten by the beetle, and that the bite made him sick?'

'I don't think noffin' about it—I nose it. What make him dream 'bout de goole so much, if 'taint 'cause he bit by the goole-bug? Ise heerd 'bout dem goole-bugs 'fore dis.'

'But how do you know he dreams about gold?'

'How I know? why, 'cause he talk about it in he sleep— dat's how I nose.'

'Well, Jup, perhaps you are right; but to what fortunate circumstances am I to attribute the honour of a visit from you today?'

'What de matter, massa?'

'Did you bring any message from Mr Legrand?'

'No, massa, I bring dis here pissel;' and here Jupiter handed me a note which ran thus:

My Dear——

Why have I not seen you for so long a time? I hope you have not been so foolish as to take offence at any little *brusquerie* of mine; but no, that is improbable.

Since I saw you I have had great cause for anxiety. I have something to tell you, yet scarcely know how to tell it, or whether I should tell it at all.

I have not been quite well for some days past, and poor old Jup annoys me, almost beyond endurance, by his well-meant attentions. Would you believe it—he had prepared a huge stick, the other day, with which to chastize me for giving him the slip, and spending the day, solus, among the hills on the mainland. I verily believe that my ill looks alone saved me a flogging.

I have made no addition to my cabinet since we met.

If you can, in any way, make it convenient, come over with Jupiter. *Do come.* I wish to see you *tonight*, upon business of importance. I assure you that it is of the *highest* importance.—Ever yours,

WILLIAM LEGRAND.

There was something in the tone of this note which gave me great uneasiness. Its whole style differed materially from that of Legrand. What could he be dreaming of? What new crotchet possessed his excitable brain? What 'business of the highest importance' could *he* possibly have to transact? Jupiter's account of him boded no good. I dreaded lest the continued pressure of misfortune had, at length, fairly unsettled the reason of my friend. Without a moment's hesitation, therefore, I prepared to accompany the negro.

Upon reaching the wharf, I noticed a scythe and three spades, all apparently new, lying in the bottom of the boat in which we were to embark.

'What is the meaning of all this, Jup?' I inquired.

'Him syfe, massa, and spade.'

'Very true; but what are they doing here?'

'Him de syfe and de spade what Massa Will sis 'pon my buying for him in de town, and de debbil's own lot of money I had to gib for 'em.'

'But what, in the name of all that is mysterious, is your "Massa Will" going to do with scythes and spades?'

'Dat's more dan *I* know, and debbil take me if I don't b'lieve 'tis more dan he know too. But it's all cum ob de bug.'

Finding that no satisfaction was to be obtained of Jupiter, whose whole intellect seemed to be absorbed by 'de bug', I now stepped into the boat, and made sail. With a fair and strong breeze we soon ran into the little cove to the northward of Fort Moultrie, and a walk of some two miles brought us to the hut. It was about three in the afternoon when we arrived. Legrand had been awaiting us in eager expectation. He grasped my hand with a nervous *empressement* which alarmed me and strengthened the suspicions already entertained. His countenance was pale even to ghastliness and his deep-set eyes glared with unnatural lustre. After some inquiries respecting his health, I asked him, not knowing what better to say, if he had yet obtained the *scarabaeus* from Lieutenant G——.

'Oh, yes,' he replied, colouring violently, 'I got it from him the next morning. Nothing should tempt me to part with that *scarabaeus*. Do you know that Jupiter is quite right about it?'

'In what way,' I asked, with a sad foreboding at heart.

'In supposing it to be a bug of *real gold*.' He said this with an air of profound seriousness, and I felt inexpressibly shocked.

'This bug is to make my fortune,' he continued, with a triumphant smile; 'to reinstate me in my family possessions. Is it any wonder, then, that I prize it? Since Fortune has thought fit to bestow it upon me, I have only to use it properly, and I shall arrive at the gold of which it is the index. Jupiter, bring me that *scarabaeus*!'

'What de bug, massa? I'd rudder not go fer trubble dat bug; you mus' git him for your own self.' Hereupon Legrand arose, with a grave and stately air, and brought me the beetle from a glass case in which it was enclosed. It was a beautiful *scarabaeus*, and, at that time, unknown to naturalists—of course a great prize in a scientific point of view. There were two round black spots near one extremity of the back, and a long one near the other. The scales were exceedingly hard and glossy, with all the appearance of burnished gold. The weight of the insect was very remarkable, and, taking all things into consideration, I could hardly blame Jupiter for his opinion respecting it; but what to make of Legrand's concordance with that opinion, I could not, for the life of me, tell.

'I sent for you,' said he, in a grandiloquent tone, when I had completed my examination of the beetle, 'I sent for you that I might have your counsel and assistance in furthering the views of Fate and of the bug—'

'My dear Legrand,' I cried, interrupting him, 'you are certainly unwell, and had better use some little precautions. You shall go to bed, and I will remain with you a few days, until you get over this. You are feverish and—'

'Feel my pulse,' said he.

I felt it, and to say the truth, found not the slightest indication of fever.

'But you may be ill and yet have no fever. Allow me this once to prescribe for you. In the first place go to bed. In the next—'

'You are mistaken,' he interposed, 'I am as well as I can expect to be under the excitement which I suffer. If you really wish me well, you will relieve this excitement.'

'And how is this to be done?'

'Very easily. Jupiter and myself are going upon an expedition into the hills, upon the mainland, and, in this expedition, we shall need the aid of some person in whom we can confide. You are the only one we can trust. Whether we succeed or fail, the excitement which you now perceive in me will be equally allayed.'

'I am anxious to oblige you in any way,' I replied; 'but do you mean to say that this infernal beetle has any connection with your expedition into the hills?'

'It has.'

'Then, Legrand, I can become a party to no such absurd proceeding.'

'I am sorry—very sorry—for we shall have to try it by ourselves.'

'Try it by yourselves! The man is surely mad!—but stay!—how long do you propose to be absent?'

'Probably all night. We shall start immediately, and be back, at all events, by sunrise.'

'And you will promise me, upon your honour, that when this freak of yours is over, and the bug business (good God!) settled to your satisfaction, you will then return home and follow my advice implicitly, as that of your physician.'

'Yes; I promise; and now let us be off, for we have no time to lose.'

With a heavy heart I accompanied my friend. We started about four o'clock—Legrand, Jupiter, the dog, and myself. Jupiter had with him the scythe and spades—the whole of which he insisted upon carrying—more through fear, it seemed to me, of trusting either of the implements within reach of his master, than from any excess of industry or complaisance. His demeanour was dogged in the extreme, and 'dat deuced bug' were the sole words which escaped his lips during the journey. For my own part, I had charge of a couple of dark lanterns, while Legrand contented himself with the *scarabaeus*, which he carried attached to the end of a bit of whip-cord; twirling it to and fro, with the air of a conjuror, as he went. When I observed this last, plain evidence of my friend's aberration of mind, I could scarcely refrain from tears. I thought it best, however, to humour his fancy, at least for the present, or until I could adopt some more energetic measures with a chance of success. In the meantime, I endeavoured, but all in vain, to sound him in regard to the object of the expedition. Having succeeded in inducing me to accompany him, he seemed unwilling to hold conversation upon any topic of minor importance, and to all my questions vouchsafed no other reply than 'we shall see!'

We crossed the creek at the head of the island by means of a skiff, and, ascending the high grounds on the shore of the mainland, proceeded in a north-westerly direction, through a tract of country excessively wild and desolate, where no trace of a human footstep was to be seen. Legrand led the way with decision; pausing only for an instant, here and there, to consult what appeared to be certain landmarks of his own contrivance upon a former occasion.

In this manner we journeyed for about two hours, and the sun was

just setting when we entered a region infinitely more dreary than any
yet seen. It was a species of tableland, near the summit of an almost
inaccessible hill, densely wooded from base to pinnacle, and inter-
spersed with huge crags that appeared to lie loosely upon the soil, and
in many cases were prevented from precipitating themselves into the
valleys below, merely by the support of the trees against which they
reclined. Deep ravines, in various directions, gave an air of still sterner
solemnity to the scene.

The natural platform to which we had clambered was thickly over-
grown with brambles, through which we soon discovered that it would
have been impossible to force our way but for the scythe; and
Jupiter, by direction of his master, proceeded to clear for us a path
to the foot of an enormously tall tulip-tree, which stood, with some
eight or ten oaks, upon the level, and far surpassed them all, and all
other trees which I had then ever seen, in the beauty of its foliage
and form, in the wide spread of its branches, and in the general majesty
of its appearance. When we reached this tree. Legrand turned to Jupiter,
and asked him if he thought he could climb it. The old man seemed a
little staggered by the question, and for some moments made no
reply. At length he approached the huge trunk, walked slowly around
it, and examined it with minute attention. When he had completed his
scrutiny, he merely said—

'Yes massa, Jup climb any tree he ebber see in his life.'

'Then up with you as soon as possible, for it will soon be too
dark to see what we are about.'

'How far mus go up, massa?' inquired Jupiter.

'Get up the main trunk first, and then I will tell you which way to
go—and here—stop! take this beetle with you.'

'De bug, Massa Will!—de goole-bug!' cried the negro, drawing
back in dismay—'what for mus tote de bug way up de tree?—d—n
if I do!'

'If you are afraid, Jup, a great big negro like you, to take hold of a
harmless little dead beetle, why you can carry it up by this string—but,
if you do not take it up with you in some way, I shall be under the
necessity of breaking your head with this shovel.'

'What de matter now, massa? said Jup, evidently shamed into
compliance; 'always want for to raise fuss wid old nigger. Was only

funnin anyhow. *Me* feered de bug! what I keer for de bug?' Here he took cautiously hold of the extreme end of the string, and, maintaining the insect as far from his person as circumstances would permit, prepared to ascend the tree.

In youth, the tulip-tree or *Liriodendron Tulipoferum*, the most magnificent of American foresters, has a trunk peculiarly smooth, and often rises to a great height without lateral branches; but, in its riper age, the bark becomes gnarled and uneven, while many short limbs make their appearance on the stem. Thus the difficulty of ascension, in the present case, lay more in semblance than in reality. Embracing the huge cylinder, as closely as possible, with his arms and knees, seizing with his hands some projections, and resting his naked toes upon others, Jupiter, after one or two narrow escapes from falling at length wriggled himself into the first great fork, and seemed to consider the whole business as virtually accomplished. The *risk* of the achievement was, in fact now over, although the climber was some sixty or seventy feet from the ground.

'Which way mus go now, Massa Will?' he asked.

'Keep up the largest branch—the one on this side,' said Legrand. The negro obeyed him promptly, and apparently with but little trouble; ascending higher and higher, until no glimpse of his squat figure could be obtained through the dense foliage which enveloped it. Presently his voice was heard in a sort of halloo.

'How much fudder is got for go?'

'How high up are you?' asked Legrand.

'Ebber so fur,' replied the negro; 'can see de sky fru de top ob de tree.'

'Never mind the sky, but attend to what I say. Look down the trunk and count the limbs below you on this side. How many limbs have you passed?'

'One, two, three, four fibe—I done pass fibe big limb, massa, pon dis side.'

'Then go climb higher.'

In a few minutes the voice was heard again, announcing that seventh limb was attained.

'Now Jup,' cried Legrand, evidently much excited. 'I want you to work your way out upon that limb as far as you can. If you see anything strange let me know.'

By this time what little doubt I might have entertained of my poor friend's insanity was put finally at rest. I had no alternative but to conclude him stricken with lunacy, and I became seriously anxious about getting him home. While I was pondering upon what was best to be done, Jupiter's voice was again heard.

'Mos feerd for to venture pon dis limb berry far—'tis dead limb putty much all de way.'

'Did you say it was a *dead* limb, Jupiter?' cried Legrand in a quavering voice.

'Yes, massa, him dead as de door-nail—done up for sartain—done deperted dis here life.'

'What in the name of heaven shall I do?' asked Legrand, seemingly in the greatest distress.

'Do!' said I, glad of an opportunity to interpose a word, 'why come home and go to bed. Come now!—that's a fine fellow. It's getting late, and, besides, you remember your promise.'

'Jupiter,' cried he, without heeding me in the least, 'do you hear me?'

'Yes, Massa Will, hear you ebber so plain.'

'Try the wood well, then, with your knife, and see if you think it *very* rotten.'

'Him rotten, massa, sure nuff,' replied the negro in a few moments, 'but not so berry rotten as mought be. Mought venture out leetle way pon de limb by myself, dat's true.'

'By yourself!—what do you mean?'

'Why, I mean de bug. Tis *berry* hebby bug. S'pose I drop him down fuss, and den de limb won't break wid just de weight ob one nigger.'

'You infernal scoundrel!' cried Legrand, apparently much relieved, 'what do you mean by telling me such nonsense as that? As sure as you drop that beetle I'll break your neck. Look here, Jupiter, do you hear me?'

'Yes, massa, needn't hollo at poor nigger dat style.'

'Well! now listen!—if you will venture out on the limb as far as you think safe, and not let go the beetle, I'll make you a present of a silver dollar as soon as you get down.'

'I'm gwine, Massa Will—deed I is,' replied the negro very promptly —'mos out to the eend now.'

'*Out to the end!*' here fairly screamed Legrand; 'do you say you are out to the end of that limb?'

'Soon be to de eend massa—o-o-o-o-oh! Lor-gor-a-marcy! what *is* dis here pon de tree?'

'Well!' cried Legrand, highly delighted, 'what is it?'

'Why taint noffin but a skull—somebody bin lef him head up de tree, and de crows done gobble ebery bit ob de meat off.'

'A skull, you say!—very well,—how is it fastened to the limb?— what holds it on?'

'Sure nuff massa; mus look. Why dis berry curous sarcumstance, pon my word—dare's a great big nail in de skull, what fastens ob it on to de tree.'

'Well now, Jupiter, do exactly as I tell you—do you hear?'

'Yes massa.'

'Pay attention, then—find the left eye of the skull.'

'Hum! hoo! dat's good! why dey ain't no eye lef at all.'

'Curse your stupidity! Do you know your right hand from your left.'

'Yes, I knows dat—knows all bout dat—'tis my left hand what I chops de wood wid.'

'To be sure! you are left-handed; and your left eye is on the same side as your left hand. Now, I suppose, you can find the left eye of the skull, or the place where the left eye has been. Have you found it?'

Here was a long pause. At length the negro asked:

'Is de lef eye of de skull pon de same side as de lef hand side of de skull too?—cause de skull ain't got not a bit ob a hand at all—nebber mind! I got de lef eye now—here de lef eye! what mus do wid it?'

'Let the beetle drop through it, as far as the string will reach—but be careful and not let go your hold of the string.'

'All dat done, Massa Will; mighty easy ting for to put de bug fru de hole—look out for him dare below!'

During this colloquy no portion of Jupiter's person could be seen; but the beetle, which he had suffered to descend, was now visible at the end of the string, and glistened, like a globe of burnished gold, in the last rays of the setting sun, some of which still faintly illumined the eminence upon which we stood. The *scarabaeus* hung quite clear of any branches, and, if allowed to fall, would have fallen at our feet.

Legrand immediately took the scythe, and cleared with it a circular space, three or four yards in diameter, just beneath the insect, and, having accomplished this, ordered Jupiter to let go the string and come down from the tree.

Driving a peg, with great nicety, into the ground, at the precise spot where the beetle fell, my friend now produced from his pocket a tape-measure. Fastening one end of this at that point of the trunk of the tree which was nearest the peg, he unrolled it till it reached the peg and thence further unrolled it, in the direction already established by the two points of the tree and the peg, for the distance of fifty feet— Jupiter clearing away the brambles with a scythe. At the spot thus attained a second peg was driven, and about this, as a centre, a rude circle, about four feet in diameter, described. Taking now a spade himself, and giving one to Jupiter and one to me, Legrand begged us to set about digging as quickly as possible.

To speak the truth, I had no special relish for such amusement at any time, and, at that particular moment, would most willingly have declined it; for the night was coming on, and I felt much fatigued with the exercise already taken; but I saw no mode of escape, and was fearful of disturbing my poor friend's equanimity by a refusal. Could I have depended, indeed, upon Jupiter's aid, I would have had no hesitation in attempting to get the lunatic home by force; but I was too well assured of the old negro's disposition, to hope that he would assist me, under any circumstances, in a personal contest with his master. I made no doubt that the latter had been infected with some of the innumerable Southern superstitions about money buried, and that his phantasy had received confirmation by the finding of the *scarabaeus*, or, perhaps, by Jupiter's obstinacy in maintaining it to be 'a bug of real gold'. A mind disposed to lunacy would readily be led away by such suggestions—especially if chiming in with favourite preconceived ideas—and then I called to mind the poor fellow's speech about the beetle's being 'the index of his fortune'. Upon the whole, I was sadly vexed and puzzled, but at length, I concluded to make a virtue of necessity—to dig with a good will, and thus the sooner to convince the visionary, by ocular demonstration, of the fallacy of the opinions he entertained.

The lanterns having been lit, we all fell to work with a zeal worthy a more rational cause; and, as the glare fell upon our persons and implements, I could not help thinking how picturesque a group we composed, and how strange and suspicious our labours must have appeared to any interloper who, by chance, might have stumbled upon our whereabouts.

We dug very steadily for two hours. Little was said; and our chief embarrassment lay in the yelpings of the dog, who took exceeding interest in our proceedings. He, at length, became so obstreperous that we grew fearful of his giving the alarm to some strangers in the vicinity, —or, rather, this was the apprehension of Legrand;—for myself, I should have rejoiced at any interruption which might have enabled me to get the wanderer home. The noise was, at length, very effectually silenced by Jupiter, who, getting out of the hole with a dogged air of deliberation, tied the brute's mouth up with one of his suspenders, and then returned, with a grave chuckle, to his task.

When the time mentioned had expired, we had reached a depth of five feet, and yet no signs of any treasure became manifest. A general pause ensued, and I began to hope that the farce was at an end. Legrand, however, although evidently much disconcerted, wiped his brow thoughtfully and recommenced. We had excavated the entire circle of four feet diameter, and now we slightly enlarged the limit, and went to the farther depth of two feet. Still nothing appeared. The gold-seeker, whom I sincerely pitied, at length clambered from the pit, with the bitterest disappointment imprinted upon every feature, and proceeded, slowly and reluctantly, to put on his coat, which he had thrown off at the beginning of his labour. In the meantime I made no remark. Jupiter at a signal from his master, began to gather up his tools. This done, and the dog having been unmuzzled, we turned in profound silence towards home.

We had taken, perhaps, a dozen steps in this direction, when, with a loud oath, Legrand strode up to Jupiter, and seized him by the collar. The astonished negro opened his eyes and mouth to the fullest extent, let fall the spades, and fell upon his kness.

'You scoundrel!' said Legrand, hissing out the syllables from between his clenched teeth—'you infernal black villain!—speak, I tell you!— answer me this instant, without prevarication!—which—which is your left eye?'

'Oh, my golly, Massa Will! ain't dis here my lef eye for sartain?' roared the terrified Jupiter, placing his hand upon his *right* organ of vision, and holding it there with a desperate pertinacy, as if in immediate dread of his master's attempt at a gouge.

'I thought so!—I knew it! hurrah!' vociferated Legrand, letting the negro go and executing a series of curvets and caracols, much to the astonishment of his valet, who, arising from his knees, looked mutely, from his master to myself, and then from myself to his master.

'Come! we must go back,' said the latter, 'the game's not up yet'; and he again led the way to the tulip-tree.

'Jupiter,' said he, when we reached its foot, 'come here! was the skull nailed to the limb with the face outwards, or with the face to the limb?'

'De face was out, massa, so dat de crows could get at de eyes good, widout any trouble.'

'Well, then, was it this eye or that through which you dropped the beetle?'—here Legrand touched each of Jupiter's eyes.

' 'Twas dis eye, massa—de lef eye—jis as you tell me,'—and here it was his right eye that the negro indicated.

'That will do—we must try it again.'

Here my friend, about whose madness I now saw, or fancied that I saw, certain indications of method, removed the peg which marked the spot where the beetle fell, to a spot about three inches to the westward of its former position. Taking, now, the tape measure from the nearest point of the trunk to the peg as before, and continuing the extension in a straight line to the distance of fifty feet, a spot was indicated, removed, by several yards, from the point at which we had been digging.

Around the new position a circle, somewhat larger than in the former instance, was now described, and we again set to work with the spade. I was dreadfully weary, but, scarcely understanding what had occasioned the change in my thoughts, I felt no longer any great aversion from the labour imposed. I had become most unaccountably interested —nay, even excited. Perhaps there was something, amid all the extravagant demeanour of Legrand—some air of forethought, or of deliberation, which impressed me. I dug eagerly, and now and then caught myself actually looking, with something that very much resembled expectation, for the fancied treasure, the vision of which had demented my unfortunate companion. At a period when such vagaries of thought most fully possessed me, and when we had been at work perhaps an hour and a half, we were again interrupted by the violent howlings of the dog. His uneasiness, in the first instance, had been, evidently, but the result of playfulness or caprice, but he now assumed a bitter and serious tone. Upon Jupiter's again attempting to muzzle him, he made furious resistance, and, leaping into the hole, tore up the mould frantically with his claws. In a few seconds he had uncovered a mass of human bones, forming two complete skeletons, intermingled with several buttons of metal, and what appeared to be the dust of decayed woollen. One or two strokes of a spade upturned the blade of a large Spanish knife, and, as we dug farther, three or four loose pieces of gold and silver coin came to light.

At sight of these the joy of Jupiter could scarcely be restrained, but the countenance of his master wore an air of extreme disappointment. He urged us, however, to continue our exertions, and the words were hardly uttered when I stumbled and fell forward, having caught the toe of my boot in a large ring of iron that lay half buried in the loose earth.

We now worked in earnest, and never did I pass ten minutes of more intense excitement. During this interval we had fairly unearthed an oblong chest of wood, which, from its perfect preservation and wonderful hardness, had plainly been subjected to some mineralising process—perhaps that of the bi-chloride of mercury. This box was three feet and a half long, three feet broad, and two and a half feet deep. It was firmly secured by bands of wrought iron, riveted, and forming a kind of open trellis-work over the whole. On each side of the chest, near the top, were three rings of iron—six in all—by means of which a firm hold could be obtained by six persons. Our utmost united endeavours served only to disturb the coffer very slightly in its bed. We at once saw the impossibility of removing so great a weight. Luckily, the sole fastenings of the lid consisted of two sliding bolts. These we threw back—trembling and panting with anxiety. In an instant, a treasure of incalculable value lay gleaming before us. As the rays of the lanterns fell within the pit, there flashed upward a glow and a glare, from a confused heap of gold and of jewels, that absolutely dazzled our eyes.

I shall not pretend to describe the feelings with which I gazed. Amazement was, of course, predominant. Legrand appeared exhausted with excitement, and spoke very few words. Jupiter's countenance wore, for some minutes, as deadly a pallor as it is possible, in the nature of things, for any negro's visage to assume. He seemed stupefied—thunderstricken. Presently he fell upon his knees in the pit, and burying his naked arms up to the elbows in gold, let them there remain, as if enjoying the luxury of a bath. At length with a deep sigh, he exclaimed, as if in a soliloquy:

'And ids all cum ob de goole-bug! de putty goole-bug! de poor little goole-bug, what I boosed in dat sabage kind of style! Ain't you shamed ob yourself, nigger?—answer me dat!'

It became necessary, at last, that I should arouse both master and valet to the expediency of removing the treasure. It was growing late, and it behoved us to make exertion, that we might get everything housed before daylight. It was difficult to say what should be done, and much time was spent in deliberation—so confused were the ideas of all. We, finally, lightened the box by removing two-thirds of its contents, when we were enabled, with some trouble, to raise it from the hole. The articles taken out were deposited among the brambles, and the dog left to guard them, with strict orders from Jupiter, neither, upon any pretence, to stir from the spot, nor to open his mouth until our return. We then hurriedly made for home with the chest; reaching the hut in safety, but after excessive toil, at one o'clock in the morning. Worn out as we were, it was not in human nature to do more immediately. We rested until two, and had supper: starting for the hills immediately afterwards, armed with three stout sacks, which, by good luck, were upon the premises. A little before four we arrived at the pit, divided the remainder of the booty, as equally as might be, among us, and, leaving the holes unfilled, again set out for the hut, at which, for the second time, we deposited our golden burthens, just as the first faint streaks of the dawn gleamed from over the tree-tops in the East.

We were now thoroughly broken down; but the intense excitement of the time denied us repose. After an unquiet slumber of some three or four hours' duration, we arose, as if by preconcert, to make examination of our treasure.

In an instant, a treasure of incalculable value lay gleaming before us.

The chest had been full to the brim, and we spent the whole day, and the greater part of the next night, in a scrutiny of its contents. There had been nothing like order or arrangement. Everything had been heaped in promiscuously. Having assorted with care, we found ourselves possessed of even vaster wealth than we had at first supposed. In coin there was rather more than four hundred and fifty thousand dollars—estimating the value of the pieces, as accurately as we could, by the tables of the period. There was not a particle of silver. All was gold of antique date and of great variety—French, Spanish, and German money, with a few English guineas, and some counters, of which we had never seen specimens before. There were several very large and heavy coins, so worn that we could make nothing of their inscriptions. There was no American money. The value of the jewels we found more difficult in estimating. There were diamonds—some of them exceedingly large and fine—a hundred and ten in all, and not one of them small; eighteen rubies of remarkable brilliancy;—three hundred and ten emeralds, all very beautiful; and twenty-one sapphires, with an opal. These stones had all been broken from their settings and thrown loose in the chest. The settings themselves, which we picked out from among the other gold, appeared to have been beaten up with hammers, as if to prevent identification. Besides all this, there was a vast quantity of solid gold ornaments: nearly two hundred massive finger and ear-rings; rich chains—thirty of these, if I remember; eighty-three very large and heavy crucifixes; five gold censers of great value; a prodigious golden punch-bowl, ornamented with richly chased vine-leaves and Bacchanalian figures; with two sword-handles exquisitely embossed, and many other smaller articles which I cannot recollect. The weight of these valuables exceeded three hundred and fifty pounds avoirdupois; and in this estimate I have not included one hundred and ninety-seven superb gold watches; three of the number being worth each five hundred dollars, if one. Many of them were very old, and as timekeepers valueless; the works having suffered more or less from corrosion—but all were rich jewelled and in cases of great worth. We estimated the entire contents of the chest, that night, at a million and a half of dollars; and upon the subsequent disposal of the trinkets and jewels (a few being retained for our own use), it was found that we had greatly under-valued the treasure.

When, at length, we had concluded our examination, and the intense excitement of the time had, in some measure, subsided, Legrand, who saw that I was dying with impatience for a solution of this extraordinary riddle, entered into a full detail of all the circumstances connected with it.

'You remember,' said he, 'the night when I handed you the rough sketch I had made of the *scarabaeus*. You recollect also that I became quite vexed at you for insisting that my drawing resembled a death's head. When you first made this assertion, I thought you were jesting; but afterwards I called to mind the peculiar spots on the back of the insect, and admitted to myself that your remark had some little foundation in fact. Still, the sneer at my graphic powers irritated me— for I am considered a good artist—and, therefore, when you handed me the scrap of parchment, I was about to crumple it up and throw it angrily into the fire.'

'The scrap of paper, you mean,' said I.

'No; it had much of the appearance of paper, and at first I supposed it to be such, but when I came to draw upon it, I discovered it at once to be a piece of very thin parchment. It was quite dirty, you remember. Well, as I was in the very act of crumpling it up, my glance fell upon the sketch at which you had been looking, and you may imagine my astonishment when I perceived, in fact, the figure of a death's-head just where it seemed to me, I had made the drawing of the beetle. For a moment I was too much amazed to think with accuracy. I knew that my design was very different in detail from this—although there was a certain similarity in general outline. Presently I took a candle, and seating myself at the other end of the room proceeded to scrutinize the parchment more closely. Upon turning it over, I saw my own sketch upon the reverse, just as I had made it. My first idea, now, was mere surprise at the really remarkable similarity of outline—at the singular coincidence involved in the fact that, unknown to me, there should have been a skull upon the other side of the parchment, immediately beneath my figure of the *scarabaeus*, and that this skull, not only in outline, but in size, should so closely resemble my drawing. I say the singularity of this coincidence absolutely stupefied me for a time. This is the usual effect of such coincidences. The mind struggles to establish a connection—a sequence of cause and effect—and, being unable to do so, suffers a species of temporary paralysis. But, when I recovered from this stupor, there dawned upon me gradually a conviction which startled me even far more than the coincidence. I began distinctly, positively, to remember that there had been *no* drawing upon the parchment when I made my sketch of the *scarabaeus*. I became perfectly certain of this; for I recollected turning up first one side and then the other, in search of the cleanest spot. Had the skull been then there, of course I could not have failed to notice it. Here was indeed a mystery which I felt it impossible to explain; but, even at that early moment, there seemed to glimmer, faintly, within the most remote and secret chambers of my intellect, a glow-worm-like conception of that truth which last night's adventure brought to so magnificent a demonstration. I arose at once, and putting the parchment securely away, dismissed all further reflection until I should be alone.

'When you had gone, and when Jupiter was fast asleep, I betook myself to a more methodical investigation of the affair. In the first place I considered the manner in which the parchment had come into my possession. The spot where we discovered the *scarabaeus* was on the coast of the mainland, about a mile eastward of the island, and but a short distance above high-water mark. Upon my taking hold of it, it gave me a sharp bite, which caused me to let it drop. Jupiter, with his accustomed caution, before seizing the insect, which had flown towards him, looked about him for a leaf, or something of that nature, by which to take hold of it. It was at this moment that his eyes, and mine also, fell upon the scrap of parchment, which I then supposed to be paper. It was lying half buried in the sand, a corner sticking up. Near the spot where we found it, I observed the remnants of the hull of what appeared to have been a ship's long-boat. The wreck seemed to have been there for a great while; for the resemblance to boat timbers could scarcely be traced.

'Well, Jupiter picked up the parchment, wrapped the beetle in it, and gave it to me. Soon afterwards we turned to go home, and on the way met Lieutenant G——. I showed him the insect, and he begged me to let him take it to the fort. Upon my consenting, he thrust it forthwith into his waistcoat pocket, without the parchment in which it had been wrapped, and which I had continued to hold in my hand during his inspection. Perhaps he dreaded my changing my mind, and thought it best to make sure of the prize at once—you know how enthusiastic he is on all subjects connected with Natural History. At the same time, without being conscious of it, I must have deposited the parchment in my own pocket.

'You remember that when I went to the table, for the purpose of making a sketch of the beetle, I found no paper where it was usually kept. I looked in the drawer, and found none there. I searched my pockets, hoping to find an old letter, when my hand fell upon the parchment. I thus detail the precise mode in which it came into my possession; for the circumstances impressed me with peculiar force.

'No doubt you will think me fanciful—but I had already established a kind of *connection*. I had put together two links of a great chain. There was a boat lying upon a seacoast, and not far from the boat was a parchment—*not a paper*—with a skull depicted upon it. You will, of course, ask "where is the connection?" I reply that the skull, or death's-head, is the well-known emblem of the pirate. The flag of the death's-head is hoisted in all engagements.

'I have said that the scrap was parchment, and not paper. Parchment is durable—almost imperishable. Matters of little moment are rarely consigned to parchment; since, for the mere ordinary purposes of drawing or writing, it is not nearly so well adapted as paper. This reflection suggested some meaning—some relevancy—in the death's-head. I did not fail to observe, also, the *form* of the parchment. Although one of its corners had been, by some accident, destroyed, it could be seen that the original form was oblong. It was just a slip, indeed, as might have been chosen for a memorandum —for a record of something to be long remembered and carefully preserved.'

'But,' I interposed, 'you say that the skull was *not* upon the parchment when you made the drawing of the beetle. How then do you trace any connection between the boat and the skull—since this latter, according to your own admission, must have been designed (God only knows how or by whom) at some period subsequent to your sketching the *scarabaeus*?'

'Ah, hereupon turns the whole mystery; although the secret, at this point, I had comparatively little difficulty in solving. My steps were sure, and could afford' but a single result. I reasoned, for example, thus: When I drew the *scarabaeus*, there was no skull apparent upon the parchment. When I had completed the drawing I gave it to you, and observed you narrowly until you returned it. *You*, therefore, did not design the skull, and no one else was present to do it. Then it was not done by human agency. And nevertheless it was done.

'At this stage of my reflections I endeavoured to remember, and *did* remember, with entire distinctness, every incident which occurred about the period in question. The weather was chilly (oh, rare and happy accident!), and a fire was blazing upon the hearth. I was heated with exercise and sat near the table. You, however, had drawn a chair close to the chimney. Just as I had placed the parchment in your hand, and as you were in the act of inspecting it, Wolf, the Newfoundland, entered, and leaped upon your shoulders. With your left hand you caressed him and kept him off, while your right, holding the parchment, was permitted to fall listlessly between your knees, and in close proximity to the fire. At one moment I thought the blaze had caught it, and was about to caution you, but, before I could speak, you had withdrawn it, and were engaged in its examination. When I considered all these particulars, I doubted not for a moment that *heat* had been the agent in bringing to light, upon the parchment, the skull which I saw designed upon it. You are well aware that chemical preparations exist, and have existed time out of mind, by means of which it is possible to write upon either paper or vellum, so that the characters shall become visible only when subjected to the action of fire. Zaffre, digested in *aqua regia*, and diluted with four times its weight of water, is sometimes employed; a green tint results. The regulus of cobalt, dissolved in spirit of nitre, gives a red. These colours disappear at longer or shorter intervals after the material written upon cools, but again becomes apparent upon the reapplication of heat.

'I now scrutinized the death's-head with care. Its outer edges—the edges of the drawing nearest the edge of the vellum—were far more *distinct* than the others. It was clear that the action of the caloric had been imperfect or unequal. I immediately kindled a fire, and subjected every portion of the parchment to a glowing heat. At first, the only effect was the strengthening of the faint lines in the skull; but, upon persevering in the experiment, there became visible, at the corner of the slip, diagonally opposite to the spot in which the

THE GOLD-BUG

death's-head was delineated, the figure of what I at first supposed
to be a goat. A closer scrutiny, however, satisfied me that it was
intended for a kid.'

'Ha! ha!' said I, 'to be sure I have no right to laugh at you—a
million and a half of money is too serious a matter for mirth—but you
are not about to establish a third link in your chain—you will not find
any especial connection between your pirates and a goat—pirates, you
know, have nothing to do with goats; they appertain to the farming
interest.'

'But I have just said that the figure was *not* that of a goat.'

'Well, a kid then—pretty much the same thing.'

'Pretty much, but not altogether,' said Legrand. 'You may have
heard of one *Captain* Kidd. I at once looked upon the figure of the
animal as a kind of punning or hieroglyphical signature. I say
signature; because its position upon the vellum suggested this idea.
The death's-head at the corner diagonally opposite, had, in the same
manner, the air of a stamp, or seal. But I was sorely put out by the
absence of all else—of the body to my imagined instrument—of the
text for my context.'

'I presume you expected to find a letter between the stamp and the
signature.'

'Something of that kind. The fact is, I felt irresistibly impressed with
a presentiment of some vast good fortune impending. I can scarcely
say why. Perhaps, after all, it was rather a desire than an actual belief;
—but do you know that Jupiter's silly words, about the bug being of
solid gold, had a remarkable effect upon my fancy? And then the series
of accidents and coincidences—these were so *very* extraordinary. Do
you observe how mere an accident it was that these events should
have occurred upon the *sole* day of all the year in which it has been,
or may be sufficiently cool for fire, and that without the fire, or
without the intervention of the dog at the precise moment in which
he appeared, I should never have become aware of the death's-head,
and so never the possessor of the treasure.'

'But proceed—I am all impatience.'

'Well; you have heard of, course, the many stories current—the
thousand vague rumours afloat about money buried, somewhere upon
the Atlantic coast, by Kidd and his associates. These rumours must

have had some foundation in fact. And that the rumours have existed so long and so continuously, could have resulted, it appeared to me, only from the circumstances of the buried treasure still *remaining* entombed. Had Kidd concealed his plunder for a time, and afterward reclaimed it, the rumours would scarcely have reached us in their present unvarying form. You will observe that the stories told are all about money-seekers, not about money-finders. Had the pirate recovered his money, there the affair would have dropped. It seemed to me that some accident—say the loss of a memorandum indicating its locality—had deprived him of the means of recovering it, and this accident had become known to his followers, who otherwise might never have heard that treasure had been concealed at all, and who, busying themselves in vain, because unguided, attempts to regain it, had first given birth, and then universal currency, to the reports which are now so common. Have you ever heard of any important treasure being unearthed along the coast?'

'Never.'

'But that Kidd's accumulations were immense, is well known. I took it for granted, therefore, that the earth still held them; and you will scarcely be surprised when I tell you that I felt a hope, nearly amounting to certainty, that the parchment so strangely found involved a lost record of the place of deposit.'

'But how did you proceed?'

'I held the vellum again to the fire, after increasing the heat, but nothing appeared. I now thought it possible that the coating of dirt might have something to do with the failure: so I carefully rinsed the parchment by pouring warm water over it, and, having done this, I placed it in a tin pan, with the skull downwards, and put the pan upon a furnace of lighted charcoal. In a few minutes, the pan having become thoroughly heated, I removed the slip, and, to my inexpressible joy, found it spotted, in several places, with what appeared to be figures arranged in lines. Again I placed it in the pan, and suffered it to remain another minute. Upon taking it off, the whole was just as you see it now.'

Here Legrand, having re-heated the parchment, submitted it to my inspection. The following characters were rudely traced, in a red tint, between the death's head and the goat:

53‡‡†305))6★;4826)4‡.)4‡);806★;48†8¶60))85;1‡(;:‡★8†83(88)
5★†;‡5(;88★96★?;8)★‡(;485);5★†2:★‡(;4956★2(5★—4)8¶8★;4069
285);)5†8)4‡‡;1(‡9;48081;8:8‡1;48†85;4(485†528806★81(‡9;48;
(88;‡(‡?34;48)4‡;161;:188;‡?;

'But,' said I, returning him the slip, 'I am as much in the dark as ever. Were all the jewels of Golconda awaiting me upon my solution of this enigma, I am quite sure that I should be unable to earn them.'

'And yet,' said Legrand, 'the solution is by no means so difficult as you might be led to imagine from the first hasty inspection of the characters. These characters, as any one might readily guess, form a cipher—that is to say, they convey a meaning; but then from what is known of Kidd, I could not suppose him capable of constructing any of the more abstruse cryptographs. I made up my mind, at once, that this was of a simple species—such, however, as would appear, to the crude intellect of the sailor, absolutely insoluble without the key.'

'And you really solved it?'

'Readily; I have solved others of an abstruseness ten thousand times greater. Circumstances, and a certain bias of mind, have led me to take interest in such riddles, and it may well be doubted whether human ingenuity can construct an enigma of the kind which human ingenuity may not, by proper application, resolve. In fact, having once established connected and legible characters, I scarcely gave a thought to the mere difficulty of developing their import.

'In the present case—indeed in all cases of secret writing—the first question regards the *language* of the cipher; for the principles of solution, so *far*, especially, as the more simple ciphers are concerned, depend upon, and are varied by, the genius of the particular idiom. In general, there is no alternative but experiment (directed by probabilities) of every tongue known to him who attempts the solution, until the true one be attained. But, with the cipher now before us all difficulty was removed by the signature. The pun upon the word "Kidd" is appreciable in no other language than the English. But for this consideration I should have begun my attempts with the Spanish and French, as the tongues in which a secret of this kind would most naturally have been written by a pirate of the Spanish main. As it was, I assumed the cryptograph to be English.

'You observe there are no divisions between the words. Had there been divisions the task would have been comparatively easy. In such cases I should have commenced with a collation and analysis of the shorter words, and, had a word of a single letter occurred, as is most likely (*a* or *I*, for example), I should have considered the solution as assured. But, there being no division, my first step was to ascertain the predominant letters, as well as the least frequent. Counting all, I constructed a table thus:

> Of the character 8 there are 33.
> ; there are 26.
> 4 there are 19.
> ‡) there are 16.
> ★ there are 13.
> 5 there are 12.
> 6 there are 11.
> † 1 there are 8.
> 0 there are 6.
> 9 2 there are 5.
> : 3 there are 4.
> ? there are 3.
> ¶ there are 2.
> —. there are 1.

'Now in English, the letter which most frequently occurs is *e*. Afterwards, the succession runs thus: *a o i d b n r s t n y c f g l m w b k p q x z*. E predominates so remarkably, that an individual sentence of any length is rarely seen, in which it is not the prevailing character.

'Here, then, we have, in the very beginning, the groundwork for something more than a mere guess. The general use which may be made of the table is obvious—but, in this particular cipher, we shall only very partially require its aid. As our predominant character is 8, we will commence by assuming it as the *e* of the natural alphabet. To verify the supposition, let us observe if the 8 be seen often in couples—for *e* is doubled with great frequency in English—in such words, for example, as "meet", "fleet", "speed", "seen", "been", "agree", etc. In the present instance we see it doubled no less than five times, although the cryptograph is brief.

'Let us assume 8, then, as *e*. Now, of all *words* in the language, "the" is most usual; let us see, therefore, whether there are not repetitions of any three characters, in the same order of collocation, the last of them being 8. If we discover repetitions of such letters, so arranged, they will most probably represent the word "the". Upon inspection, we find no less than seven such arrangements, the characters being ;48. We may, therefore, assume that; represents *t*, 4 represents *h*, and 8 represents *e*—the last being now well confirmed. Thus a great step has been taken.

'But, having established a single word, we are enabled to establish a vastly important point; that is to say, several comments and terminations of other words. Let us refer, for example, to the last instance but one, in which the combination ;48 occurs—not far from the end of the cipher. We know that the; immediately ensuing is the commencement of a word, and, of the six characters succeeding this "the", we are cognizant of no less than five. Let us set these characters down, thus, by the letters we know them to represent, leaving a space for the unknown—

teeth.

'Here we are enabled, at once, to discard the "*th*", as forming no portion of the word commencing with the first *t*; since, by experiment of the entire alphabet for a letter adapted to the vacancy, we perceive that no word can be formed of which this *th* can be a part. We are thus narrowed into.

tee,

and, going through the alphabet, if necessary, as before, we arrive at the word "tree", as the sole possible reading. We thus gain another letter, *r*, represented by (, with the words "the tree" in juxtaposition.

'Looking beyond these words, for a short distance, we again see the combination ;48, and employ it by way of *termination* to what immediately precedes. We have thus this arrangement:

the tree ;4(‡?34 the,

or, substituting the natural letters, where known, it reads thus:

the tree thr‡?3h the,

'Now, if, in place of the unknown characters, we leave blank spaces, or substitute dots, we read thus:

the tree thr. . . h the,

137

when the word *"through"* makes itself evident at once. But this discovery gives us three new letters, *o, u,* and *g,* represented by ‡, ?, and 3.

'Looking now, narrowly, through the cipher for combinations of known characters, we find, not very far from the beginning, this arrangement,

83(88, or egree,

which, plainly, is the conclusion of the word "degree", and gives us another letter, *d,* represented by †.

'Four letters beyond the word "degree", we perceive the combination

;46(;88.

'Translating the known characters, and representing the unknown by dots, as before, we read thus:

th.rtee,

an arrangement immediately suggestive of the word "thirteen", and again furnishing us with two new characters, *i* and *n* represented by 6 and ★.

'Referring, now to the beginning of the cryptograph, we find the combination,

53‡‡†.

'Translating as before, we obtain

good,

which assures us that the first letter is *A,* and that the first two words are "A good".

'It is now time that we arrange our key, as far as discovered, in a tabular form, to avoid confusion. It will stand thus:

5 represents a
† represents d
8 represents e
3 represents g
4 represents h
6 represents i
★ represents n
‡ represents o
(represents r
; represents t
? represents u

'We have, therefore, no less than eleven of the most important letters represented, and it will be unnecessary to proceed with the details of the solution. I have said enough to convince you that ciphers of this nature are readily soluble, and to give you some insight into the *rationale* of their development. But be assured the specimen before us appertains to the very simplest species of cryptograph. It now only remains to give you the full translation of the characters upon the parchment, as unriddled. Here it is:

A good glass in the bishop's hostel in the devil's seat forty-one degrees and thirteen minutes northeast and by north main branch seventh limb east side shoot from the left eye of the death's-head a bee-line from the tree through the shot fifty feet out.'

'But,' said I, 'the enigma seems still in as bad a condition as ever. How is it possible to extort a meaning from all the jargon about "devil's seats", "death's-heads", and "bishop's hostels"?'

'I confess,' replied Legrand, 'that the matter still wears a serious aspect, when regarded with a casual glance. My first endeavour was to divide the sentence into the natural division intended by the cryptographist.'

'You mean, to punctuate it?'

'Something of that kind.'

'But how was it possible to effect this?'

'I reflected that it had been a *point* with the writer to run his words together without division, so as to increase the difficulty of the solution. Now, a not over-acute man, in pursuing such an object, would be nearly certain to overdo the matter. When, in the course of his composition, he arrived at a break in his subject which would naturally require a pause, or a point, he would be exceedingly apt to run his characters, at this place, more than usually close together. If you will observe the MS., in the present instance, you will easily detect five such cases of unusual crowding. Acting upon this hint, I made the division thus:

A good glass in the bishop's hostel in the devil's seat—forty-one degrees and thirteen minutes—northeast and by north—main branch seventh

*limb east side—shoot from the left eye of the death's-head—a bee-line from
the tree through the shot fifty feet.'*

'Even this division,' said I, 'leaves me still in the dark.'

'It left me also in the dark,' replied Legrand, 'for a few days; during
which I made diligent inquiry, in the neighbourhood of Sullivan's
Island, for any building which went by the name of the "Bishop's
Hotel"; for, of course, I dropped the obsolete word "hostel". Gaining no
information on the subject, I was on the point of extending my
sphere of search, and proceeding in a more systematic manner, when,
one morning, it entered my head, quite suddenly, that this "Bishop's
Hostel" might have some reference to an old family, of the name of
Bessop, which, time out of mind, had held possession of an ancient
manorhouse, about four miles to the northward of the island. I
accordingly went over to the plantation, and reinstituted my inquiries
among the older negroes of the place. At length, one of the most aged
of the women said that she had heard of such a place as *Bessop's
Castle*, and thought that she could guide me to it, but that it was not a
castle, nor a tavern, but a high rock.

'I offered to pay her well for her trouble, and, after some demur,
she consented to accompany me to the spot. We found it without much
difficulty, when, dismissing her, I proceeded to examine the place. The
"castle" consisted of an irregular assemblage of cliffs and rocks—one of
the latter being quite remarkable for its height as well as for its
insulated and artificial appearance. I clambered to its apex, and then
felt much at a loss as to what should be next done.

'While I was busied in reflection, my eyes fell upon a narrow ledge
in the eastern face of the rock, perhaps a yard below the summit
upon which I stood. This ledge projected about eighteen inches, and was
not more than a foot wide, while a niche in the cliff just above it
gave it a rude resemblance to one of the hollow-backed chairs used
by our ancestors. I made no doubt that here was the "devil's-seat"
alluded to in the MS., and now I seemed to grasp the full secret of the
riddle.

'The "good glass", I knew, could have reference to nothing but a
telescope; for the word "glass" is rarely employed in any other sense
by seamen. Now here, I at once saw, was a telescope to be used, and

a definite point of view, *admitting no variation*, from which to use it. Nor did I hesitate to believe that the phrase, "forty-one degrees and thirteen minutes", and, "northeast and by north", were intended as directions for the levelling of the glass. Greatly excited by these discoveries, I hurried home, procured a telescope, and returned to the rock.

'I let myself down to the ledge, and found that it was impossible to retain a seat upon it except in one particular position. This fact confirmed my preconceived idea. I proceeded to use the glass. Of course, the "forty-one degrees and thirteen minutes" could allude to nothing but elevation above the visible horizon, since the horizontal direction was clearly indicated by the words, "northeast and by north". This latter direction I at once established by means of a pocket-compass; then, pointing the glass as nearly at an angle of forty-one degrees of elevation as I could do it by guess, I moved it cautiously up or down, until my attention was arrested by a circular rift or opening in the foliage of a large tree that overtopped its fellows in the distance. In the centre of this rift I perceived a white spot, but could not, at first, distinguish what it was. Adjusting the focus of the telescope, I again looked, and now made it out to be a human skull.

'Upon this discovery I was so sanguine as to consider the enigma solved: for the phrase "main branch, seventh limb, east side", could refer only to the position of the skull upon the tree, while "shoot from the left eye of the death's-head" admitted, also, of but one interpretation, in regard to a search for a buried treasure. I perceived that the design was to drop a bullet from the left eye of the skull, and that a bee-line, or, in other words, a straight line, drawn from the nearest point of the trunk through "the shot" (or the spot where the bullet fell), and thence extended to a distance of fifty feet,, would indicate a definite point—and beneath this point I thought it at least *possible* that a deposit of value lay concealed.'

'All this,' I said, 'is exceedingly clear, and, although ingenious, still simple and explicit. When you left the Bishop's Hotel, what then?'

'Why, having carefully taken the bearings of the tree, I turned homeward. The instant that I left "the devil's seat", however, the circular rift vanished; nor could I get a glimpse of it afterwards, turn as I would. What seems to me the chief ingenuity in this whole business, is the fact (for repeated experiment has convinced me it *is* a fact) that the circular opening in question is visible from no other attainable point of view than that afforded by the narrow ledge upon the face upon the rock.

'In this expedition to the "Bishop's Hotel" I had been attended by Jupiter, who had, no doubt, observed, for some weeks past, the abstraction of my demeanour, and took especial care not to leave me alone. But, on the next day, getting up very early, I contrived to give him the slip, and, went into the hills in search of the tree. After much toil I found it. When I came home at night my valet proposed to give me a flogging. With the rest of the adventure I believe you are as well acquainted as myself.'

'I suppose,' said I, 'you missed the spot, in the first attempt at digging, through Jupiter's stupidity in letting the bug fall through the right instead of through the left eye of the skull.'

'Precisely. This mistake made a difference of about two inches and a half in the "shot"—that is to say, in the position of the peg nearest the tree; and had the treasure been *beneath* the "shot", the error would have been of little moment; but the "shot", together with the nearest point of the tree, were merely two points for the establishment of a line of direction; of course the error, however trivial in the beginning, increased as we proceeded with the line, and by the time we had gone fifty feet threw us quite off the scene. But for my deep-seated impressions that treasure was here somewhere actually buried, we might have had all our labour in vain.'

'But your grandiloquence, and your conduct in swinging the beetle —how excessively odd! I was sure you were mad. And why did you insist upon letting fall the bug, instead of a bullet, from the skull?'

'Why, to be frank. I felt somewhat annoyed by your evident suspicions touching my sanity, and so resolved to punish you quietly, in my own way, by a little bit of sober mystification. For this reason I swung the beetle, and for this reason I let it fall from the tree. An observation of yours about its great weight suggested the latter idea.'

'Yes, I perceive; and now there is only one point which puzzles me. What are we to make of the skeletons found in the hole?'

'That is a question I am no more able to answer than yourself. There seems, however, only one plausible way of accounting for them—and yet it is dreadful to believe in such atrocity as my suggestion would imply. It is clear that Kidd—if Kidd indeed secreted this treasure, which I doubt not—it is clear that he must have had assistance in the labour. But this labour concluded, he may have thought it expedient to remove all participants in his secret. Perhaps a couple of blows with a mattock were sufficient, while his coadjutors were busy in the pit; perhaps it required a dozen—who shall tell?'

THE EPISODE OF THE MEXICAN SEER

Grant Allen

My name is Seymour Wilbraham Wentworth. I am brother-in-law and secretary to Sir Charles Vandrift, the South African millionaire and famous financier. Many years ago, when Charlie Vandrift was a small lawyer in Cape Town, I had the (qualified) good fortune to marry his sister. Much later, when the Vandrift estate and farm near Kimberley developed by degrees into the Cloetedorp Golcondas, Limited, my brother-in-law offered me the not unremunerative post of secretary; in which capacity I have ever since been his constant and attached companion.

He is not a man whom any common sharper can take in, is Charles Vandrift. Middle height, square build, firm mouth, keen eyes—the very picture of a sharp and successful business genius. I have only known one rogue impose upon Sir Charles, and that one rogue, as the Commissary of Police at Nice remarked, would doubtless have imposed upon a syndicate of Vidocq, Robert Houdin, and Cagliostro.

We had run across to the Riviera for a few weeks in the season. Our object being strictly rest and recreation from the arduous duties of financial combination, we did not think it necessary to take our wives out with us. Indeed, Lady Vandrift is absolutely wedded to the joys of London, and does not appreciate the rural delights of the

Mediterranean littoral. But Sir Charles and I, though immersed in affairs when at home, both thoroughly enjoy the complete change from the City to the charming vegetation and pellucid air on the terrace at Monte Carlo. We *are* so fond of scenery. That delicious view over the rocks of Monaco, with the Maritime Alps in the rear, and the blue sea in front, not to mention the imposing Casino in the foreground, appeals to me as one of the most beautiful prospects in all Europe. Sir Charles has a sentimental attachment for the place. He finds it restores and refreshens him, after the turmoil of London, to win a few hundred at roulette in the course of an afternoon among the palms and cactuses and pure breezes of Monte Carlo. The country, say I, for a jaded intellect! However, we never on any account actually stop in the Principality itself. Sir Charles thinks Monte Carlo is not a sound address for a financier's letters. He prefers a comfortable hotel on the Promenade des Anglais at Nice, where he recovers health and renovates his nervous system by taking daily excursions along the coast to the Casino.

This particular season we were snugly ensconced at the Hotel des Anglais. We had capital quarters on the first floor—salon, study, and bedrooms—and found on the spot a most agreeable cosmopolitan society. All Nice, just then, was ringing with talk about a curious impostor, known to his followers as the Great Mexican Seer, and supposed to be gifted with second sight, as well as with endless other supernatural powers. Now, it is a peculiarity of my able brother-in-law's that, when he meets with a quack, he burns to expose him; he is so keen a man of business himself that it gives him, so to speak, a disinterested pleasure to unmask and detect imposture in others. Many ladies at the hotel, some of whom had met and conversed with the Mexican Seer, were constantly telling us strange stories of his doings. He had disclosed to one the present whereabouts of a runaway husband; he had pointed out to another the numbers that would win at roulette next evening; he had shown a third the image on a screen of the man she had for years adored without his knowledge. Of course, Sir Charles didn't believe a word of it; but his curiosity was roused; he wished to see and judge for himself of the wonderful thought-reader.

'What would be his terms, do you think, for a private *séance*?' he asked of Madame Picardet, the lady to whom the Seer had successfully predicted the winning numbers.

'He does not work for money,' Madame Picardet answered, 'but for the good of humanity. I'm sure he would gladly come and exhibit for nothing his miraculous faculties.'

'Nonsense!' Sir Charles answered. 'The man must live. I'd pay him five guineas, though, to see him alone. What hotel is he stopping at?'

'The Cosmopolitan, I think,' the lady answered. 'Oh no; I remember now, the Westminster.'

Sir Charles turned to me quietly. 'Look here, Seymour,' he whispered. 'Go round to this fellow's place immediately after dinner, and offer him five pounds to give a private *séance* at once in my rooms, without mentioning who I am to him; keep the name quite quiet. Bring him back with you, too, and come straight upstairs with him, so that there may be no collusion. We'll see just how much the fellow can tell us.'

I went as directed. I found the Seer a very remarkable and interesting person. He stood about Sir Charles's own height, but was slimmer and straighter, with an aquiline nose, strangely piercing eyes, very large black pupils, and a finely-chiselled close-shaven face, like the bust of Antinous in our hall in Mayfair. What gave him the most characteristic touch, however, was his odd head of hair, curly and wavy like Paderewski's, standing out in a halo round his high white forehead and his delicate profile. I could see at a glance why he succeeded so well in impressing women; he had the look of a poet, a singer, a prophet.

'I have come round,' I said. 'to ask whether you will consent to give a *séance* at once in a friend's rooms; and my principal wishes me to add that he is prepared to pay five pounds as the price of the entertainment.'

Señor Antonio Herrera—that was what he called himself—bowed to me with impressive Spanish politeness. His dusky olive cheeks were wrinkled with a smile of gentle contempt as he answered gravely—

'I do not sell my gifts; I bestow them freely. If your friend—your anonymous friend—desires to behold the cosmic wonders that are wrought through my hands, I am glad to show them to him. Fortunately, as often happens when it is necessary to convince and confound a sceptic (for that your friend is a sceptic I feel instinctively), I chance to have no engagements at all this evening.' He ran his hand through his fine, long hair reflectively. 'Yes, I go,' he continued, as if addressing some unknown presence that hovered about the ceiling; 'I go; come with me!' Then he put on his broad sombrero, with its crimson ribbon, wrapped a cloak round his shoulders, lighted a cigarette, and strode forth by my side towards the Hotel des Anglais.

He talked little by the way, and that little in curt sentences. He seemed buried in deep thought; indeed, when we reached the door and I turned in, he walked a step or two farther on, as if not noticing to what place I had brought him. Then he drew himself up short, and gazed around him for a moment. 'Ha, the Anglais,' he said—and I may mention in passing that his English, in spite of a slight southern accent, was idiomatic and excellent. 'It is here, then; it is here!' He was addressing once more the unseen presence.

I smiled to think that these childish devices were intended to deceive Sir Charles Vandrift. Not quite the sort of man (as the City of London knows) to be taken in by hocus-pocus. And all this, I saw, was the cheapest and most commonplace conjurer's patter.

We went upstairs to our rooms. Charles had gathered together a few friends to watch the performance. The Seer entered, rapt in thought. He was in evening dress, but a red sash round his waist gave a touch of picturesqueness and a dash of colour. He paused for a moment in the middle of the salon, without letting his eyes rest on anybody or anything. Then he walked straight up to Charles, and held out his dark hand.

'Good evening,' he said. 'You are the host. My soul's sight tells me so.'

'Good shot,' Sir Charles answered. 'These fellows have to be quick-witted, you know, Mrs Mackenzie, or they'd never get on at it.'

The Seer gazed about him, and smiled blankly at a person or two whose faces he seemed to recognize from a previous existence. Then Charles began to ask him a few simple questions, not about himself, but about me, just to test him. He answered most of them with surprising correctness. 'His name? His name begins with an S I think: You call him Seymour.' He paused long between each clause, as if the facts were revealed to him slowly. 'Seymour—Wilbraham—Earl of

He walked straight up to Charles, and held out his hand.

Strafford. No, not Earl of Strafford! Seymour Wilbraham Wentworth. There seems to be some connection in somebody's mind now present between Wentworth and Strafford. I am not English. I do not know what it means. But they are somehow the same name, Wentworth and Strafford.'

He gazed around, apparently for confirmation. A lady came to his rescue.

'Wentworth was the surname of the great Earl of Strafford,' she murmured gently; 'and I was wondering, as you spoke, whether Mr Wentworth might possibly be descended from him.'

'He is,' the Seer replied instantly, with a flash of those dark eyes. And I thought this curious; for though my father always maintained the reality of the relationship, there was one link wanting to complete the pedigree. He could not make sure that the Hon. Thomas Wilbraham Wentworth was the father of Jonathan Wentworth, the Bristol horse-dealer, from whom we are descended.

'Where was I born?' Sir Charles interrupted, coming suddenly to his own case.

The Seer clapped his two hands to his forehead and held it between them, as if to prevent it from bursting. 'Africa', he said slowly, as the facts narrowed down, so to speak. 'South Africa; Cape of Good Hope; Jansenville; De Witt Street. 1840.'

'By Jove, he's correct,' Sir Charles muttered. 'He seems really to do it. Still, he may have found me out. He may have known where he was coming.'

'I never gave a hint,' I answered; 'till he reached the door, he didn't even know to what hotel I was piloting him.'

The Seer stroked his chin softly. His eye appeared to me to have a furtive gleam in it. 'Would you like me to tell you the number of a bank-note enclosed in an envelope?' he asked casually.

'Go out of the room,' Sir Charles said, 'while I pass it round the company.'

Señor Herrera disappeared. Sir Charles passed it round cautiously, holding it all the time in his own hand, but letting his guests see the number. Then he placed it in an envelope and gummed it down firmly.

The Seer returned. His keen eyes swept the company with a comprehensive glance. He shook his shaggy mane. Then he took the envelope in his hands and gazed at it fixedly. 'AF, 73549,' he answered in a slow tone. 'A Bank of England note for fifty pounds— exchanged at the Casino for gold won yesterday at Monte Carlo.'

'I see how he did that,' Sir Charles said triumphantly. 'He must have changed it there himself; and then I changed it back again. In point of fact, I remember seeing a fellow with long hair loafing about. Still, it's capital conjuring.'

'He can see through matter,' one of the ladies interposed. It was Madame Picardet. 'He can see through a box.' She drew a little gold vinaigrette, such as our grandmothers used, from her dress-pocket. 'What is in this?' she inquired, holding it up to him.

Señor Herrera gazed through it. 'Three gold coins,' he replied, knitting his brows with the effort of seeing into the box: 'one, an American five dollars; one, a French ten-franc piece; one, twenty marks, German, of the old Emperor William.'

She opened the box and passed it round. Sir Charles smiled a quiet smile.

'Confederacy!' he muttered, half to himself. 'Confederacy!'

The Seer turned to him with a sullen air. 'You want a better sign?' he said, in a very impressive voice. 'A sign that will convince you! Very well: you have a letter in your left waistcoat pocket—a crumpled-up letter. Do you wish me to read it out? I will, if you desire it.'

It may seem to those who know Sir Charles incredible, but, I am bound to admit, my brother-in-law coloured. What that letter contained I cannot say; he only answered, very testily and evasively, 'No, thank you; I won't trouble you. The exhibition you have already given us of your skill in this kind more than amply suffices.' And his fingers strayed nervously to his waistcoat pocket, as if he was half afraid, even then, Señor Herrera would read it.

I fancied too, he glanced somewhat anxiously towards Madame Picardet.

The Seer bowed courteously. 'Your will, señor, is law,' he said. 'I make it a principle, though I can see through all things, invariably to respect the secrecies and sanctities. If it were not so, I might dissolve society. For which of us is there who could bear the whole truth being told about him?' He gazed around the room. An unpleasant thrill supervened. Most of us felt this uncanny Spanish American knew really too much. And some of us were engaged in financial operations.

'For example,' the Seer continued blandly. 'I happened a few weeks ago to travel down here from Paris by train with a very intelligent man, a company promoter. He had in his bag some documents—some confidential documents:' he glanced at Sir Charles. 'You know the kind of thing, my dear sir: reports from experts—from mining engineers. You may have seen some such; marked *strictly private*.'

'They form an element in high finance,' Sir Charles admitted coldly.

'Pre-cisely,' the Seer murmured, his accent for a moment less Spanish than before. 'And, as they were marked *strictly private*, I respect, of course, the seal of confidence. That's all I wish to say. I hold it a duty, being intrusted with such powers, not to use them in a manner which may annoy or incommode my fellow-creatures.'

'Your feeling does you honour,' Sir Charles answered, with some acerbity. Then he whispered in my ear: 'Confounded clever scoundrel, Sey; rather wish we hadn't brought him here.'

Señor Herrera seemed intuitively to divine this wish, for he interposed, in a lighter and gayer tone—

'I will now show you a different and more interesting embodiment of occult power, for which we shall need a somewhat subdued arrangement of surrounding lights. Would you mind, señor host—for I have purposely abstained from reading your name on the brain of any one present—would you mind my turning down this lamp just a little? . . . So! That will do. Now, this one; and this one. Exactly! that's right.' He poured a few grains of powder out of a packet into a saucer. 'Next, a match, if you please. Thank you!' It burnt with a strange green light. He drew from his pocket a card, and produced a little ink-bottle. 'Have you a pen?' he asked.

I instantly brought one. He handed it to Sir Charles. 'Oblige me,' he said, 'by writing your name there.' And he indicated a place in the centre of the card, which had an embossed edge, with a small middle square of a different colour.

Sir Charles has a natural disinclination to signing his name without knowing why. 'What do you want with it?' he asked. (A millionaire's signature has so many uses.)

'I want you to put the card in an envelope,' the Seer replied, 'and then to burn it. After that, I shall show you your own name written in letters of blood on my arm, in your own handwriting.'

Sir Charles took the pen. If the signature was to be burned as soon as finished, he didn't mind giving it. He wrote his name in his usual firm clear style—the writing of a man who knows his worth and is not afraid of drawing a cheque for five thousand.

'Look at it long,' the Seer said, from the other side of the room. He had not watched him write it.

Sir Charles stared at it fixedly. The Seer was really beginning to produce an impression.

'Now, put it in that envelope,' the Seer exclaimed.

Sir Charles, like a lamb, placed it as directed.

The Seer strode forward. 'Give me the envelope,' he said. He took it in his hand, walked over towards the fireplace, and solemnly burnt it. 'See—it crumbles into ashes,' he cried. Then he came back to the middle of the room, close to the green light, rolled up his sleeve, and held his arm before Sir Charles. There, in blood-red letters, my brother-in-law read the name, 'Charles Vandrift', in his own hand-writing!

'I see how that's done,' Sir Charles murmured, drawing back. 'It's a clever delusion; but still, I see through it. It's like that ghost-book. Your ink was deep green; your light was green; you make me look at it long; and then I saw the same thing written on the skin of your arm in complementary colours.'

'You think so?' the Seer replied, with a curious curl of the lip.

'I'm sure of it,' Sir Charles answered.

Quick as lightning the Seer rolled up his sleeve. 'That's your name,' he cried, in a very clear voice, 'but not your whole name. What do you say, then, to my right? Is this one also a complementary colour?' He held his other arm out. There, in sea-green letters, I read the name, 'Charles O'Sullivan Vandrift'. It is my brother-in-law's full baptismal designation; but he has dropped the O'Sullivan for many years past, and, to say the truth, doesn't like it. He is a little bit ashamed of his mother's family.

Charles glanced at it hurriedly. 'Quite right,' he said, 'quite right!' But his voice was hollow. I could guess he didn't care to continue the *séance*. He could see through the man, of course; but it was clear the fellow knew too much about us to be entirely pleasant.

'Turn up the lights,' I said, and a servant turned them. 'Shall I say coffee and benedictine?' I whispered to Vandrift.

'By all means,' he answered. 'Anything to keep this fellow from further impertinences! And, I say, don't you think you'd better suggest at the same time that the men should smoke? Even these ladies are not above a cigarette—some of them.'

There was a sigh of relief. The lights burned brightly. The Seer for the moment retired from business, so to speak. He accepted a partaga with a very good grace, sipped his coffee in a corner, and chatted to the lady who had suggested Strafford with marked politeness. He was a polished gentleman.

Next morning, in the hall of the hotel, I saw Madame Picardet again, in a neat tailor-made travelling dress, evidently bound for the railway-station.

'What, off, Madame Picardet?' I cried.

She smiled, and held out her prettily-gloved hand. 'Yes, I'm off,' she answered archly. 'Florence, or Rome, or somewhere. I've drained Nice dry—like a sucked orange. Got all the fun I can out of it. Now I'm away again to my beloved Italy.'

But it struck me as odd that, if Italy was her game, she went by the omnibus which takes down to the *train de luxe* for Paris. However, a man of the world accepts what a lady tells him, no matter how improbable; and I confess, for ten days or so, I thought no more about her, or the Seer either.

At the end of that time our fortnightly pass-book came in from the bank in London. It is part of my duty, as the millionaire's secretary, to make up this book once a fortnight, and to compare the cancelled cheques with Sir Charles's counterfoils. On this particular occasion I happened to observe what I can only describe as a very grave discrepancy—in fact, a discrepancy of £5,000. On the wrong side, too. Sir Charles was debited with £5,000 more than the total amount that was shown on the counterfoils.

I examined the book with care. The source of the error was obvious.

It lay in a cheque to Self or Bearer, for £5,000, signed by Sir Charles, and evidently paid across the counter in London, as it bore on its face no stamp or indication of any other office.

I called in my brother-in-law from the salon to the study. 'Look here, Charles,' I said, 'there's a cheque in the book which you haven't entered.' And I handed it to him without comment, for I thought it might have been drawn to settle some little loss on the turf or at cards, or to make up some other affair he didn't desire to mention to me. These things will happen.

He looked at it and stared hard. Then he pursed up his mouth and gave a long low 'Whew!' At last he turned it over and remarked, 'I say, Sey, my boy, we've just been done jolly well brown, haven't we?'

I glanced at the cheque. 'How do you mean?' I inquired.

'Why, the Seer,' he replied, still staring at it ruefully. 'I don't mind the five thou., but to think the fellow should have gammoned the pair of us like that—ignominious, I call it!'

'How do you know it's the Seer?' I asked.

'Look at the green ink,' he answered. 'Besides, I recollect the very shape of the last flourish. I flourished a bit like that in the excitement of the moment, which I don't always do with my regular signature.'

'He's done us,' I answered, recognizing it. 'But how the dickens did he manage to transfer it to the cheque? This looks like your own handwriting, Charles, not a clever forgery.'

'It is,' he said. 'I admit it—I can't deny it. Only fancy him bamboozling me when I was most on my guard! I wasn't to be taken in by any of his silly occult tricks and catch-words; but it never occurred to me he was going to victimize me financially in this way. I expected attempts at a loan or an extortion; but to collar my signature to a blank cheque—atrocious!'

'How did he manage it?' I asked.

'I haven't the faintest conception. I only know those are the words I wrote. I could swear to them anywhere.'

'Then you can't protest the cheque?'

'Unfortunately, no; it's my own true signature.'

We went that afternoon without delay to see the Chief Commissary of Police at the office. He was a gentlemanly Frenchman, much less formal and red-tapey than usual, and he spoke excellent English with an American accent, having acted, in fact, as a detective in New York for about ten years in his early manhood.

'I guess,' he said slowly, after hearing our story, 'you've been victimized right here by Colonel Clay, gentlemen.'

'Who is Colonel Clay?' Sir Charles asked.

'That's just what I want to know,' the Commissary answered, in his curious American-French-English. 'He is a Colonel, because he occasionally gives himself a commission; he is called Colonel Clay, because he appears to possess an india-rubber face, and he can mould it like clay in the hands of the potter. Real name, unknown. Nationality, equally French and English. Address, usually Europe. Profession, former maker of wax figures to the Musée Grevin. Age, what he chooses. Employs his knowledge to mould his own nose and cheeks, with wax additions, to the character he desires to personate. Aquiline this time, you say. *Hein!* Anything like these photographs?'

He rummaged in his desk and handed us two.

'Not in the least,' Sir Charles answered. 'Except, perhaps, as to the neck, everything here is quite unlike him.'

'Then that's the Colonel!' the Commissary answered, with decision, rubbing his hands in glee. 'Look here,' and he took out a pencil and rapidly sketched the outline of one of the two faces—that of a bland-looking young man, with no expression worth mentioning. 'There's the Colonel in his simple disguise. Very good. Now watch me: figure to yourself that he adds here a tiny patch of wax to his nose—an aquiline bridge—just so; well, you have him right there; and the chin, ah, one touch: now, for hair, a wig: for complexion, nothing easier: that's the profile of your rascal, isn't it?'

'Exactly,' we both murmured. By two curves of the pencil, and a shock of false hair, the face was transmuted.

'He had very large eyes, with very big pupils, though,' I objected, looking close; 'and the man in the photograph here has them small and boiled-fishy.'

'That's so,' the Commissary answered. 'A drop of belladonna expands—and produces the Seer; five grains of opium contract—and give a dead-alive, stupidly-innocent appearance. Well, you leave this affair to me, gentleman. I'll see the fun out. I don't say I'll catch him for you; nobody ever yet has caught Colonel Clay; but I'll explain how he did the trick; and that ought to be consolation enough to a man of your means for a trifle of five thousand!'

'You are not the conventional French office-holder, M. le Commissaire,' I ventured to interpose.

'You bet!' the Commissary replied, and drew himself up like a captain of infantry. 'Messieurs,' he continued, in French, with the utmost dignity, 'I shall devote the resources of this office to tracing out the crime, and, if possible, to effectuating the arrest of the culpable.'

We telegraphed to London, of course, and we wrote to the bank, with a full description of the suspected person. But I need hardly add that nothing came of it.

Three days later the Commissary called at our hotel. 'Well, gentlemen,' he said, 'I am glad to say I have discovered everything!'

'What? Arrested the Seer?' Sir Charles cried.

The Commissary drew back, almost horrified at the suggestion.

'Arrested Colonel Clay?' he exclaimed, '*Mais*, monsieur, we are only human! Arrested him? No, not quite. But tracked out how he did it. That is already much—to unravel Colonel Clay, gentlemen!'

'Well, what do you make of it?' Sir Charles asked, crestfallen.

The Commissary sat down and gloated over his discovery. It was clear a well-planned crime amused him vastly. 'In the first place, monsieur,' he said, 'disabuse your mind of the idea that when monsieur your secretary went out to fetch Señor Herrera that night, Señor Herrera didn't know to whose rooms he was coming. Quite otherwise, in point of fact. I do not doubt myself that Señor Herrera, or Colonel Clay (call him which you like), came to Nice this winter for no other purpose than just to rob you.'

'But I sent for him,' my brother-in-law interposed.

'Yes; he *meant* you to send for him. He forced a card, so to speak. If he couldn't do that I guess he would be a pretty poor conjurer. He had a lady of his own—his wife, let us say, or his sister—stopping here at this hotel; a certain Madame Picardet. Through her he induced several ladies of your circle to attend his *séances*. She and they spoke to you about him, and aroused your curiosity. You may bet your bottom dollar that when he came to this room he came ready primed and prepared with endless facts about both of you.'

'What fools we have been, Sey,' my brother-in-law exclaimed. 'I see it all now. That designing woman sent round before dinner to say I wanted to meet him; and by the time you got there he was ready for bamboozling me.'

'That's so,' the Commissary answered. 'He had your name ready painted on both his arms; and he had made other preparations of still greater importance.'

'You mean the cheque. Well, how did he get it?'

The Commissary opened the door. 'Come in,' he said. And a young man entered whom we recognized at once as the chief clerk in the Foreign Department of the Crédit Marseillais, the principal bank all along the Riviera.

'State what you know of this cheque,' the Commissary said, showing it to him, for we had handed it over to the police as a piece of evidence.

'About four weeks since—' the clerk began.

'Say ten days before your *séance*,' the Commissary interposed.

'A gentleman with very long hair and an aquiline nose, dark, strange, and handsome, called in at my department and asked if I could tell him the name of Sir Charles Vandrift's London banker. He said he had a sum to pay in to your credit, and asked if we would forward it for him. I told him it was irregular for us to receive the money, as you had no account with us, but that your London bankers were Darby, Drummond, and Rothenberg, Limited.'

'Quite right,' Sir Charles murmured.

'Two days later a lady, Madame Picardet, who was a customer of ours, brought in a good cheque for three hundred pounds, signed by a first-rate name, and asked us to pay it in on her behalf to Darby, Drummond, and Rothenberg's, and to open a London account with them for her. We did so, and received in reply a cheque-book.'

'From which this cheque was taken, as I learn from the number, by telegram from London,' the Commissary put in. 'Also, that on the same day on which your cheque was cashed, Madame Picardet, in London, withdrew her balance.'

'But how did the fellow get me to sign the cheque?' Sir Charles cried. 'How did he manage the card trick?'

The Commissary produced a similar card from his pocket. 'Was that the sort of thing?' he asked.

'Precisely! A facsimile.'

'I thought so. Well, our Colonel, I find, bought a packet of such cards, intended for admission to a religious function, at a shop in the Quai Masséna. He cut out the centre, and, see here—' The Commissary turned it over, and showed a piece of paper pasted neatly over the back; this he tore off, and there, concealed behind it, lay a folded cheque, with only the place where the signature should be written showing through on the face which the Seer had presented to us. 'I call that a neat trick,' the Commissary remarked, with professional enjoyment of a really good deception.

'But he burnt the envelope before my eyes,' Sir Charles exclaimed.

'Pooh!' the Commissary answered. 'What would he be worth as a conjurer, anyway, if he couldn't substitute one envelope for another between the table and the fireplace without your noticing it? And Colonel Clay, you must remember, is a prince among conjurers.'

'Well, it's a comfort to know we've identified our man, and the woman who was with him,' Sir Charles said, with a slight sigh of relief. 'The next thing will be, of course, you'll follow them up on these clues in England and arrest them?'

The Commissary shrugged his shoulders. 'Arrest them!' he exclaimed, much amused. 'Ah, monsieur, but you are sanguine! No officer of justice has ever succeeded in arresting le Colonel Caoutchouc, as we call him in French. He is as slippery as an eel, that man. He wriggles through our fingers. Suppose even we caught him, what could we prove? I ask you. Nobody who has seen him once can ever swear to him again in his next impersonation. He is *impayable*, this good Colonel. On the day when I arrest him, I assure you, monsieur, I shall consider myself the smartest police-officer in Europe.'

'Well, I shall catch him yet,' Sir Charles answered, and relapsed into silence.

THE LEGACY

John Gordon

I enjoy it here. The blue water crumbles so delicately on the rocks that one would never believe that the sugary bubbles could be gnashed by those same broken teeth into a fearsome madman's froth. Yet it happens. Things change unexpectedly—nothing is ever quite what it seems.

I sail my boat in these warm, blue waters—wine dark, the Greeks used to call them—while my aunt still looks out on the icy whale's road of those more northern seas I knew so well when I was younger. I live very comfortably, and so does she, yet our lives have each taken a dramatic turn—and neither of us is quite what others take us to be.

My Aunt May is a very hard woman, but I owe her much. When he was alive, however, I much preferred my Uncle Philip. He had a long face and his small mouth was very near the bottom of it, a long way from his eyes which were so pale that one was aware of the pinprick of his pupils. It was a goat-like face, and could have been frightening to a boy except that the little mouth had a curl of laughter to it.

Even though we lived in the same town I was about twelve before I met him. There was a gulf between our families, although it was not of his making, at least not directly. The trouble was that he had money, and when my aunt married him she married it. In a big way.

She moved into his house on the promenade, and vanished almost completely from our sight. The rift took place before I was born and, by the time I speak of, it had become so wide that even my father, her brother, would turn a corner hastily or enter a shop if his sister should appear in the street, no matter how far away. But he was very mild-mannered and shunned a quarrel.

My mother was bolder, although it did not profit her much. I have seen her return from a chance meeting with my aunt red-faced and angry for a whole evening over the way 'that woman' had brushed her aside.

'But I've told you,' my father would say, looking worried, 'just keep out of her way.'

'Next time,' my mother would threaten, 'I'll let her know just what we think of her!'

At this, my father would try to joke. 'And have her cut Richard out of her will?'

My mother would snort.

I am Richard. And there was never the slightest chance of my Aunt May's money coming my way. I did not care. I hated her. She was, and is, a formidable woman. There is a solidity about her as though, under her woollen dress, she is made of rock; a solid chunk. She has a large head and wears glasses with thin gold rims that should be elegant yet seem to do nothing except pull all the contours of her face to a single point of irritation between the eyes. It has grown worse of late, yet even in those days it gave her an expression that warned most people away. It certainly succeeded as far as my family was concerned.

It was only by the merest chance that I ever met my uncle. It was a hot day, early in the year before the summer crowds, and the promenade was almost deserted. I was on my way home from school, taking a long way round and drawn that way by the sea which that afternoon was almost blue and very calm. I remember very well the simplicity of everything I saw—the straightness of the horizon, the parallel white line where the waves touched the beach, the yellow border of the sand where nobody was walking and, running alongside it, the white edge of the Promenade. The world consisted of parallel strips stretching to infinity, and I stood alone in the centre of it. Then a book landed on the pavement beside me. I should have been startled; I was not even faintly surprised.

I looked up to see where it had come from and I saw for the first time that I was outside my aunt's house. Above me was the balcony of the first floor. The book must have fallen from there, yet I could see no sign of how it had done so. I was stooping to pick it up when I detected, from the edge of my eye, a movement above. I hesitated and, as I straightened, the grey hair and long, pale face of my uncle appeared over the balustrade.

I did not know who it was. I had never seen him before. My aunt, however, was not entirely responsible for this because, for many years he had not been outside the house. My uncle had a crippling disease of the joints which kept him in a wheelchair but, more restricting than even that, was the fact that he and my aunt occupied only an apartment on the first floor and there were two flights of stairs to ground level—impossible for him.

The whole house was theirs, but they let the other floors to tenants. I have often heard my mother say, 'They could easily move somewhere that's easy for him—it's not as though they haven't got the money. It's that woman who keeps him there.'

This was not quite fair. It was my uncle who enjoyed the apartment for the view of the sea it gave from the balcony; it was my aunt who enjoyed the profits of letting out the rest of the house. She would never miss a chance like that although, as my mother said, they were a long way from poverty. There was an engineering works in my uncle's family, and also the boatyard where he had met and married one of the clerks in the office, my Aunt May.

'She made him a prisoner from the very first day,' my mother would say.

It was the prisoner who, having painfully levered himself from his chair, was now speaking to me.

'Would you be kind enough,' he said, 'to bring the book up to me?'

And that was how I came to enter my aunt's house. It was at the end of a long Victorian terrace built of grey stone and I had to go around the corner to get to the entrance. The door was open, but I had lost my bearings and was still in the entrance hall when I heard a door open somewhere above and my uncle telling me to come up. There were two broad flights of stairs before I reached his landing and I was gazing up the stair-well to the top of the house far overhead when I came level with him.

'Yes,' he said, 'it is a big place, young man. There is a wonderful view from the roof.'

'Great,' I said. I was very shy.

'Are you afraid of heights?'

'No.'

It pleased him to hear me say that. 'Nor was I. I used to take my telescope up there when I could manage it.'

'Great,' I repeated. It seemed to be all I could think of to say.

'I still have it. You'd certainly like to see it.'

It was an order, and as he turned his wheelchair I followed him.

In that way began a friendship that may never have happened if we had known at the outset that we were related—for I had forgotten the fact as soon as we began talking, just as I had forgotten the book I was carrying.

The room he took me into was very lofty. There was a ceiling with elaborate plaster mouldings, a chandelier and furniture of the sort I had seen in museums with pieces of cord across the seats of the chairs to prevent you sitting in them. But there was no cord here. Not that I was asked to sit, for my uncle was wheeling rapidly towards one of two pairs of tall French windows that led to the balcony. It was there his telescope stood on its tripod.

He had a passion for ships, and so had I. Once I had made that discovery, I had no difficulty in talking. My only shyness came when I remembered something that he was quite unaware of; the fact that he was entertaining his nephew. From time to time, as his smiling, rather wicked goat-face turned towards me, this secret knowledge made me blush, but I simply could not bring myself to reveal to him that I was not quite what I seemed. It would, in an odd way, have been a betrayal—he appeared to like me as I was; a stranger met by chance.

As I was leaving he picked up the book which I had eventually laid on a table.

'A lucky accident,' he said. 'I dropped the book on you, now you must drop in on me.'

He laughed at that and quite forgot to ask my name. I felt more deceitful than ever, and it was this that prevented me saying anything about what had happened when I got home. There was also the fact that, if my mother got to know, she would cross-question me without ceasing. It had to be a secret from her more than anybody else.

It could have rested there. I need never have gone back. But, of course, I did. I told myself it was the telescope that interested me, but it was the mystery, the delight in intrigue that caused me the very next afternoon to loiter along the promenade after school. There was no figure on the balcony and it was some time before I plucked up courage to go through the hallway and climb the stairs. Thoughts of my aunt were in my mind, but I was in luck for it was my uncle, leaning forward in his chair, who opened the door. He was delighted to see me.

'I was afraid I'd lost you for good,' he said. 'You left yesterday without telling me who you were.' His small mouth twitched, goat-like. 'By the way, who are you?'

I was glad to get that over with, but when I told him he slumped forward so suddenly in his chair that I thought the news had killed him. As I moved forward I stumbled over the door sill so that by the time I reached him I was almost on my knees and looking up into his face. He was not ill. He was almost helpless with laughter.

'Your aunt . . .' he said, and then laughter conquered him and he wheezed and coughed. He tried again. 'Your aunt. . . .' But once more the fit took him and he could not go on. Every time he tried to speak it was the same, and soon we were laughing together. There was no need of explanations between us from then on.

I often went to see him. Whenever I left he would give me a time for our next meeting, and I knew without being told that he was sure my aunt would not be there.

My mother was right in one respect; he *was* a prisoner, although in many ways a contented one. He loved boats and the sea, and I, who haunted the docks, was able to give him news of comings and goings, although he missed very little through his telescope. And he had his books, and his music. He was very fond of music—and so was I, but our tastes differed. It was classical music for him, and for me it wasn't.

Music was the only thing over which we seriously disagreed. Not that we quarrelled. In fact we exchanged tapes, and he allowed me to play my music on his magnificent machinery. It sounded so much better than on the little player I had at home that the beat of my stuff was heard much more often than his sort of music when I was there—although he always said there would be a time in my life when I would need it. He was right, but in a way neither of us could have foreseen.

The whole summer through our meetings continued. We enjoyed the secrecy, but it was foolish of us to think it could last.

The end did not come until the autumn. It was a wet day and, as it happened, I had left my shoes, my wet coat and my school bag on the mat just inside the door. My uncle and I were sitting at the window looking out across a leaden sea to the headland where low, grey clouds were rolling in laden with more rain, when the door behind us opened. One of my tapes was playing and we did not hear the door until it began pushing my shoes across the floor. At the same time there was an exclamation of annoyance. We turned to see my aunt in the doorway.

I was alarmed. Don't forget I was only twelve, and moreover I was in my socks. It was like being caught naked. I have never felt so defenceless. My uncle was also startled, but he was magnificent. I swear it took him less than a second to grasp the situation and act.

He was wheeling forward, a smile on his face as though pleased to welcome her and saying as he did so, 'This is Richard, my dear. Our nephew. He just happed to be passing. . . .'

'I know who it is.' The eyes behind her glasses bulged slightly like two polished stones, without warmth. And yet her face, against her nature, attempted to welcome me. My uncle again was the first to see why she wished to seem friendly. It was because there was a witness. A figure had appeared behind her in the doorway.

'Is that Mr Gibbs, my dear?' said my uncle, peering round her. 'Come in, Mr Gibbs, and meet my nephew.'

Mr Gibbs was a portly, confident man, of the same sort of bulk as my aunt but slightly taller. He had taken off his hat to shake the rain from it in the hall and when we shook hands his skin was still wet and cold, but underneath it his muscles were hard. A firm handshake is not necessarily the sign of an honest man.

'My wife sees a lot of Mr Gibbs,' said my uncle. 'She and Roland are good friends, aren't you, my dear?'

She and Mr Roland Gibbs stood side by side in their wet coats and said nothing. My uncle seemed to be enjoying himself.

'Roland,' he said, turning to me, 'is our solicitor. He takes care of all our affairs. Doubtless that is what he has been doing this afternoon.'

Mr Gibbs put up a hand and with one downward motion removed the droplets of rain from his small, black moustache. This enabled him to close his eyes and effectively keep himself out of the conversation. He was the sort of man who weighed things up before he spoke; a watcher.

My aunt was about to say something, but my uncle spoke first. 'And while you have been seeing Roland, my dear, I have had several pleasant afternoons with Richard.'

'I see,' said my aunt briefly.

And then there was silence. My aunt and the solicitor simply stood there, a yard between them. Neither was particularly tall, yet they dominated the room. The music from my tape washed inappropriately over them. My uncle noticed it and smiled.

'Richard and I have a lot in common,' he said, 'but our tastes don't always coincide. Turn it off, there's a good chap.'

In my socks I padded over to the player in the corner and retrieved my tape, while my aunt watched every step as though I was a dog that had strayed in from the promenade. I put the tape in my pocket and turned reluctantly to face them. I could not keep my eyes on hers.

'He seems very much at home,' she said. It was criminal of me.

My uncle looked up at the man. 'Please take off your coat, Roland. I am sure my wife wants you to stay.'

It seemed a very pointed thing to say and, young as I was, I was quick to notice every time that I was mentioned my uncle would bring in the man's name. Richard against Roland. But it was a very uneasy balance and I was glad when my uncle said I was on the point of leaving and despatched me. We did not arrange another meeting. Instead, he told me to telephone.

I chose a time when, according to past experience, my aunt should not have been at home, but it was her voice that answered. My uncle, she said, had been taken ill and was in bed. She hung up. I waited a day or two and then tried again. I was told he was too ill to see anyone. The end of my meetings with my uncle was as abrupt as that.

I had said nothing about any of this at home. It had somehow become too big a secret to suddenly reveal—but the change in my habits and my long silences made my mother suspect that something was amiss. When she tackled me about it I had to tell her. And when she went to the telephone my aunt met her match. That same afternoon my mother, father and I climbed to the door of my aunt's apartment.

My mother took a keen interest in everything around her. She noted the carpets on the stairs, the pieces of casual furniture on the landings, the panelling; she looked up the stair-well towards the top of the house, and down towards the basement. 'And all this is let out,' she said. 'They're worth a mint of money.'

The meeting with my aunt was, as you can imagine, frigid. My mother, all warm and reconciliation, went forward as if to kiss her, but my aunt turned away and, as though she was the proprietor of the hotel and we were dubious guests, she led us through the rooms until we came to my uncle's bedroom. It was not until we were at the door that she even acknowledged the presence of her brother, my father.

'He's ill,' she said, as though we were responsible. 'You can't stay more than a few minutes.'

My father, blushing, bowed his head. 'All right, May,' he said meekly.

I looked at him. He was overawed. The grandeur of the rooms had subdued him; he was impressed by his sister's wealth, and she recognized it and was keeping him in his place. If ever there was a moment that decided how I was to act in future, this was it. She has only herself to thank for what happened.

My uncle was propped up in bed, looking thinner than ever. But it was not the sight of him that first caught my eye; it was the wheelchair near his bed. It had always been a part of him, and now it stood there empty, like something discarded, never to be used again. It was as though, by leaving it, my uncle was slipping out of his life. I had never before come so close to seeing the consequences of death, and for a moment I was on the verge of fainting.

I do not remember very much of what happened during the next few minutes, except that my uncle and my parents were almost strangers and acted like it, awkwardly.

I remember most of my uncle's thin neck rising from the narrow shoulders of his pyjamas, and the hollow in it where a vein pulsed. But my aunt supervised everything, and in no time at all we were on our way out. We had not even taken off our coats.

She held the door and I was about to follow my parents out when my uncle called me. Without giving my aunt a chance to stop me I went straight to him. He put out a hand and I held it. It was dry and hot, and the skin was very fine over the bones.

'This has happened to me before, Richard,' he said. 'Don't worry about me.'

I nodded. He raised he eyes beyond me and I knew that his pinprick pupils were fixed on my aunt. I had heard her coming closer, and she was directly behind me when he said, still looking at her, 'I have something to say to this young man.'

'Be quick about it.'

To hear her was to know what it was like to be in prison and have your visiting hour cut short.

'Call back his mother and father,' said my uncle.

'They're on their way out,' said my aunt. Nothing was going to make her do as he wished, and I turned to obey him but she held my shoulder. My uncle saw what happened and he made a movement with his hand dismissing the idea. He seemed to want to say something else but had difficulty in breathing.

'Well?' She was impatient.

'I just want the boy to know,' he said, 'that one day he and I shall go sailing.'

'Ridiculous,' she said.

'Or he will,' said my uncle. 'He'll go sailing for me. We'll own a boat together.'

My aunt's hand was still on my shoulder. Now she pushed me to one side, stepped up to the bed and began tucking in the bedclothes like a brutally efficient nurse. There was a threat in everything she did. It's time for your rest,' she said.

A moment later she was pushing me ahead of her out of the room. I twisted my head to look at him. He smiled at me.

It was then that I did something I still have pleasure in recalling. I trod on my aunt's foot. Deliberately. She stopped with a sharp hiss of pain, and in the moment before she bustled me roughly through the doorway, I had time to smile at him. Then he winked. I winked back.

I never saw him again.

It is true that, shortly afterwards, he recovered enough to get out of bed. As far as I knew he was his old self, yet whenever I rang it was my aunt who answered the telephone and she made it quite plain that my presence would be unwelcome. My mother, of course, heard about this and was indignant, and was just working herself up to another furore when we heard about the accident.

My uncle, for the first time in years, had attempted to leave the apartment, but this had been a foolish enterprise. He and his wheelchair had been found at the foot of the stairs. My uncle was twisted, broken and dead.

'It was murder!' said my mother. 'That woman should never have left him alone.'

My father, however, sought to excuse my aunt. She was, after all, his sister. 'She had only gone out for the afternoon,' he said, 'to see their solicitor.'

My mother snorted down her nose and gave him what she called an old-fashioned look.

But the inquest agreed with my father. The coroner said it was quite clear that my uncle had wheeled himself to the landing, perhaps hoping to chat to one of the tenants, and had lost control. Unfortunately the house was empty at the time, although my aunt could not be blamed for going out to keep an important appointment. His verdict was misadventure on the part of my uncle.

So my aunt was blameless. My mother had simply spoken in haste; any suspicion was unthinkable. The facts spoke for themselves. My aunt had been with the solicitor all afternoon and, besides, my uncle was already a dying man so nothing would have been gained by hastening his end.

Yet I am sure, looking back, that even then something nagged in the recesses of my mind. However it was too uncertain—and too frightening—to be brought into the open, and moreover it was submerged in the grief I felt. I had known my uncle for only a few months, yet I wept for him.

And as for that last remark he had to me about the boat, it was only a small part of the sadness of his death. It had never been more than a daydream of his. I had put it out of my mind until, one morning, I received a letter.

It was quite a document and I had to get my father to explain it to me, but it seemed that shortly before his death my uncle had added to his will and had left me his telescope and his music. He had written that the telescope was to enable me to 'see into a brighter future,' and he hoped his music would one day 'improve the quality of my nephew's life.' As I heard the words I saw him wink again. And it was then that I remembered what he had said when we had last met. He had really wanted me to have a boat. But it was too late now. Much too late.

The letter was from my uncle's solicitor, and I could no more have gone to see Mr Roland Gibbs about my uncle's last wishes than I could my aunt. And, in fact, before two years had passed, they became one. My aunt was Mrs Roland Gibbs, and he was my new uncle.

I had nothing more to do with them until one day, long after I had left school, I ran into trouble. It was financial trouble and, oddly enough, had to do with boats. I had been running a boat repair business—not quite a boatyard—and my money had run out. The bank had been helpful, but not quite helpful enough, and the day came when I needed a loan, needed it quickly, and had nobody to turn to.

It was then that my mother came into it again. It was she who made my father approach his sister on my behalf; in fact she bullied him into going to her apartment with me one night unannounced.

We climbed the stairs I had got to know well so many years before and rang the bell. It was my new uncle who came to the door.

'Yes?' he said. He had a way of tilting back his head so that when you spoke to him you seemed to be speaking to the bristles of his moustache.

169

We told him who we were. He did not like that, but he let us in. The pebble eyes of my aunt were no greeting either. I could see what was going to happen when we mentioned money and I was prepared to pretend this was a social call and get out quickly. But my father, bless him, ploughed on.

Mr Roland Gibbs listened. His wife, sitting beside him, listened. My father's plea was brief, because he was embarrassed. When he had finished, nobody stirred for a long moment. And then Mr Gibbs got to his feet for all the world as if he had been listening to a client, not a relative, and was bringing the interview to an end.

'We'll let you know,' he said.

My father, shyly appealed to his sister. 'We haven't much time, May,' he said. 'We have to have a decision.'

'You do not understand business,' she said. 'None of you.'

They were almost the only words she said. It was quite clear what the answer would be. I wanted to shout at them, insult them by telling them the truth about themselves, but my father was beside me, blushing, already bowing his way out and I could not bear to do anything that would diminish him even further.

Gibbs stood by the door looking at his watch, impatient to see the last of us. I tried to make a dignified exit, but failed. I tripped over the door sill and stumbled out onto the landing. Gibbs did not even wait to see if I recovered my balance. The door shut firmly as I was still staggering.

I was on the verge of lunging forward to batter on the panels until he opened the door and then, I believe, I would have battered him, but something from far back stirred in my mind and restrained me. I let my father lead me away.

It was that night, sitting in my room, that I swung my telescope and began idly looking at the stars. I began making the journey through the heavens that at times I had plotted with my uncle, and as I did so the urge to recall him more completely came over me. I had his music, although I rarely played any of it—it still was not my taste, and some of it I had never heard. The little boxes on my shelf were dusty. I ran my finger along their edges and then, because it seemed to fit my mood, I lifted out one labelled 'Requiem', written in my uncle's hand. There were many tapes like it, music he had recorded from the radio.

I took something from my pocket. It was a tape cassette.

I still had the little player that could not match my uncle's elaborate machinery, but it served. I put on the tape and, as it began to turn, I swung the telescope back to the sky, when suddenly, in a way that I could not have believed possible, my uncle was with me again.

★   ★   ★   ★

Sitting on my boat now, and seeing the sea sparkle out there, I think of it as like a great snake glittering between the islands. It is everywhere, connecting everything, and I love it. But without my uncle's help that night I may never have ridden its back.

The next morning I did not go to my workshop. I had business elsewhere. And that evening, alone, I once again climbed the stairs on which my uncle had died and presented myself at my aunt's door. As before, it was my aunt's husband who answered. I smiled at him.

'I thought we had made ourselves clear last night,' he said. Over the years he had become rather stout, and indignation was making him breathless, but he was managing to be obnoxious. 'We are unable to help you.'

He began to close the door, but I put a hand on it. His indignation became icy. 'You had better go,' he said.

To his fury, I continued to smile. 'I have been thinking,' I said. He pushed on the door, but I held it. I tapped my foot on the door sill to draw his attention to it. 'It's rather high,' I said. 'You should have it lowered and then people won't trip over it.' I paused and then I added, 'And people in wheelchairs could get over it without help.'

At that his fury became ungovernable. He reached out and pushed me in the chest. As I fell back the door slammed. He was not going to be an easy man to convince. I leant on the bell. I think I must have had my thumb on the button for a full minute before the door was flung wide and Gibbs confronted me again.

'Stand there as long as you like,' he said. 'The police will soon be on their way.'

'Good,' I said, and walked past him.

My aunt had the telephone in her hand and was in the act of dialling.

'When you get through,' I said. 'I would like to have a word with them.'

She paused. The hardness of her eyes seemed to have affected her whole face.

'My uncle was too weak,' I said, 'to have got himself onto the landing. Somebody helped him.'

This was not enough to perturb her. She turned back to the dial. I let her finger move once more. Then I said, 'Somebody pushed him.'

The room had become very silent. The tall windows opened on a cloudless night. The sea chuckled far away.

'You are talking nonsense,' said my aunt, but she put down the receiver.

'Let him speak,' said her husband. 'If he is threatening us he is committing a crime.'

He moved to stand beside her. I was reminded of the day I had first seen them together, cold and wet from the rain. They were squat and heavy. It would take a great deal to shake them, and they knew it.

'Go ahead,' said Gibbs. 'And when you have finished we shall call the police.'

'No,' I said. 'I haven't got anything to say. It's your story I've come to hear. You are going to tell it to me.'

He permitted himself a smile. It moved the chunks of his face around, but it showed no humour. My aunt was quite impassive, if you can call the hatred that emanated from her a passive quality. It chilled my blood even as I walked across the room. I took something from my pocket and let them see it. It was a tape cassette.

'A Requiem,' I said. 'My uncle left it to me, and you delivered it. After all, a telescope and a few tapes you could afford. It was better than having to give me what he really wished.'

I had their attention. They were quite still as I put the cassette into its slot. I switched it on.

'Richard.' It was my uncle's voice. It was very weak; the voice of a sick man. 'I fear I have not long to live—one way or another.' He attempted to laugh, but it was too difficult. 'What I wanted you to know is that I cared for you greatly, my boy, and I meant what I said about the boat. Your aunt does not wholly agree with me, however, nor does our solicitor. They think I am too ill, too feeble-minded to be allowed to alter my will in your favour. I will try, my boy, but I fear that no matter how much my health improves they will always, between them, be able to say that I was not sufficiently in my right mind when I signed. All they will allow me to give you are my telescope and music. So I send you this message instead of a document. Enjoy the telescope, my boy; enjoy the tapes.' He began to laugh then, but feebly and soon there was no sound from the tape except the hiss as it ran through the machine. I switched it off.

My aunt and her husband had, I thought, lost a little colour, but they quickly recovered.

'Is that all?' he said.

I nodded. 'That's all he had to say.'

'Then you might as well pick it up and leave. There is nothing there that gives you a claim to anything more than you got.'

'Surely,' I said, 'it's quite clear what he meant.'

'He was right about one thing.' said Gibbs. 'His mind was giving out. That tape proves it.'

Again I nodded. I had to accept it. 'My uncle was afraid you would say that,' I said. I lifted the lid and took out the cassette. And then I shrugged, giving up. 'I suppose you might as well keep it.'

I put it back and closed the lid. 'Let me listen to it once more,' I said, 'just for old time's sake.' I switched on. It was the cruellest thing I have ever done.

They did nothing to prevent me standing there, listening. They could afford to; I was playing into their hands.

Again a voice came from the speakers—but a woman's voice this time, not my uncle's.

'I'm sorry,' I said. 'I've turned the tape over.'

Then I stopped talking to listen. We all listened. It was my aunt's voice that filled the room.

'Once he gets well again it will be too late. He and that damned boy will find a way,' she said.

'Then we'll do it,' a man's voice replied. It made the solicitor sit down very suddenly at my aunt's side. 'You will be alone in the house tomorrow?' the voice went on. 'Are you sure?'

They sat side by side like two stupid children, their eyes gone vacant as they heard themselves planning the crime of so many years before. My uncle's microphone had been listening just as they were listening now. His stereo equipment was expensive and he had often allowed me to play with it. There was a microphone that could wait for voices before it switched itself on.

I left them still listening. I am not a vindictive man, and I did not wish to gloat. Besides, there was nothing I need fear if they destroyed the tape. They were listening to a copy I had made that morning. My uncle's Requiem was in a safe place.

My aunt's husband is dead now. He had, I believe, a weak heart. But my aunt is made of sterner stuff. She has, however, become very generous to her nephew, and she continues to live in the same apartment—which I am sure is what my uncle would have wished. Neither of us was ever a vindictive man.

THE ADVENTURE OF THE SPECKLED BAND

Sir Arthur Conan Doyle

In glancing over my notes of the seventy odd cases in which I have during the last eight years studied the methods of my friend Sherlock Holmes, I find many tragic, some comic, a large number merely strange, but none commonplace; for working as he did rather for the love of his art than for the acquirement of wealth, he refused to associate himself with any investigation which did not tend towards the unusual, and even the fantastic. Of all these varied cases, however, I cannot recall any which presented more singular features than that which was associated with the well-known Surrey family of the Roylotts of Stoke Moran. The events in question occurred in the early days of my association with Holmes, when we were sharing rooms as bachelors, in Baker Street. It is possible that I might have placed them upon record before, but a promise of secrecy was made at the time, from which I have only been freed during the last month by the untimely death of the lady to whom the pledge was given. It is perhaps as well that the facts should now come to light, for I have reasons to know there are widespread rumours as to the death of Dr Grimesby Roylott which tend to make the matter even more terrible than the truth.

It was early in April, in the year '83, that I woke one morning to find Sherlock Holmes standing, fully dressed, by the side of my bed. He was a late riser as a rule, and, as the clock on the mantelpiece showed me that it was only a quarter past seven, I blinked up at him in some surprise, and perhaps just a little resentment, for I was myself regular in my habits.

'Very sorry to knock you up, Watson,' said he, 'but it's the common lot this morning. Mrs Hudson has been knocked up, she retorted upon me, and I on you.'

'What is it, then? A fire?'

'No, a client. It seems that a young lady has arrived in a considerable state of excitement, who insists upon seeing me. She is waiting now in the sitting-room. Now, when young ladies wander about the Metropolis at this hour of the morning, and knock sleepy people up out of their beds, I presume that it is something very pressing which they have to communicate. Should it prove to be an interesting case, you would, I am sure, wish to follow it from the outset. I thought at any rate that I should call you, and give you the chance.'

'My dear fellow, I would not miss it for anything.'

I had no keener pleasure than in following Holmes in his professional investigations, and in admiring the rapid deductions, as swift as intuitions, and yet always founded on a logical basis, with which he unravelled the problems which were submitted to him. I rapidly threw on my clothes, and was ready in a few minutes to accompany my friend down to the sitting-room. A lady dressed in black and heavily veiled, who had been sitting in the window, rose as we entered.

'Good morning, madam,' said Holmes cheerily. 'My name is Sherlock Holmes. This is my intimate friend and associate, Dr Watson, before whom you can speak as freely as before myself. Ha, I am glad to see that Mrs Hudson has had the good sense to light the fire. Pray, draw up to it, and I shall order you a cup of hot coffee, for I observe that you are shivering.'

'It is not cold which makes me shiver,' said the woman in a low voice, changing her seat as requested.

'What then?'

'It is fear, Mr Holmes. It is terror.' She raised her veil as she spoke, and we could see that she was indeed in a pitiable state of agitation, her face all drawn and grey, with restless, frightened eyes, like those

of some hunted animal. Her features and figure were those of a woman
of thirty, but her hair was shot with premature grey, and her expression
was weary and haggard. Sherlock Holmes ran her over with one of his
quick, all-comprehensive glances.

'You must not fear,' said he soothingly, bending forward and patting
her forearm. 'We shall soon set matters right, I have no doubt. You
have come in by train this morning, I see.'

'You know me, then?'

'No, but I observe the second half of a return ticket in the palm of
your left glove. You must have started early, and yet you had a good
drive in a dog-cart, along heavy roads, before you reached the station.'

The lady gave a violent start, and stared in bewilderment at my
companion.

'There is no mystery, my dear madam,' said he, smiling. 'The left
arm of your jacket is spattered with mud in no less than seven places.
The marks are perfectly fresh. There is no vehicle save a dog-cart
which throws up mud in that way, and then only when you sit on the
left-hand side of the driver.'

'Whatever your reasons may be, you are perfectly correct,' said she.
'I started from home before six, reached Leatherhead at twenty past,
and came in by the first train to Waterloo. Sir, I can stand this strain
no longer, I shall go mad if it continues. I have no one to turn to—
none, save only one, who cares for me, and he, poor fellow, can be of
little aid. I have heard of you, Mr Holmes; I have heard of you from
Mrs Farintosh, whom you helped in the hour of her sore need. It was
from her that I had your address. Oh, sir, do you not think you could
help me too, and at least throw a little light through the dense
darkness which surrounds me? At present it is out of my power to
reward you for your services, but in a month or two, I shall be married,
with the control of my own income, and then at least you shall not
find me ungrateful.'

Holmes turned to his desk, and unlocking it, drew out a small case-
book which he consulted.

'Farintosh,' said he. 'Ah, yes, I recall the case; it was concerned
with an opal tiara. I think it was before your time, Watson. I can only
say, madam, that I shall be happy to devote the same care to your
case as I did to that of your friend. As to reward, my profession is its

reward; but you are at liberty to defray whatever expenses I may be put to, at the time which suits you best. And now I beg that you will lay before us everything that may help us in forming an opinion upon the matter.'

'Alas!' replied our visitor. 'The very horror of my situation lies in the fact that my fears are so vague, and my suspicions depend so entirely upon small points, which might seem trivial to another, that even he to whom of all others I have a right to look for help and advice looks upon all that I tell him about it as the fancies of a nervous woman. He does not say so, but I can read it from his soothing answers and averted eyes. But I have heard, Mr Holmes, that you can see deeply into the manifold wickedness of the human heart. You may advise me how to walk amid the dangers which encompass me.'

'I am all attention, madam.'

'My name is Helen Stoner, and I am living with my step-father, who is the last survivor of one of the oldest Saxons families in England, the Roylotts of Stoke Moran, on the western border of Surrey.'

Holmes nodded his head. 'The name is familiar to me,' said he.

'The family was at one time among the richest in England, and the estate extended over the borders into Berkshire in the north, and Hampshire in the west. In the last century, however, four successive heirs were of a dissolute and wasteful disposition, and the family ruin was eventually completed by a gambler, in the days of the Regency. Nothing was left save a few acres of ground and the two-hundred-year-old house, which is itself crushed under a heavy mortgage. The last squire dragged out his existence there, living the horrible life of an aristocratic pauper; but his only son, my stepfather, seeing that he must adapt himself to the new conditions, obtained an advance from a relative, which enabled him to take a medical degree, and went out to Calcutta, where, by his professional skill and his force of character, he established a large practice. In a fit of anger, however, caused by some robberies which had been perpetrated in the house, he beat his native butler to death, and narrowly escaped a capital sentence. As it was, he suffered a long term of imprisonment, and afterwards returned to England a morose and disappointed man.

'When Dr Roylott was in India he married my mother, Mrs Stoner, the young widow of Major-General Stoner, of the Bengal

Artillery. My sister Julia and I were twins, and we were only two years old at the time of my mother's re-marriage. She had a considerable sum of money, not less than a thousand a year, and this she bequeathed to Dr Roylott entirely whilst we resided with him, with a provision that a certain annual sum should be allowed to each of us in the event of our marriage. Shortly after our return to England my mother died—she was killed eight years ago in a railway accident near Crewe. Dr Roylott then abandoned his attempts to establish himself in practice in London, and took us to live with him in the ancestral house at Stoke Moran. The money which my mother had left was enough for all our wants, and there seemed no obstacle to our happiness.

'But a terrible change came over our stepfather about this time. Instead of making friends and exchanging visits with our neighbours, who had at first been overjoyed to see a Roylott of Stoke Moran back in the old family seat, he shut himself up in his house, and seldom came out save to indulge in ferocious quarrels with whoever might cross his path. Violence of temper approaching to mania has been hereditary in the men of the family, and in my stepfather's case it had, I believe, been intensified by his long residence in the tropics. A series of disgraceful brawls took place, two of which ended in the police-court, until at last he became the terror of the village, and the folks would fly at his approach, for he is a man of immense strength, and absolutely uncontrollable in his anger.

'Last week he hurled the local blacksmith over a parapet into a stream, and it was only by paying over all the money that I could gather together that I was able to avert another public exposure. He had no friends at all save the wandering gipsies, and he would give these vagabonds leave to encamp upon the few acres of bramble-covered land which represent the family estate, and would accept in return the hospitality of their tents, wandering away with them sometimes for weeks on end. He has a passion also for Indian animals, which are sent over to him by a correspondent, and he has at this moment a cheetah and a baboon, which wander freely over his grounds, and are feared by the villagers almost as much as their master.

'You can imagine from what I say that my poor sister Julia and I had no great pleasure in our lives. No servant would stay with us, and for a long time we did all the work of the house. She was but thirty at the time of her death, and yet her hair had already began to whiten, even as mine has.'

'Your sister is dead, then?'

'She died just two years ago, and it is of her death that I wish to speak to you. You can understand that, living the life which I have described, we were little likely to see anyone of our own age and position. We had, however, an aunt, my mother's maiden sister, Miss Honoria Westphail, who lives near Harrow, and we were occasionally allowed to pay short visits at this lady's house. Julia went there at Christmas two years ago, and met there a half-pay Major of Marines, to whom she became engaged. My step-father learned of the engagement when my sister returned, and offered no objection to the marriage; but within a fortnight of the day which had been fixed for the wedding, the terrible event occurred which has deprived me of my only companion.'

Sherlock Holmes had been leaning back in his chair with his eyes closed, and his head sunk in a cushion, but he half opened his lids now, and glanced across at his visitor.

'Pray be precise as to details,' said he.

'It is easy for me to be so, for every event of that dreadful time is seared into my memory. The manor house is, as I have already said, very old, and only one wing is now inhabited. The bedrooms in this wing are on the ground floor, the sitting-rooms being in the central block of the buildings. Of these bedrooms, the first is Dr Roylott's, the second my sister's, and the third my own. There is no communication between them, but they all open out into the same corridor. Do I make myself plain?'

'Perfectly so.'

'The windows of the three rooms open out upon the lawn. The fatal night Dr Roylott had gone to his room early, though we knew that he had not retired to rest, for my sister was troubled by the smell of the strong Indian cigars which it was his custom to smoke. She left her room, therefore, and came into mine, where she sat for some time, chatting about her approaching wedding. At eleven o'clock she rose to leave me, but she paused at the door and looked back.

'"Tell me, Helen," said she, "have you ever heard anyone whistle in the dead of the night?"

'"Never," said I.

'"I suppose that you could not possibly whistle yourself in your sleep?"

'"Certainly not. But why?"

'"Because during the last few nights I have always, about three in the morning, heard a low clear whistle. I am a light sleeper, and it has awakened me. I cannot tell where it came from—perhaps from the next room, perhaps from the lawn. I thought that I would just ask you whether you had heard it."

'"No, I have not. It must be those wretched gipsies in the plantation."

'"Very likely. And yet if it were on the lawn I wonder that you did not hear it also."

'"Ah, but I sleep more heavily than you."

'"Well, it is of no great consequence at any rate," she smiled back at me, closed my door, and a few moments later I heard her key turn in the lock."

'Indeed,' said Holmes. 'Was it your custom always to lock yourselves in at night?'

'Always.'

'And why?'

'I think that I mentioned to you that the Doctor kept a cheetah and a baboon. We had no feeling of security unless our doors were locked.'

'Quite so. Pray proceed with your statement.'

'I could not sleep that night. A vague feeling of impending misfortune impressed me. My sister and I, you will recollect, were twins, and you know how subtle are the links which bind two souls which are so closely allied. It was a wild night. The wind was howling outside, and the rain was beating and splashing against the windows. Suddenly, amidst all the hubbub of the gale, there burst forth the wild scream of a terrified woman. I knew that it was my sister's voice. I sprang from my bed, wrapped a shawl round me, and rushed into the corridor. As I opened my door I seemed to hear a low whistle, such as my sister described, and a few moments later a clanging sound, as if a mass of metal had fallen. As I ran down the passage my sister's door was unlocked, and revolved slowly upon its hinges. I stared at it horror-stricken, not knowing what was about to issue from it. By the light of the corridor lamp I saw my sister appear in the opening, her face blanched with terror, her hands groping for help, her whole figure swaying to and fro like that of a drunkard. I ran to her and threw my arms round her, but at that moment her knees seemed to give way and she fell to the ground. She writhed as one who is in terrible pain, and her limbs were dreadfully convulsed. At first I thought that she had not recognized me, but as I bent over her she suddenly shrieked out in a voice which I shall never forget, "O, my God! Helen! It was the band! The speckled band!" There was something else which she would have fain have said, and she stabbed with her finger into the air in the direction of the Doctor's room, but a fresh convulsion seized her and choked her words. I rushed out, calling loudly for my step-father, and I met him hastening from his room in his dressing-gown. When he reached my sister's side she was unconscious, and though he poured brandy down her throat, and sent for medical aid from the village, all efforts were in vain, for she slowly sank and died without having recovered her consciousness. Such was the dreadful end of my sister.'

'One moment,' said Holmes; 'are you sure about this whistle and metallic sound? Could you swear to it?'

'That was what the county coroner asked me at the inquiry. It is my strong impression that I heard it, and yet among the crash of the gale, and the creaking of an old house, I may possibly have been deceived.'

'Was your sister dressed?'

'No, she was in her nightdress. In her right hand was found the charred stump of a match, and in her left a match-box.'

'Showing that she had struck a light and looked about her when the alarm took place. That is important. And what conclusions did the coroner come to?'

'He investigated the case with great care, for Dr Roylott's conduct had long been notorious in the county, but he was unable to find any satisfactory cause of death. My evidence showed that the door had been fastened upon the inner side, and the windows were blocked by old-fashioned shutters with broad iron bars, which were secured every night. The walls were carefully sounded, and were shown to be quite solid all round, and the flooring was also thoroughly examined, with the same result. The chimney is wide, but is barred up by four large staples. It is certain, therefore, that my sister was quite alone when she met her end. Besides, there were no marks of any violence upon her.'

'How about poison?'

'The doctors examined her for it, but without success.'

'What do you think that this unfortunate lady died of, then?'

'It is my belief that she died of pure fear and nervous shock, though what it was which frightened her I cannot imagine.'

'Where there gipsies in the plantation at the time?'

'Yes, there are nearly always some there.'

'Ah, and what did you gather from this allusion to a band—a speckled band?'

'Sometimes I have thought that it was merely the wild talk of delirium, sometimes that it may have referred to some band of people, perhaps to these very gipsies in the plantation. I do not know whether the spotted handkerchiefs which so many of them wear over their heads might have suggested the strange adjective which she used.'

Holmes shook his head like a man who is far from being satisfied.

'These are very deep waters,' said he; 'pray go on with your narrative.'

'Two years have passed since then, and my life has been until lately lonelier than ever. A month ago, however, a dear friend, whom I have known for many years, has done me the honour to ask my hand in marriage. His name is Armitage—Percy Armitage—the second son of Mr Armitage, of Crane Water, near Reading. My step-father has offered no opposition to the match, and we are to be married in the course of the spring. Two days ago some repairs were started in the west wing of the building, and my bedroom wall has been pierced, so that I have had to move into the chamber in which my sister died, and to sleep in the very bed in which she slept. Imagine, then, my thrill of terror when last night, as I lay awake, thinking over her terrible fate, I suddenly heard in the silence of the night the low whistle which had been the herald of her own death. I sprang up and lit the lamp, but nothing was to be seen in the room. I was too shaken to go to bed again, however, so I dressed, and as soon as it was daylight I slipped down, got a dog-cart at the Crown Inn, which is opposite, and drove to Leatherhead, from whence I have come on this morning, with the one object of seeing you and asking your advice.'

'You have done wisely,' said my friend. 'But have you told me all?'

'Yes, all.'

'Miss Roylott, you have not. You are screening your stepfather.'

'Why, what do you mean?'

For answer Holmes pushed back the frill of black lace which fringed the hand that lay upon our visitor's knee. Five little livid spots, the marks of four fingers and a thumb, were printed upon the white wrist.

'You have been cruelly used,' said Holmes.

The lady coloured deeply, and covered over her injured wrist. 'He is a hard man,' she said, 'and perhaps he hardly knows his own strength.'

There was a long silence, during which Holmes leaned his chin upon his hands and stared into the crackling fire.

'This is very deep business,' he said at last. 'There are a thousand details which I should desire to know before I decide upon our course of action. Yet we have not a moment to lose. If we were to come to Stoke Moran today, would it be possible for us to see over these rooms without the knowledge of your stepfather?'

'As it happens, he spoke of coming into town today upon some most important business. It is probable that he will be away all day, and that there would be nothing to disturb you. We have a housekeeper now, but she is old and foolish, and I could easily get her out of the way.'

'Excellent. You are not averse to this trip, Watson?'

'By no means.'

'Then we shall both come. What are you going to do yourself?'

'I have one or two things which I would wish to do now that I am in town. But I shall return by the twelve o'clock train, so as to be there in time for your coming.'

'And you may expect us early in the afternoon. I have myself some small business matters to attend to. Will you not wait and breakfast?'

'No, I must go. My heart is lightened already since I have confided my trouble to you. I shall look forward to seeing you again this afternoon.' She dropped her thick black veil over her face, and glided from the room.

'And what do you think of it all, Watson?' asked Sherlock Holmes, leaning back in his chair.

'It seems to me to be a most dark and sinister business.'

'Dark enough and sinister enough.'

'Yet if the lady is correct in saying that the flooring and walls are sound, and that the door, window, and chimney are impassable, then her sister must have been undoubtedly alone when she met her mysterious end.'

'What becomes, then, of these nocturnal whistles, and what of the very peculiar words of the dying woman?'

'I cannot think.'

'When you combine the ideas of whistles at night, the presence of a band of gipsies who are on intimate terms with this old doctor, the fact that we have every reason to believe that the doctor has an interest in preventing his step-daughter's marriage, the dying allusion to a band, and finally, the fact that Miss Helen Stoner heard a metallic clang, which might have been caused by one of those metal bars which secured the shutters falling back into their place, I think there is good ground to think that the mystery may be cleared along those lines.'

'But what, then, did the gipsies do?'

'I cannot imagine.'

'I see many objections to any such a theory.'

'And so do I. It is precisely for that reason that we are going to Stoke Moran this day. I want to see whether the objections are fatal, or if they may be explained away. But what, in the name of the devil!'

The ejaculation had been drawn from my companion by the fact that our door had been suddenly dashed open, and that a huge man framed himself in the aperture. His costume was a peculiar mixture of the professional and of the agricultural, having a black top hat, a long frock-coat, and a pair of high gaiters, with a hunting-crop swinging in his hand. So tall was he that his hat actually brushed the crossbar of the doorway, and his breadth seemed to span it across from side to side. A large face, seared with a thousand wrinkles, burned yellow with the sun, and marked with every evil passion, was turned from one to the other of us, while his deep-set, bile-shot eyes, and the high thin fleshless nose, gave him somewhat the resemblance to a fierce old bird of prey.

'Which of you is Holmes?' asked this apparition.

'My name, sir, but you have the advantage of me,' said my companion quietly.

'I am Dr Grimesby Roylott, of Stoke Moran.'

'Indeed, Doctor,' said Holmes blandly. 'Pray take a seat.'

'I will do nothing of the kind. My step-daughter has been here. I have traced her. What has she been saying to you?'

'It is a little cold for the time of the year,' said Holmes.

'What has she been saying to you?' screamed the old man furiously.

'But I have heard that the crocuses promise well,' continued my companion imperturbably.

'Ha! You put me off, do you?' said our new visitor, taking a step forward, and shaking his hunting-crop. 'I know you, you scoundrel! I have heard of you before. You are Holmes the meddler.'

My friend smiled.

'Holmes the busybody!'

His smile broadened.

'Holmes the Scotland-yard Jack-in-office.'

Holmes chuckled heartily. 'Your conversation is most entertaining,' said he. 'When you go out close the door, for there is a decided draught.'

'I will go when I have had my say. Don't you dare to meddle with my affairs. I know that Miss Stoner has been here—I traced her! I am a dangerous man to fall foul of! See here.' He stepped swiftly forward, seized the poker and bent it into a curve with his huge brown hands.

'See that you keep yourself out of my grip,' he snarled, and hurling the twisted poker into the fireplace, he strode out of the room.

'He seems a very amiable person,' said Holmes, laughing. 'I am not quite so bulky, but if he had remained I might have shown him that my grip was not much more feeble than his own.' As he spoke he picked up the steel poker, and with a sudden effort straightened it out again.

'Fancy his having the insolence to confound me with the official detective force! This incident gives zest to our investigation, however, and I only trust that our little friend will not suffer from her imprudence in allowing this brute to trace her. And now, Watson, we shall order breakfast, and afterwards I shall walk down to Doctors' Commons, where I hope to get some data which may help us in this matter.'

It was nearly one o'clock when Sherlock Holmes returned from his excursion. He held in his hand a sheet of blue paper, scrawled over with notes and figures.

'I have seen the will of the deceased wife,' said he. 'To determine its exact meaning I have been obliged to work out the present prices of the investments with which it is concerned. The total income, which at the time of the wife's death was little short of £1,100, is now through the fall in agricultural prices not more than £750. Each daughter can claim an income of £250, in case of marriage. It is evident, therefore, that if both girls had married this beauty would have had a mere pittance, while even one of them would cripple him to a serious extent. My morning's work has not been wasted, since it has proved that he has the very strongest motives for standing in the way of anything of the sort. And now, Watson, this is too serious for dawdling, especially as the old man is aware that we are interesting ourselves in his affairs, so if you are ready we shall call a cab and drive to Waterloo. I should be very much obliged if you would slip your revolver into your pocket. An Eley's No. 2 is an excellent argument with gentlemen who can twist steel pokers into knots. That and a toothbrush are, I think, all that we need.'

At Waterloo we were fortunate in catching a train for Leatherhead, where he hired a trap at the station inn, and drove for four or five miles through the lovely Surrey lanes. It was a perfect day, with a bright sun and a few fleecy clouds in the heavens. The trees and wayside hedges were just throwing out their first green shoots, and the air was full of the pleasant smell of the moist earth. To me at least there was a strange contrast between the sweet promise of the spring and this sinister quest upon which we were engaged. My companion sat in front of the trap, his arms folded, his hat pulled down over his eyes, and his chin sunk upon his breast, buried in the deepest thought. Suddenly, however, he started, tapped me on the shoulder, and pointed over the meadows.

'Look there!' said he.

A heavily-timbered park stretched up in a gentle slope, thickening into a grove at the highest point. From amidst the branches there jutted out the grey gables and high roof-tree of a very old mansion.

'Stoke Moran?' said he.

'Yes, sir, that be the house of Dr Grimesby Roylott,' remarked the driver.

'There is some building going on there,' said Holmes; 'that is where we are going.'

'There's the village,' said the driver, pointing to a cluster of roofs some distance to the left; 'but if you want to get to the house, you'll find it shorter to go over this stile, and so by the foot-path over the fields. There it is, where the lady is walking.'

'And the lady, I fancy, is Miss Stoner,' observed Holmes, shading his eyes. 'Yes, I think we had better do as you suggest.'

We got off, paid our fare, and the trap rattled back on its way to Leatherhead.

'I thought it as well,' said Holmes, as we climbed the stile, 'that this fellow should think we had come here as architects, or on some definite business. It may stop his gossip. Good afternoon, Miss Stoner. You see that we have been as good as our word.'

Our client of the morning had hurried forward to meet us with a face which spoke her joy. 'I have been waiting so eagerly for you,' she cried, shaking hands with us warmly. 'All has turned out splendidly. Dr Roylott has gone to town, and it is unlikely that he will be back before evening.'

'We have had the pleasure of making the Doctor's acquaintance,' said Holmes, and in a few words he sketched out what had occurred. Miss Stoner turned white to the lips as she listened.

'Good heavens!' she cried, 'he has followed me, then.'

'So it appears.'

'He is so cunning that I never know when I am safe from him. What will he say when he returns?'

'He must guard himself, for he may find that there is someone more cunning than himself upon his track. You must lock yourself from him tonight. If he is violent, we shall take you away to your aunt's at

'Look there!' said Holmes, pointing over the meadows.

Harrow. Now, we must make the best use of our time, so kindly take us at once to the rooms which we are to examine.'

The building was of grey, lichen-blotched stone, with a high central portion, and two curving wings, like the claws of a crab, thrown out on each side. In one of these wings the windows were broken, and blocked with wooden boards, while the roof was partly caved in, a picture of ruin. The central portion was in little better repair, but the right-hand block was comparatively modern, and the blinds in the windows, with the blue smoke curling up from the chimneys, showed that this was where the family resided. Some scaffolding had been erected against the end wall, and the stonework had been broken into, but there were no signs of any workmen at the moment of our visit. Holmes walked slowly up and down the ill-trimmed lawn, and examined with deep attention the outsides of the windows.

'This, I take it, belongs to the room in which you used to sleep, the centre one to your sister's, and the one next to the main building to Dr Roylott's chamber?'

'Exactly so. But I am now sleeping in the middle one.'

'Pending the alterations, as I understand. By the way, there does not seem to be any very pressing need for repairs at that end wall.'

'There were none. I believe that it was an excuse to move me from my room.'

'Ah! that is suggestive. Now, on the other side of this narrow wing runs the corridor from which these three rooms open. There are windows in it, of course?'

'Yes, but very small ones. Too narrow for anyone to pass through.'

'As you both locked your doors at night your rooms were unapproachable from that side. Now, would you have the kindness to go into your room, and to bar your shutters.'

Miss Stoner did so, and Holmes, after a careful examination through the open window, endeavoured in every way to force the shutter open, but without success. There was no slit through which a knife could be passed to raise the bar. Then with his lens he tested the hinges, but they were of solid iron, built firmly into the massive masonry. 'Hum!' said he, scratching his chin in some perplexity, 'my theory certainly presents some difficulty. No one could pass these shutters if they were bolted. Well, we shall see if the inside throws any light upon the matter.'

A small side-door led into the whitewashed corridor from which the three bedrooms opened. Holmes refused to examine the third chamber, so we passed at once to the second, that in which Miss Stoner was now sleeping, and in which her sister had met her fate. It was a homely little room, with a low ceiling and a gaping fire-place, after the fashion of old country houses. A brown chest of drawers stood in one corner, a narrow white-counterpaned bed in another, and a dressing-table on the left-hand side of the window. These articles, with two small wickerwork chairs, made up all the furniture in the room, save for a square of Wilton carpet in the centre. The boards round and the panelling of the walls were brown, worm-eaten oak, so old and discoloured that it may have dated from the original building of the house. Holmes drew one of the chairs into a corner and sat silent, while his eyes travelled round and round and up and down, taking in every detail of the apartment.

'Where does that bell communicate with?' he asked at last, pointing to a thick bell-rope which hung down beside the bed, the tassel actually lying upon the pillow.

'It goes to the housekeeper's room.'

'It looks newer than the other things?'

'Yes, it was only put there a couple of years ago.'

'Your sister asked for it, I suppose?'

'No, I never heard of her using it. We used always to get what we wanted for ourselves.'

'Indeed, it seemed unnecessary to put so nice a bell-pull there. You will excuse me for a few minutes while I satisfy myself as to this floor.' He threw himself down upon his face with his lens in his hand, and crawled swiftly backwards and forwards, examining minutely the cracks between the boards. Then he did the same with the woodwork with which the chamber was panelled. Finally he walked over to the bed and spent some time in staring at it, and in running his eye up and down the wall. Finally he took the bell-rope in his hand and gave it a brisk tug.

'Why, it's a dummy,' said he.

'Won't it ring?'

'No, it is not even attached to a wire. This is very interesting. You can see now that it is fastened to a hook just above where the little opening of the ventilator is.'

'How very absurd! I never noticed that before.'

'Very strange!' muttered Holmes, pulling at the rope. 'There are one or two very singular points about this room. For example, what a fool a builder must be to open a ventilator in another room, when, with the same trouble, he might have communicated with the outside air!'

'This is also quite modern,' said the lady.

'Done about the same time as the bell-rope,' remarked Holmes.

'Yes, there were several little changes carried out about that time.'

'They seem to have been of a most interesting character—dummy bell-ropes, and ventilators which do not ventilate. With your permission, Miss Stoner, we shall now carry our researches into the inner apartment.'

Dr Grimesby Roylott's chamber was larger than that of his stepdaughter, but was as plainly furnished. A camp bed, a small wooden shelf full of books, mostly of a technical character, an arm-chair beside the bed, a plain wooden chair against the wall, a round table, and a large iron safe were the principal things which met the eye. Holmes walked slowly round and examined each and all of them with the keenest interest.

'What's in here?' he asked, tapping the safe.

'My stepfather's business papers.'

'Oh! you have seen inside, then!'

'Only once, some years ago. I remember that it was full of papers.'

'There isn't a cat in it, for example?'

'No. What a strange idea!'

'Well, look at this!' He took up a small saucer of milk which stood on the top of it.

'No; we don't keep a cat. But there is a cheetah and a baboon.'

'Ah, yes, of course! Well, a cheetah is just a big cat, and yet a saucer of milk does not go very far in satisfying its wants, I dare say. There is one point which I should wish to determine.' He squatted down in front of the wooden chair, and examined the seat of it with the greatest attention.

'Thank you. That is quite settled,' said he, rising and putting his lens in his pocket. 'Hullo! here is something interesting!'

The object which had caught his eye was a small dog lash hung on one corner of the bed. The lash, however, was curled upon itself, and tied so as to make a loop of whipcord.

'What do you make of that, Watson?'

'It's a common enough lash. But I don't know why it should be tied.'

'That is not quite so common, is it? Ah, me! it's a wicked world, and when a clever man turns his brain to crime it is the worst of all. I think that I have seen enough now, Miss Stoner, and, with your permission, we shall walk out upon the lawn.'

I had never seen my friend's face so grim, or his brow so dark, as it was when we turned from the scene of this investigation. We had walked several times up and down the lawn, neither Miss Stoner nor myself liking to break in upon his thoughts before he roused himself from his reverie.

'It is very essential, Miss Stoner,' said he, 'that you should absolutely follow my advice in every respect.'

'I shall most certainly do so.'

'The matter is too serious for any hesitation. Your life may depend upon your compliance.'

'I assure you that I am in your hands.'

'In the first place, both my friend and I must spend the night in your room.'

Both Miss Stoner and I gazed at him in astonishment.

'Yes, it must be so. Let me explain. I believe that that is the village inn over there?'

'Yes, that is the "Crown",'

'Very good. Your windows would be visible from there?'

'Certainly.'

'You must confine yourself to your room, on pretence of a headache, when your step-father comes back. Then when you hear him retire for the night, you must open the shutters of your window, undo the hasp, put your lamp there as a signal to us, and then withdraw with everything which you are likely to want into the room which you used to occupy. I have no doubt that, in spite of the repairs, you could manage there for one night.'

'Oh, yes, easily.'

'The rest you will leave in our hands.'

'But what will you do?'

'We shall spend the night in your room, and we shall investigate the cause of this noise which has disturbed you.'

'I believe, Mr Holmes, that you have already made up your mind,' said Miss Stoner, laying her hand upon my companion's sleeve.

'Perhaps I have.'

'Then for pity's sake tell me what was the cause of my sister's death.'

'I should prefer to have clearer proofs before I speak.'

'You can at least tell me whether my own thought is correct, and if she died from some sudden fright.'

'No, I do not think so. I think that there was probably some more tangible cause. And now, Miss Stoner, we must leave you, for if Dr Roylott returned and saw us, our journey would be in vain. Goodbye, and be brave, for if you will do what I have told you, you may rest assured that we shall soon drive away the dangers that threaten you.'

Sherlock Holmes and I had no difficulty in engaging a bedroom and sitting-room at the Crown Inn. They were on the upper floor, and from our window we could command a view of the avenue gate, and of the inhabited wing of Stoke Moran Manor House. At dusk we saw Dr Grimesby Roylott drive past, his huge form looming up beside the little figure of the lad who drove him. The boy had some slight difficulty in undoing the heavy iron gates, and we heard the hoarse roar of the Doctor's voice, and saw the fury with which he shook his clenched fists at him. The trap drove on, and a few minutes later we saw a sudden light spring up among the trees as the lamp was lit in one of the sitting-rooms.

'Do you know, Watson,' said Holmes, as we sat together in the gathering darkness, 'I have really some scruples as to taking you tonight. There is a distinct element of danger.'

'Can I be of assistance?'

'Your presence might be invaluable.'

'Then I shall certainly come.'

'It is very kind of you.'

'You speak of danger. You have evidently seen more in these rooms than was visible to me.'

'No, but I fancy that I may have deduced a little more. I imagine that you saw all I did.'

'I saw nothing remarkable save the bell-rope, and what purpose that could answer I confess is more than I can imagine.'

'You saw the ventilator, too?'

'Yes, but I do not think that it is such a very unusual thing to have a small opening between two rooms. It was so small that a rat could hardly pass through.'

'I knew that we should find a ventilator before ever we came to Stoke Moran.'

'My dear Holmes!'

"Oh, yes, I did. You remember in her statement she said that her sister could smell Dr Roylott's cigar. Now, of course that suggests at once that there must be a communication between the two rooms. It could only be a small one, or it would have been remarked upon at the coroner's inquiry. I deduced a ventilator.'

'But what harm can there be in that?'

'Well, there is at least a curious coincidence of dates. A ventilator is made, a cord is hung, and a lady who sleeps in the bed dies. Does not that strike you?'

'I cannot as yet see any connection.'

'Did you observe anything very peculiar about that bed?'

'No.'

'It was clamped to the floor. Did you ever see a bed fastened like that before?'

'I cannot say that I have.'

'The lady could not move her bed. It must always be in the same relative position to the ventilator and to the rope—for so we may call it, since it was clearly never meant for a bell-pull.'

'Holmes,' I cried, 'I seem to see dimly what you are hitting at. We are only just in time to prevent some subtle and horrible crime.'

'Subtle enough and horrible enough. When a doctor goes wrong he is the first of criminals. He has nerve and he has knowledge. Palmer and Pritchard were among the heads of their profession. This man strikes even deeper, but I think, Watson, that we shall be able to strike deeper still. But we shall have horrors enough before the night is over: for goodness' sake let us have a quiet pipe, and turn our minds for a few hours to something more cheerful.'

★   ★   ★   ★

About nine o'clock the light among the trees was extinguished, and all was dark in the direction of the Manor House. Two hours passed slowly away, and then, suddenly, just at the stroke of eleven, a single bright light shone out right in front of us.

'That is our signal,' said Holmes, springing to his feet; 'it comes from the middle window.' As we passed out he exchanged a few words with the landlord, explaining that we were going on a late visit to an acquaintance, and that it was possible that we might spend the night there. A moment later we were out on the dark road, a chill wind blowing in our faces, and one yellow light twinkling in front of us through the gloom to guide us on our sombre errand.

There was little difficulty in entering the grounds, for unrepaired breaches gaped in the old park wall. Making our way among the trees, we reached the lawn, crossed it, and were about to enter through the window, when out from a clump of laurel bushes there darted what seemed to be a hideous and distorted child, who threw itself on the grass with writhing limbs, and then ran swiftly across the lawn into the darkness.

'My God!' I whispered, 'did you see it?'

Holmes was for the moment as startled as I. His hand closed like a vice upon my wrist in agitation. Then he broke into a low laugh, and put his lips to my ear.

'It is a nice household,' he murmured, 'that is the baboon.'

I had forgotten the strange pets which the Doctor affected. There was a cheetah, too; perhaps we might find it upon our shoulders at any moment. I confess that I felt easier in my mind when, after following Holmes's example and slipping off my shoes, I found myself inside the bedroom. My companion noiselessly closed the shutters, moved the lamp onto the table, and cast his eyes round the room. All was as we had seen it in the day-time. Then creeping up to me and making a trumpet of his hand, he whispered into my ear again so gently that it was all that I could do to distinguish the words:

'The least sound would be fatal to our plans.'

I nodded to show that I had heard.

'We must sit without a light. He would see it through the ventilator.'

I nodded again.

'Do not go to sleep; your very life may depend upon it. Have your pistol ready in case we should need it. I will sit on the side of the bed, and you in that chair.'

I took out my revolver and laid it on the corner of the table.

Holmes had brought up a long thin cane, and this he placed upon the bed beside him. By it he laid the box of matches and the stump of a candle. Then he turned down the lamp and we were left in darkness.

How shall I ever forget that dreadful vigil? I could not hear a sound, not even the drawing of a breath, and yet I knew that my companion sat open-eyed, within a few feet of me, in the same state of nervous tension in which I was myself. The shutters cut off the least ray of light, and we waited in absolute darkness. From outside came the occasional cry of a night-bird, and once at our very window a long drawn, cat-like whine, which told us that the cheetah was indeed at liberty. Far away we could hear the deep tones of the parish clock, which boomed out every quarter of an hour. How long they seemed, those quarters! Twelve o'clock, and one, and two, and three, and still we sat waiting silently for whatever might befall.

Suddenly there was the momentary gleam of a light up in the direction of the ventilator, which vanished immediately, but was succeeded by a strong smell of burning oil and heated metal. Someone in the next room had lit a dark lantern. I heard a gentle sound of movement, and then all was silent once more, though the smell grew stronger. For half an hour I sat with straining ears. Then suddenly another sound became audible—a very gentle, soothing sound, like that of a small jet of steam escaping continually from a kettle. The instant that we heard it, Holmes sprang from the bed, struck a match, and lashed furiously with his cane at the bell-pull.

'You see it, Watson?' he yelled. 'You see it?'

But I saw nothing. At the moment when Holmes struck the light I heard a low, clear whistle, but the sudden glare flashing into my weary eyes made it impossible for me to tell what it was at which my friend lashed so savagely. I could, however, see that his face was deadly pale, and filled with horror and loathing.

He had ceased to strike, and was gazing up at the ventilator, when suddenly there broke from the silence of the night the most horrible cry to which I have ever listened. It swelled up louder and louder, a hoarse yell of pain and fear and anger all mingled in the one dreadful shriek. They say that away down in the village, and even in the distant parsonage, that cry raised the sleepers from their beds. It struck cold to our hearts, and I stood gazing at Holmes, and he at me, until the last echoes of it had died away into the silence from which it rose.

'What can it mean?' I gasped.

'It means that it is all over,' Holmes answered. 'And perhaps, after all, it is for the best. Take your pistol, and we shall enter Dr Roylott's room.'

With a grave face he lit the lamp, and led the way down the corridor. Twice he struck at the chamber door without any reply from within. Then he turned the handle and entered, I at his heels, with the cocked pistol in my hand.

It was a singular sight which met our eyes. On the table stood a dark lantern with the shutter half open, throwing a brilliant beam of light upon the iron safe, the door of which was ajar. Beside this table, on the wooden chair, sat Dr Grimesby Roylott, clad in a long grey dressing-gown, his bare ankles protruding beneath, and his feet thrust into red heelless Turkish slippers. Across his lap lay the short stock with the long lash which we had noticed during the day. His chin was cocked upwards, and his eyes were fixed in a dreadful rigid stare at the corner of the ceiling. Round his brow he had a peculiar yellow band, with brownish speckles, which seemed to be bound tightly round his head. As we entered he made neither sound nor motion.

'The band! the speckled band!' whispered Holmes.

I took a step forward. In an instant his strange headgear began to move, and there reared itself from among his hair the squat diamond-shaped head and puffed neck of a loathsome serpent.

'It was a swamp adder!' cried Holmes—' the deadliest snake in India. He has died within ten seconds of being bitten. Violence does, in truth, recoil upon the violent, and the schemer falls into the pit which he digs for another. Let us thrust this creature back into its den, and we can then remove Miss Stoner to some place of shelter, and let the county police know what has happened.'

As he spoke he drew the dog whip swiftly from the dead man's lap, and throwing the noose round the reptile's neck, he drew it from its horrid perch, and carrying it at arm's length, threw it into the iron safe, which he closed upon it.

*   *   *   *

Such are the true facts of the death of Dr Grimesby Roylott, of Stoke Moran. It is not necessary that I should prolong a narrative which has already run to too great a length by telling how we broke the sad news to the terrified girl, how we conveyed her by the morning train to the care of her good aunt at Harrow, of how the slow process of official inquiry came to the conclusion that the Doctor met his fate while indiscreetly playing with a dangerous pet. The little which I had yet to learn of the case was told me by Sherlock Holmes as we travelled back next day.

'I had,' said he, 'come to an entirely erroneous conclusion, which shows, my dear Watson, how dangerous it always is to reason from insufficient data. The presence of the gipsies, and the use of the word "band", which was used by the poor girl, no doubt, to explain the appearance which she had caught a horrid glimpse of by the light of her match, were sufficient to put me upon an entirely wrong scent. I can only claim the merit that I instantly reconsidered my position when, however, it became clear to me that whatever danger threatened an occupant of the room could not come either from the window or the door. My attention was speedily drawn, as I have already remarked to you, to this ventilator, and to the bell-rope which hung down to the bed. The discovery that this was a dummy, and that the bed was clamped to the floor, instantly gave rise to a suspicion that the rope was there as a bridge for something passing through the hole, and coming to the bed. The idea of a snake instantly occurred to me, and when I coupled it with my knowledge that the Doctor was furnished with a supply of creatures from India, I felt that I was probably on the right track. The idea of using a form of poison which could not possibly be discovered by any chemical test was just such a one as would occur to a clever and ruthless man who had had an Eastern training. The rapidity with which such a poison would take effect would also, from his point of view, be an advantage. It would be a sharp-eyed coroner indeed who could distinguish the two little dark punctures which would show where the poison fangs had done their work. Then I thought of the whistle. Of course, he must recall the snake before the morning light revealed it to the victim. He had trained it, probably by the use of the milk which we saw, to return to him when summoned. He would put it through the ventilator at the hour that he thought best, with the certainty that it would crawl down the rope, and land on the bed. It might or might not bite the occupant, perhaps she might escape every night for a week, but sooner or later she must fall a victim.

'I had come to these conclusions before ever I had entered his room. An inspection of his chair showed me that he had been in the habit of standing on it, which, of course, would be necessary in order that he should reach the ventilator. The sight of the safe, the saucer of milk, and the loop of whipcord were enough to finally dispel any doubts which may have remained. The metallic clang heard by Miss Stoner was obviously caused by her father hastily closing the door of his safe upon its terrible occupant. Having once made up my mind, you know the steps which I took in order to put the matter to the proof. I heard the creature hiss, as I have no doubt that you did also, and I instantly lit the light and attacked it.'

'With the result of driving it through the ventilator.'

'And also with the result of causing it to turn upon its master at the other side. Some of the blows of my cane came home, and roused its snakish temper, so that it flew upon the first person it saw. In this way I am no doubt indirectly responsible for Dr Grimesby Roylott's death, and I cannot say that it is likely to weigh very heavily upon my conscience.'

THE NAMELESS MAN

Rodriguez Ottolengui

Mr Barnes was sitting in his private room, with nothing of special importance to occupy his thoughts, when his office boy announced a visitor.

'What name?' asked Mr Barnes.

'None!' was the reply.

'You mean,' said the detective, 'that the man did not give you his name. He must have one, of course. Show him in.'

A minute later the stranger entered, and, bowing courteously, began the conversation at once.

'Mr Barnes, the famous detective, I believe?' said he.

'My name is Barnes,' replied the detective. 'May I have the pleasure of knowing yours?'

'I sincerely hope so,' continued the stranger. 'The fact is, I suppose I have forgotten it.'

'Forgotten your name?' Mr Barnes scented an interesting case, and became doubly attentive.

'Yes!' said the visitor. 'That is precisely my singular predicament. I seem to have lost my identity. That is the object of my call. I wish to discover who I am. As I am evidently a full-grown man, I can certainly claim that I have a past history, but to me that past is entirely a blank. I awoke this morning in this condition, yet apparently in possession of all my faculties, so much so that I at once saw the advisability of consulting a first-class detective, and, upon inquiry, I was directed to you.'

'Your case is most interesting, from my point of view, I mean. To you, of course, it must seem unfortunate. Yet it is not unparalleled. There have been many such cases recorded, and, for your temporary relief, I may say that sooner or later, complete restoration of memory usually occurs. But now, let us try to unravel your mystery as soon as possible, that you may suffer as little inconvenience as there need be. I would like to ask you a few questions?'

'As many as you like, and I will do my best to answer.'

'Do you think that you are a New Yorker?'

'I have not the least idea, whether I am or not.'

'You say you were advised to consult me. By whom?'

'The clerk at the Waldorf Hotel, where I slept last night.'

'Then, of course, he gave you my address. Did you find it necessary to ask him how to find my offices?'

'Well, no, I did not. That seems strange, does it not? I certainly had no difficulty in coming here. I suppose that must be a significant fact, Mr Barnes?'

'It tends to show that you have been familiar with New York, but we must still find out whether you live here or not. How did you register at the hotel?'

'M. J. G. Remington, City.'

'You are sure that Remington is not your name?'

'Quite sure. After breakfast this morning I was passing through the lobby when the clerk called me twice by that name. Finally, one of the hall-boys touched me on the shoulder and explained that I was wanted at the desk. I was very much confused to find myself called "Mr Remington", a name which certainly is not my own. Before I fully realized my position, I said to the clerk, "Why do you call me Remington?" and he replied, "Because you registered under that name." I tried to pass it off, but I am sure that the clerk looks upon me as a suspicious character.'

'What baggage have you with you at the hotel?'

'None. Not even a satchel.'

'May there not be something in your pockets that would help us; letters, for example?'

'I am sorry to say that I have made a search in that direction but found nothing. Luckily I did have a pocket-book though.'

'Much money in it?'

'In the neighbourhood of five hundred dollars.'

Mr Barnes turned to his table and made a few notes on a pad of paper. While he was so engaged his visitor took out a fine gold watch, and, after a glance at the face, was about to return it to his pocket when Mr Barnes wheeled around in his chair, and said:

'That is a handsome watch you have there. Of a curious pattern too. I am rather interested in old watches.'

The stranger seemed confused for an instant, and quickly put up his watch, saying:

'There is nothing remarkable about it. Merely an old family relic. I value it more for that than anything else. But about my case, Mr Barnes, how long do you think it will take to restore my identity to me? It is rather awkward to go about under a false name.'

'I should think so,' said the detective. 'I will do my best for you, but you have given me absolutely no clue to work upon, so that it is impossible to say what my success will be. Still I think forty-eight hours should suffice. At least in that time I ought to make some discoveries for you. Suppose you call again on the day after tomorrow at noon precisely. Will that suit you?'

'Very well, indeed. If you can tell me who I am at that time I shall be more convinced that you are a great detective, as I have been told.'

He arose and prepared to go, and upon the instant Mr Barnes touched a button under his table with his foot, which caused a bell to ring in a distant part of the building, no sound of which penetrated the private office. Thus anyone could visit Mr Barnes in his den, and might leave unsuspicious of the fact that a spy would be awaiting him out in the street who would shadow him persistently day and night until recalled by his chief. After giving the signal, Mr Barnes held his strange visitor in conversation a few moments longer to allow his spy opportunity to get to his post.

'How will you pass the time away, Mr Remington?' said he. 'We may as well call you by that name, until I find your true one.'

'Yes, I suppose so. As to what I shall do during the next forty-eight hours, why, I think I may as well devote myself to seeing the sights. It is a remarkably pleasant day for a stroll, and I think I will visit your beautiful Central Park.'

'A capital idea. By all means, I would advise occupation of that kind. It would be best not to do any business until your memory is restored to you.'

'Business. Why, of course, I can do no business.'

'No! If you were to order any goods, for example, under the name of Remington, later on when you resume your proper identity, you might be arrested as an impostor.'

'By George, I had not thought of that. My position is more serious than I had realized. I thank you for the warning. Sight-seeing will assuredly be my safest plan for the next two days.'

'I think so. Call at the time agreed upon, and hope for the best. If I should need you before then, I will send to your hotel.'

Then, saying 'Good morning,' Mr Barnes turned to his desk again, and, as the stranger looked at him before stepping out of the room, the detective seemed engrossed with some papers before him. Yet scarcely had the door closed upon the retreating form of his recent visitor, when Mr Barnes looked up, with an air of expectancy. A moment later a very tiny bell in a drawer of his desk rang, indicating that the man had left the building, the signal having been sent to him by one of his employees, whose business it was to watch all departures, and notify his chief. A few moments later Mr Barnes himself emerged, clad in an entirely different suit of clothing, and with such an alteration in the colour of his hair, that more than a casual glance would have been required to recognize him.

When he reached the street the stranger was nowhere in sight, but Mr Barnes went to a doorway opposite, and there he found, written in blue pencil, the word 'up', whereupon he walked rapidly up town as far as the next corner, where once more he examined a door-post, upon which he found the word 'right', which indicated the way the man ahead of him had turned. Beyond this he could expect no signals, for the spy shadowing the stranger did not know positively that his chief would take part in the game. Two signals which he had written on the doors were merely a part of a routine, and intended to aid Mr

He deftly removed a pocket-handkerchief from the tail of his coat.

Barnes should he follow; but if he did so, he would be expected to be in sight of the spy by the time the second signal were reached. And so it proved in this instance, for as Mr Barnes turned the corner to the right, he easily discerned his man about two blocks ahead, and presently was near to see "Remington" also.

The pursuit continued until Mr Barnes was surprised to see him enter the Park, thus carrying out his intention as stated in his interview with the detective. Entering at the Fifth Avenue gate he made his way towards the menagerie, and here a curious incident occurred. The stranger had mingled with the crowd in the monkey-house, and was enjoying the antics of the mischievous little animals, when Mr Barnes, getting close behind him, deftly removed a handkerchief from the tail of his coat and swiftly transferred it to his own.

On the day following, shortly before noon, Mr Barnes walked quickly into the reading-room of the Fifth Avenue Hotel. In one corner there is a handsome mahogany cabinet, containing three compartments, each of which is entered through double doors, having glass panels in the upper half. About these panels are draped yellow silk curtains, and in the centre of each appears a white porcelain numeral. These compartments are used as public telephone stations, the applicant being shut in, so as to be free from the noise of the outer room.

Mr Barnes spoke to the girl in charge, and then passed into the compartment numbered '2'. Less than five minutes later Mr Leroy Mitchel came into the reading-room. His keen eyes peered about him, scanning the countenances of those busy with the papers or writing, and then he gave the telephone girl a number, and went into the compartment numbered '1'. About ten minutes elapsed before Mr Mitchel came out again, and, having paid the toll, he left the hotel. When Mr Barnes emerged, there was an expression of extreme satisfaction upon his face. Without lingering, he also went out. But instead of following Mr Mitchel through the main lobby to Broadway, he crossed the reading-room and reached 23rd Street through the side door. Thence he proceeded to the station of the Elevated Railroad, and went up town. Twenty minutes later he was ringing the bell of Mr Mitchel's residence. The buttons, who answered his summons, informed him that his master was not at home.

'He usually comes in to luncheon, however, does he not?' asked the detective.

'Yes, sir,' responded the boy.

'Is Mrs Mitchel at home?'

'No sir.'

'Miss Rose?'

'Yes, sir.'

'Ah! Then I'll wait. Take my card to her.'

Mr Barnes passed into the luxurious drawing-room, and was soon joined by Rose, Mr Mitchel's adopted daughter.

'I am sorry papa is not at home, Mr Barnes,' said the little lady, 'but he will surely be in to luncheon, if you will wait.'

'Yes, thank you, I think I will. It is quite a trip up, and, being here, I may as well stop awhile and see your father, though the matter is not of any great importance.'

'Some interesting case, Mr Barnes? If so, do tell me about it. You know I am almost as much interested in your cases as papa is.'

'Yes, I know you are, and my vanity is flattered. But I am sorry to say I have nothing on hand at present worth relating. My errand is a very simple one. Your father was saying, a few days ago, that he was thinking of buying a bicycle, and yesterday, by accident, I came across a machine of an entirely new make, which seems to me superior to anything yet produced. I thought he might be interested to see it, before deciding what kind to buy.'

'I am afraid you are too late, Mr Barnes. Papa has bought a bicycle already.'

'Indeed! What style did he choose?'

'I really do not know, but it is down in the lower hall, if you care to look at it.'

'It is hardly worth while, Miss Rose. After all, I have no interest in the new model, and if your father has found something that he likes, I won't even mention the other to him. It might only make him regret his bargain. Still, on second thoughts, I will go down with you, if you will take me, into the dining-room and show me the head of that moose which your father had been bragging about killing. I believe it has come back from the taxidermist's?'

'Oh, yes! He is just a monster. Come on!'

They went down to the dining-room, and Mr Barnes expressed great admiration about the moose's head, and praised Mr Mitchel's skill as a marksman. But he had taken a moment to scrutinize the bicycle which stood in the hall-way, while Rose was opening the blinds in the dining-room. Then they returned to the drawing-room, and after a little more conversation Mr Barnes departed, saying that he could not wait any longer, but he charged Rose to tell her father that he particularly desired him to call at noon on the following day.

Promptly at the time appointed, Remington walked into the office of Mr Barnes, and was announced. The detective was in his private room. Mr Leroy Mitchel had been admitted but a few moments before.

'Ask Mr Remington in,' said Mr Barnes to his boy, and when that gentleman entered, before he could show surprise to find a third party present, the detective said:

'Mr Mitchell, this is the gentleman whom I wish you to meet. Permit me to introduce to you, Mr Mortimer J. Goldie, better known to the sporting fraternity as G. J. Mortimer, the champrion short-distance bicycle rider, who recently rode a mile in the phenomenal time of 1·56, on a quarter-mile track.'

As Mr Barnes spoke, he gazed from one to the other of his companions, with a half-quizzical, and wholly pleased expression on his face. Mr Mitchel appeared much interested, but the newcomer was evidently greatly astonished. He looked blankly at Mr Barnes a moment, then dropped into a chair with the query:

'How in the name of conscience did you find that out?'

'That much was not very difficult,' replied the detective. 'I can tell you more; indeed I can supply your whole past history, provided your memory has been sufficiently restored for you to recognize my facts as true.'

Mr Barnes looked at Mr Mitchel and winked one eye in a most suggestive manner, at which that gentleman burst out into hearty laughter, finally saying:

'We may as well admit that we are beaten, Goldie. Mr Barnes has been too much for us.'

'But I want to know how he has done it,' persisted Mr Goldie.

'I have no doubt that Mr Barnes will gratify you. Indeed, I am as curious as you are to know by what means he has arrived at his quick solution of the problem which we set him.'

'I will enlighten you as to detective methods with pleasure,' said Mr Barnes. 'Let me begin with the visit made to me by this gentleman two days ago. At the very outset his statement aroused my suspicion, though I did my best not to let him think so. He announced to me that he had lost his identity, and I promptly told him that his case was not uncommon. I said that, in order that he might feel sure that I did not doubt his tale. But truly his case, if he were telling the truth, was absolutely unique. Men have lost recollection of their past, and even have forgotten their names. But I have never before heard of a man who had forgotten his name, *and at the same time knew that he had done so.*'

'A capital point, Mr Barnes,' said Mr Mitchel. 'You were certainly shrewd to suspect fraud so early.'

'Well, I cannot say that I suspected fraud so soon, but the story was so unlikely, that I could not believe it immediately. I therefore was what I might call analytically attentive during the rest of the interview. The next point worth noting which came out was that although he had forgotten himself, he had not forgotten New York, for he admitted having come to me without special guidance.'

'I remember that,' interrupted Mr Goldie, 'and I think I even said to you at the time that it was significant.'

'And I told you that it at least showed that you had been familiar with New York. This was better proven when you said that you would spend the day at Central Park, and when, after leaving here, you had no difficulty to find your way thither.'

'Do you mean to say that you had me followed? I made sure that no one was after me.'

'Well, yes, you were followed,' said Mr Barnes, with a smile. 'I had a spy after you, and I follwed you as far as the Park myself. But let me come to the other points in your interview and my deductions. You told me that you had registered as "M. J. G. Remington". This helped me considerably, as we shall see presently. A few minutes later you took out your watch, and in that little mirror over my desk, which I use occasionally when I turn my back upon a visitor, I noted that there was an inscription on the outside of the case. I turned and asked you something about the watch, when you hastily returned it to your pocket, with the remark that it was "an old family relic". Now can you explain how you could have known that, supposing that you had forgotten who you were?'

'Neatly caught, Goldie,' laughed Mr Mitchel. 'You certainly made a mess of it there.'

'It was an asinine slip,' said Mr Goldie, laughing also.

'Now then,' continued Mr Barnes, 'you readily see that I had good reason for believing that you had not forgotten your name. On the contrary, I was positive that your name was a part of the inscription on the watch. What, then, could be your purpose in pretending otherwise? I did not discover that for some time. However, I decided to go ahead, and find you out if I could. Next I noted two things. Your coat opened once, so that I saw, pinned to your vest, a bicycle badge, which I recognized as the emblem of the League of American Wheelmen.'

'Oh! Oh!' cried Mr Mitchel. 'Shame on you, Goldie, for a blunderer.'

'I had entirely forgotten the badge,' said Mr Goldie.

'I also observed,' the detective went on, 'little indentations on the sole of your shoe, as you had your legs crossed, which satisfied me that you were a rider even before I observed the badge. Now, then, we come to the name, and the significance thereof. Had you really lost your memory, the choosing of a name when you registered at the hotel, would have been a haphazard matter of no importance to me. But as soon as I decided that you were imposing upon me, I knew that your choice of a name had been a deliberate act of the mind; one from which deductions could be drawn.'

'Ah! Now we come to the interesting part,' said Mr Mitchel. 'I love to follow a detective when he uses his brains.'

'The name as registered, and I examined the registry myself to make sure, was odd. Three initials are unusual. A man without memory, and therefore not quite sound mentally, would hardly have chosen so many. Then why had it been done in this instance? What more natural than that these initials represented the true name? In assuming an alias, it is the most common method to transpose the real name in some way. At least it was a working hypothesis. Then the last name might be very significant. "Remington". The Remingtons make guns, sewing-machines, typewriters, and bicycles. Now, this man was a bicycle rider, I was sure. If he chose his own initials as a part of the alias, it was possible that he selected "Remington" because it was familiar to him. I even imagined that he might be an agent for Remington bicycles, and I had arrived at that point during our interview, when I advised him not to buy anything until his identity was restored. But I was sure of my quarry, when I stole a handkerchief from him at the park, and found the initials "M.J.G." upon the same.'

'Marked linen on your person!' exclaimed Mr Mitchel. 'Worse and worse! We'll never make a successful criminal of you, Goldie.'

'Perhaps not! I shan't cry over it.'

'I felt sure of my success by this time,' continued Mr Barnes, 'yet at the very next step I was baulked. I looked over a list of L.A.W. members and could not find a name to fit my initials, which shows, as you will see presently, that, as I may say, "too many clues spoil the broth." Without the handkerchief I would have done better. Next I secured a catalogue of the Remingtons, which gave a list of their authorized agents, and again I failed. Returning to my office I received information from my spy, sent in by messenger, which promised to open a way for me. He had followed you about, Mr Goldie, and I must say you played your part very well, so far as avoiding acquaintances is concerned. But at last you went to a public telephone, and called up someone. My man saw the importance of discovering to whom you had spoken, and bribed the telephone attendant to give him the information. All that he learned, however, was that you had spoken to the public station at the Fifth Avenue Hotel. My spy thought that this was inconsequent, but it proved to me at once that there was collusion, and that your man must have been at the other station by previous appointment. As that was at noon, a few minutes before the same hour on the following day, that is to say, yesterday, I went to the Fifth Avenue Hotel telephone and secreted myself in the middle compartment, hoping to hear what your partner might say to you. I failed in this, as the boxes are too well made to permit sound to pass from one to the other; but imagine my gratification to see Mr Mitchel himself go into the box.'

'And why?' asked Mr Mitchel.

'Why, as soon as I saw you, I comprehended the whole scheme. It was you who had concocted the little diversion to test my ability. Thus, at last, I understood the reason for the pretended loss of identity. With the knowledge that you were in it, I was more than ever determined to get at the facts. Knowing that you were out, I hastened to your house, hoping for a chat with little Miss Rose, as the most likely member of your family to get information from.'

'Oh, fie! Mr Barnes,' said Mr Mitchel, 'to play upon the innocence of childhood! I am ashamed of you!'

'All's fair, etc. Well, I succeeded. I found Mr Goldie's bicycle in your hall-way, and, as I suspected, 'twas a Remington. I took the number and hurried down to the agency, where I readily discovered that wheel number 5,086 is ridden by G. J. Mortimer, one of their regular racing team. I also learned that Mortimer's private name is Mortimer J. Goldie. I was much pleased at this, because it showed how good my reasoning had been about the alias, for you observe that the racing name is merely a transposition of the family name. The watch, of course, is a prize, and the inscription would have proved that you were imposing upon me, Mr Goldie, had you permitted me to see it.'

'Of course. That was why I put it back in my pocket.'

'I said just now,' said Mr Barnes, 'that without the stolen handkerchief I would have done better. Having it, when I looked over the L.A.W. list I went through the "G's" only. Without it I should have looked through the "G's", "J's", and "M's", not knowing how the letters may have been transposed. In that case I should have found "G. J. Mortimer", and the initials would have proved that I was on the right track.'

'You have done well, Mr Barnes,' said Mr Mitchel. 'I asked Goldie to play the part of a nameless man for a few days, to have some fun with you. But you have had fun with us, it seems. Though, I am conceited enough to say, that had it been possible for me to play the principal part, you would not have pierced my identity so soon.'

'Oh! I don't know,' said Mr Barnes. 'We are both of us a little egotistical, I fear.'

'Undoubtedly. Still, if I ever set another trap for you, I will assign myself the chief rôle.'

'Nothing would please me better,' said Mr Barnes. 'But, gentlemen, as you have lost in this little game, it seems to me that someone owes me a dinner, at least!'

'I'll stand the expense with pleasure,' said Mr Mitchel.

'Not at all,' interrupted Mr Goldie. 'It was through my blundering that we lost, and I'll pay the piper.'

'Settle it between you,' cried Mr Barnes. 'But let us walk on. I am getting hungry.'

Whereupon they adjourned to Delmonico's.

THE QUICK BROWN FOX

Edmund Crispin

The port had been round several times, and Wakefield's temperamental dogmatism was by now somewhat inflamed by it.

'Just the same,' he said, irrupting upon a discussion whose origin and purpose no one could clearly remember, 'detective stories *are* anti-social, and no amount of sophistries can disguise the fact. It's quite impossible to suppose that criminals don't collect useful information from them, fantastic and far-fetched though they usually are. No one, I think'—here he glared belligerently at his fellow-guests—'will attempt to contest *that*. And further—'

'*I* contest it,' said Gervase Fen; and Wakefield groaned dismally. 'For all the use criminals make of them, the members of the Detection Club might as well be a chorus of voices crying in the wilderness. Look at the papers and observe what, in spite of detective fiction, criminals actually do. They buy arsenic at the chemist's, signing their own names in the Poisons Book, and then put stupendous quantities of it in their victim's tea. They leave their fingerprints on every possible object in the corpse's vicinity. They invariably forget that burnt paper, if it isn't reduced to dust, can be reconstituted and read. They spend, with reckless abandon, stolen bank-notes whose serial numbers they must know are in the possession of the police. . . .

'No, on the whole I don't think criminals get much help from detective stories. And if by any chance they *are* addicts, that fact by itself is almost certain to scupper them, since their training in imaginary crime—which is almost always extremely complicated—tends to make them over-elaborate in the contriving of their own actual misdeeds; and that, of course, means that they're easy game. . . . For instance, there was the Munsey case.'

'It has always been my opinion,' said Wakefield to the ceiling, 'that after-dinner conversation should be general rather than anecdotal. Moreover—'

'I'd known the family slightly,' said Fen, unperturbed, 'over quite a long period of years. There were five of them, you remember: George Munsey, a little, round, chuckling man who'd made money on the Stock Exchange; his wife Dorothy, vague and stately and benign, who acquired something of a reputation as a poetess in the earlier twenties and lost it again, conclusively, in the later; Judith and Eleanor, the two daughters, aged twenty-two and twenty-five respectively, and both uncommonly pretty; and George Munsey's sister Ellen, a dour, disapproving woman who battened on them, being herself genuinely penniless. With the exception of Judith, they all endured Aunt Ellen very patiently; and Judith's dislike of her hadn't, I think, any rational basis, but was more in the nature of a violent temperamental aversion such as does sometimes crop up between dissimilar personalities. Aunt Ellen didn't reciprocate it, by the way: if anything, she was rather fonder of Judith than of the others.

'Aunt Ellen apart, they were a well-to-do family, since Mrs Munsey and Judith and Eleanor had all inherited substantially from Mrs Munsey's father. However, they kept no servants, preferring, on the whole, to lead a mildly Bohemian existence, looking after themselves. Their house was—is, I suppose I should say—in St John's Wood; and I was staying there myself on the night of the murder.

'I'd travelled up from Oxford to deal with some odd scraps of business and to get myself a new portable typewriter (eventually it was a second-hand one I bought, in Holborn). On the following morning I had to attend a Ministry of Education conference, and I was proposing to stay overnight at the Athenaeum. At lunch-time, however, I chanced on George Munsey in the Author's Club bar, and when he heard how I

was placed he suggested I should stay with him instead. I warned him
I'd have to work—there was a long memorandum to be typed out
for presentation at the M. of E. conference—but he was quite agreeable
to that; and so at about half-past two in the afternoon I duly appeared
on his doorstep, typewriter and all.

'I wasn't the only guest, it transpired. The second spare bedroom
was occupied by Eleanor's current *fiancé*, an overhandsome but
tolerably pleasant young man called Tony Odell, the owner (I was told)
of a chain of milk bars in the West End. In addition to being
Eleanor's *fiancé*, he was Judith's ex-*fiancé*; and I gathered, indirectly,
that it was he rather than Judith who had been primarily responsible
for the breaking-off of their engagement. However, none of the three
seemed much discomfited by the exchange, and until the next day
I wasn't in the least aware of anything's being amiss in the house.

'On arrival, I found that Judith was in the kitchen, concocting
something or other; that Aunt Ellen was upstairs refreshing herself
with an afternoon nap; and that the other four—Mr and Mrs Munsey,
Eleanor and Odell—were playing Racing Demon in the drawing-
room. Now, I have a fondness for Racing Demon, so having dumped
my bag and typewriter in my room, I joined in; and the five of us
played uninterruptedly for the next two hours. At half-past four, on the
Munsey's departing in a body to make tea, I retrieved my typewriter
and settled down in the library to work. There I stayed—recruited by
food and drink which the family brought in to me at irregular
intervals—until nearly midnight. I hadn't any occasion to leave the
library, so I've no idea what the others did with themselves; and I
don't remember that anything more eventful happened to me, during
the remainder of the day, than having to put a new ribbon into my
machine. By the time I'd finished my job they'd all gone to bed, and I
wasn't at all sorry to follow them.

'But the next morning, Odell being not yet up and the others
unitedly engaged in cooking breakfast, Judith took me aside, in a state
of considerable agitation, and confided to me certain matters which I
must confess disturbed me a good deal. Summarized—for conciseness'
and Wakefield's sake—what she told me was as follows:

'She'd heard me come up to bed at midnight, and having finished
her book, and being still sleepless, had set off, as soon as the closing

She was curious to know what he was up to.

of my bedroom door signalled me out of the way (she was a modest child, and apparently had very little on), to fetch a magazine from the hall. Arriving at the head of the stairs, however, she had looked down and seen Odell slip quietly out of the drawing-room and into the library, whence shortly afterwards she heard the rattle of my typewriter, which I'd left down there. In the normal way she wouldn't have thought much about this, but Odell's manner had struck her as distinctly furtive, and she was curious to know what he was up to. She hid in the hall cloaks closet, therefore, until after about ten minutes Odell emerged and crept upstairs to his room. Then she went into the library to see if she could find any indication of what he'd been doing there. Well, she did in fact find something, and in due course showed it to me. . . .' Fen broke off rather abruptly; and when he resumed, it was to say: 'You know that when you're using thin typing-paper you usually put a backing-sheet behind the sheet you're actually typing on?'

Haldane nodded. 'Yes, I know.'

'That's what he'd done. And he'd left the backing-sheet in the waste-paper basket. And you could read what he'd typed by the indentations on it. And what he'd typed was not in the least pleasant.'

Fen paused to refill his glass. 'As I recall it,' he went on after a moment, 'the message ran like this: "*You remember what happened at Manchester on December 4th 1945? So do I. But a thousand pounds might persuade me, I think, to forget about it. I'll write again and tell you where to leave the money. It will be the worse for you if you try to find out who I am.*"'

Haldane nodded again. 'Blackmail,' he murmured thoughtfully.

'Quite so. But there was just one odd thing about the message on that revealing backing-sheet, and that was its heading. It consisted of four words: "*The quick brown fox*".'

There was an instant's bemused silence. Someone said: 'What on earth . . .?'

'Yes. A little mystifying, I agree. But anyway, there it was—and there too, more importantly, was the impress of the blackmail note. And if Odell was blackmailing someone in the house, then the situation required very delicate handling indeed. Judith wanted my advice, naturally enough' ('Tcha,' said Wakefield), 'as to what she ought to do. But I never had a chance to give it her, because it was at that point in our conversation that we heard Eleanor's scream. Eleanor had gone to call her *fiancé* down to breakfast, and had found him dead in his bed.

'Well, the police came, and the Ministry awaited me vainly, and as soon as the routine of the investigation was over, Superintendant Yolland took me into consultation. The facts he had to offer were singularly unenlightening. Odell had been killed by a single blow on the forehead. The weapon was a heavy brass poker from the drawing-room, and no great strength would have been needed to wield it effectively. Death had occurred between 5 and 6 a.m. and had been instantaneous. There were no fingerprints and no helpful traces of any kind.

'Naturally, I felt bound to tell the Superintendent what Judith had told me; and by way of response, he produced for my inspection two sheets of typing-paper which he'd found hidden away in one of Odell's drawers. The first one I looked at bore, in faint and spidery typescript, the blackmail message I've already quoted—but *not* the odd superscription. The second sheet was identical with the first in every possible respect, *except* that it was addressed, like the backing-sheet, to The Quick Brown Fox. And that being so—'

'That being so,' Wakefield interrupted, 'you didn't, I trust, have to do any very strenuous thinking in order to solve your mystery.'

'You think the solution obvious?' said Fen mildly.

'I think it child's play,' said Wakefield with much complacency. 'With what, after all, does one associate the words "The quick brown fox"? One associates them, of course, with the sentence "The quick brown fox jumps over the lazy dog", which has the peculiarity of containing all the letter of the alphabet. To cut a long story short, Odell wasn't *writing* a blackmail note: he was *copying* one, *in order to find out if it had been typed on that particular typewriter.* In other words, he was not a blackmailer, but a blackmailer's victim.

He started to type out the Quick Brown Fox sentence, as a means of comparison, and then decided it would be simpler just to copy the complete message. And the original, together with his copy, was naturally enough found in his drawer. I take it that he wasn't the man to accede meekly to blackmail, and that he'd made up his mind to find out who was threatening him; at which the blackmailer took fright and brained him while he slept.

'As to who the blackmailer was, that's easy, too. As I understand it, both messages *were* in fact typed on Professor Fen's machine.' Fen assented. 'Just so. Well, then, between the time Professor Fen entered the house and the time Odell made his copy, what opportunity was there for anyone to use the typewriter? One, and one only—the period during which Professor Fen was playing Racing Demon in the drawing-room. And—well, we know there were only two people who weren't uninterruptedly engaged in that game: to wit, Judith and Aunt Ellen. Judith you can eliminate on the simple grounds that if she'd been the blackmailer she'd scarcely have told Professor Fen what she did tell him. And that leaves Aunt Ellen. . . . Did you ever find out anything about Odell and Manchester and that date?'

'Yes,' said Fen. 'Odell (and that wasn't his real name) had deserted from the army on that date and in that place. And Aunt Ellen, who'd been in the A.T.S., had had to do, at one time, with the dossiers relating to deserters. In one of those dossiers she'd seen a photograph of Odell, and consequently she recognized him the first time he entered the house.'

'She didn't attempt to deny having recognized him?'

'Oh no. She couldn't very well deny it, because—having discreetly checked back to make sure she hadn't made a mistake—she'd confided the facts to Judith after Odell became engaged to Eleanor; and Judith had advised her to do and say nothing, on the grounds that Odell had a first-rate fighting record, and that his desertion, at the end of the war, was therefore a technical rather than a moral offence.'

'Well,' said Wakefield smugly, 'I'm not asserting that on the case I've outlined you could convict Aunt Ellen of the *murder*—even though it's pretty certain she did it. But she was arrested, I take it, for the blackmail?'

'Oh dear no. You see, Wakefield,' said Fen with aggravating kindness, 'your answer to the problem, though immensely cogent and logical, has one grave defect: it doesn't happen to be the right answer.'

Wakefield was much offended. 'If it *isn't* the right answer,' he returned sourly, 'that's because you've not given me all the relevant facts.'

'Oh, but I have. You remember my telling you about changing the ribbon in my typewriter?'

'Yes.'

'And you remember my saying that one of the blackmail messages was in "a faint and spidery typescript"?'

'So it would be, if it was typed in the afternoon, before you changed the ribbon.'

'But you remember also, no doubt, my saying that apart from The Quick Brown Fox, the second sheet was identical with the first *in every possible respect*?'

For once Wakefield was bereft of speech; he subsided, breathing heavily through his nose.

'Therefore,' said Fen, '*both* messages were in faint, spidery typescript. Therefore they were *both* typed while I was playing Racing Demon. And therefore Judith's story about Odell and the typewriter and the blackmail was a deliberate pack of lies from beginning to end.

'Under police examination she broke down and confessed to the murder; and in due course she was tried and convicted, though the death sentence was eventually commuted to life imprisonment. She hated Odell for jilting her in favour of her sister; and if she hadn't planted the messages in Odell's room, and spun me her fairy-tales about blackmail in a sophisticated, double-bluff attempt to incriminate Aunt Ellen, she might have got away with the killing. But the trouble was, she read detective stories; and what she dreamed up—in the hope that everyone would make the deductions Wakefield has just been making, and probe no further—was in consequence a detective-story device. . . . I hope no one will imagine I'm mocking at detective-story devices. In point of fact, I dote on them. But so long as criminals take them for a model, the police are going to have a very easy time; because, like the wretched Judith, your genuinely murderous addict will dig his cunning and complicated pits for the investigators, only, in the upshot, to fall head first into one of them himself.'

JOHNNY ONE-EYE

Damon Runyon

This cat I am going to tell you about is a very small cat, and in fact it is only a few weeks old, consequently it is really nothing but an infant cat. To tell the truth, it is just a kitten.

It is grey and white and very dirty and its fur is all frowzled up, so it is a very miserable-looking little kitten to be sure the day it crawls through a broken basement window into an old house in East Fifty-third Street over near Third Avenue in the city of New York and goes from room to room saying merouw, merouw in a low, weak voice until it comes to a room at the head of the stairs on the second story where a guy by the name of Rudolph is sitting on the floor thinking of not much.

One reason Rudolph is sitting on the floor is because there is nothing else to sit on as this is an empty house that is all boarded up for years and there is no furniture whatever in it, and another reason is that Rudolph has a .38 slug in his side and really does not feel like doing much of anything but sitting. He is wearing a derby hat and his overcoat as it is in the wintertime and very cold and he has an automatic Betsy on the floor beside him and naturally he is surprised quite some when the little kitten comes merouwing into the room and he picks up the Betsy and points it at the door in case anyone he does not wish to see is with the kitten. But when he observes that it is all alone, Rudolph puts the Betsy down again and speaks to the kitten as follows:

'Hello, cat,' he says.

Of course the kitten does not say anything in reply except merouw but it walks right up to Rudolph and climbs on his lap, although the chances are if it knows who Rudolph is it will hightail it out of there quicker than anybody can say scat. There is enough daylight coming through the chinks in the boards over the windows for Rudolph to see that the kitten's right eye is in bad shape, and in fact it is bulged half out of its head in a most distressing manner and it is plain to be seen that the sight is gone from this eye. It is also plain to be seen that the injury happened recently and Rudolph gazes at the kitten a while and starts to laugh and says like this:

'Well, cat,' he says, 'you seem to be scuffed up almost as much as I am. We make a fine pair of invalids here together. What is your name, cat?'

Naturally the kitten does not state its name but only goes merouw and Rudolph says, 'All right, I will call you Johnny. Yes,' he says, 'your tag is now Johnny One-Eye.'

Then he puts the kitten in under his overcoat and pretty soon it gets warm and starts to purr and Rudolph says:

'Johnny,' he says, 'I will say one thing for you and that is you are plenty game to be able to sing when you are hurt as bad as you are. It is more than I can do.'

But Johnny only goes merouw again and keeps on purring and by and by it falls sound asleep under Rudolph's coat and Rudolph is wishing the pain in his side will let up long enough for him to do the same.

Well, I suppose you are saying to yourself, what is this Rudolph doing in an old empty house with a slug in his side, so I will explain that the district attorney is responsible for this situation. It seems that the DA appears before the grand jury and tells it that Rudolph is an extortion guy and a killer and I do not know what all else, though some of these statements are without doubt a great injustice to Rudolph as, up to the time the DA makes them, Rudolph does not kill anybody of any consequence in years.

It is true that at one period of his life he is considered a little wild

'Hello, cat' he says.

but this is in the 1920s when everybody else is, too, and for seven or eight years he is all settled down and is engaged in business organization work, which is very respectable work indeed. He organizes quite a number of businesses on a large scale and is doing very good for himself. He is living quietly in a big hotel all alone, as Rudolph is by no means a family guy, and he is highly spoken of by one and all when the DA starts poking his nose into his affairs, claiming that Rudolph has no right to be making money out of the businesses, even though Rudolph gives these businesses plenty of first-class protection.

In fact, the DA claims that Rudolph is nothing but a racket guy and a great knock to the community, and all this upsets Rudolph no little when it comes to his ears in a roundabout way. So he calls up his lawbooks and requests legal advice on the subject and lawbooks says the best thing he can think of for Rudolph to do is to become as inconspicuous as possible right away but to please not mention to anyone that he gives this advice.

Lawbooks says he understands the DA is requesting indictments and is likely to get them and furthermore that he is rounding up certain parties that Rudolph is once associated with and trying to get them to remember incidents in Rudolph's early career that may not be entirely to his credit. Lawbooks says he hears that one of these parties is a guy by the name of Cute Freddy and that Freddy makes a deal with the DA to lay off of him if he tells everything he knows about Rudolph, so under the circumstances a long journey by Rudolph will be in the interest of everybody concerned.

So Rudolph decides to go on a journey but then he gets to thinking that maybe Freddy will remember a little matter that Rudolph long since dismissed from his mind and does not wish to have recalled again, which is the time he and Freddy did a job on a guy by the name of The Icelander in Troy years ago and he drops around to Freddy's house to remind him to be sure not to remember this.

But it seems that Freddy, who is an important guy in business organization work himself, though in a different part of the city than Rudolph, mistakes the purpose of Rudolph's visit and starts to out with his rooty-toot-toot and in order to protect himself it is necessary for Rudolph to take his Betsy and give Freddy a little tatooing. In fact,

Rudolph practically crockets his monogram on Freddy's chest and leaves him exceptionally deceased.

But as Rudolph is departing from the neighbourhood, who bobs up but a young guy by the name of Buttsy Fagan, who works for Freddy as a chauffeur and one thing and another, and who is also said to be able to put a slug through a keyhole at forty paces without touching the sides though I suppose it will have to be a pretty good-sized keyhole. Anyway, he takes a long-distance crack at Rudolph as Rudolph is rounding a corner, but all Buttsy can see of Rudolph at the moment is a little piece of his left side and this is what Buttsy hits, although no one knows it at the time, except of course Rudolph, who just keeps on departing.

Now this incident causes quite a stir in police circles, and the DA is very indignant over losing a valuable witness and when they are unable to locate Rudolph at once, a reward of five thousand dollars is offered for information leading to his capture alive or dead and some think they really mean dead. Indeed, it is publicly stated that it is not a good idea for anyone to take any chances with Rudolph as he is known to be armed and is such a character as will be sure to resent being captured, but they do not explain that this is only because Rudolph knows the DA wishes to place him in the old rocking chair at Sing Sing and that Rudolph is quite allergic to the idea.

Anyway, the cops go looking for Rudolph in Hot Springs and Miami and every other place except where he is, which is right in New York wandering around town with the slug in his side, knocking at the doors of old friends requesting assistance. But all the old friends do for him is to slam the doors in his face and forget they ever see him, as the DA is very tough on parties who assist guys he is looking for, claiming that this is something most illegal called harbouring fugitives. Besides Rudolph is never any too popular at best with his old friends as he always plays pretty much of a lone duke and takes the big end of everything for his.

He cannot even consult a doctor about the slug in his side as he knows that nowadays the first thing a doctor will do about a guy with a gunshot wound is to report him to the cops, although Rudolph can remember when there was always a sure-footed doctor around who would consider it a privilege and a pleasure to treat him and keep his trap closed about it. But of course this was in the good old days and Rudolph can see they are gone forever. So he just does the best he can about the slug and goes on wandering here and there and around and about and the blats keep printing his picture and saying, where is Rudolph?

Where he is some of the time is in Central Park trying to get some sleep, but of course even the blats will consider it foolish to go looking for Rudolph there in such cold weather, as he is known as a guy who enjoys his comfort at all times. In fact, it is comfort that Rudolph misses more than anything as the slug is commencing to cause him great pain and naturally the pain turns Rudolph's thoughts to the author of same and he remembers that he once hears somebody say that Buttsy lives over in East Fifty-third Street.

So one night Rudolph decides to look Buttsy up and cause him a little pain in return and he is moseying through Fifty-third when he gets so weak he falls down on the sidewalk in front of the old house and rolls down a short flight of steps that lead from the street level to a little railed-in area-way and ground floor or basement door and before he stops rolling he brings up against the door itself and it creaks open inward as he bumps it. After he lays there awhile Rudolph can see that the house is empty and he crawls on inside.

Then when he feels stronger, Rudolph makes his way upstairs because the basement is damp and mice keep trotting back and forth over him and eventually he winds up in the room where Johnny One-Eye finds him the following afternoon and the reason Rudolph settles down in this room is because it commands the stairs. Naturally, this is important to a guy in Rudolph's situation, though after he is sitting there for about fourteen hours before Johnny comes along he can see that he is not going to be much disturbed by traffic. But he considers it a very fine place, indeed, to remain planted until he is able to resume his search for Buttsy.

Well, after a while Johnny One-Eye wakes up and comes from under the coat and looks at Rudolph out of his good eye and Rudolph waggles his fingers and Johnny plays with them, catching one finger in his front paws and biting it gently and this pleases Rudolph no little as he never before has any personal experience with a kitten. However, he remembers observing one when he was a boy down in

Houston Street, so he takes a piece of paper out of his pocket and makes a little ball of it and rolls it along the floor and Johnny bounces after it very lively indeed. But Rudolph can see that the bad eye is getting worse and finally he says to Johnny like this:

'Johnny,' he says, 'I guess you must be suffering more than I am. I remember there are some pet shops over on Lexington Avenue not far from here and when it gets good and dark I am going to take you out and see if we can find a cat croaker to do something about your eye. Yes, Johnny,' Rudolph says, 'I will also get you something to eat. You must be starved.'

Johnny One-Eye says merouw to this and keeps on playing with the paper ball but soon it comes on dark outside and inside, too, and, in fact, it is so dark inside that Rudolph cannot see his hand before him. Then he puts his Betsy in a side pocket of his overcoat and picks up Johnny and goes downstairs, feeling his way in the dark and easing along a step at a time until he gets to the basement door. Naturally, Rudolph does not wish to strike any matches because he is afraid someone outside may see the light and get nosey.

By moving very slowly, Rudolph finally gets to Lexington Avenue and while he is going along he remembers the time he walks from 125th Street in Harlem down to 110th with six slugs in him and never feels as bad as he does now. He gets to thinking that maybe he is not the guy he used to be, which of course is very true as Rudolph is now forty-odd years of age and is fat around the middle and getting bald, and he also does some thinking about what a pleasure it will be to him to find this Buttsy and cause him the pain he is personally suffering.

There are not many people in the streets and those that are go hurrying along because it is so cold and none of them pay any attention to Rudolph or Johnny One-Eye either, even though Rudolph staggers a little now and then like a guy who is rummed up, although of course it is only weakness. The chances are he is also getting a little feverish and lightheaded because finally he stops a cop who is going along swinging his arms to keep warm and asks him if he knows where there is a pet shop and it is really most indiscreet of such a guy as Rudolph to be interviewing cops. But the cop just points up the street and goes on without looking twice at Rudolph and Rudolph laughs and pokes Johnny with a finger and says:

'No, Johnny One-Eye,' he says, 'the cop is not a dope for not recognizing Rudolph. Who can figure the hottest guy in forty-eight states to be going along a street with a little cat in his arms? Can you, Johnny?'

Johnny says merouw and pretty soon Rudolph comes to the pet shop the cop points out. Rudolph goes inside and says to the guy like this:

'Are you a cat croaker?' Rudolph says. 'Do you know what to do about a little cat that has a hurt eye?'

'I am a kind of a vet,' the guy says.

'Then take a glaum at Johnny One-Eye here and see what you can do for him,' Rudolph says.

Then he hands Johnny over to the guy and the guy looks at Johnny a while and says:

'Mister,' he says, 'the best thing I can do for this cat is to put it out of its misery. You better let me give it something right now. It will just go to sleep and never know what happens.'

Well, at this, Rudolph grabs Johnny One-Eye out of the guy's hands and puts him under his coat and drops a duke on the Betsy in his pocket as if he is afraid the guy will take Johnny away from him again and he says to the guy like this:

'No, no, no,' Rudolph says. 'I cannot bear to think of such a thing. What about some kind of an operation? I remember they take a bum lamp out of Joe the Goat at Bellevue one time and he is okay now.'

'Nothing will do your cat any good,' the guy says. 'It is a goner. It will start having fits pretty soon and die sure. What is the idea of trying to save such a cat as this? It is no kind of cat to begin with. It is just a cat. You can get a million like it for a nickel.'

'No,' Rudolph says, 'this is not just a cat. This is Johnny One-Eye. He is my only friend in the world. He is the only living thing that ever comes pushing up against me warm and friendly and trust me in my whole life. I feel sorry for him.'

'I feel sorry for him, too,' the guy says. 'I always feel sorry for animals that get hurt and for people.'

'I do not feel sorry for people,' Rudolph says. 'I only feel sorry for Johnny One-Eye. Give me some kind of stuff that Johnny will eat.'

'Your cat wants milk,' the guy says. 'You can get some at the delicatessen store down at the corner. Mister,' he says, 'you look sick yourself. Can I do anything for you?'

But Rudolph only shakes his head and goes on out and down to the delicatessen joint where he buys a bottle of milk and this transaction reminds him that he is very short in the moo department. In fact, he can find only a five-dollar note in his pockets and he remembers that he has no way of getting any more when this runs out, which is a very sad predicament indeed for a guy who is accustomed to plenty of moo at all times.

Then Rudolph returns to the old house and sits down on the floor again and gives Johnny One-Eye some of the milk in his derby hat as he neglects buying something for Johnny to drink out of. But Johnny offers no complaint. He laps up the milk and curls himself into a wad in Rudolph's lap and purrs.

Rudolph takes a swig of the milk himself but it makes him sick for by this time Rudolph is really far from being in the pink of condition. He not only has the pain in his side but he has a heavy cold which he probably catches from lying on the basement floor or maybe sleeping in the park and he is wheezing no little. He commences to worry that he may get too ill to continue looking for Buttsy, as he can see that if it is not for Buttsy he will not be in this situation, suffering the way he is, but on a long journey to some place.

He takes to going off into long stretches of a kind of stupor and every time he comes out of one of these stupors the first thing he does is to look around for Johnny One-Eye and Johnny is always right there either playing with the paper ball or purring in Rudolph's lap. He is a great comfort to Rudolph but after a while Rudolph notices that Johnny seems to be running out of zip and he also notices that he is running out of zip himself especially when he discovers that he is no longer able to get to his feet.

It is along in the late afternoon of the day following the night Rudolph goes out of the house that he hears someone coming up the stairs and naturally he picks up his Betsy and gets ready for action when he also hears a very small voice calling kitty, kitty, kitty, and he realizes that the party that is coming can be nobody but a child. In fact, a minute later a little pretty of maybe six years of age comes into the room all out of breath and says to Rudolph like this:

'How do you do?' she says. 'Have you seen my kitty?'

Then she spots Johnny One-Eye in Rudolph's lap and runs over and sits down beside Rudolph and takes Johnny in her arms and at first Rudolph is inclined to resent this and has a notion to give her a good boffing but he is too weak to exert himself in such a manner.

'Who are you?' Rudolph says to the little pretty, 'and,' he says, 'where do you live and how do you get in this house?'

'Why,' she says, 'I am Elsie, and I live down the street and I am looking everywhere for my kitty for three days and the door is open downstairs and I know kitty likes to go in doors that are open so I came to find her and here she is.'

'I guess I forgot to close it last night,' Rudolph says. 'I seem to be very forgetful lately.'

'What is your name?' Elsie asks, 'and why are you sitting on the floor in the cold and where are all your chairs? Do you have any little girls like me and do you love them dearly?'

'No,' Rudolph says. 'By no means and not at all.'

'Well,' Elsie says, 'I think you are a nice man for taking care of my kitty. Do you love kitty?'

'Look,' Rudolph says, 'his name is not kitty. His name is Johnny One-Eye, because he has only one eye.'

'I call her kitty,' Elsie says. 'But,' she says, 'Johnny One-Eye is a nice name too and if you like it best I will call her Johnny and I will leave her here with you to take care of always and I will come to see her every day. You see,' she says, 'if I take Johnny home Buttsy will only kick her again.'

'Buttsy?' Rudolph says. 'Do I hear you say Buttsy? Is his other name Fagan?'

'Why, yes,' Elsie says, 'Do you know him?'

'No,' Rudolph says, 'but I hear of him. What is he to you?'

'He is my new daddy,' Elsie says. 'My other one and my best one is dead and so my mamma makes Buttsy my new one. My mamma says Buttsy is her mistake. He is very mean. He kicks Johnny and hurts her eye and makes her run away. He kicks my mamma too. Buttsy kicks everybody and everything when he is mad and he is always mad.'

'He is a louse to kick a little cat,' Rudolph says.

'Yes,' Elsie says, 'that is what Mr O'Toole says he is for kicking my mamma but my mamma says it is not a nice word and I am never to say it out loud.'

'Who is Mr O'Toole?' Rudolph says.

'He is the policeman,' Elsie says. 'He lives across the street from us and he is very nice to me. He says Buttsy is the word you say just now, not only for kicking my mamma but for taking her money when she brings it home from work and spending it so she cannot buy me nice things to wear. But do you know what?' Elsie says. 'My mamma says some day Buttsy is going far away and then she will buy me lots of things and send me to school and make me a lady.'

Then Elsie begins skipping around the room with Johnny One-Eye in her arms and singing I am going to be a lady, I am going to be a lady, until Rudolph has to tell her to pipe down because he is afraid somebody may hear her. And all the time Rudolph is thinking of Buttsy and regretting that he is unable to get on his pins and go out of the house.

'Now I must go home,' Elsie says, 'because this is a night Buttsy comes in for his supper and I have to be in bed before he gets there so I will not bother him. Buttsy does not like little girls. Buttsy does not like little kittens, Buttsy does not like little anythings. My mamma is afraid of Buttsy and so am I. But,' she says, 'I will leave Johnny here with you and come back tomorrow to see her.'

'Listen, Elsie,' Rudolph says, 'does Mr O'Toole come home tonight to his house for his supper, too?'

'Oh, yes,' Elsie says. 'He comes home every night. Sometimes when there is a night Buttsy is not coming in for his supper my mamma lets me go over to Mr O'Toole's and I play with his dog Charley but you must never tell Buttsy this because he does not like O'Toole either. But this is a night Buttsy is coming and that is why my mamma tells me to get in early.'

Now Rudolph takes an old letter out of his inside pocket and a pencil out of another pocket and he scribbles a few lines on the envelope and stretches himself out on the floor and begins groaning, oh, oh, oh, and then he says to Elsie like this:

'Look, Elsie,' he says, 'you are a smart little kid and you pay strict attention to what I am going to say to you. Do not go to bed tonight until Buttsy gets in. Then,' Rudolph says, 'you tell him you come in this old house looking for your cat and that you hear somebody groaning like I do just now in the room at the head of the stairs and that you find a guy who says his name is Rudolph lying on the floor so sick he cannot move. Tell him the front door of the basement is open. But,' Rudolph says, 'you must not tell him that Rudolph tells you to say these things. Do you understand?'

'Oh,' Elsie says, 'do you want him to come here? He will kick Johnny again if he does.'

'He will come here, but he will not kick Johnny.' Rudolph says. 'He will come here, or I am the worst guesser in the world. Tell him what I look like, Elsie. Maybe he will ask you if you see a gun. Tell him you do not see one. You do not see a gun, do you, Elsie?'

'No,' Elsie says, 'only the one in your hand when I first come in but you put it under your coat. Buttsy has a gun and Mr O'Toole has a gun but Buttsy says I am never, never to tell anybody about this or he will kick me the way he does my mamma.'

'Well,' Rudolph says, 'you must not remember seeing mine, either. It is a secret between you and me and Johnny One-Eye. Now,' he says, 'if Buttsy leaves the house to come and see me, as I am pretty sure he will, you run over to Mr O'Toole's house and give him this note, but do not tell Buttsy or your mamma either about the note. If Buttsy does not leave, it is my hard luck, but you give the note to Mr O'Toole anyway. Now tell me what you are to do, Elsie,' Rudolph says, 'so I can see if you have got everything correct.'

'I am to go on home and wait for Buttsy,' she says, 'and I am to tell him Rudolph is lying on the floor of this dirty old house with a fat stomach and a big nose making noises and that he is very sick and the basement door is open and there is no gun if he asks me, and when Buttsy comes to see you I am to take this note to Mr O'Toole but Buttsy and my mamma are not to know I have the note and if Buttsy does not leave I am to give it to Mr O'Toole anyway and you are to stay here and take care of Johnny my kitten.'

'That is swell,' Rudolph says. 'Now you run along.'

So Elsie leaves and Rudolph sits up against the wall because his side feels easier this way and Johnny One-Eye is in his lap purring very low and the dark comes on until it is blacker inside the room than in the middle of a tunnel and Rudloph feels that he is going into another stupor and he has a tough time fighting it off.

Afterwards some of the neighbours claim they remember hearing a shot inside the house and then two more in quick succession and then all is quiet until a little later when Officer O'Toole and half a dozen other cops and an ambulance with a doctor come busting into the street and swarm into the joint with their guns out and their flashlights going. The first thing they find is Buttsy at the foot of the stairs with two bullet wounds close together in his throat, and naturally he is real dead.

Rudolph is still sitting against the wall with what seems to be a small bundle of bloody fur in his lap but which turns out to be what is left of this little cat I am telling you about, although nobody pays any attention to it at first. They are more interested in getting the come-alongs on Rudolph's wrists but before they move him he pulls his clothes aside and shows the doctor where the slug is in his side and the doctor take one glaum and shakes his head and says:

'Gangrene,' he says. 'I think you have pneumonia too, from the way you are blowing.'

'I know,' Rudolph says. 'I know this morning. Not much chance, hey, croaker?'

'Not much,' the doctor says.

'Well, cops,' Rudolph says, 'load me in. I do not suppose you want Johnny, seeing that he is dead.'

'Johnny who?' one of the cops say.

'Johnny One-Eye,' Rudolph says. 'This little cat here in my lap. Buttsy shoots Johnny's only good eye out and takes most of his noodle with it. I never see a more wonderful shot. Well, Johnny is better off but I feel sorry about him as he is my best friend down to the last.'

Then he begins to laugh and the cop asks him what tickles him so much and Rudolph says:

'Oh,' he says, 'I am thinking of the joke on Buttsy. I am positive he will come looking for me, all right, not only because of the little alter-cation between Cute Freddy and me but because the chances are Buttsy is greatly embarrassed by not tilting me over the first time, as of course he never knows he wings me. Furthermore,' Rudolph says, 'and this

is the best reason of all, Buttsy will realize that if I am in his neighbourhood it is by no means a good sign for him, even if he hears I am sick.

'Well,' Rudolph says, 'I figure that with any kind of a square rattle
I will have a better chance of nailing him than he has of nailing me,
but that even if he happens to nail me, O'Toole will get my note in
time to arrive here and nab Buttsy on the spot with his gun on him.
And,' Rudolph says, 'I know it will be a great pleasure to the DA to
settle Buttsy for having a gun on him.

'But,' Rudolph says, 'as soon as I hear Buttsy coming on the
sneaksby up the stairs, I can see I am taking all the worst of it because
I am now wheezing like a busted valve and you can hear me a block
away except when I hold my breath, which is very difficult indeed,
considering the way I am already greatly tuckered out. No,' Rudolph
says, 'it does not look any good for me as Buttsy keeps coming up the
stairs, as I can tell he is doing by a little faint creak in the boards now
and then. I am in no shape to manoeuvre around the room and pretty
soon he will be on the landing and then all he will have to do is to
wait there until he hears me which he is bound to do unless I stop
breathing altogether. Naturally,' Rudolph says, 'I do not care to risk a
blast in the dark without knowing where he is as something tells me
Buttsy is not a guy you can miss in safety.

'Well,' Rudolph says, 'I notice several times before this that in the
dark Johnny One-Eye's good glim shines like a big spark, so when
I feel Buttsy is about to hit the landing, although of course I cannot
see him, I flip Johnny's ball of paper across the room to the wall just
opposite the door and tough as he must be feeling Johnny chases after it
when he hears it light. I figure Buttsy will hear Johnny playing with the
paper and see his eye shining and think it is me and take a pop at it
and that his gun flash will give me a crack at him.

'It all works out just like I dope it,' Rudolph says, 'but,' he says, 'I
never give Buttsy credit for being such a marksman as to be able to hit
a cat's eye in the dark. If I know this, maybe I will never stick Johnny
out in front the way I do. It is a good thing I never give Buttsy a second
shot. He is a lily. Yes,' Rudolph says, 'I can remember when I can use a
guy like him.'

'Buttsy is no account,' the cop says. 'He is a good riddance. He is
the makings of a worse guy than you.'

'Well,' Rudolph says, 'it is a good lesson to him for kicking a little cat.'

Then they take Rudolph to a hospital and this is where I see him and piece out this story of Johnny One-Eye, and Officer O'Toole is at Rudolph's bedside keeping guard over him, and I remember that not long before Rudolph chalks out he looks at O'Toole and says to him like this:

'Copper,' he says, 'there is no chance of them out-juggling the kid on the reward moo, is there?'

'No,' O'Toole says, 'no chance. I keep the note you send me by Elsie saying she will tell me where you are. It is information leading to your capture just as the reward offer states. Rudolph,' he says, 'it is a nice thing you do for Elsie and her mother, although,' he says, 'it is not nearly as nice as icing Buttsy for them.'

'By the way, copper,' Rudolph says, 'there is the remainders of a pound note in my pants pocket when I am brought here. I want you to do me a favour. Get it from the desk and buy Elsie another cat and name it Johnny, will you?'

'Sure,' O'Toole says. 'Anything else?'

'Yes,' Rudolph says, 'be sure it has two good eyes.'

PHILOMEL COTTAGE

Agatha Christie

'Goodbye, darling.'

'Goodbye, sweetheart.'

Alix Martin stood leaning over the small rustic gate, watching the retreating figure of her husband as he walked down the road in the direction of the village.

Presently he turned a bend and was lost to sight, but Alix still stayed in the same position, absent-mindedly smoothing a lock of the rich brown hair which had blown across her face, her eyes far away and dreamy.

Alix Martin was not beautiful, nor even, strictly speaking, pretty. But her face, the face of a woman no longer in her first youth, was irradiated and softened until her former colleagues of the old office days would hardly have recognized her. Miss Alix King had been a trim business-like young woman, efficient, slightly brusque in manner, obviously capable and matter-of-fact.

Alix had graduated in a hard school. For fifteen years, from the age of eighteen until she was thirty-three, she had kept herself (and for seven years of the time an invalid mother) by her work as a shorthand typist. It was the struggle for existence which had hardened the soft lines of her girlish face.

True, there had been romance—of a kind—Dick Windyford, a fellow clerk. Very much of a woman at heart, Alix had always known without seeming to know that he cared. Outwardly they had been friends, nothing more. Out of his slender salary Dick had been hard put to it to provide for the schooling of a younger brother. For the moment he could not think of marriage.

And then suddenly deliverance from daily toil had come to the girl in the most unexpected manner. A distant cousin had died, leaving her money to Alix—a few thousand pounds, enough to bring in a couple of hundred a year. To Alix it was freedom, life, independence. Now she and Dick need wait no longer.

But Dick reacted unexpectedly. He had never directly spoken of his love to Alix; now he seemed less inclined to do so than ever. He avoided her, became morose and gloomy. Alix was quick to realize the truth. She had become a woman of means. Delicacy and pride stood in the way of Dick's asking her to be his wife.

She liked him none the worse for it, and was indeed deliberating as to whether she herself might not take the first step, when for the second time the unexpected descended upon her.

She met Gerald Martin at a friend's house. He fell violently in love with her, and within a week they were engaged. Alix, who had always considered herself 'not the falling-in-love kind', was swept clean off her feet.

Unwittingly she had found the way to arouse her former lover. Dick Windyford had come to her stammering with rage and anger.

'The man's a perfect stranger to you! You know nothing about him!'

'I know that I love him.'

'How can you know—in a week?'

'It doesn't take everyone eleven years to find out that they're in love with a girl,' cried Alix angrily.

His face went white.

'I've cared for you ever since I met you. I thought that you cared also.'

Alix was truthful.

'I thought so too,' she admitted. 'But that was because I didn't know what love was.'

Then Dick had burst out again. Prayers, entreaties, even threats—

threats against the man who had supplanted him. It was amazing to Alix to see the volcano that existed beneath the reserved exterior of the man she had thought she knew so well.

Her thoughts went back to that interview now, on this sunny morning, as she leant on the gate of the cottage. She had been married a month, and she was idyllically happy. Yet, in the momentary absence of her husband who was everything to her, a tinge of anxiety invaded her perfect happiness. And the cause of that anxiety was Dick Windyford.

Three times since her marriage she had dreamed the same dream. The environment differed, but the main facts were always the same. *She saw her husband lying dead and Dick Windyford standing over him, and she knew clearly and distinctly that his was the hand which had dealt the fatal blow.*

But horrible though that was, there was something more horrible still—horrible, that was, on awakening, for in the dream it seemed perfectly natural and inevitable. *She Alix Martin, was glad that her husband was dead*; she stretched out grateful hands to the murderer, sometimes she thanked him. The dream always ended the same way, with herself clasped in Dick Windyford's arms.

★　　★　　★　　★

She had said nothing of this dream to her husband, but secretly it had perturbed her more than she liked to admit. Was it a warning—a warning against Dick Windyford?

Alix was roused from her thoughts by the sharp ringing of the telephone bell from within the house. She entered the cottage and picked up the receiver. Suddenly she swayed, and put out a hand against the wall.

'Who did you say was speaking?'

'Why, Alix, what's the matter with your voice? I wouldn't have known it. It's Dick.'

'Oh!' said Alix. 'Oh! Where—where are you?'

'At the "Traveller's Arms"—that's the right name, isn't it? Or don't you even know of the existence of your village pub? I'm on my holiday—doing a bit of fishing here. Any objections to my looking you two good people up this evening after dinner?'

'No,' said Alix sharply. 'You mustn't come.'

There was a pause, and then Dick's voice, with a subtle alteration in it, spoke again.

'I beg your pardon,' he said formally. 'Of course I won't bother you—'

Alix broke in hastily. He must think her behaviour too extraordinary. It *was* extraordinary. Her nerves must be all to pieces.

'I only meant that we were—engaged tonight,' she explained, trying to make her voice sound as natural as possible. 'Won't you—won't you come to dinner tomorrow night?'

But Dick evidently noticed the lack of cordiality in her tone.

'Thanks very much,' he said, in the same formal voice, 'but I may be moving on any time. Depends if a pal of mine turns up or not. Goodbye, Alix.' He paused, and then added hastily, in a different tone: 'Best of luck to you, my dear.'

Alix hung up the receiver with a feeling of relief.

'He mustn't come here,' she repeated to herself. 'He mustn't come here. Oh, what a fool I am! To imagine myself into a state like this. All the same, I'm glad he's not coming.'

She caught up a rustic rush hat from a table, and passed out into the garden again, pausing to look up at the name carved over the porch: Philomel Cottage.

'Isn't it a very fanciful name?' she had said to Gerald once before they were married. He had laughed.

'You little Cockney,' he had said affectionately. 'I don't believe you have ever heard a nightingale. I'm glad you haven't. Nightingales should sing only for lovers. We'll hear them together on a summer's evening outside our own home.'

And at the remembrance of how they had indeed heard them, Alix, standing in the doorway of her home, blushed happily.

It was Gerald who had found Philomel Cottage. He had come to Alix bursting with excitement. He had found the very spot for them— unique—a gem—the chance of a lifetime. And when Alix had seen it she too was captivated. It was true that the situation was rather lonely —they were two miles from the nearest village—but the cottage itself was so exquisite, with its old-world appearance and its solid comfort of bathrooms, hot-water, electric light, and telephone, that she fell a victim to its charm immediately. And then a hitch occurred. The owner, a rich man who had made it his whim, declined to let it. He would only sell.

Gerald Martin, though possessed of a good income, was unable to touch his capital. He could raise at most a thousand pounds. The owner was asking three. But Alix, who had set her heart on the place, came to the rescue. Her own capital was easily realized, being in bearer bonds. She would contribute half of it to the purchase of the home. So Philomel Cottage became their very own, and never for a minute had Alix regretted the choice. It was true that servants did not appreciate the rural solitude—indeed, at the moment they had none at all—but Alix, who had been starved of domestic life, thoroughly enjoyed cooking dainty little meals and looking after the house.

The garden, which was magnificently stocked with flowers, was attended to by an old man from the village who came twice a week.

As she rounded the corner of the house, Alix was surprised to see the old gardener in question busy over the flower beds. She was surprised because his days for work were Mondays and Fridays, and today was Wednesday.

'Why, George, what are you doing here?' she asked, as she came towards him.

The old man straightened up with a chuckle, touching the brim of an aged cap.

'I thought as how you'd be surprised, ma'am. But 'tis this way. There be a fête over to Squire's on Friday, and I sez to myself, I sez, neither Mr Martin nor yet his good lady won't take it amiss if I comes for once on a Wednesday instead of a Friday.'

'That's quite all right,' said Alix. 'I hope you'll enjoy yourself at the fête.'

'I reckon to,' said George simply. 'It's a fine thing to be able to eat your fill and know all the time as it's not you as is paying for it. Squire allus has a proper sit-down tea for 'is tenants. Then I thought too, ma'am, as I might as well see you before you goes away so as to learn your wishes for the borders. You'll have no idea when you'll be back, ma'am, I suppose?'

'But I'm not going away.'

George stared at her.

'Bain't you going to Lunnon tomorrow?'

'No. What put such an idea into your head?'

George jerked his head over his shoulder.

'Met maister down to village yesterday. He told me you was both going away to Lunnon tomorrow, and it was uncertain when you'd be back again.'

'Nonsense,' said Alix, laughing. You must have misunderstood him.'

All the same, she wondered exactly what it could have been that Gerald had said to lead the old man into such a curious mistake. Going to London? She never wanted to go to London again.

'I hate London,' she said suddenly and harshly.

'Ah!' said George placidly. 'I must have been mistook somehow, and yet he said it plain enough, it seemed to me. I'm glad you're stopping on here. I don't hold with all this gallivanting about, and I don't think nothing of Lunnon. *I've* never needed to go there. Too many moty cars—that's the trouble nowadays. Once people have got a moty car, blessed if they can stay still anywheres. Mr Ames, wot used to have this house—nice, peaceable sort of gentleman he was until he bought one of them things. Hadn't had it a month before he put up this cottage for sale. A tidy lot he'd spent on it, too, with taps in all the bedrooms, and the electric light and all. "You'll never see your money back," I sez to him. "But," he sez to me, "I'll get every penny of two thousand pounds for this house." And sure enough, he did.'

'He got three thousand,' said Alix, smiling.

'Two thousand,' repeated George. 'The sum he was asking was talked of at the time.'

'It really was three thousand,' said Alix.

'Ladies never understand figures,' said George, unconvinced. 'You'll not tell me that Mr Ames had the face to stand up to you, and say three thousand brazen-like in a loud voice?'

'He didn't say it to me,' said Alix; 'he said it to my husband.'

George stooped again to his flower bed.

'The price was two thousand,' he said obstinately.

Alix did not trouble to argue with him. Moving to one of the further beds, she began to pick an armful of flowers.

As she moved with her fragrant posy towards the house, Alix noticed a small, dark-green object peeping from between some leaves in one of the beds. She stopped and picked it up, recognizing it for her husband's pocket diary.

She opened it, scanning the entries with some amusement. Almost from the beginning of their married life she had realized that the impulsive and emotional Gerald had the uncharacteristic virtues of neatness and method. He was extremely fussy about meals being punctual, and always planned his day ahead with the accuracy of a timetable.

Looking through the diary, she was amused to notice the entry on the date of 14 May: 'Marry Alix St Peter's 2.30.'

'The big silly,' murmured Alix to herself, turning the pages. Suddenly she stopped.

'"Wednesday, 18 June"—why, that's today.'

In the space for that day was written in Gerald's neat, precise hand: '9 p.m.' Nothing else. What had Gerald planned to do at 9 p.m.? Alix wondered. She smiled to herself as she realized that had this been a story, like those she had so often read, the diary would doubtless have furnished her with some sensational revelation. It would have had in it for certain the name of another woman. She fluttered the back pages idly. There were dates, appointments, cryptic references to business deals, but only one woman's name—her own.

Yet as she slipped the book into her pocket and went on with her flowers to the house, she was aware of a vague uneasiness. Those words of Dick Windyford's recurred to her almost as though he had been at her elbow repeating them: 'The man's a perfect stranger to you. You know nothing about him.'

It was true. What did she know about him? After all, Gerald was forty. In forty years there must have been women in his life. . . .

Alix shook herself impatiently. She must not give way to these thoughts. She had a far more instant preoccupation to deal with. Should she, or should she not, tell her husband that Dick Windyford had rung her up?

There was the possibility to be considered that Gerald might have already run across him in the village. But in that case he would be sure to mention it to her immediately upon his return, and matters would be taken out of her hands. Otherwise—what? Alix was aware of a distinct desire to say nothing about it.

If she told him, he was sure to suggest asking Dick Windyford to Philomel Cottage. Then she would have to explain that Dick had proposed himself, and that she had made an excuse to prevent his coming. And when he asked her why she had done so, what could she say? Tell him her dreams? But he would only laugh—or, worse, see that she attached an importance to it which he did not.

In the end, rather shamefacedly, Alix decided to say nothing. It was the first secret she had ever kept from her husband, and the consciousness of it made her feel ill at ease.

★   ★   ★   ★

When she heard Gerald returning from the village shortly before lunch, she hurried into the kitchen and pretended to be busy with the cooking so as to hide her confusion.

It was evident at once that Gerald had seen nothing of Dick Windyford. Alix felt at once relieved and embarrassed. She was definitely committed now to a policy of concealment.

It was not until after their simple evening meal, when they were sitting in the oak-beamed living-room with the windows thrown open to let in the sweet night air scented with the perfume of the mauve and white stocks outside, that Alix remembered the pocket diary.

'Here's something you've been watering the flowers with,' she said, and threw it into his lap.

'Dropped it in the border, did I?'

'Yes; I know all your secrets now.'

'Not guilty,' said Gerald, shaking his head.

'What about your assignation at nine o'clock tonight?'

'Oh! that—' He seemed taken aback for a moment, then he smiled as though something afforded him particular amusement. 'It's an assignation with a particularly nice girl, Alix. She's got brown hair and blue eyes and she's very like you.'

'I don't understand,' said Alix, with mock severity. 'You're evading the point.'

'No, I'm not. As a matter of fact, that's a reminder that I'm going to develop some negatives tonight, and I want you to help me.'

DETECTIVE STORIES

Gerald Martin was an enthusiastic photographer. He had a somewhat old-fashioned camera, but with an excellent lens, and he developed his own plates in a small cellar which he had had fitted up as a dark room.

'And it must be done at nine o'clock precisely,' said Alix teasingly.

Gerald looked a little vexed.

'My dear girl,' he said, with a shade of testiness in his manner, 'one should always plan a thing for a definite time. Then one gets through one's work properly.'

Alix sat for a minute or two in silence, watching her husband as he lay in his chair smoking, his dark head flung back and the clear-cut lines of his clean-shaven face showing up against the sombre background. And suddenly, from some unknown source, a wave of panic surged over her, so that she cried out before she could stop herself: 'Oh, Gerald, I wish I knew more about you!'

Her husband turned an astonished face upon her.

'But my dear Alix, you do know all about me. I've told you of my boyhood in Northumberland, of my life in South Africa, and these last ten years in Canada which have brought me success.'

'Oh! business!' said Alix scornfully.

Gerald laughed suddenly.

'I know what you mean—love affairs. You women are all the same. Nothing interests you but the personal element.'

Alix felt her throat go dry, as she muttered indistinctly: 'Well, but there must have been—love affairs. I mean—if I only knew—'

There was silence again for a minute or two. Gerald Martin was frowning, a look of indecision on his face. When he spoke it was gravely, without a trace of his former bantering manner.

'Do you think it wise, Alix, this—Bluebeard's chamber business? There have been women in my life; yes, I don't deny it. You wouldn't believe me if I did deny it. But I can swear to you truthfully that not one of them meant anything to me.'

There was a ring of sincerity in his voice which comforted the listening wife.

'Satisfied, Alix?' he asked with a smile. Then he looked at her with a shade of curiosity.

'What has turned your mind on to these unpleasant subjects tonight of all nights?'

246

Alix got up and began to walk about restlessly.

'Oh, I don't know,' she said. 'I've been nervy all day.'

'That's odd,' said Gerald, in a low voice, as though speaking to himself. 'That's very odd.'

'Why is it odd?'

'Oh, my dear girl, don't flash out at me so. I only said it was odd because as a rule you're so sweet and serene.'

Alix forced a smile.

'Everything's conspired to annoy me today,' she confessed. 'Even old George had got some ridiculous idea into his head that we were going away to London. He said you had told him so.'

'Where did you see him?' asked Gerald sharply.

'He came to work, today instead of Friday.'

'Damned old fool,' said Gerald angrily.

Alix stared in surprise. Her husband's face was convulsed with rage. She had never seen him so angry. Seeing her astonishment Gerald made an effort to regain control of himself.

'Well, he is a damned old fool,' he protested.

'What can you have said to make him think that?'

'I? I never said anything. At least—oh, yes, I remember; I made some weak joke about being "off to London in the morning," and I suppose he took it seriously. Or else he didn't hear properly. You undeceived him, of course?'

He waited anxiously for her reply.

'Of course, but he's the sort of old man who if once he gets an idea in his head—well, it isn't easy to get it out again.'

Then she told him of George's insistence on the sum asked for the cottage.

Gerald was silent for a minute or two, then he said slowly:

'Ames was willing to take two thousand in cash and the remaining thousand on mortgage. That's the origin of that mistake, I fancy.'

'Very likely,' agreed Alix.

Then she looked up at the clock, and pointed to it with a mischievous finger.

'We ought to be getting down to it, Gerald. Five minutes behind schedule.'

A very peculiar smile came over Gerald Martin's face.

247

'I've changed my mind,' he said quietly; 'I shan't do any photography tonight.'

★   ★   ★   ★

A woman's mind is a curious thing. When she went to bed that Wednesday night Alix's mind was contented and at rest. Her momentarily assailed happiness reasserted itself, triumphant as of yore.

But by the evening of the following day she realized that some subtle forces were at work undermining it. Dick Windyford had not rung up again, nevertheless she felt what she supposed to be his influence at work. Again and again those words of his recurred to her: *'The man's a perfect stranger. You know nothing about him.'* And with them came the memory of her husband's face, photographed clearly on her brain, as he said: 'Do you think it wise, Alix, this—Bluebeard's chamber business?' Why had he said that?

There had been warning in them—a hint of menace. It was as though he had said in effect: 'You had better not pry into my life, Alix. You may get a nasty shock if you do.'

By Friday morning Alix had convinced herself that there *had* been a woman in Gerald's life—a Bluebeard's chamber that he had sedulously sought to conceal from her. Her jealousy, slow to awaken, was now rampant.

Was it a woman he had been going to meet that night at 9 p.m.? Was his story of photographs to develop a lie invented upon the spur of the moment?

Three days ago she would have sworn that she knew her husband through and through. Now it seemed to her that he was a stranger of whom she knew nothing. She remembered his unreasonable anger against old George, so at variance with his usual good-tempered manner. A small thing, perhaps, but it showed her that she did not really know the man who was her husband.

There were several little things required on Friday from the village. In the afternoon Alix suggested that she should go for them whilst Gerald remained in the garden; but somewhat to her surprise he opposed this plan vehemently, and insisted on going himself whilst she remained at home. Alix was forced to give way to him, but his insistence surprised and alarmed her. Why was he so anxious to prevent her going to the village?

Suddenly an explanation suggested itself to her which made the whole thing clear. Was it not possible that, whilst saying nothing to her, Gerald had indeed come across Dick Windyford? Her own jealousy, entirely dormant at the time of their marriage, had only developed afterwards. Might it not be the same with Gerald? Might he not be anxious to prevent her seeing Dick Windyford again? This explanation was so consistent with the facts, and so comforting to Alix's perturbed mind, that she embraced it eagerly.

Yet when tea-time had come and passed she was restless and ill at ease. She was struggling with a temptation that had assailed her ever since Gerald's departure. Finally, pacifying her conscience with the assurance that the room did need a thorough tidying, she went upstairs to her husband's dressing-room She took a duster with her to keep up the pretence of housewifery.

'If I were only sure,' she repeated to herself. 'If I could only be *sure*.'

In vain she told herself that anything compromising would have been destroyed ages ago. Against that she argued that men do sometimes keep the most damning piece of evidence through an exaggerated sentimentality.

In the end Alix succumbed. Her cheeks burning with the shame of her action, she hunted breathlessly through packets of letters and documents, turned out the drawers, even went through the pockets of her husband's clothes. Only two drawers eluded her; the lower drawer of the chest of drawers and the small right-hand drawer of the writing-desk were both locked. But Alix was by now lost to all shame. In one of those drawers she was convinced that she would find evidence of this imaginary woman of the past who obsessed her.

She remembered that Gerald had left his keys lying carelessly on the sideboard downstairs. She fetched them and tried them one by one. The third key fitted the writing-table drawer. Alix pulled it open eagerly. There was a cheque-book and a wallet stuffed well with notes, and at the back of the drawer a packet of letters tied up with a piece of tape.

Her breath coming unevenly, Alix untied the tape. Then a deep, burning blush overspread her face, and she dropped the letters back into the drawer, closing and relocking it. For the letters were her own, written to Gerald Martin before she married him.

She turned now to the chest of drawers, more with a wish to feel that she had left nothing undone than from any expectations of finding what she sought.

To her annoyance none of the keys on Gerald's bunch fitted the drawer in question. Not to be defeated, Alix went into the other rooms and brought back a selection of keys with her. To her satisfaction the key of the spare room wardrobe also fitted the chest of drawers. She unlocked the drawer and pulled it open. But there was nothing in it but a roll of newspaper clippings already dirty and discoloured with age.

Alix breathed a sigh of relief. Nevertheless, she glanced at the clippings, curious to know what subject had interested Gerald so much that he had taken the trouble to keep the dusty roll. They were nearly all American papers, dated some seven years ago, and dealing with the trial of the notorious swindler and bigamist, Charles Lemaitre. Lemaitre had been suspected of doing away with his women victims. A skeleton had been found beneath the floor of one of the houses he had rented, and most of the women he had 'married' had never been heard of again.

He had defended himself from the charge with consummate skill, aided by some of the best legal talent in the United States. The Scottish verdict of 'Not Proven' might perhaps have stated the case best. In its absence, he was found Not Guilty on the capital charge, though sentenced to a long term of imprisonment on the other charges preferred against him.

Alix remembered the excitement caused by the case at the time, and also the sensation aroused by the escape of Lemaitre some three years later. He had never been recaptured. The personality of the man and his extraordinary power over women had been discussed at great length in the English papers at the time, together with an account of his excitability in court, his passionate protestations, and his occasional sudden physical collapses, due to the fact that he had a weak heart, though the ignorant accredited it to his dramatic powers.

There was a picture of him in one of the clippings Alix held, and she studied it with some interest—a long-bearded, scholarly looking gentleman.

Who was it the face reminded her of? Suddenly, with a shock, she realized that it was Gerald himself. The eyes and brow bore a strong resemblance to his. Perhaps he had kept the cutting for that reason. Her eyes went on to the paragraph beside the picture. Certain dates, it seemed, had been entered in the accused's pocket-book, and it was contended that these dates were when he had done away with his victims. Then a woman gave evidence and identified the prisoner positively by the fact that he had a mole on his left wrist, just below the palm of the hand.

Alix dropped the papers and swayed as she stood. *On his left wrist, just below the palm, her husband had a small scar.*

The room whirled round her. Afterwards it struck her as strange that she should have leaped at once to such absolute certainty. Gerald Martin was Charles Lemaitre! She knew it, and accepted it in a flash. Disjointed fragments whirled through her brain, like pieces of a jig-saw puzzle fitting into place.

The money paid for the house—her money—her money only; the bearer bonds she had entrusted to his keeping. Even her dream appeared in its true significance. Deep down in her, her subconscious self had always feared Gerald Martin and wished to escape from him. And it was to Dick Windyford this self of hers had looked for help. That, too, was why she was able to accept the truth so easily, without doubt or hesitation. She was to have been another of Lemaitre's victims. Very soon, perhaps. . . .

A half-cry escaped her as she remembered something. *Wednesday 9 p.m.* The cellar, with the flagstones that were so easily raised! Once before he had buried one of his victims in a cellar. It had been all planned for Wednesday night. But to write it down beforehand in that methodical manner—insanity! No, it was logical. Gerald always made a memorandum of his engagements: murder was to him a business proposition like any other.

But what had saved her? What could possibly have saved her? Had he relented at the last minute? No. In a flash the answer came to her —*old George.*

She understood now her husband's uncontrollable anger. Doubtless he had paved the way by telling every one he met that they were going to London the next day. Then George had come to work unexpectedly, had mentioned London to her, and she had contradicted the story. Too risky to do away with her that night, with old George repeating that conversation. But what an escape! If she had not happened to mention that trivial matter—Alix shuddered.

But there was no time to be lost. She must get away at once—before he came back. She hurriedly replaced the roll of clippings in the drawer, shut it, and locked it.

And then she stayed motionless as though frozen to stone. She heard the creak of the gate into the road. *Her husband had returned.*

For a moment Alix stayed as though petrified, then she crept on tiptoe to the window, looking out from behind the shelter of the curtain.

Yes, it was her husband. He was smiling to himself and humming a little tune. In his hand he held an object which almost made the terrified girl's heart stop beating. It was a brand-new spade.

Alix leaped to a knowledge born of instinct. *It was to be tonight.*

But there was still a chance. Gerald, humming his little tune, went round to the back of the house.

Without hesitating a moment, she ran down the stairs and out of the cottage. But just as she emerged from the door, her husband came round the other side of the house.

'Hallo,' he said, 'where are you running off to in such a hurry?'

Alix strove desperately to appear calm and as usual. Her chance was gone for the moment, but if she was careful not to arouse his suspicions, it would come again later. Even now, perhaps. . . .

'I was going to walk to the end of the lane and back,' she said in a voice that sounded weak and uncertain to her own ears.

'Right,' said Gerald. 'I'll come with you.'

'No—please, Gerald. I'm—nervy, headachy—I'd rather go alone.'

He looked at her attentively. She fancied a momentary suspicion gleamed in his eye.

'What's the matter with you, Alix? You're pale—trembling.'

'Nothing.' She forced herself to be brusque—smiling. 'I've got a headache, that's all. A walk will do me good.'

'Well, it's no good your saying you don't want me,' declared Gerald, with his easy laugh. 'I'm coming, whether you want me or not.'

She dared not protest further. If he suspected that she *knew*. . . .

With an effort she managed to regain something of her normal manner. Yet she had an uneasy feeling that he looked at her sideways every now and then, as though not quite satisfied. She felt that his suspicions were not completely allayed.

When they returned to the house he insisted on her lying down, and brought some eau-de-Cologne to bathe her temples. He was, as ever, the devoted husband. Alix felt herself as helpless as though bound hand and foot in a trap.

Not for a minute would he leave her alone. He went with her into the kitchen and helped her to bring in the simple cold dishes she had already prepared. Supper was a meal that choked her, yet, she forced herself to eat, and even to appear gay and natural. She knew now that she was fighting for her life. She was alone with this man, miles from help, absolutely at his mercy. Her only chance was so to lull his suspicions that he would leave her alone for a few moments—long enough for her to get to the telephone in the hall and summon assistance. That was her only hope now.

A momentary hope flashed over her as she remembered how he had abandoned his plan before. Suppose she told him that Dick Windyford was coming up to see them that evening?

The words trembled on her lips—then she rejected them hastily. This man would not be baulked a second time. There was a determination, an elation, underneath his calm bearing that sickened her. She would only precipitate the crime. He would murder her there and then, and calmly ring up Dick Windyford with a tale of having been suddenly called away. Oh! if only Dick Windyford were coming to the house this evening! If Dick. . . .

A sudden idea flashed into her mind. She looked sharply sideways at her husband as though she feared that he might read her mind. With the forming of a plan, her courage was reinforced. She became so completely natural in manner that she marvelled at herself.

She made the coffee and took it out to the porch where they often sat on fine evenings.

'By the way,' said Gerald suddenly, 'we'll do those photographs later.'

Alix felt a shiver run through her, but she replied, nonchalantly; 'Can't you manage alone? I'm rather tired tonight.'

'It won't take long.' He smiled to himself. 'And I can promise you you won't be tired afterwards.'

The words seemed to amuse him. Alix shuddered. Now or never was the time to carry out her plan.

She rose to her feet.

'I'm just going to telephone to the butcher,' she announced nonchalantly. 'Don't you bother to move.'

'To the butcher? At this time of night?'

'His shop's shut, of course, silly. But he's in his house all right. And tomorrow's Saturday, and I want him to bring me some veal cutlets early, before someone else grabs them off him. The old dear will do anything for me.'

She passed quickly into the house, closing the door behind her. She heard Gerald say: 'Don't shut the door,' and was quick with her light reply: 'It keeps the moths out. I hate moths. Are you afraid I'm going to make love to the butcher, silly?'

Once inside, she snatched down the telephone receiver and gave the number of the 'Traveller's Arms'. She was put through at once.

'Mr Windyford? Is he still there? Can I speak to him?'

Then her heart gave a sickening thump. The door was pushed open and her husband came into the hall.

'Do go away, Gerald,' she said pettishly. 'I hate any one listening when I'm telephoning.'

He merely laughed and threw himself into a chair.

'Sure it really is the butcher you're telephoning to?' he quizzed.

Alix was in despair. Her plan had failed. In a minute Dick Windyford would come to the phone. Should she risk all and cry out an appeal for help?

And then, as she nervously depressed and released the little key in the receiver she was holding, which permits the voice to be heard or not heard at the other end, another plan flashed into her head.

'It will be difficult,' she thought to herself. 'It means keeping my head, and thinking of the right words, and not faltering for a moment, but I believe I could do it. I *must* do it.'

And at that minute she heard Dick Windyford's voice at the other end of the 'phone.

Alix drew a deep breath. Then she depressed the key firmly and spoke.

Alix drew a deep breath. Then she depressed the key firmly and spoke.

'*Mrs Martin speaking—from Philomel Cottage. Please come* (she released the key) tomorrow morning with six nice veal cutlets (she depressed the key again). *It's very important* (she released the key). Thank you very much, Mr Hexworthy; you don't mind my ringing you up so late, I hope, but those veal cutlets are really a matter of (she depressed the key again) *life or death* (she released it). Very well—tomorrow morning (she depressed it) *as soon as possible.*

She replaced the receiver on the hook and turned to face her husband, breathing hard.

'So that's how you talk to your butcher, is it?' said Gerald.

'It's the feminine touch,' said Alix lightly.

She was simmering with excitement. He had suspected nothing. Dick, even if he didn't understand, would come.

She passed into the sitting-room and switched on the electric light. Gerald followed her.

'You seem very full of spirits now?' he said, watching her curiously.

'Yes,' said Alix. 'My headache's gone.'

She sat down in her usual seat and smiled at her husband as he sank into his own chair opposite her. She was saved. It was only five-and-twenty past eight. Long before nine o'clock Dick would have arrived.

'I didn't think much of that coffee you gave me,' complained Gerald. 'It tasted very bitter.'

'It's a new kind I was trying. We won't have it again if you don't like it, dear.'

Alix took up a piece of needlework and began to stitch. Gerald read a few pages of his book. Then he glanced up at the clock and tossed the book away.

'Half-past eight. Time to go down to the cellar and start work.'

The sewing slipped from Alix's fingers.

'Oh, not yet. Let us wait until nine o'clock.'

'No, my girl—half-past eight. That's the time I fixed. You'll be able to get to bed all the earlier.'

'But I'd rather wait until nine.'

'You know when I fix a time, I always stick to it. Come along, Alix. I'm not going to wait a minute longer.'

Alix looked up at him, and in spite of herself she felt a wave of

PHILOMEL COTTAGE

terror slide over her. The mask had been lifted. Gerald's hands were
twitching, his eyes were shining with excitement, he was continually
passing his tongue over his dry lips. He no longer cared to conceal his
excitement.

Alix thought: 'It's true—*he can't wait*—he's like a madman.'

He strode over to her, and jerked her onto her feet with a hand on
her shoulder.

'Come on, my girl—or I'll carry you there.'

His tone was gay, but there was an undisguised ferocity behind it
that appalled her. With a supreme effort she jerked herself free and
clung cowering against the wall. She was powerless. She couldn't get
away—she couldn't do anything—and he was coming towards her.

'Now, Alix—'

'No—no.'

She screamed, her hands held out impotently to ward him off.

'Gerald—stop—I've got something to tell you, something to
confess—'

He did stop.

'To confess?' he said curiously.

'Yes, to confess.' She had used the words at random, but she went
on desperately, seeking to hold his arrested attention.

A look of contempt swept over his face.

'A former lover, I suppose,' he sneered.

'No,' said Alix. 'Something else. You'd call it, I expect—yes, you'd
call it a crime.'

And at once she saw that she had struck the right note. Again his
attention was arrested, held. Seeing that, her nerve came back to her.
She felt mistress of the situation once more.

'You had better sit down again,' she said quietly.

She herself crossed the room to her old chair and sat down. She even
stooped and picked up her needlework. But behind her calmness she
was thinking and inventing feverishly; for the story she invented must
hold his interest until help arrived.

'I told you,' she said slowly, 'that I had been a shorthand-typist for
fifteen years. That was not entirely true. There were two intervals.
The first occurred when I was twenty-two. I came across a man, an
elderly man with a little property. He fell in love with me and asked

257

me to marry him. I accepted. We were married.' She paused. 'I induced him to insure his life in my favour.'

She saw a sudden keen interest spring up in her husband's face, and went on with renewed assurance:

'During the war I worked for a time in a hospital dispensary. There I had the handling of all kinds of rare drugs and poisons.'

She paused reflectively. He was keenly interested now, not a doubt of it. The murderer is bound to have an interest in murder. She had gambled on that, and succeeded. She stole a glance at the clock. It was five-and-twenty to nine.

'There is one poison—it is a little white powder. A pinch of it means death. You know something about poisons, perhaps?'

She put the question in some trepidation. If he did, she would have to be careful.

'No,' said Gerald; 'I know very little about them.'

She drew a breath of relief.

'You have heard of hyoscine, of course? This is a drug that acts much the same way, but is absolutely untraceable. Any doctor would give a certificate of heart failure. I stole a small quantity of this drug and kept it by me.'

She paused, marshalling her forces.

'Go on,' said Gerald.

'No. I'm afraid. I can't tell you. Another time.'

'Now,' he said impatiently. 'I want to hear.'

'We had been married a month. I was very good to my elderly husband, very kind and devoted. He spoke in praise of me to all the neighbours. Everyone knew what a devoted wife I was. I always made his coffee myself every evening. One evening, when we were alone together, I put a pinch of the deadly alkaloid in his cup—'

Alix paused, and carefully re-threaded her needle. She, who had never acted in her life, rivalled the greatest actress in the world at this moment. She was actually living the part of the cold-blooded poisoner.

'It was very peaceful. I sat watching him. Once he gasped a little and asked for air. I opened the window. Then he said he could not move from his chair. *Presently he died.*'

She stopped, smiling. It was a quarter to nine. Surely they would come soon.

'How much,' said Gerald, 'was the insurance money?'

'About two thousand pounds. I speculated with it, and lost it. I went back to my office work. But I never meant to remain there long. Then I met another man. I had stuck to my maiden name at the office. He didn't know I had been married before. He was a younger man, rather good-looking, and quite well off. We were married quietly in Sussex. He didn't want to insure his life, but of course he made a will in my favour. He liked me to make his coffee myself just as my first husband had done.'

Alix smiled reflectively, and added simply: 'I make very good coffee.'

Then she went on:

'I had several friends in the village where we were living. They were very sorry for me, with my husband dying suddenly of heart failure one evening after dinner. I didn't quite like the doctor. I don't think he suspected me, but he was certainly very surprised at my husband's sudden death. I don't quite know why I drifted back to the office again. Habit, I suppose. My second husband left about four thousand pounds. I didn't speculate with it this time; I invested it. Then, you see—'

But she was interrupted. Gerald Martin, his face suffused with blood, half choking, was pointing a shaking forefinger at her.

'The coffee—my God! the coffee!'

She stared at him.

'I understand now why it was bitter. You devil! You've been up to your tricks again.'

His hands gripped the arms of his chair. He was ready to spring upon her.

'You've poisoned me.'

Alix retreated from him to the fire-place. Now, terrified, she opened her lips to deny—and then paused. In another minute he would spring upon her. She summoned all her strength. Her eyes held his steadily, compellingly.

'Yes,' she said. 'I poisoned you. Already the poison is working. At this minute you can't move from your chair—you can't move—'

If she could keep him there—even a few minutes. . . .

Ah! what was that? Footsteps on the road. The creak of the gate.

Then footsteps on the path outside. The outer door opening.

'*You can't move,*' she said again.

Then she slipped past him and fled headlong from the room to fall fainting into Dick Windyford's arms.

'My God! Alix,' he cried.

Then he turned to the man with him, a tall, stalwart figure in policeman's uniform.

'Go and see what's been happening in that room.'

He laid Alix carefully down on a couch and bent over her.

'My little girl,' he murmured. 'My poor little girl. What have they been doing to you?'

Her eyelids fluttered and her lips just murmured his name.

Dick was aroused by the policeman's touching him on the arm.

'There's nothing in that room, sir, but a man sitting in a chair. Looks as though he'd had some kind of bad fright, and—'

'Yes?'

'Well, sir, he's—dead.'

They were startled by hearing Alix's voice. She spoke as though in some kind of dream, her eyes still closed.

'*And presently,*' she said, almost as though she were quoting from something, '*he died—*'

THE INFALLIBLE GODAHL

Frederick Irving Anderson

Oliver Armiston never was much of a sportsman with a rod or gun—though he could do fancy work with a pistol in a shooting gallery. He had, however, one game from which he derived the utmost satisfaction. Whenever he went travelling, which was often, he invariably caught his train by the tip of the tail, so to speak, and hung on till he could climb aboard. In other words he believed in close connections. He had a theory that more valuable dollars-and-cents time and good animal heat are wasted warming seats in stations waiting for trains than by missing them. The sum of joy to his methodical mind was to halt the slamming gates at the last fraction of the last second with majestic upraised hand, and to stroll aboard his parlour car with studied deliberation, while the train crew were gnashing their teeth in rage and swearing to get even with the gateman for letting him through.

Yet Mr Armiston never missed a train. A good many of them tried to miss him, but none ever succeeded. He reckoned time and distance so nicely that it really seemed as if his trains had nothing else half so important as waiting until Mr Oliver Armiston got aboard.

On this particular June day he was due in New Haven at two. If he failed to get there at two o'clock he could very easily arrive at three. But an hour is sixty minutes, and a minute is sixty seconds; and, further, Mr Armiston having passed his word that he would be there at two o'clock, surely would be.

On this particular day, by the time Armiston finally got to the Grand Central the train looked like an odds-on favourite. In the first place he was still in his bed at an hour when another and less experienced traveller would have been watching the clock in the station waiting room. In the second place, after kissing his wife in that absent-minded manner characteristic of true love, he became tangled in a Broadway traffic crush at the first corner. Scarcely was he extricated from this when he ran into a Socialist mass meeting at Union Square. It was due only to the wits of his chauffeur that the taxicab was extricated with very little damage to the surrounding human scenery. But our man of method did not fret. Instead he buried himself in his book, a treatise on Cause and Effect, which at that moment was lulling him with soothing sentiment:

'There is no such thing as accident. The so-called accidents of everyday life are due to the preordained action of correlated causes, which is inevitable and over which man has no control.'

This was comforting, but not much to the point, when Oliver Armiston looked up and discovered he had reached 23rd Street and had come to a halt. A sixty-foot truck, with an underslung burden consisting of a sixty-ton steel girder, had at this point suddenly developed weakness in its off hind-wheel and settled down on the pavement across the right of way like a tired elephant. This, of course, was not an accident. It was due to a weakness in the construction of that wheel—a weakness that had from the beginning been destined to block street cars and taxicabs at this particular spot at this particular hour.

Mr Armiston dismounted and walked a block. Here he hailed a second taxicab and soon was spinning north again at a fair speed, albeit the extensive building operations in Fourth Avenue had made the street well-nigh impassable.

The roughness of the pavement merely shook up his digestive apparatus and gave it zest for the fine luncheon he was promising himself the minute he stepped aboard his train. His new chauffeur got lost three times in the maze of traffic about the Grand Central

Station. This, however, was only human, seeing that the railroad company changed the map of 42nd Street every twenty-four hours during the course of the building of its new terminal.

Mr Armiston at length stepped from his taxicab, gave his grip to a porter and paid the driver from a huge roll of bills. This same roll was no sooner transferred back to his pocket than a nimble-fingered pickpocket removed it. This again was not an accident. That pickpocket had been waiting there for the last hour for that roll of bills. It was preordained, inevitable. And Oliver Armiston had just thirty seconds to catch his train by the tail and climb aboard. He smiled contentedly to himself.

It was not until he called for his ticket that he discovered his loss. For a full precious second he gazed at the hand that came away empty from his money pocket, and then:

'I find I left my purse at home,' he said with a grand air he knew how to assume on occasions. 'My name is Mr Oliver Armiston.'

Now Oliver Armiston was a name to conjure with.

'I don't doubt it,' said the ticket agent dryly. 'Mr Andrew Carnegie was here yesterday begging car fare to 125th Street, and Mr John D. Rockefeller quite frequently drops in and leaves his dollar watch in hock. Next!'

And the ticket agent glared at the man blocking the impatient line and told him to move on.

Armiston flushed crimson. He glanced at the clock. For once in his life he was about to experience that awful feeling of missing his train. For once in his life he was about to be robbed of that delicious sensation of hypnotizing the gate-keeper and walking majestically down that train platform that extends northwards under the train shed a considerable part of the distance towards Yonkers. Twenty seconds. Armiston turned round, still holding his ground, and glared concentrated malice at the man next in line. That man was in a hurry. In his hand he held a bundle of bills. For a second, the thief-instinct that is latent in us all suggested itself to Armiston. There within reach of his hand was the money, the precious paltry dollar bills that stood between him and his train. It scared him to discover that he, an upright and honoured citizen, was almost in the act of grabbing them like a common pickpocket.

Then a truly remarkable thing happened. The man thrust his handful of bills at Armiston.

'The only way I can raise this blockade is to bribe you,' he said, returning Armiston's glare. 'Here—take what you want—and give the rest of us a chance.'

With the alacrity of a blind beggar miraculously cured by the sight of much money, Armiston grabbed the handful, extracted what he needed for his ticket, and thrust the rest back into the waiting hand of his unknown benefactor. He caught the gate by a hair. So did his unknown friend. Together they walked down the platform, each matching the other's leisurely pace with his own. They might have been two potentates, so deliberately did they catch this train. Armiston would have liked very much to thank this person, but the other presented so forbidding an exterior that it was hard to find a point of attack. By force of habit Armiston boarded the parlour car, quite forgetting he did not have money for a seat. So did the other. The unknown thrust a bill at the porter. 'Get me two chairs,' he said. 'One is for this gentleman.'

Once inside and settled, Armiston renewed his efforts to thank this strange person. That person took a card from his pocket and handed it to Armiston.

'Don't run away with the foolish idea,' he said tartly, 'that I have done you a service willingly. You were making me miss my train, and I took this means of bribing you to get you out of my way. That, is all, sir. At your leisure you may send me your cheque for the trifle.'

'A most extraordinary person!' said Armiston to himself. 'Let me give you my card,' he said to the other. 'As to the service rendered, you are welcome to your own ideas on that. For my part I am very grateful.'

The unknown took the proffered card and thrust it in his waistcoat pocket without glancing at it. He swung his chair round and opened a magazine, displaying a pair of broad unneighbourly shoulders. This was rather disconcerting to Armiston, who was accustomed to have his card act as an Open Sesame!

'Damn his impudence!' he said to himself. 'He takes me for a mendicant. I'll make copy of him!'

This was the popular author's way of getting even with those who offended his tender sensibilities.

Two things worried Armiston: One was his luncheon—or rather the absence of it; and the other was his neighbour. This neighbour, now that Armiston had a chance to study him, was a young man, well set up. He had a fine bronzed face that was not half so surly as his manner. He was now buried up to his ears in a magazine, oblivious of everything about him, even the dining-car porter, who strode down the aisle and announced the first call to lunch in the dining car.

'I wonder what the fellow is reading,' said Armiston to himself. He peeped over the man's shoulder and was interested at once, for the stranger was reading a copy of a magazine called by the vulgar 'The White Sepulchre'. It was the pride of this magazine that no man on earth could read it without the aid of a dictionary. Yet this person seemed to be enthralled. And what was more to the point, and vastly pleasing to Armiston, the man was at that moment engrossed in one of Armiston's own effusions. It was one of his crime stories that had won him praise and lucre. It concerned the Infallible Godahl.

These stories were pure reason incarnate in the person of a scientific thief. The plot was invariably so logical that it seemed more like the output of some machine than of a human mind. Of course the plots were impossible, because the fiction thief had to be an incredible genius to carry out the details. But nevertheless they were highly entertaining, fascinating and dramatic at one and the same time.

And this individual read the story through without winking an eyelash—as though the mental effort cost him nothing—and then, to Armiston's delight, turned back to the beginning and read it again. The author threw out his chest and shot his cuffs. It was not often that such unconscious tribute fell to his lot. He took the card of his unknown benefactor. It read:

Mr J. Borden Benson

THE TOWERS   NEW YORK CITY

'Humph!' snorted Armiston. 'An aristocrat—and a snob too!'

At this moment the aristocrat turned in his chair and handed the magazine to his companion. All his bad humour was gone.

'Are you familiar,' he asked 'with this man Armiston's work? I mean these scientific thief stories that are running now.'

'Ye-yes. Oh, yes,' sputtered Armiston, hastily putting the other's card away. 'I—in fact, you know—I take them every morning before breakfast.'

In a way this was the truth, for Armiston always began his day's writing before breakfasting.

Mr Benson smiled—a very fine smile at once boyish and sophisticated.

'Rather a heavy diet early in the morning, I should say,' he replied. 'Have you read this last one then?'

'Oh, yes,' said the delighted author.

'What do you think of it?' asked Benson.

The author puckered his lips.

'It is on a par with the others,' he said.

'Yes,' said Benson thoughtfully. 'I should say the same thing. And when we have said that there is nothing left to say. They are truly a remarkable product. Quite unique, you know. And yet,' he said, frowning at Armiston, 'I believe that this man Armiston is to be ranked as the most dangerous man in the world today.'

'Oh, I say—' began Armiston. But he checked himself, chuckling. He was very glad Mr Benson had not looked at his card.

'I mean it,' said the other decidedly. 'And you think so yourself, I fully believe. No thinking man could do otherwise.'

'In just what way? I must confess I have never thought of his work as anything but pure invention.'

It was truly delicious. Armiston would certainly make copy of this person.

'I will grant,' said Benson, 'that there is not a thief in the world today clever enough—brainy enough—to take advantage of the suggestions put forth in these stories. But some day there will arise a man to whom they will be as simple as an ordinary blueprint, and he will profit accordingly. This magazine, by printing these stories, is merely furnishing him with his tools, showing him how to work. And the worst of it is—'

'Just a minute,' said the author. 'Agreeing for the moment that these stories will be the tools of Armiston's hero in real life some day, how about the popular magazines? They print ten such stories to one of these by Armiston.'

'Ah, my friend,' said Benson, 'you forget one thing; the popular magazines deal with real life—the possible, the usual. And in that very thing they protect the public against sharpers, by exposing the methods of those same sharpers. But with Armiston—no. Much as I enjoy him as an intellectual treat, I am afraid—'

He didn't finish his sentence. Instead he fell to shaking his head, as though in amazement at the devilish ingenuity of the author under discussion.

'I am certainly delighted,' thought that author, 'that my disagreeable benefactor did not have the good grace to look at my card. This really is most entertaining.' And then aloud, and treading on thin ice. 'I should be very glad to tell Oliver what you say and see what he has to say about it.'

Benson's face broke into a wreath of wrinkles:

'Do you know him? Well, I declare! That is a privilege. I heartily wish you would tell him.'

'Would you like to meet him? I am under no obligation to you. I can arrange a little dinner for a few of us.'

'No,' said Benson, shaking his head; 'I would rather go on reading him without knowing him. Authors are so disappointing in real life. He may be some puny, anaemic little half-portion, with dirty fingernails and all the rest that goes with genius. No offence to your friend! Besides, I am afraid I might quarrel with him.'

'Last call for lunch in the dinin' cy-yah-aa,' sang the porter. Armiston was looking at his fingernails as the porter passed. They were manicured once a day.

'Come lunch with me,' said Benson heartily. 'I should be pleased to have you as my guest. I apologize for being rude to you at the ticket window, but I did want to catch this train mighty bad.'

Armiston laughed. 'Well, you have paid my car fare,' he said, 'and I won't deny I am hungry enough to eat a hundred-and-ten-pound rail. I will let you buy me a meal, being penniless.'

Benson arose, and as he drew out his handkerchief the card Armiston had given him fluttered into that worthy's lap. Armiston closed his hand over it, chuckling again. Fate had given him the chance of preserving his incognito with this person as long as he wished. It would be a rare treat to get him ranting again about the author Armiston.

But Armiston's host did not rant against his favourite author. In fact he was so enthusiastic over that man's genius that the same qualities which he decried as a danger to society in his opinion only added lustre to the work. Benson asked his guest innumerable questions as to the personal qualities of his ideal, and Armiston shamelessly constructed a truly remarkable person. The other listened entranced.

'No, I don't want to know him,' he said. 'In the first place I haven't the time, and in the second I'd be sure to start a row. And then there is another thing: if he is half the man I take him to be from what you say, he wouldn't stand for people fawning on him and telling him what a wonder he is. That's about what I should be doing, I am afraid.'

'Oh,' said Armiston, 'he isn't as bad as that. He is a—well, a sensible chap, with clean fingernails and all that, you know, and he gets his haircut once every three weeks, the same as the rest of us.'

'I am glad to hear you say so, Mr—er. . . .'

Benson fell to chuckling.

'By gad,' he said, 'here we have been talking with each other for an hour, and I haven't so much as taken a squint at your card to see who you are!'

He searched for the card Armiston had given him.

'Call it Brown,' said Armiston, lying gorgeously and with a feeling of utmost righteousness. 'Martin Brown, single, read-and-write, colour, white, laced shoes and derby hat, as the police say.'

'All right, Mr Brown; glad to know you. We will have some cigars. You have no idea how much you interest me, Mr Brown. How much does Armiston get for his stories?'

'Every word he writes brings him the price of a good cigar. I should say he makes forty thousand a year.'

'Humph! That is better than Godahl, his star creation, could bag as a thief, I imagine, let alone the danger of getting snipped with a pistol ball on a venture.'

Armiston puffed up his chest and shot his cuffs again.

'How does he get his plots?'

Armiston knitted his ponderous brows. 'There's the rub,' he said. 'You can talk about so-and-so much a word until you are deaf, dumb and blind. But, after all, it isn't the number of words or how they are strung together that makes a story. It is the idea. And ideas are scarce.'

'I have an idea that I have always wanted to have Armiston get hold of, just to see what he could do with it. If you will pardon me, to my way of thinking the really important thing isn't the ideas, but how to work out the details.'

'What's your idea?' asked Armiston hastily. He was not averse to appropriating anything he encountered in real life and dressing it up to suit his taste. 'I'll pass it on to Armiston, if you say so.'

'Will you? That's capital. To begin with,' Mr Benson said as he twirled his brandy glass with long, lean, silky fingers—a hand Armiston thought he would not like to have handle him in a rage— 'to begin with, Godahl, this thief, is not an ordinary thief, he is a high-brow. He has made some big hauls. He must be a very rich man now— eh? You see that he is quite real to me. By this time, I should say, Godahl has acquired such a fortune that thieving for mere money is no longer an object. What does he do? Sit down and live on his income? Not much. He is a person of refined tastes with an eye for the aesthetic. He desires art objects, rare porcelains, a gem of rare cut or colour set by Benvenuto Cellini, a Leonardo da Vinci—did Godahl steal the Mona Lisa, by the way? He is the most likely person I can think of—or perhaps a Gutenberg Bible. Treasures, things of exquisite beauty to look at, to enjoy in secret, not to show to other people. That is the natural development of this man Godahl, eh?'

'Splendid!' exclaimed Armiston, his enthusiasm getting the better of him.

'Have you ever heard of Mrs Billy Wentworth?' asked Benson.

'Indeed, I know her well,' said Armiston, his guard down.

'Then you must surely have seen her white ruby?'

'White ruby! I never heard of such a thing. A white ruby?'

'Exactly. That's just the point. Neither have I. But if Godahl heard of a white ruby the chances are he would possess it—especially if it were the only one of its kind in the world.'

'Gad! I do believe he would, from what I know of him.'

'And especially,' went on Benson, 'under the circumstances. You know the Wentworths have been round a good deal. They haven't been over-scrupulous in getting things they wanted. Now Mrs Wentworth—but before I go on with this weird tale I want you to understand me. It is pure fiction—an idea for Armiston and his wonderful Godahl. I am merely suggesting the Wentworths as fictitious characters.'

'I understand,' said Armiston.

'Mrs Wentworth might very well possess this white ruby. Let us say she stole it from some potentate's household in the Straits Settlements. She gained admittance by means of the official position of her husband. They can't accuse her of theft. All they can do is to steal the gem back from her. It is a sacred stone of course. They always are in fiction stories. And the usual tribe of jugglers, rug-peddlers, and so on—all disguised, you understand—have followed her to America, seeking a chance, not on her life, not to commit violence of any kind, but to steal that stone.

'She can't wear it,' went on Benson. 'All she can do is to hide it away in some safe place. What is a safe place? Not a bank. Godahl could crack a bank with his little finger. So might those East Indian fellows, labouring under the call of religion. Not in a safe. That would be folly.'

'How then?' put in Armiston eagerly.

'Ah, there you are! That's for Godahl to find out. He knows, let us say, that these foreigners in one way or another have turned Mrs Wentworth's apartments upside down. They haven't found anything. He knows that she keeps that white ruby in that house. Where is it? Ask Godahl! Do you see the point? Has Godahl ever cracked a nut like that? No. Here he must be the cleverest detective in the world and the cleverest thief at the same time. Before he can begin thieving he must make his blue-prints.

'When I read Armiston,' continued Benson, 'that is the kind of problem that springs up in my mind. I am always trying to think of some knot this wonderful thief would have to employ his best powers to unravel. I think of some weird situation like this one. I say to myself: "Good! I will write that. I will be as famous as Armiston. I will create another Godahl." But,' he said with a wave of his hands, 'what is the result? I tie the knot, but I can't untie it. The trouble is, I am not a Godahl. And this man Armiston, as I read him, is Godahl.

He must be, or else Godahl could not be made to do the wonderful things he does. Hello! New Haven already? Mighty sorry to have you go, old chap. Great pleasure. When you get to town let me know. Maybe I will consent to meet Armiston.'

Armiston's first care on returning to New York was to remember the providential loan by which he had been able to keep his record clean of never missing a train. He counted out the sum of bills, wrote a polite note, signed it 'Martin Brown', and despatched it by messenger to J. Borden Benson, The Towers. The Towers, the address Mr Borden's card bore, is an ultra-fashionable apartment hotel in Lower Fifth Avenue. It maintains all the pomp and solemnity of an English ducal castle. Armiston remembered having on a remote occasion taken dinner there with a friend and the recollection always gave him a chill. It was like dining among ghosts of kings, so grand and funereal was the air that pervaded everything.

Armiston, who could not forbear curiosity as to his queer benefactor, took occasion to look him up in the Blue Book and the Club Directory, and found that J. Borden Benson was quite some personage, several lines being devoted to him. This was extremely pleasing. Armiston had been thinking of that white-ruby yarn. It appealed to his sense of the dramatic. He would work it up in his best style, and on publication have a fine laugh on Benson by sending him an autographed copy and thus waking that gentleman up to the fact that it really had been the great Armiston in person he had befriended and entertained. What a joke it would be on Benson, thought the author; not without an intermixture of personal vanity, for even a genius such as he was not blind to flattery properly applied, and Benson unknowingly had laid it on thick.

'And, by gad,' thought the author, 'I will use the Wentworths as the main characters, as the victims of Godahl! They are just the people to fit into such a romance. Benson put money in my pocket, though he didn't suspect it. Lucky he didn't know what shifts we popular authors are put to for plots.'

Suiting the action to the word, Armiston and his wife accepted the next invitation they received from the Wentworths.

Mrs Wentworth, be it understood, was a lion hunter. She was forever trying to gather about her such celebrities as Armiston the author,

Brackens the painter, Johanssen the explorer, and others. Armiston had always withstood her wiles. He always had some excuse to keep him away from her gorgeous table, where she exhibited her lions to her simpering friends.

There were many undesirables sitting at the table, idle-rich youths, girls of the fast hunting set, and so on, and they all gravely shook the great author by the hand and told him what a wonderful man he was. As for Mrs Wentworth, she was too highly elated at her success in roping him for sane speech, and she fluttered about him like a hysterical bridesmaid. But, Armiston noted with relief, one of his pals was there —Johanssen. Over cigars and cognac he managed to buttonhole the explorer.

'Johanssen,' he said, 'you have been everywhere.'

'You are mistaken there,' said Johanssen. 'I have never before tonight been north of 59th Street in New York.'

'Yes, but you have been in Java and Ceylon and the Settlements. Tell me, have you ever heard of such a thing as a white ruby?'

The explorer narrowed his eyes to a slit and looked queerly at his questioner. 'That's a queer question,' he said in a low voice, 'to ask in this house.'

Armiston felt his pulse quicken. 'Why?' he asked, assuming an air of surprised innocence.

'If you don't know,' said the explorer shortly, 'I certainly will not enlighten you.'

'All right; as you please. But you haven't answered my question yet. Have you ever heard of a white ruby?'

'I don't mind telling you that I have heard of such a thing—that is, I have heard there is a ruby in existence that is called the white ruby. It isn't really white, you know; it has a purplish tinge. But the old heathen who rightly owns it likes to call it white, just as he likes to call his blue and grey elephants white.'

'Who owns it?' asked Armiston, trying his best to make his voice sound natural. To find in this manner that there was some parallel for the mystical white ruby of which Benson had told him appealed strongly to his superdeveloped dramatic sense. He was now as keen on the scent as a hound.

Johanssen took to drumming on the tablecloth. He smiled to

himself and his eyes glowed. Then he turned and looked sharply at his questioner.

'I suppose,' he said, 'that all things are grist to a man of your trade. If you are thinking of building a story round a white ruby I can think of nothing more fascinating. But, Armiston,' he said, suddenly altering his tone and almost whispering, 'if you are on the track of *the* white ruby let me advise you now to call off your dogs and keep your throat whole. I think I am a brave man. I have shot tigers at ten paces —held my fire purposely to see how charmed a life I really did bear. I have been charged by mad rhinos and by wounded buffaloes, have walked across a clearing where the air was being punctured with bullets as thick as holes in a mosquito screen. But,' he said, laying his hand on Armiston's arm, 'I have never had the nerve to hunt the white ruby.'

'Capital!' exclaimed the author.

'Capital, yes, for a man who earns his bread and gets his excitement by sitting at a typewriter and dreaming about these things. But take my word for it, it isn't capital for a man who gets his excitement by doing this thing. Hands off, my friend!'

'It really does exist then?'

Johanssen puckered his lips. 'So they say,' he said.

'What's it worth?'

'Worth? What do you mean by worth? Dollars and cents? What is your child worth to you. A million, a billion—how much? Tell me. No, you can't. Well, that's just what the miserable stone is worth to the man who rightfully owns it. Now let's quit talking nonsense. There's Billy Wentworth shooing the men into the drawing-room. I suppose we shall be entertained this evening by some of the hundred-dollar-a-minute songbirds, as usual. It's amazing what these people will spend for mere vulgar display when there are hundreds of families starving within a mile of this spot!'

Two famous singers sang that night. Armiston did not have much opportunity to look over the house. He was now fully determined to lay the scene of his story in this very house. At leavetaking the sugar-sweet Mrs Billy Wentworth drew Armiston aside and said:

'It's rather hard on you to ask you to sit through an evening with these people. I will make amends by asking you to come to me some night when we can be by ourselves. Are you interested in rare curios? Yes, we all are. I have some really wonderful things I want you to see. Let us make it next Tuesday, with a little informal dinner, just for ourselves.'

Armiston then and there made the lion hunter radiantly happy by accepting her invitation to sit at her board as a family friend instead of as a lion.

As he put his wife into their automobile he turned and looked at the house. It stood opposite Central Park. It was a copy of some French château in grey sandstone, with a barbican, and overhanging towers, and all the rest of it. The windows of the street floor peeped out through deep embrasures and were heavily guarded with iron latticework.

'Godahl will have the very devil of a time breaking in there,' he chuckled to himself. Late that night his wife awakened him to find out why he was tossing about so.

'That white ruby has got on my nerves,' he said cryptically, and she, thinking he was dreaming, persuaded him to try to sleep again.

Great authors must really live in the flesh, at times at least, the lives of their great characters. Otherwise these great characters would not be so real as they are. Here was Armiston, who had created a superman in the person of Godahl the thief. For ten years he had written nothing else. He had laid the life of Godahl out in squares, thought for him, dreamed about him, set him to new tasks, gone through all sorts of queer adventures with him. And this same Godahl had amply repaid him. He had raised the author from the ranks of struggling amateurs to a position among the most highly paid fiction writers in the United States. He had brought him ease and luxury. Armiston did not need the money any more. The serial rights telling of the exploits of this Godahl had paid him handsomely. The book of Godahl's adventures had paid him even better, and had furnished him yearly with a never-failing income, like government bonds, but at a much higher rate of interest. Even though the crimes this Godahl had committed were all on paper, nevertheless Godahl was a living being to his creator. More—he was Armiston, and Armiston was Godahl.

It was not surprising, then, that when Tuesday came Armiston awaited the hour with feverish impatience. Here, as his strange friend had so thoughtlessly and casually told him, was an opportunity for the great Godahl to outdo even himself. Here was an opportunity for Godahl to be the greatest detective in the world, in the first place, before he could carry out one of his sensational thefts.

So it was Godahl, not Armiston, who helped his wife out of their automobile that evening and mounted the splendid steps of the Wentworth mansion. He cast his eyes aloft; took in every inch of the facade.

'No,' he said, 'Godahl cannot break in from the street. I must have a look at the back of the house.'

He cast his eyes on the ironwork that guarded the deep windows giving on the street.

It was not iron after all, but chilled steel sunk into armoured concrete. The outposts of this house were as safely guarded as the vault of the United States Mint.

'It's got to be from the inside,' he said, making mental note of this fact.

The butler was stone-deaf. This was rather singular. Why should a family of the standing of the Wentworths employ a man as head of their city establishment who was stone-deaf? Armiston looked at the man with curiosity. He was still in middle age. Surely, then, he was not retained because of years of service. No, there was something more than charity behind this. He addressed a casual word to the man as he handed him his hat and cane. His back was turned and the man did not reply. Armiston turned and repeated the sentence in the same tone. The man watched his lips in the bright light of the hall.

'A lip-reader, and a dandy,' thought Armiston, for the butler seemed to catch every word he said.

'Fact Number 2!' said the creator of Godahl the thief.

He felt no compunction at thus noting the most intimate details of the Wentworth establishment. An accident had put him on the track of a rare good story, and it was all copy. Besides, he told himself, when he came to write the story he would disguise it in such a way that no one reading it would know it was about the Wentworths. If their establishment happened to possess the requisite setting for a great story, surely there was no reason why he should not take advantage of that fact.

The great thief—he made no bones of the fact to himself that he had come here to help Godahl—accepted the flattering greeting of his hostess with the grand air that so well fitted him. Armiston was tall and thin, with slender fingers and a touch of grey in his wavy hair, for all his youthful years, and he knew how to wear clothes. Mrs Wentworth was proud of him as a social ornament, even aside from his glittering fame as an author. And Mrs Armiston was well born, so there was no jar in their being received in the best house of the town.

The dinner was truly delightful. Here Armiston saw, or thought he saw, one of the reasons for the deaf butler. The hostess had him so trained that she was able to catch her servant's eye and instruct him in this or that trifle by merely moving her lips. It was almost uncanny, thought the author, this silent conversation the deaf man and his mistress were able to carry on unnoticed by the others.

'By gad, it's wonderful! Godahl, my friend, underscore that note of yours referring to the deaf butler. Don't miss it. It will take a trick.'

Armiston gave his undivided attention to his hostess as soon as he found Wentworth entertaining Mrs Armiston and thus properly dividing the party. He persuaded her to talk by a cleverly pointed question here and there; and as she talked, he studied her.

'We are going to rob you of your precious white ruby, my friend,' he thought humorously to himself; 'and while we are laying our wires there is nothing about you too small to be worthy of our attention.'

Did she really possess the white ruby? Did this man Benson know anything about the white ruby? And what was the meaning of the strange actions of his friend Johanssen when approached on the subject in this house? His hostess came to have a wonderful fascination for him. He pictured this beautiful creature so avid in her lust for rare gems that she actually did penetrate the establishment of some heathen potentate in the Straits simply for the purpose of stealing the mystic stone. 'Have you ever, by any chance, been in the Straits'? he asked indifferently.

'Wait,' Mrs Wentworth said with a laugh as she touched his hand lightly; 'I have some curios from the Straits, and I will venture to say you have never seen their like.'

Half an hour later they were all seated over coffee and cigarettes in

Mrs Wentworth's boudoir. It was indeed a strange place. There was scarcely a single corner of the world that had not contributed something to its furnishing. Carvings of teak and ivory; hangings of sweet-scented vegetable fibres; lamps of jade; queer little gods, all sitting like Buddha with their legs drawn up under them, carved out of jade or sardonyx; scarfs of baroque pearls; Darjeeling turquoises—Armiston had never before seen such a collection. And each item had its story. He began to look on this frail little woman with different eyes. She had been and seen and done, and the tale of her life, what she had actually lived, outshone even that of the glittering rascal Godahl, who was standing beside him now and directing his ceaseless questions. 'Have you any rubies?' he asked.

Mrs Wentworth bent before a safe in the wall. With swift fingers she whirled the combination. The keen eyes of Armiston followed the bright knob like a cat.

'Fact Number 3!' said the Godahl in him as he mentally made note of the numbers. 'Five—eight—seven—four—six. That's the combination.'

Mrs Wentworth showed him six pigeon-blood rubies.

'This one is pale,' he said carelessly, holding a particularly large stone up to the light. 'Is it true that occasionally they are found white?'

His hostess looked at him before answering. He was intent on a deep-red stone he held in the palm of his hand. It seemed a thousand miles deep.

'What a fantastic idea!' she said. She glanced at her husband, who had reached out and taken her hand in a naturally affectionate manner.

'Fact Number 4!' mentally noted Armiston. 'Are not you in mortal fear of robbery with all this wealth?'

Mrs Wentworth laughed lightly.

'That is why we live in a fortress,' she said.

'Have you never, then, been visited by thieves?' asked the author boldly.

'Never!' she said.

'A lie,' thought Armiston. 'Fact Number 5! We are getting on swimmingly.'

'I do not believe that even your Godahl the Infallible could get in here,' Mrs Wentworth said. 'Not even the servants enter this room.

He began to look on this frail little woman with different eyes.

That door is not locked with a key; yet it locks. I am not much of a housekeeper,' she said lazily, 'but such housekeeping as is done in this room is all done by these poor little hands of mine.'

'No! Most amazing! May I look at the door?'

'Yes, Mr Godahl,' said the woman, who had lived more lives than Godahl himself.

Armiston examined the door, this strange device that locked without a key, apparently indeed without a lock, and came away disappointed.

'Well, Mr Godahl?' his hostess said tauntingly. He shook his head in perplexity.

'Most ingenious,' he said; and then suddenly: 'Yet I will venture that if I turned Godahl loose on this problem he would solve it.'

'What fun!' she cried, clapping her hands.

'You challenge him?' asked Armiston.

'What nonsense is this!' cried Wentworth, coming forward.

'No nonsense at all,' said Mrs Wentworth. 'Mr Armiston has just said that his Godahl could rob me. Let him try. If he can—if mortal man can gain the secrets of ingress and egress of this room—I want to know it. I don't believe mortal man can enter this room.'

Armiston noted a strange glitter in her eyes.

'Gad! She was born to the part! What a woman!' he thought. And then aloud:

'I will set him to work. I will lay the scene of his exploit in—say—Hungary, where this room might very well exist in some feudal castle. How many people have entered this room since it was made the storehouse of all this wealth?'

'Not six besides yourself,' replied Mrs Wentworth.

'Then no one can recognize it if I describe it in a story—in fact, I will change the material details. We will say that it is not jewels Godahl is seeking. We will say that it is a—'

Mrs Wentworth's hand touched his own. The tips of her fingers were cold. 'A white ruby,' she said.

'Gad! What a thoroughbred!' he exclaimed to himself—or to Godahl. And then aloud: 'Capital! I will send you a copy of the story autographed.'

The next day he called at The Towers and sent up his card to Mr

Benson's apartments. Surely a man of Benson's standing could be trusted with such a secret. In fact it was evidently not a secret to Benson, who in all probability was one of the six Mrs Wentworth said had entered that room. Armiston wanted to talk the matter over with Benson. He had given up his idea of having fun with him by sending him a marked copy of the magazine containing his tale. His story had taken complete possession of him, as always had been the case when he was at work dispatching Godahl on his adventures.

'If that ruby really exists,' Armiston said, 'I don't know whether I shall write the story or steal the ruby for myself. Benson is right. Godahl should not steal any more for mere money. He is after rare, unique things now. And I am Godahl. I feel the same way myself.'

A valet appeared, attired in a gorgeous livery. Armiston wondered why any self-respecting American would consent to don such raiment, even though it was the livery of the great Benson family.

'Mr Armiston, sir,' said the valet, looking at the author's card he held in his hand. 'Mr Benson sailed for Europe yesterday morning. He is spending the summer in Norway. I am to follow on the next steamer. Is there any message I can take to him, sir? I have heard him speak of you, sir.'

Armiston took the card and wrote on it in pencil:

> *I called to apologize. I am Martin Brown. The chance was*
> *too good to miss. You will pardon me, won't you?*

For the next two weeks Armiston gave himself over to his dissipation, which was accompanying Godahl on this adventure. It was a formidable task. The secret room he placed in a Hungarian castle, as he had promised. A beautiful countess was his heroine. She had seen the world, mostly in man's attire, and her escapades had furnished vivacious reading for two continents. No one could possibly connect her with Mrs Billy Wentworth. So far it was easy. But how was Godahl to get into this wonderful room where the countess had hidden this wonderful rare white ruby? The room was lined with chilled steel. Even the door—this he had noted when he was examining that peculiar portal—was lined with layers of steel. It could withstand any known tool.

However, Armiston was Armiston, and Godahl was Godahl. He got into that room. He got the white ruby!

The manuscript went to the printers, and the publishers said that Armiston had never done anything like it since he started Godahl on his astonishing career.

He banked the cheque for his tale, and as he did so he said: 'Gad I would a hundred times rather possess that white ruby. Confound the thing! I feel as if I had not heard the last of it.'

Armiston and his wife went to Maine for the summer without leaving their address. Along in the early fall he received by registered mail, forwarded by his trusted servant at the town house, a package containing the envelope he had addressed to J. Borden Benson, The Towers. Furthermore it contained the dollar bill he had dispatched to that individual, together with his note which he had signed 'Martin Brown'. And across the note, in the most insulting manner, was written in coarse, greasy blue-pencil lines:

Damnable impertinence. I'll cane you the first time I see you.

And no more. That was enough of course—quite sufficient.

In the same mail came a note from Armiston's publishers, saying that his story 'The White Ruby' was scheduled for publication in the October number, out 25 September. This cheered him up. He was anxious to see it in print. Late in September they started back to town.

'Aha!' he said as he sat reading his paper in the parlour car. He had caught this train by the veriest tip of its tail and upset the running schedule in the act. 'Aha! I see my genial friend, J. Borden Benson, is in town, contrary to custom at this time of year. Life must be a great bore to that snob.'

A few days after arriving in town he received a package of advance copies of the magazine containing his story, and he read the tale of the 'White Ruby' as if he had never seen it before. On the cover of one copy, which he was to dispatch to his grumpy benefactor, J. Borden Benson, he wrote:

Charmed to be caned. Call any time. See contents.
Oliver Armiston.

On the other he wrote:

Dear Mrs Wentworth,
  See how simple it is to pierce your fancied security!

He dispatched these two magazines with a feeling of glee. No sooner had he done so, however, than he learned that the Wentworths had not yet returned from Newport. The magazine would be forwarded to them no doubt. The Wentworths' absence made the tale all the better, for in his story Armiston had insisted on Godahl's breaking into the castle and solving the mystery of the keyless door during the season when the château was closed and strung with a perfect network of burglar alarms connecting with the *Gendarmerie* in the nearby village.

That was the twenty-fifth day of September. The magazine was put on sale that morning.

On the twenty-sixth day of September Armiston bought a late edition of an afternoon paper from a leather-lunged boy who was hawking 'Extra'! in the street. Across the first page the headlines met his eye:

ROBBERY AND MURDER IN THE WENTWORTH MANSION!

Private watchmen, summoned by burglar alarm at ten o'clock this morning, find servant with skull crushed on floor of mysterious steel-doored room. Murdered man's pockets filled with rare jewels. Police believe he was murdered by a confederate who escaped.

THE WENTWORTH BUTLER, STONE-DEAF, HAD JUST
RETURNED FROM NEWPORT TO OPEN HOUSE
AT TIME OF MURDER.

★   ★   ★   ★

It was ten o'clock that night when an automobile drew up at Armiston's door, and a tall man with a square jaw, square shoes and a square moustache alighted. This was Deputy Police Commissioner

Byrnes, a professional detective whom the new administration had drafted into the city's service from the government secret service.

Byrnes was admitted and as he advanced to the middle of the drawing-room, without so much as a nod to the ghostlike Armiston who stood shivering before him, he drew a package of papers from his pocket.

'I presume you have seen all the evening papers,' he said, spitting his words through his half-closed teeth with so much show of personal malice that Armiston—never a brave man in spite of his Godahl—cowered before him.

Armiston shook his head dumbly at first, but at length he managed to say: 'Not all; no.'

The Deputy Commissioner with much deliberation drew out the latest extra and handed it to Armiston without a word.

It was the *Evening News*. The first page was divided down its entire length by a black line. On one side, and occupying four columns, was a word-for-word reprint of Armiston's story, 'The White Ruby'.

On the other, the facts in deadly parallel, was a graphic account of the robbery and murder at the home of Billy Wentworth. The parallel was glaring in the intensity of its dumb accusation. On the one side was the theoretical Godahl, working his masterly way of crime, step by step; and on the other was the plagiarism of Armiston's story, following the intricacies of the master mind with copy-book accuracy.

The editor, who must have been a genius in his way, did not accuse. He simply placed the fiction and the fact side by side and let the reader judge for himself. It was masterly. If, as the law says, the mind that conceives, the intelligence that directs, a crime is more guilty than the very hand that acts, then Armiston here was both thief and murderer. Thief, because the white ruby had actually been stolen. Mrs Billy Wentworth, rushed to the city by special train, attended by doctors and nurses, now confirmed the story of the theft of the ruby. Murderer, because in the story Godahl had for once in his career stooped to murder as the means, and had triumphed over the dead body of his confederate, scorning, in his joy at possessing the white ruby, the paltry diamonds, pearls and red rubies with which his confederate had crammed his pockets.

Armiston seized the police official by his lapels.

'The butler!' he screamed. 'The butler! Yes, the butler. Quick, or he will have flown.'

Byrnes gently disengaged the hands that had grasped him.

'Too late,' he said. 'He has already flown. Sit down and quiet your nerves. We need your help. You are the only man in the world who can help us now.'

When Armiston was himself again he told the whole tale, beginning with his strange meeting with J. Borden Benson on the train, and ending with his accepting Mrs Wentworth's challenge to have Godahl break into the room and steal the white ruby. Byrnes nodded over the last part. He had already heard that from Mrs Wentworth, and there was the autographed copy of the magazine to show for it.

'You say that J. Borden Benson told you of this white ruby in the first place.'

Armiston again told, in great detail, the circumstances, all the humour now turned into grim tragedy.

'That is strange,' said the ex-secret-service chief. 'Did you leave your purse at home or was your pocket picked?'

'I thought at first that I had absent-mindedly left it at home. Then I remembered having paid the chauffeur out of the roll of bills, so my pocket must have been picked.'

'What kind of a looking man was this Benson?'

'You must know him,' said Armiston.

'Yes, I know him; but I want to know what he looked like to you. I want to find out how he happened to be so handy when you were in need of money.'

Armiston described the man minutely.

The Deputy sprang to his feet. 'Come with me,' he said; and they hurried into the automobile and soon drew up in front of The Towers.

Five minutes later they were ushered into the magnificent apartment of J. Borden Benson. That worthy was in his bath preparing to retire for the night.

'I don't catch the name,' Armiston and the Deputy heard him cry through the bathroom door to his valet.

'Mr Oliver Armiston, sir.'

'Ah, he has come for his caning, I expect. I'll be there directly.'

He did not wait to complete his toilet, so eager was he to see the author. He strode out in a brilliant bathrobe and in one hand he carried an alpenstock. His eyes glowed in anger. But the sight of Byrnes surprised as well as halted him.

'Do you mean to say this is J. Borden Benson?' cried Armiston to Byrnes, rising to his feet and pointing at the man.

'The same,' said the Deputy; 'I swear it. I know him well! I take it he is not the gentleman who paid your car fare to New Haven.'

'Not by a hundred pounds!' exclaimed Armiston as he surveyed the huge bulk of the elephantine clubman.

The forced realization that the stranger he had hitherto regarded as a benefactor was not J. Borden Benson at all, but someone who had merely assumed that worthy's name while he was playing the conceited author as an easy dupe, did more to quiet Armiston's nerves than all the sedatives his doctor had given him. It was a badly dashed popular author who sat down with the Deputy Commissioner in his library an hour later. He would gladly have consigned Godahl to the bottom of the sea; but it was too late. Godahl had taken the trick.

'How do you figure it?' Armiston asked, turning to the Deputy.

'The beginning is simple enough. It is the end that bothers me,' said the official. 'Your bogus J. Borden Benson is, of course, the brains of the whole combination. Your infernal Godahl has told us just exactly how this crime was committed. Now your infernal Godahl must bring the guilty parties to justice.'

It was plain to be seen that the police official hated Godahl worse than poison, and feared him too.

'Why not look in the Rogues' Gallery for this man who befriended me on the train?'

The chief laughed.

'For the love of Heaven, Armiston, do you, who pretend to know all about scientific thievery, think for a moment that the man who took your measure so easily is of the class of crooks who get their pictures in the Rogues' Gallery? Talk sense!'

'I can't believe you when you say he picked my pocket.'

'I don't care whether you believe me or not; he did, or one of his pals did. It all amounts to the same thing, don't you see? First, he wanted to get acquainted with you. Now the best way to get into your good graces was to put you unsuspectingly under obligation to him.

So he robs you of your money. From what I have seen of you in the last few hours it must have been like taking candy from a child. Then he gets next to you in line. He pretends that you are merely some troublesome toad in his path. He gives you money for your ticket, to get you out of his way so he won't miss his train. His train! Of course his train is your train. He puts you in a position where you have to make advances to him. And then, grinning to himself all the time at your conceit and gullibility, he plays you through your pride, your Godahl. Think of the creator of the great Godahl falling for a trick like that!'

Byrnes's last words were the acme of biting sarcasm.

'You admit yourself that he is too clever for you to put your hands on.'

'And then,' went on Byrnes, not heeding the interruption, 'he invites you to lunch and tells you what he wants you to do for him. And you follow his lead like a sheep at the tail of the bellwether! Great Scott, Armiston! I would give a year's salary for one hour's conversation with that man.'

Armiston was beginning to see the part this queer character had played; but he was in a semi-hysterical state, and, like a woman in such a position, he wanted a calm mind to tell him the whole thing in words of one syllable, to verify his own dread.

'What do you mean?' he asked. 'I don't quite follow. You say he tells me what he wants me to do.'

Byrnes shrugged his shoulders in disgust; then, as if resigned to the task before him, he began his explanation.

'Here, man, I will draw a diagram for you. This gentleman friend of yours—we will call him John Smith for convenience—wants to get possession of this white ruby. He knows that it is in the keeping of Mrs Billy Wentworth. He knows you know Mrs Wentworth and have access to her house. He knows that she stole this bauble and is frightened to death all the time. Now John Smith is a pretty clever chap. He handled the great Armiston like hot putty. He had exhausted his resources. He is baffled and needs help. What does he do? He reads the stories about the great Godahl. Confidentially, Mr Armiston, I will tell you that I think your great Godahl is mush. But that is neither here nor there. If you can sell him as a gold brick, all right. But Mr John

Smith is struck by the wonderful ingenuity of this Godahl. He says;
"Ha! I will get Godahl to tell me how to get this gem!"

'So he gets hold of yourself, sir, and persuades you that you are
playing a joke on him by getting him to rant and rave about the great
Godahl. Then—and here the villain enters—he says: "Here is a thing
the great Godahl cannot do. I dare him to do it." He tells you about
the gem, whose very existence is quite fantastic enough to excite
the imagination of the wonderful Armiston. And by clever suggestion
he persuades you to play the plot at the home of Mrs Wentworth. And
all the time you are chuckling to yourself, thinking what a rare joke
you are going to have on J. Borden Benson when you send him an
autographed copy and show him that he was talking to the distinguished
genius all the time and didn't know it. That's the whole story, sir. Now
wake up!'

Byrnes sat back in his chair and regarded Armiston with the smile
a pedagogue bestows on a refractory boy whom he has just flogged
soundly.

'I will explain further,' he continued. 'You haven't visited the house
yet. You can't. Mrs Wentworth, for all she is in bed with four dozen
hot-water bottles, would tear you limb from limb if you went there.
And don't you think for a minute she isn't able to. That woman is
a vixen.'

Armiston nodded gloomily. The very thought of her now sent him
into a cold sweat.

'Mr Godahl, the obliging,' continued the Deputy, 'notes one thing
to begin with: the house cannot be entered from the outside. So it must
be an inside job. How can this be accomplished? Well, there is the deaf
butler. Why is he deaf? Godahl ponders. Ha! He has it! The
Wentworths are so dependent on servants that they must have them
round them at all times. This butler is the one who is constantly about
them. They are worried to death by their possession of this white ruby.
Their house has been raided from the inside a dozen times. Nothing is
taken, mind you. They suspect their servants. This thing haunts them,
but the woman will not give up this foolish bauble. So she has as her major
domo a man who cannot understand a work in any language unless
he is looking at the speaker and is in a bright light. He can only
understand the lips. Handy, isn't it? In a dull light or with their backs

287

turned they can talk about anything they want to. This is a jewel of a butler.

'But,' added Byrnes, 'one day a man calls. He is a lawyer. He tells the butler he is heir to a fortune—fifty thousand dollars. He must go to Ireland to claim it. Your friend on the train—he is the man of course—sends your butler to Ireland. So this precious butler is lost. They must have another. Only a deaf one will do. And they find just the man they want—quite accidentally, you understand. Of course it is Godahl, with forged letters saying he has been in service in great houses. Presto! The great Godahl himself is now the butler. It is simple enough to play deaf. You say this is fiction. Let me tell you this: six weeks ago the Wentworths actually changed butlers. That hasn't come out in the papers yet.'

Armiston, who had listened to the Deputy's review of his story listlessly, now sat up with a start. He suddenly exclaimed gleefully:

'But my story didn't come out till two days ago!'

'Ah, yes; but you forget that it has been in the hands of your publishers for three months. A man who was clever enough to dupe the great Armiston wouldn't shirk the task of getting hold of a proof of that story.'

Armiston sank deeper into his chair.

'Once Godahl got inside the house the rest was simple. He corrupted one of the servants. He opened the steel-lined door with the flame of an oxyacetylene blast. As you say in your story that flame cuts steel like wax; he didn't have to bother about the lock. He simply cut the door down. Then he put his confederate in a good humour by telling him to fill his pockets with the diamonds and other junk in the safe, which he obligingly opens. One thing bothers me, Armiston. How did you find out about that infernal contraption that killed the confederate?'

Armiston buried his face in his hands. Byrnes rudely shook him.

'Come,' he said; 'you murdered that man, though you are innocent. Tell me how.'

'Is this the third degree?' said Armiston.

'It looks like it,' said the Deputy grimly as he gnawed at his stubby moustache. Armiston drew a long breath, like one who realizes how hopeless is his situation. He began to speak in a low tone.

All the while the Deputy glared at Godahl's inventor with his accusing eye.

'When I was sitting in the treasure room with the Wentworths and my wife, playing auction bridge, I dismissed the puzzle of the door as easily solved by means of the brazing flame. The problem was not to get into the house, or into this room, but to find the ruby. It was not in the safe.'

'No, of course not. I suppose your friend on the train was kind enough to tell you that. He had probably looked there himself.'

'Gad! He did tell me that, come to think of it. Well, I studied that room. I was sure the white ruby, if it really existed, was within ten feet of me. I examined the floor, the ceiling, the walls. No result. But,' he said, shivering as if in a draught of cold air, 'there was a chest in that room made of Lombardy oak.' The harassed author buried his face in his hands. 'Oh, this is terrible!' he moaned.

'Go on,' said the Deputy in his colourless voice.

'I can't. I tell it all in the story, Heaven help me!'

'I know you tell it all in the story,' came the rasping voice of Byrnes; 'but I want you to tell it to me. I want to hear it from your own lips—as Armiston; you understand, whose devilry has just killed a man; not as your damnable Godahl.'

'The chest was not solid oak,' went on Armiston. 'It was solid steel covered with oak to disguise it.'

'How did you know that?'

'I had seen it before.'

'Where?'

'In Italy fifteen years ago, in a decayed castle, back through the Soldini Pass from Lugano. It was the possession of an old nobleman, a friend of a friend of mine.'

'Humph!' grunted the Deputy. And then: 'Well, how did you know it was the same one?'

'By the inscription carved on the front. It was—but I have told all this in print already. Why need I go over it all again.'

'I want to hear it again from your own lips. Maybe there are some points you did not tell in print. Go on!'

'The inscription was "*Sanctus Dominus*".'

The Deputy smiled grimly.

'Very fitting, I should say. Praise the Lord with the most diabolical engine of destruction I have ever seen.'

'And then,' said Armiston, 'there was the owner's name—"Arno Petronii". Queer name that.'

'Yes,' said the Deputy dryly. 'How did you hit on this as the receptacle for the white ruby?'

'If it were the same one I saw in Lugano—and I felt sure it was—it was certain death to attempt to open it—that is, for one who did not know how. Such machines were common enough in the Middle Ages. There was an obvious way to open it. It was meant to be obvious. To open it that way was inevitable death. It released tremendous springs that crushed anything within a radius of five feet. You saw that?'

'I did,' said the Deputy, and he shuddered as he spoke. Then, bringing his fierce face within an inch of the cowering Armiston, he said:

'You knew the secret spring by which that safe could be opened as simply as a shoebox, eh?'

Armiston nodded his head.

'But Godahl did not,' he said. 'Having recognized this terrible chest,' went on the author, 'I guessed it must be the hiding place of the jewel—for two reasons: in the first place Mrs Wentworth had avoided showing it to us. She passed it by as a mere bit of curious furniture. Second, it was too big to go through the door or any one of the windows. They must have gone to the trouble of taking down the wall to get that thing in there. Something of a task, too, considering it weighs about two tons.'

'You didn't bring out that point in your story.'

'Didn't I? I fully intended to.'

'Maybe,' said the Deputy, watching his man sharply, 'it so impressed your friend who paid your car fare to New Haven that he clipped it out of the manuscript when he borrowed it.'

'There is no humour in this affair, sir, if you will pardon me,' said Armiston.

'That is quite true. Go ahead.'

'The rest you know, Godahl, in my story—the thief in real life—had to sacrifice a life to open that chest. So he corrupted a small kitchen servant, filling his pockets with these other jewels, and told him to touch the spring.'

'You murdered that man in cold blood,' said the Deputy, rising and pacing the floor. 'The poor deluded devil, from the looks of what's left of him, never let out a whimper, never knew what hit him. Here, take some more of this brandy. Your nerves are in a bad way.'

'What I can't make out is this,' said Armiston after a time. 'There was a million dollars' worth of stuff in that room that could have been put into a quart measure. Why did not this thief, who was willing to go to all the trouble to get the white ruby, take some of the jewels? Nothing is missing besides the white ruby, as I understand it. Is there?'

'No,' said the Deputy. 'Not a thing. Here comes a messenger boy.'

'For Mr Armiston? Yes,' he said to the entering maid. The boy handed him a package for which the Deputy signed.

'This is for you,' he said, turning to Armiston as he closed the door. 'Open it.'

When the package was opened the first object to greet their eyes was a roll of bills.

'This grows interesting,' said Byrnes. He counted the money. 'Thirty-nine dollars. Your friend evidently is returning the money he stole from you at the station. What does he have to say for himself? I see there is a note?'

He reached over and took the paper out of Armiston's hands. It was ordinary bond stationery, with no identifying marks of any consequence. The note was written in bronze ink, in a careful copperplate hand, very small and precise. It read:

Most Excellency Sir:
Herewith, most honoured dollars I am dispatching complete.
Regretful extremely of sad blood being not to be prevented.
Accept trifle from true friend.

That was all.

'There's a jeweller's box,' said Byrnes. 'Open it.'

Inside the box was a lozenge-shaped diamond about the size of a little fingernail. It hung from a tiny bar of silver, highly polished and devoid of ornament. On the back under the clasp-pin were several microscopic characters.

There were several obvious clues to be followed—the messenger boy, the lawyers who induced the deaf butler to go to Ireland on what later proved to be a wild-goose chase, the employment agency through which the new butler had been secured, and so on. But all of these avenues proved too respectable to yield results. Deputy Byrnes had early arrived at his own conclusions, by virtue of the knowledge he had gained as government agent, yet to appease the popular indignation he kept up a desultory search for the criminal.

It was natural that Armiston should think of his friend Johanssen at this juncture. Johanssen possessed that wonderful Oriental capacity of aloofness which we Westerners are so ready to term indifference or lack of curiosity.

'No, I thank you,' said Johanssen. 'I'd rather not mix in.'

The pleadings of the author were in vain. His words fell on deaf ears.

'If you will not lift a hand because of your friendship for me,' said Armiston bitterly, 'then think of the law. Surely there is something due to justice, when both robbery and bloody murder have been committed!'

'Justice!' cried Johanssen in scorn. 'Justice, you say! My friend, if you steal for me, and I reclaim by force that which is mine, is that injustice? If you cannot see the idea behind that surely, then, I cannot explain it to you.'

'Answer one question,' said Armiston. 'Have you any idea who the man was I met on the train?'

'For your own peace of mind—yes. As a clue leading to what you so glibly term justice—pshaw! Tonight's sundown would be easier for you to catch than this man if I know him. Mind you, Armiston, I do not know. But I believe. Here is what I believe:

'In a dozen courts of kings and petty princelings that I know of in the East there are Westerners retained as advisers—fiscal agents they usually call them. Usually they are American or English, or occasionally German.

'Now I ask you a question. Say that you were in the hire of a heathen prince, and a grievous wrong were done that prince, say, by a thoughtless woman who had not the least conception of the beauty of an idea she has outraged. Merely for the possession of a bauble, valueless to her except to appease vanity, she ruthlessly rode down a superstition that was as holy to this prince as your own belief in Christ is to you. What would you do?'

Without waiting for Armiston to answer, Johanssen went on:

'I know a man—You say this man you met on the train had wonderful hands, did he not? Yes, I thought so. Armiston I know a man who would not sit idly by and smile to himself over the ridiculous fuss occasioned by the loss of an imperfect stone—off-colour, badly cut, and everything else. Neither would he laugh at the superstition behind it. He would say to himself: "This superstition is older by several thousand years than I or my people." And this man, whom I know, is brave enough to right that wrong himself if his underlings failed.'

'I follow,' said Armiston dully.

'But,' said Johanssen, leaning forward and tapping the author on the knee—'but the task proves too big for him. What did he do? He asked the cleverest man in the world to help him. And Godahl helped him. That,' said Johanssen, interrupting Armiston with a raised finger, 'is the story of the white ruby. The Story of the White Ruby, you see, is something infinitely finer than mere vulgar robbery and murder, as the author of Godahl the Infallible conceived it.'

Johanssen said a great deal more. In the end he took the lozenge-shaped diamond pendant and put the glass on the silver bar, that his friend might see the inscription on the back. He told him what the inscription signified—'Brother of a King', and, furthermore, how few men alive possessed the capacity for brotherhood.

'I think,' said Armiston as he was about to take his leave, 'that I will travel in the Straits this winter.'

'If you do,' said Johanssen, 'I earnestly advise you to leave your Godahl and his decoration at home.'

THE BLAST OF THE BOOK

G.K. Chesterton

Professor Openshaw always lost his temper, with a loud bang, if anybody called him a Spiritualist; or a believer in Spiritualism. This, however, did not exhaust his explosive elements; for he also lost his temper if anybody called him a disbeliever in Spiritualism. It was his pride to have given his whole life to investigating Psychic Phenomena; it was also his pride never to have given a hint of whether he thought they were really psychic or merely phenomenal. He enjoyed nothing so much as to sit in a circle of devout Spiritualists and give devastating descriptions of how he had exposed medium after medium and detected fraud after fraud: for indeed he was a man of much detective talent and insight, when once he had fixed his eye on an object, and he always fixed his eye on a medium, as a highly suspicious object. There was a story of his having spotted the same Spiritualistic mountebank under three different disguises: dressed as a woman, a white-bearded old man, and a Brahmin of a rich chocolate brown. These recitals made the true believers rather restless, as indeed they were intended to do; but they could hardly complain, for no Spiritualist denies the existence of fraudulent mediums; only the Professor's flowing narrative might well seem to indicate that all mediums were fraudulent.

But woe to the simple-minded and innocent Materialist (and

Materialists as a race are rather innocent and simple-minded) who, presuming on this narrative tendency, should advance the thesis that ghosts were against the laws of nature, or that such things were only old superstitions; or that it was all tosh, or, alternately, bunk. Him would the Professor, suddenly reversing all his scientific batteries, sweep from the field with a cannonade of unquestionable cases and unexplained phenomena, of which the wretched rationalist had never heard in his life, giving all the dates and details, stating all the attempted and abandoned natural explanations; stating everything, indeed, except whether he, John Oliver Openshaw, did or did not believe in Spirits; and that neither Spiritualist nor Materialist could ever boast of finding out.

Professor Openshaw, a lean figure with pale leonine hair and hypnotic blue eyes, stood exchanging a few words with Father Brown, who was a friend of his, on the steps outside the hotel where both had been breakfasting that morning and sleeping the night before. The Professor had come back râther late from one of his grand experiments, in general exasperation, and was still tingling with the fight that he always waged alone and against both sides.

'Oh, I don't mind you,' he said laughing. 'You don't believe in it even if it's true. But all these people are perpetually asking me what I'm trying to prove. They don't seem to understand that I'm a man of science. A man of science isn't trying to prove anything. He's trying to find out what will prove itself.'

'But he hasn't found out yet,' said Father Brown.

'Well, I have some little notions of my own, that are not quite so negative as most people think,' answered the Professor, after an instant of frowning silence; 'anyhow, I've begun to fancy that if there is something to be found, they're looking for it along the wrong line. It's all too theatrical; it's showing off, all their shiny ectoplasm and trumpets and voices and the rest; all on the model of old melodramas and mouldy historical novels about the Family Ghost. If they'd go to history instead of historical novels, I'm beginning to think they'd really find something. But not Apparitions.'

'After all,' said Father Brown, 'Apparitions are only Appearances. I suppose you'd say the Family Ghost is only keeping up appearances.'

The Professor's gaze, which had commonly a fine abstracted

295

character, suddenly fixed and focused itself as it did on a dubious medium. It had rather the air of a man screwing a strong magnifying-glass into his eye. Not that he thought the priest was in the least like a dubious medium; but he was startled into attention by his friend's thought following so closely on his own.

'Appearances!' he muttered, 'crikey, but it's odd you should say that just now. The more I learn, the more I fancy they lose by merely looking for appearances. Now if they'd look a little into Disappearances—'

'Yes,' said Father Brown, 'after all, the real fairy legends weren't so very much about the appearance of famous fairies; calling up Titania or exhibiting Oberon by moonlight. But there were no end of legends about people *disappearing,* because they were stolen by the fairies. Are you on the track of Kilmeny or Thomas the Rhymer?'

'I'm on the track of ordinary modern people you've read of in the newspapers,' answered Openshaw. 'You may well stare; but that's my game just now; and I've been on it for a long time. Frankly, I think a lot of psychic appearances could be explained away. It's the disappearances I can't explain, unless they're psychic. These people in the newspapers who vanish and are never found—if you knew the details as I do . . . and now only this morning I got confirmation; an extraordinary letter from an old missionary, quite a respectable old boy. He's coming to see me at my office this morning. Perhaps you'd lunch with me or something; and I'd tell the results—in confidence.'

'Thanks; I will—unless,' said Father Brown modestly, 'the fairies have stolen me by then.'

With that they parted and Openshaw walked round the corner to a small office he rented in the neighbourhood; chiefly for the publication of a small periodical, of psychical and psychological notes of the priest and most agnostic sort. He had only one clerk, who sat at a desk in the outer office, totting up figures and facts for the purposes of the printed report; and the Professor paused to ask if Mr Pringle had called. The clerk answered mechanically in the negative and went on mechanically adding up figures; and the Professor turned towards the inner room that was his study. 'Oh, by the way, Berridge,' he added, without turning round, 'if Mr Pringle comes, send him straight in to me. You needn't interrupt your work; I rather want those notes finished tonight if possible. You might leave them on my desk tomorrow, if I am late.'

And he went into his private office, still brooding on the problem which the name of Pringle had raised; or rather, perhaps, had ratified and confirmed in his mind. Even the most perfectly balanced of agnostics is partially human; and it is possible that the missionary's letter seemed to have greater weight as promising to support his private and still tentative hypothesis. He sat down in his large and comfortable chair, opposite the engraving of Montaigne; and read once more the short letter from the Rev Luke Pringle, making the appointment for that morning. No man knew better than Professor Openshaw the marks of the letter of the crank; the crowded details; the spidery handwriting; the unnecessary length and repetition. There were none of these things in this case; but a brief and businesslike typewritten statement that the writer had encountered some curious cases of Disappearance, which seemed to fall within the province of the Professor as a student of psychic problems. The Professor was favourably impressed; nor had he any unfavourable impression, in spite of a slight movement of surprise, when he looked up and saw that the Rev Luke Pringle was already in the room.

'Your clerk told me I was to come straight in,' said Mr Pringle apologetically, but with a broad and rather agreeable grin. The grin was partly masked by masses of reddish-grey beard and whiskers; a perfect jungle of a beard, such as is sometimes grown by white men living in the jungles; but the eyes above the snub nose had nothing about them in the least wild or outlandish. Oppenshaw had instantly turned on them that concentrated spotlight or burning-glass of sceptical scrutiny which he turned on many men to see if they were mountebanks or maniacs; and, in this case, he had a rather unusual sense of reassurance. The wild beard might have belonged to a crank, but the eyes completely contradicted the beard; they were full of that quite frank and friendly laughter which is never found in the faces of those who are serious frauds or serious lunatics. He would have expected a man with those eyes to be a Philistine, a jolly sceptic, a man who shouted out shallow but hearty contempt for ghosts and spirits; but anyhow, no professional humbug could afford to look so frivolous as that. The man was buttoned up to the throat in a shabby old cape, and only his broad limp hat suggested the cleric; but missionaries from wild places do not always bother to dress like clerics.

'You probably think all this is another hoax, Professor,' said Mr Pringle, with a sort of abstract enjoyment, 'and I hope you will forgive my laughing at your very natural air of disapproval. All the same, I've got to tell my story to somebody who knows, because it's true. And, all joking apart, it's tragic as well as true. Well, to cut it short, I was missionary in Nya-Nya, a station in West Africa, in the thick of the forests, where almost the only other white man was the officer in command of the district, Captain Wales; and he and I grew rather thick. Not that he liked missions; he was, if I may say so, thick in many ways; one of those square-headed, square-shouldered men of action who hardly need to think, let alone believe. That's what makes it all the queerer. One day he came back to his tent in the forest, after a short leave, and said he had gone through a jolly rum experience, and didn't know what to do about it. He was holding a rusty old book in a leather binding, and he put it down on a table beside his revolver and an old Arab sword he kept, probably as a curiosity. He said this book had belonged to a man on the boat he had just come off; and the man swore that nobody must open the book, or look inside it; or else they would be carried off by the devil, or disappear, or something. Wales said this was all nonsense, of course; and they had a quarrel; and the upshot seems to have been that this man, taunted with cowardice or superstition, actually did look into the book; and instantly dropped it; walked to the side of the boat—'

'One moment,' said the Professor, who had made one or two notes. 'Before you tell me anything else. Did this man tell Wales where he had got the book, or who it originally belonged to?'

'Yes,' replied Pringle, now entirely grave. 'It seems he said he was bringing it back to Dr Hankey, the Oriental traveller now in England, to whom it originally belonged, and who had warned him of its strange properties. Well, Hankey is an able man and a rather crabbed and sneering sort of man; which makes it queerer still. But the point of Wales's story is much simpler. It is that the man who had looked into the book walked straight over the side of the ship, and was never seen again.'

'Do you believe it yourself?' asked Openshaw after a pause.

'Well, I do,' replied Pringle. 'I believe it for two reasons. First, that Wales was an entirely unimaginative man; and he added one touch that only an imaginative man could have added. He said that the man walked straight over the side on a still and calm day; but there was no splash.'

The Professor looked at his notes for some seconds in silence; and then said; 'And your other reason for believing it?'

'My other reason,' answered the Rev Luke Pringle, 'is what I saw myself.'

There was another silence; until he continued in the same matter-of-fact way. Whatever he had, he had nothing of the eagerness with which the crank, or even the believer, tried to convince others.

'I told you that Wales put down the book on the table beside the sword. There was only one entrance to the tent; and it happened that I was standing in it, looking out into the forest, with my back to my companion. He was standing by the table grumbling and growling about the whole business; saying it was tomfoolery in the twentieth century to be frightened of opening a book; asking why the devil he shouldn't open it himself. Then some instinct stirred in me and I said that he had better not do that, it had better be returned to Dr Hankey. "What harm could it do?" he said restlessly. "What harm did it do?" I answered obstinately. "What happened to your friend on the boat?" He didn't answer, indeed I didn't know what he could answer; but I pressed my logical advantage in mere vanity. "If it comes to that," I said, "what is your version of what really happened on the boat?" Still he didn't answer; and I looked round and saw that he wasn't there.

'The tent was empty. The book was lying on the table; open but on its face, as if he had turned it downwards. But the sword was lying on the ground near the other side of the tent; and the canvas of the tent showed a great slash, as if somebody had hacked his way out with the sword. The gash in the tent gaped at me; but showed only the dark glimmer of the forest outside. And when I went across and looked through the rent I could not be certain whether the tangle of the tall plants and the undergrowth had been bent or broken; at least not farther than a few feet. I have never seen or heard of Captain Wales from that day.

'I wrapped the book up in brown paper, taking good care not to look at it; and I brought it back to England, intending at first to return it to Dr Hankey. Then I saw some notes in your paper suggesting a hypothesis about such things; and I decided to stop on the way and put the matter before you; as you have a name for being balanced and having an open mind.'

Professor Openshaw laid down his pen and looked steadily at the man on the other side of the table; concentrating in that single stare all his long experience of many entirely different types of humbug, and even some eccentric and extraordinary types of honest men. In the ordinary way, he would have begun with the healthy hypothesis that the story was a pack of lies. On the whole he did incline to assume that it was a pack of lies. And yet he could not fit the man into his story; if it were only that he could not see that sort of liar telling that sort of lie. The man was not trying to look honest on the surface, as most quacks and impostors do; somehow, it seemed all the other way; as if the man *was* honest, in spite of something else that was merely on the surface. He thought of a good man with one innocent delusion; but again the symptoms were not the same; there was even a sort of virile indifference; as if the man did not care much about his delusion, if it was a delusion.

'Mr Pringle,' he said sharply, like a barrister making a witness jump, 'where is this book of yours now?'

The grin reappeared on the bearded face which had grown grave during the recital.

'I left it outside,' said Mr Pringle. 'I mean in the outer office. It was a risk, perhaps; but the less risk of the two.'

'What do you mean?' demanded the Professor. 'Why didn't you bring it straight in here?'

'Because,' answered the missionary, 'I knew that as soon as you saw it, you'd open it—before you had heard the story. I thought it possible you might think twice about opening it—after you'd heard the story.'

Then after a silence he added: 'There was nobody out there but your clerk; and he looked a stolid steady-going specimen, immersed in business calculations.'

Openshaw laughed unaffectedly. 'Oh, Babbage,' he cried, 'your magic tomes are safe enough with him, I assure you. His name's Berridge—but I often call him Babbage; because he's so exactly like a

Calculating Machine. No human being, if you can call him a human being, would be less likely to open other people's brown paper parcels. Well, we may as well go and bring it in now; though I assure you I will consider seriously the course to be taken with it. Indeed, I tell you frankly,' and he stared at the man again, 'that I'm not quite sure whether we ought to open it here and now, or send it to this Dr Hankey.'

The two had passed together out of the inner into the outer office; and even as they did so, Mr Pringle gave a cry and ran forward towards the clerk's desk. For the clerk's desk was there; but not the clerk. On the clerk's desk lay a faded old leather book, torn out of it's brown-paper wrappings, and lying closed, but as if it had just been opened. The clerk's desk stood against the wide window that looked out into the street; and the window was shattered with a huge ragged hole in the glass; as if a human body had been shot through it into the world without. There was no other trace of Mr Berridge.

Both the two men left in the office stood as still as statues; and then it was the Professor who slowly came to life. He looked even more judicial than he had ever looked in his life, as he slowly turned and held out his hand to the missionary.

'Mr Pringle,' he said, 'I beg your pardon, I beg your pardon only for thoughts that I have had; and half-thoughts at that. But nobody could call himself a scientific man and not face a fact like this.'

'I suppose,' said Pringle doubtfully, 'that we ought to make some inquiries. Can you ring up his house and find out if he has gone home?'

'I don't know that he's on the telephone,' answered Openshaw, rather absently; 'he lives somewhere up Hampstead way, I think. But I suppose somebody will inquire here, if his friends or family miss him.'

'Could we furnish a description,' asked the other, 'if the police want it?'

'The police!' said the Professor, starting from his reverie. 'A description. . . . Well, he looked awfully like everybody else, I'm afraid, except for goggles. One of those clean-shaven chaps. But the police . . . look here, what *are* we to do about this mad business?'

'I know what I ought to do,' said the Rev Mr Pringle firmly, 'I am going to take this book straight to the only original Dr Hankey,

The window was shattered with a huge ragged hole in the glass.

and ask him what the devil it's all about. He lives not very far from here, and I'll come straight back and tell you what he says.'

'Oh, very well,' said the Professor at last, as he sat down rather wearily; perhaps relieved for the moment to be rid of the responsibility. But long after the brisk and ringing footsteps of the little missionary had died away down the street, the Professor sat in the same posture, staring into vacancy like a man in a trance.

He was still in the same seat and almost in the same attitude, when the same brisk footsteps were heard on the pavement without and the missionary entered, this time, as a glance assured him, with empty hands.

'Dr Hankey,' said Pringle gravely, 'wants to keep the book for an hour and consider the point. Then he asks us both to call and he will give us his decision. He specially desired, Professor, that you should accompany me on the second visit.'

Openshaw continued to stare in silence; then he said, suddenly:

'Who the devil is Dr Hankey?'

'You sound rather as if you meant he was the devil,' said Pringle, smiling, 'and I fancy some people have thought so. He had quite a reputation in your own line; but he gained it mostly in India, studying local magic and so on, so perhaps he's not so well known here. He is a yellow skinny little devil with a lame leg, and a doubtful temper; but he seems to have set up in an ordinary respectable practice in these parts, and I don't know anything definitely wrong about him—unless it's wrong to be the only person who can possibly know anything about all this crazy affair.'

Professor Openshaw rose heavily and went to the telephone; he rang up Father Brown, changing the luncheon engagement to a dinner, that he might hold himself free for the expedition to the house of the Anglo-Indian doctor; after that he sat down again, lit a cigar and sank once more into his own unfathomable thoughts.

$$\star \quad \star \quad \star \quad \star$$

Father Brown went round to the restaurant appointed for dinner, and kicked his heels for some time in a vestibule full of mirrors and palms in pots; he had been informed of Openshaw's afternoon engagement, and, as the evening closed-in dark and stormy round the glass and the green plants, guessed that it had produced something unexpected and unduly prolonged. He even wondered for a moment whether the Professor would turn up at all; but when the Professor eventually did, it was clear that his own more general guesses had been justified. For it was a very wild-eyed and even wild-haired Professor who eventually drove back with Mr Pringle from the expedition to the North of London, where suburbs are still fringed with heathy wastes and scraps of common, looking more sombre under the rather thunderstorm sunset. Nevertheless, they had apparently found the house, standing a little apart though within hail of other houses; they had verified the brass-plate duly engraved: 'J. I. Hankey, MD, MRCS'. Only they did not find J. I. Hankey, MD, MRCS. They found only what a nightmare whisper had already subconsciously prepared them to find: a commonplace parlour with the accursed volume lying on the table, as if it had just been read; and beyond, a backdoor burst open and a faint trail of footsteps that ran a little way up so steep a garden path that it seemed that no lame man could have run up so lightly. But it was a lame man who had run; for in those few steps there was the mis-shapen unequal mark of some sort of surgical boot; then two marks of that boot alone (as if the creature had hopped) and then nothing. There was nothing further to be learnt from Dr J. I. Hankey, except that he had made his decision. He had read the oracle and received the doom.

When the two came into the entrance under the palms, Pringle put the book down suddenly on a small table, as if it burned his fingers. The priest glanced at it curiously; there was only some rude lettering on the front with a couplet:

> *They that looked into this book*
> *Them the Flying Terror took;*

and underneath, as he afterwards discovered, similar warnings in Greek, Latin and French. The outer two had turned away with a natural impulsion towards drinks, after their exhaustion and bewilderment; and Openshaw had called to the waiter, who brought cocktails on a tray.

'You will dine with us, I hope,' said the Professor to the missionary; but Mr Pringle amiably shook his head.

'If you'll forgive me,' he said, 'I'm going to wrestle with this book and this business by myself somewhere. I suppose I couldn't use your office for an hour or so?'

'I suppose—I'm afraid it's locked,' said Openshaw in some surprise.

'You forgot there's a hole in the window.' The Rev Luke Pringle gave the very broadest of all his broad grins and vanished into the darkness without.

'A rather odd fellow, that, after all,' said the Professor, frowning.

He was rather surprised to find Father Brown talking to the waiter who had brought the cocktails, apparently about the waiter's most private affairs; for there was some mention of a baby who was now out of danger. He commented on the fact with some surprise, wondering how the priest came to know the man; but the former only said, 'Oh, I dine here every two or three months, and I've talked to him now and then.'

The Professor, who himself dined there about five times a week, was conscious that he had never thought of talking to the man; but his thoughts were interrupted by a strident ringing and a summons to the telephone. The voice on the telephone said it was Pringle; it was rather a muffled voice, but it might well be muffled in all those bushes of beard and whisker. Its message was enough to establish identity.

'Professor,' said the voice, 'I can't stand it any longer. I'm going to look for myself. I'm speaking from your office and the book is in front of me. If anything happens to me, this is to say goodbye. No—it's no good trying to stop me. You wouldn't be in time anyhow. I'm opening the book now. I . . .'

Openshaw thought he heard something like a sort of thrilling or shivering yet almost soundless crash; then he shouted the name of Pringle again and again, but he heard no more. He hung up the receiver, and, restored to a superb academic calm, rather like the calm of despair, went back and quietly took his seat at the dinner-table. Then, as coolly as if he were describing the failure of some small silly trick at a séance, he told the priest every detail of this monstrous mystery.

'Five men have now vanished in this impossible way,' he said. 'Every one is extraordinary; and yet the one case I simply can't get over is my clerk, Berridge. It's just because he was the quietest creature that he's the queerest case.'

'Yes,' replied Father Brown, 'it was a queer thing for Berridge to do, anyway. He was awfully conscientious. He was always so jolly careful to keep all the office business separate from any fun of his own. Why, hardly anybody knew he was quite a humorist at home and—'

'Berridge!' cried the Professor. 'What on earth are you talking about? Did you know him?'

'Oh, no,' said Father Brown carelessly, 'only as you say I know the waiter. I've often had to wait in your office, till you turned up; and of course I passed the time of day with poor Berridge. He was rather a card. I remember he once said he would like to collect valueless things, as collectors did the silly things they thought valuable. You know the old story about the woman who collected valueless things.'

'I'm not sure I know what you're talking about,' said Openshaw. 'But even if my clerk was eccentric (and I never knew a man I should have thought less so), it wouldn't explain what happened to him; and it certainly wouldn't explain the others.'

'What others?' asked the priest.

The Professor stared at him and spoke distinctly, as if to a child:

'My dear Father Brown, Five Men have disappeared.'

Father Brown gazed back at his host with equal steadiness and spoke with equal distinctness. Nevertheless, the Professor required the words repeated, and they were repeated as distinctly.

'I say that no men have disappeared.'

'My dear Professor Openshaw, no men have disappeared.'

After a moment's silence, he added, 'I suppose the hardest thing is to convince anybody that $o + o + o = o$. Men believe the oddest things if they are a series; that is why Macbeth believed the three words of the three witches; though the first was something he knew himself; and the last something he could only bring about himself. But in your case the middle term is the weakest of all.'

'What do you mean?'

'You saw nobody vanish. You did not see the man vanish from the boat. You did not see the man vanish from the tent. All that rests on the word of Mr Pringle, which I will not discuss just now. But you'll admit this; you would never have taken his word yourself, *unless* you had seen it confirmed by your clerk's disappearance; just as Macbeth would never have believed he would be king, if he had not been confirmed in believing he would be Cawdor.'

'That may be true,' said the Professor, nodding slowly. 'But *when* it was confirmed, I knew it was the truth. You say I saw nothing myself. But I did; I saw my own clerk disappear. Berridge did disappear.'

'Berridge did not disappear,' said Father Brown. 'On the contrary.'

'What the devil do you mean by "on the contrary"?'

'I mean,' said Father Brown, 'that he never disappeared. He appeared.'

Openshaw stared across at his friend, but the eyes had already altered in his head, as they did when they concentrated on a new presentation of a problem. The priest went on:

'He appeared in your study, disguised in a bushy red beard and buttoned up in a clumsy cape, and announced himself as the Rev Luke Pringle. And you had never noticed your own clerk enough to know him again, when he was in so rough-and-ready a disguise.'

'But surely,' began the Professor.

'Could you describe him for the police?' asked Father Brown. 'Not you. You probably knew he was clean-shaven and wore tinted-glasses; and merely taking off those glasses was a better disguise than putting on anything else. You had never seen his eyes any more than his soul; jolly laughing eyes. He had planted his absurd book and all the properties; then he calmly smashed the window, put on the beard and cape and walked into your study; knowing that you had never looked at him in your life.'

'But why should he play me such an insane trick?' demanded Openshaw.

'Why, *because* you had never looked at him in your life,' said Father Brown; and his hand slightly curled and clinched, as if he might have struck the table, if he had been given to gesture. 'You called him the Calculating Machine, because that was all you ever used him for. You never found out even what a stranger strolling into your office could find out, in five minutes' chat: that he was a character; that he was full of antics; that he had all sorts of views on you and your theories and your reputation for "spotting" people. Can't you understand his itching to prove that you couldn't spot your own clerk? He has nonsense notions of all sorts. About collecting useless things; for instance. Don't you know the story of the woman who bought the two most useless things; an old doctor's brass-plate and a wooden leg? With those your ingenious clerk created the character of the remarkable Dr Hankey; as easily as the visionary Captain Wales. Planting them in his own house—'

'Do you mean that place we visited beyond Hampstead was Berridge's own house?' asked Openshaw.

'Did *you* know his house—or even his address?' retorted the priest. 'Look here, don't think I'm speaking disrespectfully of you or your work. You are a great servant of truth and you know I could never be disrespectful to that. You've seen through a lot of liars, when you put your mind to it. But don't *only* look at liars. Do, just occasionally, look at honest men—like the waiter.'

'Where is Berridge now?' asked the Professor, after a long silence.

'I haven't the least doubt,' said Father Brown, 'that he is back in your office. In fact, he came back into your office at the exact moment when the Rev Luke Pringle read the awful volume and faded into the void.'

There was another long silence and then Professor Openshaw laughed; with the laugh of a great man who is great enough to look small. Then he said abruptly:

'I suppose I do deserve it; for not noticing the nearest helpers I have. But you must admit the accumulation of incidents was rather formidable. Did you *never* feel just a momentary awe of the awful volume?'

'Oh, that,' said Father Brown. 'I opened it as soon as I saw it lying there. It's all blank pages. You see, I am not superstitious '

THE TEA-LEAF

Edgar Jepson & Robert Eustace

Arthur Kelstern and Hugh Willoughton met in the Turkish bath in Duke Street, St James's, and rather more than a year later in that Turkish bath they parted. Both of them were bad-tempered men, Kelstern cantankerous and Willoughton violent. It was, indeed, difficult to decide which was the worse-tempered; and when I found that they had suddenly become friends, I gave that friendship three months. It lasted nearly a year.

When they did quarrel they quarrelled about Kelstern's daughter Ruth. Willoughton fell in love with her and she with him, and they became engaged to be married. Six months later, in spite of the fact that they were plainly very much in love with one another, the engagement was broken off. Neither of them gave any reason for breaking it off. My belief was that Willoughton had given Ruth a taste of his infernal temper and got as good as he gave.

Not that Ruth was at all a Kelstern to look at. Like the members of most of the old Lincolnshire families, descendants of the Vikings and the followers of Canute, one Kelstern is very like another Kelstern, fair-haired, clear-skinned, with light blue eyes and a good bridge to the nose. But Ruth had taken after her mother; she was dark, with a straight nose, dark-brown eyes of the kind often described as liquid, dark-brown hair, and as kissable lips as ever I saw. She was a proud, self-sufficing, high-spirited girl, with a temper of her own. She needed it to live with that cantankerous old brute Kelstern. Oddly enough, in spite of the fact that he always would try to bully her, she was fond of him; and I will say for him that he was very fond of her. Probably she was the only creature in the world of whom he was really fond. He was an expert in the application of scientific discoveries to industry; and she worked with him in his laboratory. He paid her five hundred a year, so that she must have been uncommonly good.

He took the breaking off of the engagement very hard indeed. He would have it that Willoughton had jilted her. Ruth took it hard, too; her warm colouring lost some of its warmth; her lips grew less kissable and set in a thinner line. Willoughton's temper grew worse than ever; he was like a bear with a perpetually sore head. I tried to feel my way with both him and Ruth with a view to help to bring about a reconciliation. To put it mildly, I was rebuffed. Willoughton swore at me; Ruth flared up and told me not to meddle in matters that didn't concern me. Nevertheless, my strong impression was that they were missing one another badly and would have been glad enough to come together again if their stupid vanity could have let them.

Kelstern did his best to keep Ruth furious with Willoughton. One night I told him—it was no business of mine; but I never did give a tinker's curse for his temper—that he was a fool to meddle and had much better leave them alone. It made him furious, of course; he would have it that Willoughton was a dirty hound and a low blackguard—at least those were about the mildest things he said of him. Given his temper and the provocation, nothing less could be expected. Moreover, he was looking a very sick man and depressed.

He took immense trouble to injure Willoughton. At his clubs, the Athenaeum, the Devonshire, and the Savile, he would display considerable ingenuity in bringing the conversation round to him; then he would declare that he was a scoundrel of the meanest type. Of course, it did Willoughton harm, though not nearly as much as Kelstern desired, for Willoughton knew his job as few engineers knew it; and it is very hard indeed to do much harm to a man who really knows his job. People have to have him. But of course it did him some harm; and Willoughton knew that Kelstern was doing it. I came across two men who told me that they had given him a friendly hint. That did not improve *his* temper.

An expert in the construction of those ferro-concrete buildings which are rising up all over London, he was as distinguished in his sphere as Kelstern in his. They were alike not only in the matters of brains and bad temper; but I think that their minds worked in very much the same way. At any rate, both of them seemed determined not to change their ordinary course of life because of the breaking off of that engagement.

It had been the habit of both of them to have a Turkish bath, at the baths in Duke Street, at four in the afternoon on the second and last Tuesday in every month. To that habit they stuck. The fact that they must meet on those Tuesdays did not cause either of them to change his hour of taking his Turkish bath by the twenty minutes which would have given them no more than a passing glimpse of one another. They continued to take it, as they always had, simultaneously. Thick-skinned? They were thick-skinned. Neither of them pretended that he did not see the other; he scowled at him; and he scowled at him most of the time. I know this, for sometimes I had a Turkish bath myself at that hour.

It was about three months after the breaking off of the engagement that they met for the last time at that Turkish bath, and there parted for good.

Kelstern had been looking ill for about six weeks; there was a greyness and a drawn look to his face; and he was losing weight. On the second Tuesday in October he arrived at the bath punctually at four, bringing with him, as was his habit, a thermos flask full of a very delicate China tea. If he thought that he was not perspiring freely enough he would drink it in the hottest room; if he did perspire freely enough, he would drink it after his bath. Willoughton arrived about two minutes later. Kelstern finished undressing and went into the bath a couple of minutes before Willoughton. They stayed in the hot room about the same time; Kelstern went into the hottest room about a minute after Willoughton. Before he went into it he sent for his thermos flask, which he had left in the dressing-room, and took it into the hottest room with him.

As it happened, they were the only two people in the hottest room;

and they had not been in it two minutes before the four men in the hot room heard them quarrelling. They heard Kelstern call Willoughton a dirty hound and a low blackguard, among other things, and declare he would do him in yet. Willoughton told him to go to the devil twice. Kelstern went on abusing him, and presently Willoughton fairly shouted: 'Oh, shut up, you old fool! Or I'll make you!'

Kelstern did not shut up. About two minutes later Willoughton came out of the hottest room, scowling, walked through the hot room into the shampooing room, and put himself into the hands of one of the shampooers. Two or three minutes after that a man of the name of Helston went into the hottest room and fairly yelled. Kelstern was lying back on a couch, with the blood still flowing from a wound over his heart.

There was a devil of a hullabaloo. The police were called in; Willoughton was arrested. Of course he lost his temper and, protesting furiously that he had had nothing whatever to do with the crime, abused the police. That did not incline them to believe him.

After examining the room and the dead body the detective-inspector in charge of the case came to the conclusion that Kelstern had been stabbed as he was drinking his tea. The thermos flask lay on the floor and some of the tea had evidently been spilt, for some tea-leaves—the tea in the flask must have been carelessly strained off the leaves by the maid who filled it—lay on the floor about the mouth of the empty flask. It looked as if the murderer had taken advantage of Kelstern's drinking his tea to stab him while the flask rather blocked his vision and prevented him from seeing what he would be at.

The case would have been quite plain sailing but for the fact that they could not find the weapon. It had been easy enough for Willoughton to take it into the bath in the towel in which he was draped. But how had he got rid of it? Where had he hidden it? A Turkish bath is no place to hide anything in. It is as bare as an empty barn—if anything barer; and Willoughton had been in the barest part of it. The police searched every part of it—not that there was much point in doing that, for Willoughton had come out of the hottest room and gone through the hot room into the shampooers' room. When Helston started shouting 'Murder!' he had rushed back with the shampooers to the hottest room and there he had stayed. Since it was obvious that he had committed the murder, the shampooers and the bathers had kept their eyes on him. They were all of them certain that he had not left them to go to the dressing-room; they would not have allowed him to do so.

It was obvious that he must have carried the weapon into the bath, hidden in the folds of the towel in which he was draped, and brought it away in the folds of that towel. He had laid the towel down beside the couch on which he was being shampooed; and there it still lay when they came to look for it, untouched, with no weapon in it, with no traces of blood on it. There was not much in the fact that it was not stained with blood, since Willoughton could have wiped the knife, or dagger, or whatever weapon he used, on the couch on which Kelstern lay. There were no marks of any such wiping on the couch; but the blood, flowing from the wound, might have covered them up. But why was the weapon not in the towel?

There was no finding that weapon.

Then the doctors who made the autopsy came to the conclusion that the wound had been inflicted by a circular, pointed weapon nearly three-quarters of an inch in diameter. It had penetrated rather more than three inches, and, supposing that its handle was only four inches long, it must have been a sizable weapon, quite impossible to overlook. The doctors also discovered a further proof of the theory that Kelstern had been drinking tea when he was stabbed. Halfway down the wound they found two halves of a tea-leaf which had evidently fallen onto Kelstern's body, been driven into the wound, and cut in half by the weapon. Also they discovered that Kelstern was suffering from cancer. This fact was not published in the papers; I heard it at the Devonshire.

Willoughton was brought before the magistrates, and to most people's surprise did not reserve his defence. He went into the witness-box and swore that he had never touched Kelstern, that he had never had anything to touch him with, that he had never taken any weapon into the Turkish bath and so had had no weapon to hide, that he had never even seen any such weapon as the doctors described. He was committed for trial.

The papers were full of the crime; every one was discussing it; and the question which occupied everyone's mind was: where had Willoughton hidden the weapon? People wrote to the papers to suggest that he had ingeniously put in some place under everybody's eyes and that it had been overlooked because it was so obvious. Others suggested that, circular and pointed, it must be very like a thick lead-pencil, that it was a thick lead-pencil; and that was why the police had overlooked it in their search. The police had not overlooked any thick lead-pencil; there had been no thick lead-pencil to overlook. They hunted England through—Willoughton did a lot of motoring— to discover the man who had sold him this curious and uncommon weapon. They did not find the man who had sold it to him; they did not find a man who sold such weapons at all. They came to the conclusion that Kelstern had been murdered with a piece of steel, or iron, rod filed to a point like a pencil.

In spite of the fact that only Willoughton *could* have murdered Kelstern, I could not believe that he had done it. The fact that Kelstern was doing his best to injure him professionally and socially was by no means a strong enough motive. Willoughton was far too intelligent a man not to be very well aware that people do not take much notice of statements to the discredit of a man whom they need to do a job for them; and for the social injury he would care very little. Besides, he might very well injure, or even kill, a man in one of his tantrums; but his was not the kind of bad temper that plans a cold-blooded murder; and if ever a murder had been deliberately planned, Kelstern's had.

I was as close a friend as Willoughton had, and I went to visit him in prison. He seemed rather touched by my doing so, and grateful. I learnt that I was the only person who had done so. He was subdued and seemed much gentler. It might last. He discussed the murder readily enough, and naturally with a harassed air. He said quite frankly that he did not expect me, in the circumstances, to believe that he had not committed it; but he had not, and he could not for the life of him conceive who had. I did believe that he had not committed it; there was something in his way of discussing it that wholly convinced me. I told him that I was quite sure that he had not killed Kelstern; and he looked at me as if he did not believe the assurance. But again he looked grateful.

Ruth was grieving for her father; but Willoughton's very dangerous plight to some degree distracted her mind from her loss. A woman can quarrel with a man bitterly without desiring to see him hanged;

and Willoughton's chance of escaping hanging was not at all a good one. But she would not believe for a moment that he had murdered her father.

'No; there's nothing in it—nothing whatever,' she said firmly. 'If dad had murdered Hugh I could have understood it. He had reasons— or at any rate he had persuaded himself that he had. But whatever reason had Hugh for murdering dad? It's all nonsense to suppose that he'd mind dad's trying all he knew to injure him as much as that. All kinds of people are going about trying to injure other people in that way, but they don't really injure them very much; and Hugh knows that quite well.'

'Of course they don't; and Hugh wouldn't really believe that your father was injuring him much,' I said. 'But you're forgetting his infernal temper.'

'No, I'm not,' she protested. 'He might kill a man in one of his rages on the spur of the moment. But this wasn't the spur of the moment. Whoever did it had worked the whole thing out and came along with the weapon ready.'

I had to admit that that was reasonable enough. But who had done it? I pointed out to her that the police had made careful inquiries about everyone in the bath at the time, the shampooers and the people taking their baths, but they found no evidence whatever that any one of them had at any time had any relations, except that of shampooer, with her father.

'Either it was one of them, or somebody else who just did it and got right away, or there's a catch somewhere,' she said, frowning thoughtfully.

'I can't see how there can possibly have been anyone in the bath, except the people who are known to have been there,' said I. 'In fact, there can't have been.'

Then the Crown subpoenaed her as a witness for the prosecution. It seemed rather unnecessary and even a bit queer, for it could have found plenty of evidence of bad blood between the two men without dragging her into it. Plainly it was bent on doing all it knew to prove motive enough. Ruth worked her brain so hard trying to get to the bottom of the business that there came a deep vertical wrinkle just above her right eyebrow that stayed there.

On the morning of the trial I called for her after breakfast to drive her down to the New Bailey. She was pale, and looked as if she had had a poor night's rest, and, naturally enough, she seemed to be suffering from an excitement she found hard to control. It was not like her to show any excitement she might be feeling.

She said in an excited voice: 'I think I've got it!' and would say no more.

We had of course, been in close touch with Willoughton's solicitor, Hamley; and he had kept seats for us just behind him. He wished to have Ruth to hand to consult should some point turn up on which she could throw light, since she knew more than anyone about the relations between Willoughton and her father. I had timed our arrival very well; the jury had just been sworn in. Of course, the court was full of women, the wives of peers and bookmakers and politicians, most of them overdressed and over-scented.

Then the judge came in; and with his coming the atmosphere of the court became charged with that sense of anxious strain peculiar to trials for murder. It was rather like the atmosphere of a sick-room in a case of fatal illness, but worse.

Willoughton came into the dock looking under the weather and very much subdued. But he was certainly looking dignified, and he said that he was not guilty in a steady enough voice.

Greatorex, the leading counsel for the Crown, opened the case for the prosecution. There was no suggestion in his speech that the police had discovered any new fact. He begged the jury not to lay too much stress on the fact that the weapon had not been found. He had to, of course.

Then Helston gave evidence of finding that Kelstern had been stabbed, and he and the other three men who had been with him in the hot room gave evidence of the quarrel they had overheard between Willoughton and the dead man, and that Willoughton came out of the hottest room scowling and obviously furious. One of them, a fussy old gentleman of the name of Underwood, declared that it was the bitterest quarrel he had ever heard. None of the four of them could throw any light on the matter of whether Willoughton was carrying the missing weapon in the folds of the towel in which he was draped; all of them were sure that he had nothing in his hands.

Willoughton came into the dock looking very much subdued.

The medical evidence came next. In cross-examining the doctors who had made the autopsy, Hazeldean, Willoughton's counsel, established the fact quite definitely that the missing weapon was of a fair size; that its rounded blade must have been over half an inch in diameter and between three and four inches long. They were of the opinion that to drive a blade of that thickness into the heart a handle of at least four inches in length would be necessary to give a firm enough grip. They agreed that it might very well have been a piece of a steel, or iron, rod sharpened like a pencil. At any rate, it was certainly a sizeable weapon, not one to be hidden quickly or to disappear wholly in a Turkish bath. Hazeldean could not shake their evidence about the tea-leaf; they were confident that it had been driven into the wound and cut in half by the blade of the missing weapon, and that went to show that the wound had been inflicted while Kelstern was drinking his tea.

Detective-Inspector Brackett, who was in charge of the case, was cross-examined at great length about his search for the missing weapon. He made it quite clear that it was nowhere in that Turkish bath, neither in the hot rooms, nor the shampooing room, nor the dressing-rooms, nor the vestibule, nor the office. He had had the plunge bath emptied; he had searched the roofs, though it was practically certain that the skylight above the hot room, not the hottest, had been shut at the time of the crime. In re-examination he scouted the idea of Willoughton's having had an accomplice who had carried away the weapon for him. He had gone into that matter most carefully.

The shampooer stated that Willoughton came to him scowling so savagely that he wondered what had put him into such a bad temper. In cross-examining him, Arbuthnot, Hazeldean's junior, made it clearer than ever that, unless Willoughton had already hidden the weapon in the bare hottest room, it was hidden in the towel. Then he drew from the shampooer the definite statement that Willoughton had set down the towel beside the couch on which he was shampooed; that he had hurried back to the hot rooms in front of the shampooer; that the shampooer had come back from the hot rooms, leaving Willoughton still in them discussing the crime, to find the towel lying just as Willoughton had set it down, with no weapon in it and no trace of blood on it.

Since the inspector had disposed of the possibility that an accomplice had slipped in, taken the weapon from the towel, and slipped out of the bath with it, this evidence really made it clear that the weapon had never left the hottest room.

Then the prosecution called evidence of the bad terms on which Kelstern and Willoughton had been. Three well-known and influential men told the jury about Kelstern's efforts to prejudice Willoughton in their eyes and the damaging statements he had made about him. One of them had felt it to be his duty to tell Willoughton about this; and Willoughton had been very angry. Arbuthnot, in cross-examining, elicited the fact that any damaging statement that Kelstern made about anyone was considerably discounted by the fact that everyone knew him to be in the highest degree cantankerous.

I noticed that during the end of the cross-examination of the shampooer and during this evidence Ruth had been fidgeting and turning to look impatiently at the entrance to the court, as if she were expecting someone. Then, just as she was summoned to the witness-box, there came in a tall, stooping, grey-headed, grey-bearded man of about sixty, carrying a brown-paper parcel. His face was familiar to me, but I could not place him. He caught her eye and nodded to her. She breathed a sharp sigh of relief, and bent over and handed a letter she had in her hand to Willoughton's solicitor and pointed out the grey-bearded man to him. Then she went quietly to the witness-box.

Hamley read the letter and at once bent over and handed it to Hazeldean and spoke to him. I caught a note of excitement in his hushed voice. Hazeldean read the letter and appeared to grow excited too. Hamley slipped out of his seat and went to the grey-bearded man, who was still standing just inside the door of the porch, and began to talk to him earnestly.

Greatorex began to examine Ruth; and naturally I turned my attention to her. His examination was directed also to show on what bad terms Kelstern and Willoughton had been. Ruth was called on to tell the jury some of Kelstern's actual threats. Then he questioned Ruth about her own relations with Willoughton and the breaking off of the engagement and its infuriating effect on her father. She admitted that he had been very bitter about it, and had told her that he was resolved to do his best to do Willoughton in. I thought that she went out of her way to emphasize this resolve of Kelstern's. It seemed to me likely to prejudice the jury still more against Willoughton, making them sympathize with a father's righteous indignation, and making yet more obvious that he was a dangerous enemy. Yet she would not admit that her father was right in believing that Willoughton had jilted her.

Hazeldean rose to cross-examine Ruth with a wholly confident air. He drew from her the fact that her father had been on excellent terms with Willoughton until the breaking off of the engagement.

Then Hazeldean asked: 'It is a fact that since the breaking off of your engagement the prisoner has more than once begged you to forgive him and renew it?'

'Four times,' said Ruth.

'And you refused?'

'Yes,' said Ruth. She looked at Willoughton queerly and added: 'He wanted a lesson.'

The judge asked: 'Did you intend, then, to forgive him ultimately?'

Ruth hesitated; then she rather evaded a direct answer; she scowled frankly at Willoughton, and said: 'Oh, well, there was no hurry. He would always marry me if I changed my mind and wanted to.'

'And did your father know this?' asked the judge.

'No. I didn't tell him. I was angry with Mr Willoughton,' Ruth replied.

There was a pause. Then Hazeldean started on a fresh line.

In sympathetic accents he asked: 'Is it a fact that your father was suffering from cancer in a painful form?'

'It was beginning to grow very painful,' said Ruth sadly.

'Did he make a will and put all his affairs in order a few days before he died?'

'Three days,' said Ruth.

'Did he ever express an intention of committing suicide?'

'He said that he would stick it out for a little while and then end it all,' said Ruth. She paused and added: '*And that is what he did do.*'

One might almost say that the court started. I think that everyone in it moved a little, so that there was a kind of rustling murmur.

'Will you tell the court your reasons for that statement?' said Hazeldean.

Ruth seemed to pull herself together—she was looking very tired —then she began in a quiet, even voice: 'I never believed for a moment that Mr Willoughton murdered my father. If my father had murdered Mr Willoughton it would have been a different matter. Of course, like everybody else, I puzzled over the weapon; what it was and where it had got to. I did not believe that it was a pointed piece of a half-inch steel rod. If anybody had come to the Turkish bath meaning to murder my father and hide the weapon, they wouldn't have used one so big and so difficult to hide, when a hat-pin would have done just as well and could be hidden much more easily. But what puzzled me most was the tea-leaf in the wound. All the other tea-leaves that came out of the flask were lying on the floor. Inspector Brackett told me they were. And I couldn't believe that one tea-leaf had fallen onto my father at the very place above his heart at which the point of the weapon had penetrated the skin and got driven in by it. It was too much of a coincidence for me to swallow. But I got no nearer understanding it than any one else.'

She paused to ask if she might have a glass of water, for she had been up all night and was very tired. It was brought to her.

Then she went on in the same quiet voice: 'Of course, I remembered that dad had talked of putting an end to it; but no one with a wound like that could get up and hide the weapon. So it was impossible that he had committed suicide. Then, the night before last, I dreamt that I went into the laboratory and saw a piece of steel rod, pointed, lying on the table at which my father used to work.'

'Dreams!' murmured Greatorex, a trifle pettishly, as if he was not pleased with the way things were going.

'I didn't think much of the dream, of course,' Ruth went on. 'I had been puzzling about it all so hard for so long that it was only natural to dream about it. But after breakfast I had a sudden feeling that the secret was in the laboratory if I could find it. I did not attach any importance to the feeling; but it went on growing stronger; and after lunch I went to the laboratory and began to hunt.

'I looked through all the drawers and could find nothing. Then I went round the room looking at everything and into everything, instruments and retorts and tubes and so on. Then I went into the middle of the floor and looked slowly round the room pretty hard.

Against the wall, near the door, lying ready to be taken away, was a gas cylinder. I rolled it over to see what gas had been in it and found no label on it.'

She paused to look round the court as if claiming its best attention; then she went on: 'Now that was very queer, because every gas cylinder must have a label on it—so many gases are dangerous. I turned on the tap of the cylinder and nothing came out of it. It was quite empty. Then I went to the book in which all the things which come in are entered, and found that ten days before dad died he had had a cylinder of CO_2 and seven pounds of ice. Also he had had seven pounds of ice every day till the day of his death. It was the ice and the CO_2 together that gave me the idea. CO_2, carbon dioxide, has a very low freezing-point: -80 degrees centigrade. As liquid CO_2 comes out of the cylinder and mixes with air it turns into fine snow; and that snow, if you compress it, makes the hardest and toughest ice possible. It flashed on me that dad could have collected this snow and forced it into a mould and made a weapon that would not only inflict that wound but would evaporate very quickly! Indeed, in that heat you'd have to see the wound inflicted to know what had done it.'

She paused again to look round the court at about as rapt a lot of faces as any narrator could desire. Then she went on: 'I knew that that was what he had done. I knew it for certain. Carbon dioxide ice would make a hard, tough dagger, and it would evaporate quickly in the hottest room of a Turkish bath and leave no smell because it is scentless. So there wouldn't be any weapon. And it explained the tea-leaf, too. Dad had made a carbon dioxide dagger perhaps a week before he used it, perhaps only a day. And he had put it into the thermos flask as soon as he had made it. The thermos flask keeps out the heat as well as the cold, you know. But to make sure that it couldn't melt at all, he kept the flask in ice till he was ready to use the dagger. It's the only way you can explain that tea-leaf. It came out of the flask sticking to the point of the dagger and was driven into the wound!'

She paused again, and one might almost say that the court heaved a deep sigh of relief.

'But why didn't you go straight to the police with this theory?' asked the judge.

'But that wouldn't have been any good,' she protested quickly. 'It was no use my knowing it myself; I had to make other people believe it; I had to find evidence. I began to hunt for it. I felt in my bones that there was some. What I wanted was the mould in which dad compressed the carbon dioxide snow and made the dagger. I found it!'

She uttered the words in a tone of triumph and smiled at Willoughton; then she went on: 'And least, I found bits of it. In the box into which we used to throw odds and ends, scraps of material, damaged instruments, and broken test-tubes I found some pieces of vulcanite; and I saw at once that they were bits of a vulcanite container. I took some wax and rolled it into a rod about the right size, and then I pieced the container together on the outside of it—at least most of it—there are some small pieces missing. It took me nearly all night. But I found the most important bit—*the pointed end!*'

She dipped her hand into her handbag and drew out a black object about nine inches long and three-quarters of an inch thick, and held it up for everyone to see.

Someone, without thinking, began to clap; and there came a storm of applause that drowned the voice of the clerk calling for order.

When the applause died down, Hazeldean, who never misses the right moment, said: 'I have no more questions to ask the witness, my lord,' and sat down.

That action seemed to clinch it in my eyes, and I have no doubt it clinched it in the eyes of the jury.

The judge leant forward and said to Ruth in a rather shocked voice: 'Do you expect the jury to believe that a well-known man like your father died in the act of deliberately setting a trap to hang the prisoner?'

Ruth looked at him, shrugged her shoulders, and said, with a calm acceptance of the facts of human nature one would expect to find only in a much older woman: 'Oh, well, daddy was like that. And he certainly believed he had very good reason for killing Mr Willoughton.'

There was that in her tone and manner which made it absolutely certain that Kelstern was not only like that, but that he had acted according to his nature.

Greatorex did not re-examine Ruth; he conferred with Hazeldean. Then Hazeldean rose to open the case for the defence. He said that he would not waste the time of the court, and that, in view of the fact that Miss Kelstern had solved the problem of her father's death, he would only call one witness, Professor Mozley.

The grey-headed, grey-bearded, stooping man, who had come to the court so late, went into the witness-box. Of course his face had been familiar to me; I had seen his portrait in the newspapers a dozen times. He still carried the brown-paper parcel.

In answer to Hazeldean's questions he stated that it was possible, not even difficult, to make a weapon of carbon dioxide hard enough and tough enough and sharp enough to inflict such a wound as that which had caused Kelstern's death. The method of making it was to fold a piece of chamois leather into a bag, hold that bag with the left hand, protected by a glove, over the nozzle of a cylinder containing liquid carbon dioxide, and open the valve with the right hand. Carbon dioxide evaporates so quickly that its freezing-point, -80 degrees centigrade, is soon reached; and it solidifies in the chamois-leather bag as a deposit of carbon dioxide snow. Then turn off the gas, spoon that snow into a vulcanite container of the required thickness, and ram it down with a vulcanite plunger into a rod of the required hardness. He added that it was advisable to pack the container in ice while filling it and ramming down the snow. Then put the rod into a thermos flask; and keep it till it is needed.

'And you have made such a rod?' said Hazeldean.

'Yes,' said the professor, cutting the string of the brown-paper parcel. 'When Miss Kelstern hauled me out of bed at half-past seven this morning to tell me her discoveries, I perceived at once that she had found the solution of the problem of her father's death, which had puzzled me considerably. I had breakfast quickly and got to work to make such a weapon myself for the satisfaction of the court. Here it is.'

He drew a thermos flask from the brown paper, unscrewed the top of it, and inverted it. There dropped into his gloved hand a white rod, with a faint sparkle to it, about eight inches long. He held it out for the jury to see, and said:

'This carbon dioxide ice is the hardest and toughest ice we know of; and I have no doubt that Mr Kelstern killed himself with a similar rod. The difference between the rod he used and this is that his rod was pointed. I had no pointed vulcanite container; but the container that

Miss Kelstern pieced together is pointed. Doubtless Mr Kelstern had it specially made, probably by Messrs Hawkins and Spender.'

He dropped the rod back into the thermos flask and screwed on the top.

Hazeldean sat down, Greatorex rose.

'With regard to the point of the rod, Professor Mozley, would it remain sharp long enough to pierce the skin in that heat?' he asked.

'In my opinion it would,' said the professor. 'I have been considering that point, and bearing in mind the fact that Mr Kelstern would from his avocation be very deft with his hands, and being a scientific man would know exactly what to do, he would have the rod out of the flask and the point in position in very little more than a second—perhaps less. He would, I think, hold it in his left hand and drive it home by striking the butt of it hard with his right. The whole thing would not take him two seconds. Besides, if the point of the weapon had melted the tea-leaf would have fallen off it.'

'Thank you,' said Greatorex, and turned and conferred with the Crown solicitors.

Then he said: 'We do not propose to proceed with the case, my lord.'

The foreman of the jury rose quickly and said: 'And the jury doesn't want to hear anything more, my lord. We're quite satisfied that the prisoner isn't guilty.'

'Very good,' said the judge, and he put the question formally to the jury, who returned a verdict of 'Not guilty.' He discharged Willoughton.

I came out of the court with Ruth and we waited for Willoughton.

Presently he came out of the door and stopped and shook himself. Then he saw Ruth and came to her. They did not greet one another. She just slipped her hand through his arm; and they walked out of the New Bailey together.

We made a good deal of noise, cheering them.

STRONG BROTHER JOHN

Herbert Shaw

The night was hot and thunderous. Old Armitage, waiting deferentially by the table, seemed to be fixed, a part of the room itself, the room that was close and stuffy with deepening shadows.

'You must forget there's such a thing as work,' said John Bridal kindly. 'It's too long since you've had a holiday!' He laughed. 'Those noises you think you've heard, you know.'

'But I did hear them, sir!' Old Armitage, Bridal's sole servant for nine years, spoke apologetically. 'And if you didn't insist upon it, sir, I wouldn't be going this night!'

'I do insist. You'll come back fit and well after six weeks, and you'll hear no noises then. Very likely I'll have a change myself. Goodbye, Armitage, and mind you take a good rest. If I do decide to go away, I'll write you. We'll give up the house, perhaps; it's far too big. I hope you'll have a pleasant time. Take care of yourself.'

'Thank you, sir.'

'Goodbye, then. I'll light the lamp myself.'

But long after the door below had shut John Bridal left the lamp unlit. He sat thinking of Christopher. Christopher, who had been in prison, was to be his next visitor now. Prison—that was Christopher's finish so far as he was concerned, thought John, who had helped him many times. This must be the last time. Strange that Christopher, not two years younger and with every bit as clever a brain as his own, should have gone such a different road.

The clock struck the hour at which he had told Christopher to come. He had hurried back from his special day's work in the neighbouring town, to get Armitage properly packed off before Christopher should arrive. For Armitage probably thought that the scapegrace of the family was dead, and there was no need for him to know otherwise.

He got up to light the lamp, and heard a little rustling sound, somewhere across the room—one of Armitage's noises. The moment passed; the match was steady as he lit the lamp. Not till he had carefully turned up the wick did he look round. On the settee against the wall, which had been in deep shadow half an hour before, a man sprawled easily. It was Christopher. Already on his face, though they had not seen one another now for some years, was that faint smile. 'Curse him!' thought John.

'Did Armitage let you in?' he asked.

'Don't be afraid. I came though the old gap in the back hedge and let myself in. Amused myself looking round this work-room, where you make all your money. Then I lay doggo on this settee. Dear old Armitage—I wish I could have spoken to him. How well you've made him think that he owes his very life to you!'

'Where would he be without me? He's past proper employment.'

Christopher stretched his stiff legs. 'Or you without him? Down in the town they talk of you as an eccentric who seldom stirs from this room of yours, who sees few but Armitage from one year's end to the other. They've forgotten what you're like. Don't worry, John; I took good care nobody recognized me. You haven't changed much.'

Christopher laughed as his hand went up to his short hair.

'You'd know where I'd been resting without my letter, I think. There isn't quite the same likeness now that you've taken to glasses —and you've got that wig just a shade the wrong colour. I told you you'd go bald, last time we met. You remember?'

'No,' said John shortly. 'Why did you want to see me?'

'The old reason, of course,' said Christopher. 'I'm broke. So I'm penitent. I should have liked to have kept out of prison, but there you are. It happened. One learns things, even there—you'd be surprised.'

'At the end of your rope now?'

'Quite. You see,' said Christopher simply, 'prison puts the bar up against a chap.' The smile had gone, and Christopher was changed; he spoke gently. 'I know what you want to say, John. It was a lesson. And will be, while I live.'

This mood in which he had never yet caught Christopher was agreeable to John, who hated him. He had always been jealous of Christopher, the 'mother's boy'. It was right that the man who had gone wrong should come as a suppliant, should talk like this to the man who had succeeded. The novelty of feeling acknowledged power over Christopher was a pleasant thing.

'You've been very good to me, John. If you'll only help me again, I'll chuck fooling with things, and do my best.'

'A wasted life,' said John. He stood up and looked down on him. 'If I come to your rescue now, it's on a clear understanding that it's for the last time. And that I do not see you again.'

'Why, of course, if you wish it. I am in your hands.'

'For any help from me, you are to leave England, with a promise not to return. I have thought it all out very carefully. You understand?'

'Quite.'

'Very well.' John pulled open the top drawer on the right of the big table. 'I have bought you a passage to Australia, sailing tomorrow. I will give you, in addition, two hundred and ten pounds.'

'The condition being that you finish with me entirely?'

'Exactly.'

'It isn't a great sum, is it?' asked the younger brother thoughtfully. 'I don't want to go back to the old quarrel, but it was always my mother's intention, as you know, to leave me part of her fortune. Dying suddenly, she left everything in father's hands. I was her favourite. You were his. You were like him. And at the finish you had everything. I hadn't even the younger son's share. I had nothing. You're rather a thief, John.'

'I would have dealt otherwise with you if you had ordered your life differently.'

'I think not, John.'

'Well, let's have things clear. What would you expect me to do?'

'I met young Carruthers in the town yesterday. You've not done very much with the Bridal name there, John. Carruthers was black-guarding you to all and sundry in a saloon bar. He didn't remember me, but I gathered he had been running some enterprise for you, and you had given him the sack. I thought if there was a job going, I might take his place.'

John said brutally: 'I wouldn't trust you with a job. I was a fool to trust Carruthers; because I did, he's swindled me right and left. I only took him on because I knew his father, and I treated him as an equal —gave him every opportunity. He's one of your breed.'

'Thank you,' said Christopher.

'I told him I'd prosecute. He wrote me a threatening letter, and I went to see him at his rooms today. He got very angry. Then he whined, like the weak fool he is!—said he'd do away with himself. He'd been taking drugs.' John pulled out from his pocket a little squat bottle of white tabloids, and put them on the table. 'Veronal—I took these away from his desk. But he can buy some more for all I care, if he hasn't changed his mind by this evening. I left him shouting his weak threats. He's no good!'

'Another parallel with me?' questioned the younger brother.

'Yes. There's no job for you, Christopher. Besides, it's likely I may be giving up all business, and going away. I've given you lots of chances. There's only my offer for your last chance. Nothing beyond.'

'Then I'll take it,' said Christopher. He thought oddly of drunken Carruthers, white-faced, crying: 'John Bridal thinks he's very strong, but I'll pull him down—if it's the last thing I do!'

'I thought you would. I'll get the money, and then I've done with you.'

John Bridal passed to the other end of the room, beyond the radius of the lamp. And suddenly eight square feet of the wall moved outwards, the two high bookshelves moving as well, and John took a package from the hidden safe.

Christopher said: 'There's a good idea, by Jove! Who'd know there there was a safe there?'

'Clever enough,' said John. 'It was my own idea. You'd never find the way to open it in a hundred years, short of burning down the house, though you went over every inch of the floor and wall. It cost me a small fortune, but I'm very fond of it.'

'I suppose so,' assented Christopher, and got up carelessly to look across the table into the cave where Brother John kept his notes and gold. And suddenly Christopher was round the table, and the heavy chair in which John had sat ran noisily on its casters. Now Christopher was sitting in the chair, and the back of it was firmly against the inside of that solid door which was part of the wall itself.

'Did you think you had me as a mouldy beggar at last, John? Half-crying for your two hundred pounds, afraid lest you'd not give it. You were wrong to think it, John.'

'I'll phone the police station,' said John calmly.

'I nipped the wire,' returned Christopher.

Then John rang the bell, and they heard the forlorn pealing of it in the crazy old house.

'Armitage has gone. You might have invested in a few servants, John, with all your money. You've been letting the whole property go down. The lodge empty, and that gap still in the back hedge. It's not fair of you.'

A moment passed. 'Well, then?' asked John Bridal.

'I want five thousand pounds,' said Christopher. 'A comparatively small percentage of what should have been mine, if my mother's wishes had been carried out. The door doesn't shut till I've got it.'

John Bridal laughed.

'You're strong, John, and I know you ached to get rid of me for good, but it's the little chances upset everything. In the prison hospital I learnt of this secret safe of yours. The man in the next bed to mine helped to make it. He died. Do you think I'd have written to you else? If you hadn't been so pleased to see me penitent, you would never have dreamed of opening it while I was here. You'd have sent me your cursed dole of money, your ticket, and the rest.'

'I was never bluffed yet,' remarked John Bridal. 'You don't get it, Christopher.'

'I'm perfectly ready to fight for it,' said Christopher. 'You see, I planned this thing, so far as I could. That you did open the safe was luck!'

'Do you think I keep that amount of money in the house?'

'I am sure you do. No, I warn you, John. That way's no good! This door doesn't shut!'

For suddenly he saw that John had a big pocket-knife open in his hand, and, even as he spoke, John made a queer jump forward, with the hatred of half a lifetime concentrated in that one action. And Christopher, swinging round in the chair just in time to escape the lunge, lifted himself very quickly to his feet, and hit, short and hard.

He caught John full on the face, and John went over, doubled and sideways; Christopher hardly knew he had really hit him till he heard the strange noise the other's head made on a long iron box in the bottom of the safe. And immediately he thought with disgust that he would have to put his arms round John, to help him to get to his feet again after a blow like that.

But John made no faint movement of any kind, lying there quaintly huddled, his wig the least bit out of place to show the different skin-colouring above the line that the wearing of it had made. Christopher wanted to whisper 'John,' but could not conquer his aversion to saying the name.

Instead, he fingered the passage-paper, reading it mechanically. What stupid names they gave these boats. Three minutes had gone when he went to his knees, and found that John did not breathe.

After that his brain was a very perfect working-instrument indeed, and everything was absurdly easy, except that the thing at his feet got in his way while he ransacked the safe, and transferred the notes to the drawers in the table. And John was ugly when he had been robbed of the wig that Christopher adjusted carefully on himself.

Damn it, he wasn't Christopher any more. There wasn't any Christopher, now. He was John. He mustn't forget. John was going away; he had told Armitage so. There would only have to be a note to Armitage to say as much. Tell him not to come back to the old house.

Not that it would matter if the old chap did come back. Jove, no! That ingenious safe of which nobody knew was a fine thing.

One thing, when this job was over, there wasn't the slightest need to hurry. He could go away like a gentleman in the morning. Well, it was no good jibbing. He would have to get those ugly, sprawling legs and feet inside. Then, thank goodness, you shut the thing for good.

He shut it.

Nobody would ever open the safe again. There had been a visitor of whom it was natural to want no remembrance. Now!

He hit short and hard. John went over, doubled and fell sideways.

The door was shut, and there was no trace whatever of the line of its opening. 'You would now go down into the garden you used to know and have some fresh air.' The room looked a perfect orderly picture now. 'You would have to change your habits, and to be tidy always—like John.' Christopher was talking to himself aloud. . . .

It was rather jolly in the garden till he heard the creaking of the gate. Lucky he had brought down John's glasses. When he got settled, wherever he lived, he would put his foot down on visitors. He didn't want them. And with that thought he walked easily down to the gate, with one look at the lighted windows above him.

The stranger just inside the gate said pleasantly: 'How do you do, sir. I've not seen you since you had the burglar, ages ago. I'm very sorry to bother you, but I wonder if you would give me five minutes.'

'Certainly,' said Christopher.

'Thank you, sir,' said the visitor, and followed him in. 'I won't keep you any longer than I can help, I'm sure.'

'Take a chair,' said Christopher. And, sitting in the vacant throne of strong Brother John, he waited. It was perfectly all right, but he might have pushed home that right-hand top drawer. It looked untidy, open.

'Well, sir,' said the Superintendent from the town, 'young Carruthers was in your employ in offices at Ridgmour Street, I believe?'

Christopher nodded.

'And you saw him this morning?'

'Yes.'

'We think, sir, that you may be able to help us in getting the facts of an unfortunate occurrence which will, of course, be a great shock to you. Mr Carruthers was found dead this evening from poison. Veronal, the doctor says.'

Christopher Bridal moved comfortably in his chair. 'Oh, *he* committed suicide,' he remarked in the pleasant ordinary voice of a man agreeing with a casual remark about its being a hot day.

The information caused an utter change in the officer's mind. He was bringing no news, then. Queer that his listener was already aware of the tragedy. The training of his profession concealed his surprise.

'Quite so, Mr Bridal. The strange thing is that on the little table by Mr Carruthers were two glasses. One, half-empty, contained whisky and soda only, and at first it looked suicide, as you said. But the other glass, all but empty, had contained whisky and soda *and* veronal. I thought the story would interest you, because Mr Carruthers, delirious when he was found, had your name constantly on his lips. He was blackguarding you up hill and down dale. He said more than that, too. We just thought you might be able to tell us something that would help us. Mr Carruthers, you see, went so far as to say that you had poisoned him. Absurd, but—'

The Superintendent broke off suddenly with an exclamation of surprise that he could not control. A glimmering of a new job, on rather different lines, that badly wanted to be attended to at once, came to Christopher.

Only he could not remember at the moment what the job that wanted doing was. He could only remember that it was a jolly clever trick of that young Carruthers. Carruthers the weakling, a cowardly suicide, had set this trap for the man with whom he had quarrelled. John would have got out of it somehow. But Brother John was laughing in company with Carruthers. Brother John was the strong man still.

His visitor was fingering the tiny squat bottle of veronal tabloids that John Bridal had taken away out of young Carruthers's reach. At the same time he was reading the terms of a passage to Australia, sailing on the next day. Presently he came round to Christopher's side of the table, and Christopher, whose face was white, made no movement to stop him. It occurred to the Superintendent that the drawers were stuffed full of banknotes. Premeditation written plain!

'I'm afraid you're ill, Mr Bridal,' he said. Then, pocketing the bottle of veronal, he looked towards the open windows, and whistled like a schoolboy. The sound of deliberate and heavy footsteps on the broad gravel path round the house came plainly into the room.

'I wish to God you'd push those drawers in!' cried Christopher petulantly. 'Can't you see how damnably untidy they make the place!'

'We'd better be getting along,' said the Superintendent, looking warily at his prisoner. But he knew that the handcuffs would not be needed. The other was a beaten man. For Brother John, dead though he was, was still in power.

MR DUCKWORTH'S NIGHT OUT

Michael Gilbert

The curious and involved transaction which is recorded in the annals of Gabriel Street under the title of 'Herring Jam' may be traced to its beginning in the Court of Mr Whitcomb, the South Borough stipendiary Magistrate.

Detective-Inspector Patrick Petrella, who was there on duty, was reminded of a remark once made to him by Sergeant Drage of the British Railways police to the effect that the travelling public were divisable into three classes. One, people who travelled without tickets; two, people who stole goods in transit; and three, people who defaced posters.

In the dock when he arrived Petrella found an apple-cheeked old lady accused of travelling from Wimbledon to Charing Cross with a threepenny ticket. Her defence, which she was conducting herself, was that she had asked for a ticket to the Kennington Oval, but the booking clerk had misheard her.

'But surely, madam,' said Mr Whitcomb with the courtesy for which he was renowned, 'it costs more than threepence to travel from Wimbledon to the Oval.'

Certainly, agreed the old lady, but since the booking clerk was clearly stone-deaf, what was more likely than that when *she* had said the Kennington Oval, *he* had thought she said Collier's Wood.

'But did it not occur to you that the fare to the Oval must be more than threepence?'

The old lady rode this one off. She said that she always paid exactly what booking clerks asked for. In her experience, sometimes they asked for more, sometimes less. She never argued with them.

'And why,' said Mr Whitcomb, who believed in leaving no avenue unexplored, 'if you had been given a ticket to Collier's Wood, in mistake for a ticket to the Oval, did you ultimately alight at Charing Cross?'

The old lady said she had mistaken it for Trafalgar Square.

It took some time to get his one sorted out ('absolute discharge—coupled with a severe warning) and then Ronald Duckworth was called forward. Mr Duckworth was charged with an act of wilful damage, committed on the premises of the London Passenger Transport Board, in that he, on the previous Tuesday, had attempted to tear down a poster at Borough High Street underground station, the property of Barleymow Breakfast Bricks Ltd, the said poster advertising their wares.

Mr Duckworth pleaded guilty, and an LPTB Inspector stated that at about five minutes past eleven on the evening before last, one of the porters at Borough High Street station, a Mr Sampson, returning to the platform, had observed the accused, who had apparently thought he was alone, seize a loose corner of the advertisement in question and tear it sharply in an upward direction.

'Are you perhaps not fond of Barleymow's Breakfast Bricks?' inquired Mr Whitcomb with every evidence of sympathy.

Mr Duckworth said no. It wasn't that—it was just an impulse.

Mr Whitcombe said that such impulses, though understandable (he much preferred porridge himself) ought to be resisted. He ordered Mr Duckworth to pay the costs of the prosecution and bound him over conditionally on his undertaking to leave all posters, however offensive the products they advertised, alone for the next twelve months.

Mr Duckworth departed thankfully. The next case was Petrella's, and it was not one which he viewed with any enthusiasm at all.

The charge, against Albert Mundy, was one of receiving goods well knowing them to be stolen goods. The facts were simple enough. Mr Mundy, an electrician working in the Wandsborough power station, had purchased a television set from a man he had met in the saloon bar of a public house.

They had had a few drinks and the man had told Mundy a long story of a mix-up which had resulted in the man being in possession of two television sets. 'It's a brand-new set,' he said. 'I've got it outside in the car now. I'd be glad to get rid of it for half what I paid for it.'

Mr Mundy was not only an electrician. He knew quite a lot about television sets. It was, as he saw when he went out to inspect it, a brand-new one. The maker's and wholesaler's labels were still on it.

Even if (as Mr Mundy half suspected) it contained some hidden defect, he was confident that he could put it right, and it was still a staggering bargain. He hurried home, produced the money from a reserve which he kept under a loose floorboard, and clinched the deal. The set proved to be in perfect condition. It also, unfortunately, turned out to have been one of a consignment of twelve stolen in transit between Manchester and Tooley Street goods depot—probably at the depot itself.

There was a good deal to be said on both sides: on the side of Mr Mundy, that he was an honest citizen with a hitherto unblemished record, and that he had no positive proof that the set was a stolen one; on the side of the authorities, that Mr Mundy had himself admitted that he thought the deal a fishy one, and that people who buy television sets for half the list price from strangers in public houses, must take the consequences of their actions.

There was also a third powerful, but unexpressed, argument—that several million pounds' worth of goods was being lost every year by pilfering in transport, a loss which fell on the transport services, their insurers, and, ultimately, on the public.

It was a very close thing, and the sweat stood in beads on Mr Mundy's forehead before the magistrate finally decided to give weight to his previously blameless record and dismiss the case.

Petrella thought that substantial justice had been done. Mr Mundy had been given a bad fright. To imprison him would have been bad luck on Mr Mundy's family and would not have hurt the real criminals —those who stole and organized a stealing. For the losses were now so large and so regular that they had a look of organization about them.

'We do what we can,' said Sergeant Drage. 'We can't watch the men at work. To do that properly you'd need one railway policeman for each worker. Anyway, most of them are honest enough. The few who aren't do a disproportionate amount of damage. It's worse towards Christmas—more stuff about and a lot of casual labour taken on for the holiday season.'

'If you can't watch them, how do you hope to stop them?'

'Keep your eyes and ears open. Make the place as difficult as we can to get in and out, and organize snap searches when they come off duty.'

'I see,' said Petrella. 'The old ring-fence system. You can't stop them taking it, but you can make it difficult for them to get away with it.'

Superintendent Benjamin held monthly conferences at Causeway, which the Detective-Inspectors in charge of stations attended. Petrella from Gabriel Street, Groves from the Commons, and Merriam from Tooley Street. In October, and again in November, the first item on his agenda, displacing even such established favourites as shoplifting and juvenile delinquency, was thefts from the railways.

'The insurance companies are starting to kick,' said Benjamin. 'They're bullying the Commissioner, the Commissioner's given a rocket to District, and the tail-end of the stick's landed on me.'

'Isn't it really a job for the railway police?' said Merriam.

'Surely,' said Benjamin. 'But once stuff's been stolen, it's our job too. If they can't stop them lifting it, we must stop them disposing of it. At least, that's the idea. We've got three big goods yards plumb in our area—Tooley Street, Red Cross, and Bricklayers Arms. What I suggest is—'

He went on to lay down certain principles for patrolling outside these depots. They were sound enough, in their way, but his subordinates knew as well as Benjamin did that it was like trying to watch an acre of rabbit warren with one man and one dog.

It was in the second week in November that Mr Duckworth reappeared in Mr Whitcomb's court. The charge this time had rather more serious elements in it.

It appeared that the staff of Southwark underground station had been on the point of closing down for the night. The last passenger train had gone through, and the last passenger, as they imagined, had been shepherded out into the street. Happening to come down to the platform for a final look-round, the porter had heard a suspicious noise from inside the closet where cleaning materials and other odds and ends were stored.

Being a man of discretion, he had fetched the station-master and the ticket collector before investigating, and the three of them had then returned to the platform. The closet door was open, and the accused, who must have been hiding in the cubicle, was engaged in tearing down a number of posters affixed only that morning to the wall of the station.

Mr Duckworth, who looked even more embarrassed than on the previous occasion, again pleaded guilty and said that he had again acted on impulse.

'As I said on the previous occasion,' observed Mr Whitcomb, 'it is understandable that a man might have a sudden, and perhaps overmastering, impulse to tear down a poster. But to secrete yourself in a cupboard, after the station had been closed for the night, and then come out and start systematically to pull down posters hardly seems to me to be conduct which could be properly described as impulsive.'

Mr Duckworth looked unhappy, and said that he was very sorry. Mr Whitcomb, a copy of the record of the earlier case in front of him, pondered for a few minutes, and then announced that he was far from happy about the matter. He wished further inquiries to be made (the court missioner sighed audibly) and he would put back Mr Duckworth's case for one week. He understood that the accused was a respectable family man. He could have bail on his own recognizances.

Petrella, who was in court in connection with another matter, caught the missioner at the door and said, 'When you've finished with him, let me have a go at him.'

'Have him first if you like,' said the missioner. 'He's daft as a coot. His mother was probably frightened by a railway poster when she was a girl.'

'I'm not sure,' said Petrella. He had, by now, a fairly extensive knowledge of the cranks, crackpots, and fanatics who took up so much police time and afforded such entertaining copy for the court reporters of the leading evening newspapers; but he was far from convinced that Mr Duckworth was a crank or crackpot.

So he took Duckworth out and bought him a cup of tea, and listened with infinite patience to the story of his life. Mr Duckworth was an interior decorator, and an amateur of the late war, during which he served with credit in an artillery regiment, rising to the rank of sergeant. He had a wife and three children (whose photographs Petrella inspected). He was a supporter of Charlton Athletic, and a keen darts player. And, he added, there was nothing at all wrong with his eyes.

Petrella felt that they might now be approaching the heart of the mystery. He ordered second cups of tea for both of them.

'Nothing wrong with my eyes at all,' repeated Mr Duckworth.

'Who suggested there was?' said Petrella.

'No one actually suggested it,' said Mr Duckworth crossly. 'It was just that—look here, if I tell you this story from the beginning, will you promise not to laugh at me?'

'I never laugh on duty,' said Petrella.

'No, I mean that. It's—it's quite mad. It's sort of fourth dimensional. You know what I mean?'

'Science fiction?' suggested Petrella helpfully.

'That's right—that's just what I mean! You walk out of one life into another. That's why I'd rather people thought I was a crook than they thought I was cracked, if you follow me.'

'Lots of people think like that,' said Petrella. 'Just tell me about it.'

It was, in its elements, quite a simple story. Mr Duckworth had been attending a reunion at the regimental headquarters in North London, a function he attended annually and which was, as he put it, 'the one time in the year he really let his hair down.'

Being an old soldier, before plunging into the fray, he had carefully secured his line of retreat. The nearest station to the headquarters in question was Highgate Archway, on the Northern line. His home station was Collier's Wood, on the same line. The last train left Highgate at ten minutes before midnight.

With these essential facts firmly engraved in his memory, Mr Duckworth had settled down to enjoy himself in congenial company, had drunk quite a few pints of beer and a couple (but, he thought, not more than a couple) of whiskies, and had caught his train at Highgate with two minutes to spare. As soon as the train started he fell asleep.

He settled down to a period of reflection.

An indeterminate number of minutes later he had wakened with a start and with the strong conviction that he had reached his own station and was about to be carried past it. The train, sure enough, was stationary, and the doors were open. There was not a moment to lose. Fortunately, he was sitting in a seat near to, and facing, the doors, and just as they closed he hurled himself between them.

The doors shut behind him, the train jerked into motion, and disappeared. A solitary porter, in the far distance, also disappeared, leaving Mr Duckworth still dazed from the combined effects of sleep and drink, alone on the platform.

His overmastering desire was to sit down somewhere for a few minutes and recuperate. Behind him, at the far end of the platform, was a recess which had possibly once contained a seat. It seemed to Mr Duckworth to be exactly what he wanted. He got his back comfortably against one end, his feet against the other, and settled down to a period of reflection.

When he opened his eyes he was in darkness—a sort of dim-blue darkness, broken by one very bright light.

His head, he said, was comparatively clear. He had discovered earlier that no matter how much beer he drank, give him half an hour's sleep, and he'd be more or less all right.

Petrella interrupted to say, 'How long do you think you had been asleep?

'Difficult to say,' said Mr Duckworth, but not, he thought, more than half an hour. He had then staggered to his feet and had seen that the bright light was a small floodlight at platform level. It was so placed that it lit up the platform side of the station which (he was clear-headed enough to note) was not one of the modern type, all gleaming tiles and cement, but quite an old-fashioned one with upright wooden billboards.

The light, as he observed when he reached it, was shining directly onto one of these billboards—almost as if it had been placed there purposely to illuminate it. The effect was emphasized by the fact that the billboards on both sides were blank.

'I take it,' said Petrella, 'you'd realized by this time you weren't at Collier's Wood?'

'Oh, yes. I realized I'd jumped off the train too soon and should have a long walk home. I wasn't worried about being locked up in the station. If there were lights on, there must be people still working. The next bit is something I can't remember very clearly at all. I thought I heard a noise behind me, a sort of scraping noise—and then the ceiling fell on me. Or that's what it felt like. Something hard and heavy landed on top of my head, and before I had time to feel anything else, I was falling forward and—well, the next thing I knew, I was opening my eyes. It was five o'clock of a perishing grey morning, and I was on a seat, just off the road, in the middle of South Borough Common.'

He waited, defiantly, for comment.

Petrella said, 'You might have dreamed it all, of course. Someone might have given you a lift back from the reunion and tried to find out where you lived. You were too pickled to give him your address, so he propped you up on the seat to cool off. Not very friendly, but it could have happened.'

'All right,' said Mr Duckworth. 'Then how do you account for the fact that I'd still had my ticket with me? I found it in my waistcoat pocket.'

'Then,' agreed Petrella, 'it might have happened just as you said. You butted in on something you weren't meant to see, got slugged and dumped.'

'I thought that out for myself,' said Mr Duckworth. 'Only not quite as quickly, because I had a nasty lump on the back of my head—that wasn't imaginary. It was sore as hell—and the father and mother of a hangover—and I had my wife to deal with. She'd got into a real state and gone to the police, and then when I turned up—'

'I can imagine that bit,' said Petrella.

'Yes, well, I thought about it, and I had the same idea as you. I thought I'd start by finding what station it really was.'

'That shouldn't have been too difficult,' said Petrella. 'Most of the stations on that bit of line have been modernized, and besides, you saw at least one of the advertisements—the one the light was shining on.'

'That's just it,' said Mr Duckworth.

'*Didn't* you see it?'

'Yes. I did. And I wish I hadn't. It's been getting me down. Here's where you've promised not to laugh. What I saw—and I saw it quite clearly—and if I shut my eyes I can see it now—what I saw was three

343

lines of writing, with one word on each line. It said *GET HERRING JAM.*'

Petrella stared at him.

'Now, be honest,' said Mr Duckworth. 'Isn't that where you start thinking I've got a screw loose? If you do, you're not the only one. I began to think it myself.'

Petrella said, 'You say you can visualize it? What sort of print was it, and how were the three lines arranged?'

'Ordinary capital letters. On the large side, but not enormous. The *GET* was on the top and a bit to the left. The middle line was *HERRING*—that ran right across. The *JAM* was the bottom line and a bit to the right.'

'I see,' said Petrella. 'I suppose there isn't some other advertisement rather like—'

'I've been up and down every perishing station between Waterloo and Balham twenty times and there's nothing like it at all—nothing remotely like it! Most of 'em are pictures of girls. There's some in writing, like notices telling you to buy Premium Bonds and drink somebody or other's stout.'

'But no herrings?'

'Not a fish among 'em. That's how I got the idea that it might have been an advertisement that had been covered up with another one. They change 'em about once a week. So—'

Light dawned on Petrella.

'So you started pulling off the new ones to see what the old ones said underneath.'

'It'd sort of got me by that time,' said Mr Duckworth. 'I can't explain it. But what I felt was, if I can find that advert, then perhaps I can find out what happened to me that night. If I can't—well, maybe I'm mad, I expect you think I'm mad anyway.'

'No,' said Petrella slowly. 'I don't think you're mad at all.'

*　　*　　*　　*

He said the same thing to Mr Wetherall that evening. Mr Wetherall was headmaster of the South Borough Secondary School, and when Petrella had fallen out with two landladies in succession (in both cases over the peculiar hours he kept and his excessive use of the telephone) Wetherall had suggested to Petrella that he set up house in the two empty rooms below his own in the big house in Brinkman Road. It was a bit far from Gabriel Street, but otherwise it suited Petrella perfectly. It had been great fun furnishing the rooms, and he enjoyed an occasional after-dinner gossip with Mr Wetherall.

'I don't think I'd have started trespassing and pulling down advertisements,' said Mr Wetherall. 'I'd have gone to one of the big agents who does advertising on the Underground, and asked him to find out what advertisements were showing that week.'

'You might have,' said Petrella, 'and so might I, and the agent might have told us. But not someone like Mr Duckworth.'

'Have you located the station?'

'I've had a shot at it. The trouble is that going from Highgate to Collier's Wood, Mr Duckworth could have gone one of two ways— via Charing Cross—that's the West End route—or via Bank. All the stations on the West End route are modern tile and chromium jobs. But one or two of the stations on the Bank route would fit. London Bridge, Southwark, and Borough High Street are all possibles.'

'Since you've done some work on it, I take it you don't think he made the whole thing up?'

'No, I don't,' said Petrella. 'But I couldn't explain why.'

Mr Wetherall puffed his horrible pipe for a few seconds and then said: 'No, you can't, can you? I mean, you can't tell how you know when people are telling the truth, but it's a fact that you can. I've found that often with boys.' He reflected again and said, 'I think you'd better have a word with my friend, Raynor-Hasset. He'll tell you all you want to know about the London railway system. He used to be a schoolmaster, but he's retired now. He lives in one of those little houses up on the Heath. I'll give him a ring and let him know you're coming.'

Petrella knew that Mr Wetherall seldom made recommendations idly. So the following evening he called on Mr Raynor-Hasset. Mr Wetherall's friend had a corvine face and a slight stoop, as if much of his life had been spent in exploring places with low roofs.

'I don't imagine,' he said, when they had settled down in front of the fire, 'that you have ever heard of the Spurs?'

'The Spurs?'

'Not the football team,' said Mr Raynor-Hasset with a thin smile. 'The Society for the Prevention of Unused Railway lines. I have the honour to be their secretary.'

'I'm afraid not,' said Petrella. 'What do you do?'

'Just as speleologists explore the recesses and convolutions of our caves, we delight in tracking down the railway lines which run under this great city. It is a curious fact but once a railway line has been constructed, it may be covered over—but it is hardly ever filled in again.'

'I suppose not.'

'Most people imagine, when they think about it, that our main railways lines stop well short of the centre of London. The Northern ones at Euston, Kings Cross, and St Pancras. The Southern ones at Waterloo and Victoria. It is far from true, of course. I could name you half a dozen ways of crossing London from north to south by steam train. I conducted a special trip along the Blackfriars, Holborn, Kentish Town line myself last year. And did you know that there was an old but still usable railway line, part of the original Charing Cross-Bayswater switch, which runs within a hundred yards of the Eros statue in Piccadilly? The entrance to it is through a shop—'

Petrella listened, entranced, as Mr Raynor-Hasset described and expounded to him that curious system of disused passages and tunnels, of unsuspected tracks, of forgotten stairways and phantom stations (akin to the traces in the human system of some dread but dead disease) which the private enterprise of our railway pioneers had left under the unsuspecting surface of London.

During an interval, while his host brewed cocoa for them, Petrella explained the idea which had come into his head.

Mr Raynor-Hasset cleared the table and spread on it a map of large scale. 'It's a very feasible idea,' he said. 'I think that the Tooley Street Goods Yard would be one to start with. You have had losses from there—serious losses. Quite so. You'll note that although it is now linked to London Bridge by part of the ordinary Southern system, its previous history is far from simple. It began life as a private depot for goods coming up the river to St Saviour's Dock—a horse-drawn tramway connected it to Dockhead; or you could get at it under the river by the old subway—it's disused now—that came out at Stanton's Wharf. Plenty of possibilities there. As for the underground stations —Mr Raynor-Hasset shook his head. 'If people had any idea what lay behind those shiny, well-lit platforms, they'd be pretty surprised.'

He consulted his chart again. 'If I had to make a guess I'd say that the connection lies between Tooley Street and Southwark. And I'll tell you why. Southwark underground must be within a very short distance of the connecting line which the old Brighton and South Coast —who shared London Bridge with the South Eastern and Chatham —ran across to Waterloo. It was never a great success, as passengers found it just as easy to go straight through from London Bridge, and it was closed to traffic in the eighties. You can see it marked here.'

Petrella followed the spidery lines on the map and found his excitement kindling.

'I really believe,' he said, 'that you must be right.'

'There's no need to rely on guesswork. Why don't we go and see?'

Petrella looked at him.

'With your authority,' said Mr Raynor-Hasset, 'and my experience, I should anticipate no difficulty. I take it you can square it with the authorities.'

'Yes, certainly.'

'Then I suggest tomorrow night. We will meet at—shall we say, eleven o'clock at Bermondsey South? The old station, on the north side of the Rotherhithe Road. Dress in your oldest clothes.'

$$\star \qquad \star \qquad \star \qquad \star$$

At a few minutes after eleven the following night Petrella was following Mr Raynor-Hasset down a flight of wooden steps. At the bottom of the steps a man was waiting for them.

'I've opened her up,' he said. 'Had to use a pint of oil. Must be five years since anyone went through there.'

'Almost exactly five years,' said Mr Raynor-Hasset. 'I took a party along there myself. Thank you very much, Sam. 'Some coins changed hands. 'You lock up behind. We'll probably be coming out at Waterloo.'

'I'll give 'em a ring,' said Sam. The door opened into what looked, at first sight, like a brick wall, but which was in fact the bricked-up

347

entrance to a railway tunnel. It shut behind them with a solid thud, cutting off light, air, and sound.

'I should have asked you before we started,' said Mr Raynor-Hasset, 'whether you suffered at all from claustrophobia.'

'I don't think so,' said Petrella. 'I've never really found out.'

'One man I took with me was so severely overcome that he fell flat on his face and when I endeavoured to assist him he bit me—in the left leg. Straight ahead now.'

It was quite easy going. The rails were gone, and the old permanent way had become covered, in the course of time, by a thin deposit of dried earth mixed with soot from the tunnel roof. The only discomfort was the dust they kicked up as they walked.

'Ventilation is sometimes a problem,' said Mr Raynor-Hasset. 'It was originally quite adequate, but one or two of the shafts have become blocked with the passage of time. In a really old tunnel I have used a safety lamp, but we should be all right here.' He paused to consult the map, and a pedometer which was pinned to the front of his coat. 'There's an air shaft somewhere here. Yes—you can catch a glimpse of the sky.'

Petrella looked up a narrow opening and was pleased to see the stars winking back at him. The light of the torch shone on something white. It was a tiny heap of bones.

'A dog, I should imagine,' said Mr Raynor-Hasset. 'On we go. We've much ground to cover.'

They went on in silence. Petrella soon lost count of time and distance. His guide used his torch sparingly, and as they paced forward into the blackness, Petrella began to feel the oppression of the entombed, a consciousness of the weight of earth above him. The air grew thicker, and was there—or was it his imagination—greater difficulty in breathing?

'We must,' he said, his voice coming out in a startling croak, 'we must be nearly the other side of London by now.'

Mr Raynor-Hasset halted, clicked on his torch, and said, 'One mile and nearly one furlong. By my calculations we are just passing under Bricklayers Arms depot. We go past the north-east corner, and then we should swing through nearly a quarter turn to the right. . . . Yes, here we are. Better keep an eye for possible entrances on our left.'

He kept his torch alight for two hundred yards, but the brick walls remained unbroken. Ahead of them pink beads winked and flushed in the light, retreating before them.

'Rats,' said Mr Raynor-Hasset. 'But a timid bunch. I carry a few Guy Fawkes squibs to throw at them, but I've never had to use them.'

They walked on in silence.

Petrella, who was gradually becoming acclimatized, calculated that they had gone forward another mile when Mr Raynor-Hasset spoke again.

'Can you feel,' he said, 'a slight dampness?'

'It's less dusty, certainly.'

'There's a water seepage here. Nothing serious—some defect in drainage. We must be almost under the old Leather market.'

Petrella tried to visualize the geography of that part of London.

'In that case,' he said, 'we shouldn't be far from Tooley Street.'

'About two hundred yards.'

The torch came on again. Ahead of them the surface shone, black and slimy. The smell was unspeakable. Even Mr Raynor-Hasset noticed it.

'Quite fresh, isn't it?' he said. 'We'll keep the torch on now for a bit.'

When they came to it, the side entrance was easy to see. It sloped upward, gently, to the right. Mr Raynor-Hasset took a compass bearing and marked his map.

'I should think there's no doubt at all,' he said. 'That's an old loading track and it goes straight to Tooley Street depot. You'll probably find it comes out in a loading pit. Do you wish to follow it?'

But Petrella's eyes were on the ground. 'Could you point your torch here a moment,' he said. 'Look. That's not five years old.'

It was a cigarette carton.

'No, indeed,' said Mr Raynor-Hasset. 'And those, I think, are footprints. How very interesting!'

Clearly to be seen in the mud was a beaten track of men's boot prints that led from the mouth of the shaft and onward up the tunnel.

'Keep your torch on them,' said Petrella. 'This is going to save me a lot of trouble.'

'It looks as if an army has passed this way.'

An army of soldier-ants, thought Petrella. An army bearing burdens.

349

Four hundred yards, and the line of footprints turned into a track branching down to the left. Mr Raynor-Hasset again checked his position, and said, 'Southwark underground station, or I'm a Dutchman.'

They went sharply down for a short distance, then the track levelled out, ran along, and climbed again, finally emerging into a circular ante-chamber. Above their heads an iron staircase spiralled upwards into the gloom.

'Southwark,' said Mr Raynor-Hasset, 'was one of those stations which was developed forward. I mean that when they redesigned it, they put in a moving staircase at the far end, with the lifts, and closed the old emergency stair shaft altogether. This is what we have come out into.'

But Petrella was not listening to him. The light of the torch had revealed, strewn around the foot of the staircase, an astonishing jumble of cartons, crates, boxes, sacks, and containers of every shape and size.

'This is where they unpack the stuff,' he said. 'I wonder where they store it. Can we get out onto the platform?'

'Certainly. I think this must be the way.'

There was a door in the boarding ahead of them, secured by three stout bolts.

'What time is it?'

'Just after two o'clock.'

'Should be all right,' said Petrella.

He slid the bolts and swung the door open. They stepped through and found themselves on the platform of Southwark underground station, lit only by the ghostly blue lamps which shine all night to guide the maintenance trolleys.

'What are we looking for?' said Mr Raynor-Hasset.

'There must, I think, be more storage space. Have you a knife? It would be about here, I'd guess. Hold the torch steady a moment.'

Petrella slid the blade between the boards, choosing the place with precision. He felt a latch lifting and levered strongly with the knife blade. A section of boarding hinged out towards them.

'Good gracious,' said Mr Raynor-Hasset mildly.

The deep recess contained, stacked on shelves and floor, an

astonishing assortment of goods. There were piled cartons of cigarettes, wooden boxes with the stamp of a well-known whisky firm, portable typewriters, wireless and television sets, bales of textiles, a pair of sporting rifles, boxes of shoes, cases of tinned food.

'A producer-to-consumer service,' said Petrella grimly.

His mind was already busy constructing exactly the sort of police trap that would be necessary: two cars in the street above, to catch the people when they came to collect; men in the tunnel itself, beyond the opening, to seal the far end; and a very cautious reconnaissance to find out how the Tooley Street end worked.

He was standing on the platform, thinking about all this when suddenly he started to laugh. Mr Raynor-Hasset edged perceptibly away.

'It's quite all right,' said Petrella. 'I'm not going to start biting you in the leg. Hold the torch on that wall. Now watch while I open and shut those two doors.'

Mr Raynor-Hasset did so, and then himself gave a dry cackle. 'Very ingenious,' he said.

Two advertisements stood next to each other on the billboard. They were very close, with only a thin margin between them.

When the doors were shut the two advertisements read:

THIS YEAR'S TARGET
BUY YOURSELF ANOTHER   RING PARK 0906
PREMIUM BOND   JAMES BOND & SONS
                             Everything for your car

When both doors were opened, most of the left-hand advertisement and most of the right-hand advertisement were nearly cut away; and when the cut-away parts vanished into the darkness of the opened doors, all that remained of the adjoining advertisements was:

GET
HER RING
JAM

'I couldn't help thinking,' said Petrella, 'that we have, at least, set Mr Duckworth's mind at rest.'

Acknowledgments

The publishers would like to extend their grateful thanks to the following authors, publishers and others for kindly granting them permission to reproduce the copyrighted extracts and stories included in this anthology.

THE IVY COTTAGE MYSTERY and THE 'NICOBAR' BULLION CASE from *The Chronicles of Martin Hewitt*. Reprinted by kind permission of Ward Lock Limited.

THE SECRET GARDEN and THE BLAST OF THE BOOK from *The Father Brown Stories* by G. K. Chesterton. Reprinted by kind permission of the Estate of G. K. Chesterton and Dodd Mead & Company, Inc.

THE TWO BOTTLES by Freeman Wills Crofts, from *The Evening Standard Detective Book*. Reprinted by kind permission of The Evening Standard.

A BABY IS MISSING by Alistair Cooke. Reprinted by kind permission of Granada Publishing Limited and Random House Inc.

THE EPISODE OF THE MEXICAN SEER by Grant Allen. Reprinted by kind permission of Penguin Books Ltd.

THE LEGACY by John Gordon. © 1980 John Gordon.

THE ADVENTURE OF THE SPECKLED BAND by Sir Arthur Conan Doyle. Reprinted by kind permission of John Murray (Publishers) Ltd and Jonathan Clowes Limited.

THE NAMELESS MAN by Rodriguez Ottolengui, from *The American Rivals of Sherlock Holmes*. Reprinted by kind permission of A. D. Peters Ltd.

THE QUICK BROWN FOX by Edmund Crispin, from *The Evening Standard Detective Book*. Reprinted by kind permission of The Evening Standard.

JOHNNY ONE-EYE from *Runyon First to Last* by Damon Runyon. Reprinted by kind permission of Constable Publishers and J. B. Lippincott Co.

PHILOMEL COTTAGE by Agatha Christie. Reprinted by kind permission of Hughes Massie Limited.

STRONG BROTHER JOHN by Herbert Shaw. Reprinted by kind permission of Curtis Brown Ltd.

MR DUCKWORTH'S NIGHT OUT by Michael Gilbert. Reprinted by kind permission of Curtis Brown Ltd and the author.

Every effort has been made to clear copyrights and the publishers trust that their apologies will be accepted for any errors or omissions.